Hard to Have Heroes

Hard to Have Heroes

Buddy Mays

UNIVERSITY OF
NEW MEXICO PRESS

ALBUQUERQUE

Printed in the United States of America

17 16 15 14 13 12   1 2 3 4 5 6

Library of Congress Cataloging-in-Publication Data

Mays, Buddy.

   Hard to have heroes / Buddy Mays.

      p. cm.

   ISBN 978-0-8263-5204-0 (pbk. : alk. paper) — ISBN 978-0-8263-5205-7 (electronic)

   1. Teenagers—New Mexico—Fiction. 2. Life change events—Fiction. I. Title.

   PS3613.A9726H37 2012

   813'.6—dc23

                              2012012166

Design and Layout: Melissa Tandysh

Composed in 10.8/14 Minion Pro Regular

Display type Bodoni Bold Compressed

As you get older it is harder to have heroes, but it is sort of necessary.

—ERNEST HEMINGWAY

1

The Panther Piss King
Goes West

According to a tattered family journal passed down through the decades to any female family member who volunteered to keep it safe and up to date, the following is an account of how fourteen-year-old Noah Odell, dictionary aficionado and collector of "dead soldiers," came to be residing with his widowed mother in a sturdy but somewhat battered two-bedroom, one-bath, shingle-roofed frame house in Gold Hill, Oregon, in the very rainy spring month of April 1957. This is the very same Noah Odell, of course, who, along with his mother and uncle, two friends, a crazy kid, and a dozen half-naked Apache Indians with unloaded rifles, brought the U.S. Army to its knees at a place called Outhouse Overlook in New Mexico.

This is how it happened. Eighty-eight years and one month earlier, on March 8, 1869, G.W. (General Washington) Odell, who was Noah's great-great-grandfather, loaded six rooms of homemade furniture, ten sides of salted bacon, a year's supply of dried beans and flour, and a dozen jugs of fiery, homemade liquor—known affectionately to friends, family, and hundreds of satisfied customers in Anderson County, Pennsylvania, as "panther piss"—aboard a flatboat in Pittsburg, bound for St. Louis. He was reluctantly accompanied by his wife Maude; six sons—Jefferson, Henry, William, John Adams, Eli, and Geoffrey—aged ten through sixteen; a daughter named Lucia, aged seventeen; and a polychromatic menagerie of three pigs, ten chickens, a pair of Jersey milk cows, and a team of four prized trotting horses.

G.W. told the flatboat captain that he was off to seek his fortune in the new state of Oregon, but why, at age thirty-nine, he had abandoned the security of a prolific, sixty-acre farm and a healthy business distilling moonshine on the side in Wyattsville, Pennsylvania, has always remained a mystery. The farm produced a substantial harvest of corn and wheat each year, even through the hard days of the Civil War, and had been settled by G.W.'s grandfather in the very early 1800s. The "shine" operation—for which he had been dubbed the "panther piss king" by satisfied local menfolk who refused to pay federal taxes on something as essential as a good, stiff drink—was growing and ever popular. According to the Odell family journal, this was G.W.'s secret shine recipe, which he shared with no one outside the family.

WHAT YOU NEED

20 pounds dried whole-kernel white corn, no dirt or dead bugs
10 gallons pure spring water
2 cups yeast
½ keg sweet wildflower honey
8 or 10 large peaches, peeled and pitted *or* 5 pounds fresh, ripe, pitted cherries
1 spoonful copperhead snake spit (venom)

MAKE THE MASH

Put dried corn in a gunnysack and get sack wet with warm water. Put sack in a dark place (potato cellar works good) and keep warm and wet for 10 days. Watch for corn to sprout. When corn sprouts and new shoots are as long as a coon claw, pour kernels into a big tub of clean water and wash them good. Scrub off all sprouts and roots, then drain off water, sprouts, and roots. Take the butt end of an oak board and mash corn, making sure all kernels get cracked. Pour in 10 gallons boiling spring water and then add honey and peaches and snake spit. Stir good and then let sit. When cool, mix in yeast and cover up with wet gunnysacks, except leave a thumbhole for vent. This here's the mash.

COOK THE WHISKEY

Let mash sit for a week. When it stinks to high heaven, filter through a pillercase and pour into still. Be sure your worm ain't broke or crimped anywheres. Build slow wood fire under still and cook fir-ment till gone. Catch new whiskey in charred oak barrel as it comes out of worm and let it sit for 1 week before using.

Occasionally G.W. had mentioned his desire to go "prospectin'," but the comment usually came only after he had consumed half a jug or so of this potent homemade hooch. He'd never bothered to say what he wanted to prospect for, nor did he ever even mention the subject when he was sober. G.W.'s wife Maude always assumed it was the shine talking, not the man, and as the years passed, she paid less and less attention to her husband's inebriated rambling. By the time she discovered her mistake around about February in 1869, it was too late. Without asking anyone's permission, least of all his wife's, G.W. sold the sixty acres of wheat and corn fields, the four-bedroom house, tool shed, barn, and well-insulated, two-hole out-house with hand-carved and sanded wooden seats for six hundred dollars in gold and fractional currency.

During the tedious month of flatboat life that followed—down the Ohio River to Cairo, Illinois, then up the Mississippi to St. Louis —little of importance happened, and the days were excruciatingly uneventful. The flatboat was not attacked by wild Indians, nor set upon by bandits, nor even grounded on a sandbar. The weather was clear and mild, and the flatboat captain—a tall, good looking man in his late thirties named Jack Fletcher—was a "pleasant, well-informed frontiersman," to quote the Odell journal. Captain Jack must have felt a bit sorry for Maude and the children, however, because he generously offered G.W. the benefit of his twenty years' experience on the frontier—something that most frontiersmen didn't do unless they were being paid. Jack told G.W. frankly that if he didn't have his act together when he headed west from St. Louis, he wouldn't have a chance in hell of making it to Oregon. Horses, for example, were fine for dragging plows and pulling buggies, but they had little staying power. And because horses could not live on the wild prairie grasses along the Oregon Trail, they would most certainly die of starvation within a few weeks. Captain Jack suggested oxen instead; they were slower, but sturdier and more dependable, and they could live quite well on prairie grass. He advised G.W. to keep the cows and chickens, to sell the furniture, and to trade the pigs for carpenter and lumbering tools, staples, and rifle ammunition. Saws, axes, shovels, and salt, sugar, and other spices, he told G.W., would be valuable items in a land that had few stores.

When the boat at last hailed St. Louis in mid-April 1869, G.W. took heed of the captain's counsel. He immediately traded his four prized but useless trotting horses and twenty dollars for two yokes of burly oxen. He gave away most of the handcrafted furniture and swapped the pigs and a few dollars for a variety of axes, hammers, saws, splitting wedges, nails, salt, and vegetable seeds. He bought gunpowder by the keg and lead balls by the gross weight. Finally, he purchased a twenty-one-foot-long, slightly used Conestoga wagon from a local merchant for a hundred dollars, gave most of the panther piss to the flatboat captain and his crew and drank what he could of the remainder, and three days later, when he sobered up, loaded his family, food, livestock, and wagon onto a steamer bound for Independence, Missouri.

The upstream run took four days. At Independence Landing, G.W. shelled out another two hundred dollars and joined one of the last wagon trains bound for Oregon's Willamette Valley along the Oregon Trail. The train consisted of seventeen families with covered wagons, a trio of guides who doubled as hunters and blacksmiths, eighty-one head of livestock, a passel of dogs, and a wagon master with the improbable name of M.T. Crapper. Later that same year, the transcontinental railroad would be completed, and wagon travel to the West would quickly become a thing of the past. Because G.W. wasn't exactly sure where he wanted to go in Oregon, however, it seemed only fitting that he should take the slowest way to get there.

ACCORDING TO THE Odell journal, the long, dusty trip west on the two-thousand-mile-long Oregon Trail was without *major* calamity, although a few minor ones occurred. Two weeks out from Independence, G.W.'s eldest son Geoffrey—for no apparent reason other than nearsightedness—mistook his right foot for a rattlesnake and blew away three of his toes with a .64-caliber Lancaster hunting rifle. Wagon Master Crapper cleaned and dressed the wound and allowed as how it wasn't a dangerous injury but Geoffrey would probably have trouble walking for a while. Banished to the wagon seat of the Conestoga beside his mother and sister, Geoffrey was overjoyed with guilt at the prospect of having to ride, not walk, the remaining 1,720 miles to Oregon.

Another minor catastrophe was that two thirds of the Odell's bacon supply quickly spoiled in the heat and had to be discarded along the wayside. Food was not a problem, luckily, because wild animals were abundant, and the three hunter-guides accompanying the wagon train provided everyone with plenty of bison, elk, and deer meat. What *was* a problem, though, was the fact that after missing two menstrual cycles, seventeen-year-old Lucia tearfully told her mother that she was probably pregnant. Her condition, she said, was the result of a short but sweet tryst with the handsome flatboat captain Jack Fletcher while most crew and passengers were ashore for a few hours in Cairo, Illinois. Lucia asked what she should do: kill herself or pick up a heavy boulder thrice daily and hope for the best. Do nothing and mention it not, Maude Odell told her daughter. What with Geoffrey's foot and the rotting bacon, G.W. had enough problems to deal with.

The wagon train spent three days at Fort Laramie on the North Platte River in early July, resting the animals and restocking supplies. Thereafter, however, it rolled westward for fifteen hours a day, every day of the week, even on the Sabbath. By early September 1869, just as the days were beginning to get noticeably cooler and the summer green leaves of the aspen trees in the high country were starting to metamorphose into autumn gold, the wagon master advised the travelers that they were within three hundred miles of the Columbia River. Not a single wild Indian had been spotted along the way (although, now nearly six months pregnant, Lucia was showing signs of her own little papoose), and only three members of the train had been lost—those on Geoffrey's starboard foot.

G.W. Odell was about to change all that. Early one morning a few days later, with a range of tall, snow-capped, conical-shaped peaks in sight to the west, he informed Wagon Master Crapper that he and his family were traveling no farther toward the Willamette Valley and would be leaving the wagon train within a day or two. Why he made such an unexpected and downright bizarre decision is conjecture since no one ever knew why G.W. Odell did anything, probably not even himself. Leave he did, however.

The following morning, over Maude's protests and as of yet unaware of Lucia's pending parturition, G.W. forewent the protection of numbers and turned his wagon due west toward the foothills of the lower Oregon Cascades. Mr. Crapper told G.W. that if he traveled straight toward the mountains, he would intersect the Beckett wagon road, which ran from the Columbia River south to the Klamath Indian Agency within a day or two. If he turned south on the Beckett road, he would reach the recently founded settlement of Prine, 150 miles to the south, where food and supplies were available.

With their two skinny and exhausted dairy cows tied to the back of the wagon on lead ropes so they couldn't stray and the four trail-weary chickens that had survived the trip in a wooden coop strapped to the side, the Odells made slow but steady progress across the arid, sagebrush-dotted Oregon prairie. Water was scarce and the going was tough, especially where ancient volcanic eruptions had corrugated the landscape with black-walled basalt canyons or created mile-wide fields of melon-sized lava boulders. Food was plentiful, however; the boys shot pronghorn antelope and jackrabbits for fresh meat, and Maude and Lucia picked late-season blackberries and gathered wild onions. Sure enough, three days after leaving the wagon train, they intersected the Beckett road and followed it south to Prine, a small settlement of ranchers and merchants nestled in a valley along the Crooked River. There, they bought supplies at the tiny general mercantile, rested a day or two, then left the Beckett road and once again headed due west.

It took three more days to reach the foothills of the Cascades. On the evening of the third day, the family camped along a clear water creek in a fertile, pine-filled valley. That very evening, a massive storm that had been hugging Oregon's Pacific coast for several days turned inland and barreled across the Coast Range and into the Cascades, goaded by powerful Pacific winds. By morning, three feet of powdery snow had fallen in the little valley in which the Odells were camped, effectively blocking movement in any direction. Unable to proceed with whatever plan he had formulated, if any, at least until the snow melted, G.W. figured he might as well stay put. He knew full well that his family of nine would probably not survive a harsh mountain winter living in a wagon. "Nine *now*," said Maude, "but soon to be ten," and she related Lucia's condition to her husband, adding cheerfully that the situation was only temporary.

G.W. Odell surprised everyone by not getting angry. Instead, as the snow began to melt, he and the boys got to work. The surrounding wilderness was filled with elk, deer, and wild turkey, and while John Adams and Eli went hunting, everyone else began chopping down lodgepole pines and hauling them to a small, grassy knoll at the edge of a nearby meadow with the oxen. Within two weeks, they had erected a one-story log cabin, twenty feet wide and thirty feet long, atop the knoll. The structure was without windows and had just one door and only a crude fireplace made of river stones and mud in one corner for heating and cooking. The inside, however, was dry and windproof and fairly snug when a fire was crackling in the fireplace. The nearby stream, which Maude named Tumble Creek, gave quick access to water. When the cabin's roof had been covered with a layer of clay and the walls were at last chinked with mud and moss, the Odells transferred what few pieces of furniture they had retained in St. Louis from wagon to cabin and moved in. Their four chickens, including one rooster, moved in with them. It was certainly no mansion, but it was far more comfortable than the canvas-topped Conestoga.

As the early snow melted and a late, warm Indian summer settled in over the eastern Cascades, the work began in earnest. Maude and Lucia cooked, washed clothes, and smoked elk and deer meat in a hastily constructed smokehouse near the creek. They organized the cabin and its contents and made sure the oxen and cattle got plenty to eat. The menfolk cut and stacked a winter's supply of dead lodgepole pine firewood and began to harvest and stack meadow grass for cattle and oxen fodder during the oncoming winter. In early November, the creek filled up with a run of spawning Chinook salmon, and fried fish quickly became a family favorite. By the time late autumn turned to early winter and the really icy evenings arrived, every humanly thing that could be done to make the Odell family comfortable had been done. Living on beans, bread, elk stew, deer steak, and smoked or salted salmon, they spent a comfortable, if somewhat cramped and smelly, winter.

WHEN APRIL FINALLY arrived and he found himself and his family in good health, G.W. changed his way of thinking. He had never given much credence to Providence, God's mercy, the Lord's way, or any other "Christian mishmash," and though he had allowed his wife to name their second son Eli after a character in the Bible, it was only because she threatened to invite her mother to come and visit for an entire summer if he didn't. G.W. had never been to church in his life and had never allowed grace to be recited at meals unless company was present. He was basically a heathen, and glad to be so.

But after careful consideration, he began to think that maybe he had judged the mishmash too harshly. In early December, Lucia had given birth without complications to a seven-pound baby boy she had named Fletcher. Geoffrey's gunshot wound had healed completely; with only two toes on his right foot, he still had trouble walking long distances, but he got around the cabin and yard just fine with assistance from a whittled pine cane. The chickens were laying, and the oxen and cattle had survived the winter without harm, protected from the wind and snow by a dugout shelter with a mud and grass roof hastily built for them in the fall.

With all this in mind, G.W. figured that someone somewhere wanted him to stay where he was. At the first hint of spring thaw, the family went to work. From dawn till dusk they labored shoulder to shoulder, clearing, cutting, planting, and building. By September the Odell homestead had been transformed into a true family farm. G.W. and the boys had added three additional rooms to the cabin, a spring house for cold storage, a chicken coop, a well-insulated privy, and a small but snug lodgepole pine barn for the livestock. Their productive, quarter-acre garden, tended mostly by Maude and Lucia, was providing the family with beans, tomatoes, squash, cabbages, and onions, and a narrow strip of land along Tumble Creek had been cleared and planted with corn. Twice, G.W. and Geoffrey made the four-day round trip to Prine with oxen and wagon: once to file a homestead claim on their land and buy panes of glass for the cabin's new windows, and again in the early fall to trade fresh garden vegetables and two of their oxen for much needed supplies and a riding horse.

G.W. never did find time to go prospecting, even though a major gold strike that brought thousands of miners and prospectors into western and southern Oregon had been made in 1851. Most of the gold was gone by 1870, however, and G.W. just never bothered. Between hunting trips, farming, chopping wood, building, and occasional skirmishes with passing bands of Indians, he and his sons didn't have much time for anything. For a while, in fact, the Indians required a good bit of the Odells' time. Small bands of nomadic Northern Paiute, most of them holdovers from the so-called Snake War that claimed thousands of lives in Oregon from 1864 to 1868, raided the Odell homestead on numerous occasions and caused considerable worry with their short, sharp assaults on the house and livestock. According to the Odell journal, these all took place in midsummer 1871. None of the Odells were injured, but after losing several dozen warriors to the withering barrage of lead balls from seven large-caliber Lancaster rifles and a 17-gauge Greener short-barreled shotgun, the Paiute found they were totally outgunned. Word got around and the Indians henceforth gave the Odell farm a wide berth indeed. We can only assume that whoever was passing the ammunition was also passing around a jug of brand new panther piss, distilled from the corn harvest of the previous year. Because there are no copperheads in Oregon and never have been, G.W. was probably harvesting his "snake spit"—the most important ingredient of his shine recipe—from timber rattlesnakes.

Between 1871 and 1885, a number of settler families searching for fertile farmland arrived in what had become known as Odell Valley. After rigid scrutiny by Maude and G.W. (who made sure they had either livestock or goods to trade or marriageable daughters to court), many were encouraged to remain. By 1890 Odell Valley was populated by perhaps fifty families. Narrow strips of winter wheat and yellow field corn lined the rich, silty banks of Tumble Creek, and neat, well-built farmhouses dotted the hillsides above the stream where the ponderosa and lodgepole pine forests had been cleared. G.W. Odell, who was now sixty years of age and known to almost everyone as "The General," had developed a lucrative and widespread distillery empire that stretched eastward into Idaho, south to the California border, and west all the way to the coast. His sons—even Geoffrey with the bum foot—had married and started farms or local businesses of their own. Lucia—now thirty-eight and well on her way to spinsterhood—had not found a mate, but as the community's postmistress and owner of Odell General Mercantile, she had created a comfortable niche for herself. Twenty-one-year-old Fletcher was the trusted general foreman of G.W.'s panther piss business and was making more money than he could ever dream of spending.

Only John Adams, third eldest of the Odell sons, could not seem to find his proper place in the community. He had married a sweet Pennsylvania Quaker girl named Myrtle and built her a pretty, split-pine cabin in a meadow above Tumble Creek, but he was simply not cut out to be a farmer. His corn crop failed, his chickens died, the garden wilted, and the cows quit giving milk. In the spring of 1892 the couple finally abandoned Odell Valley and moved south and west across the Cascades to the booming lumber town of Ashland, where John Adams found a job as scaler and trimmer in Waymaker's Sawmill. The job paid well and the couple prospered.

They purchased a single-story frame house near the edge of town, and a few years later Myrtle gave birth to a healthy baby boy named Ira. John Adams had seniority at the mill by this time and was offered a foreman's position by the owners. In a fit of contentment he allowed as how things couldn't get much better, and in that he was perfectly correct. On a bright October morning, while supervising the trial run of a new, steam-powered "head" saw used to cut massive pine logs into cants, one of John Adams's dangling suspender straps tangled in the blade's four-inch teeth, and without so much as a "good-bye" or a "see you later," he was converted into hamburger.

The mill's owners took good care of Myrtle, and she never again had to worry about money. When Ira turned sixteen, he too entered the lumber business, but in the accounting end only. Whereas Ira had finished eighth grade by the skin of his teeth, he was perhaps not the most indefectible bookkeeper, but neither was he a dummy, having heard the tale of his father's transmogrification numerous times. Ira married a young Ashland girl named Mabel when he was twenty and also fathered one son, a strapping twelve-pound boy named Carl William. Carl finished high school and joined the navy, and when his hitch was over—luckily well before the start of World War II—he married a robust young Scot-Irish farm girl named Ethel Boggs, who everyone knew as "Ek." Born poor on a red dirt farm in the Oklahoma panhandle and certainly familiar with hardships, Ethel made a good wife. The couple bought a small, two-bedroom frame house with a worn out cedar-shake roof and an oversized front lawn on the corner of Jacoby Street and Sixth Avenue in the mining and railroad town of Gold Hill, where Carl trained on the job as an electrician at the nearby Rogue River Hydroelectric Plant. He was eventually given a permanent position as the night engineer with the main task of keeping the plant's two ancient and unreliable turbines in running condition. It was steady work that paid the bills, put food on the table, and allowed Carl and Ethel to have their first baby—a son they named Noah—in a hospital.

Things were going along just peachy for Carl and his new family until one freezing night in the winter of 1947. Trying to locate an intermittent but troublesome short circuit in the turbine's prehistoric wiring, Carl slipped on a patch of ice and pitched head first into the plant's ten-thousand-gallon holding reservoir. He remained there, clinging to an iron railing in the icy water for three hours until he was finally discovered by the morning watch, but he died a week later of rigorous and raging pneumonia.

Ethel Odell received no compensation whatsoever for Carl's death from the hydroelectric plant. Grandpa Ira and Grandma Mabel were basically senile and didn't even attend their son's funeral, let alone offer their daughter-in-law any financial help. Ethel had no savings, but she and four-year-old Noah each got a check from Social Security every month for twenty-two dollars. Forty-four dollars a month—one dollar and forty cents a day—didn't go very far, even in 1947. Nonetheless, with what she could make by sewing or repairing clothing for neighbors and working part time at a local grocery store, it was enough to buy ten pounds of pinto beans and a twenty-pound sack of potatoes each month, pay the water and electric bills, and keep Noah in clothes, just barely.

2

The Rainy Day,
Southern Oregon Blues

In the very rainy month of March 1957, police in Eugene, Oregon, arrested a local house painter named Arnold Ashley when he strode naked as a jaybird into the Greyhound bus station and demanded a one-way ticket to the Sahara Desert. Ashley obviously had no money, and he was described by the ticket agent as "unblinking and drooling slightly from the corners of his mouth." Later at the police station, Ashley explained that he had been held prisoner in his home for the previous two weeks by a malicious flock of corpulent white ducks, all of them armed with bright yellow umbrellas. Guarded day and night by at least two of the wicked waterfowl, Ashley told police that they brandished their brollies like swords, poking and prodding him about the house as though he were a cow in a feedlot. His clothing had all been taken and burned, he claimed, and the dastardly ducks insisted he do all the cooking, laundry, bed making, and general scut work while they lounged about the house reading magazines or listening to *Fibber McGee and Molly* or the Grand Ole Opry on the radio. In desperation, Ashley finally stole a butcher knife from the kitchen, waited for the proper moment, and on a rainy midnight dreary, dispatched his guards by lopping off their heads. He then quickly made his escape out the back door and found his way to the Greyhound station from which he hoped to go somewhere warm and dry and duckless and start a new life.

Deducing fowl play, police officers made a search of Ashley's home. They found no deceased white ducks or yellow umbrellas, but they *did* discover the partial remains of Ashley's wife. Her head had been plucked and cleaned and her mouth had been stuffed with slices of apple and onion, and the whole gruesome mess had been roasted over slow heat in the oven. What happened to the rest of Dora Ashley, officers could only speculate. Ashley himself was committed to the state mental hospital for the criminally insane in Salem, where he spent the rest of his unnatural life. Psychiatrists allowed as to how he was incurably afflicted with the "Too Much Rain" syndrome and had simply gone quackers.

In northwest Washington's very rainy Skagit County, Mrs. Kay Kosomovitch, the trophy wife of retired banker and avid golfer Rubin Kosomovitch, notified the local constabulary that upon returning home from a three-day shopping trip to Seattle that morning that she could find no sign of her husband and that there was no indication that he had even occupied the premises during her absence. Their bed was still neatly made exactly as she had left it, and there were no dirty dishes in the sink, no filthy clothes thrown on the floor, and no stinky underwear stuffed into the closets. Kay's white toy poodle Mandilina hadn't been fed or watered since her departure, and the poor creature had managed to survive only by eating garbage and drinking from the toilet bowl.

The Kosomovitch family was well-to-do and well known in Skagit County, and the sheriff quickly organized a search party. Half an hour later, deputies located a bloated and quite lifeless Rubin locked in a small storage shed behind the house. A handwritten suicide note found at the scene explained that because the rain was going to last forever, he would never again have the chance to go golfing nor the opportunity to use the brand new set of golf clubs given to him by his lovely young wife that very Christmas. The county coroner attributed Rubin's death to "acute dietary indiscretion" brought on by swallowing at least half a dozen new golf balls. Kay Kosomovitch, however, knew her husband's death had been caused by one thing and one thing only. Too much rain. One week after the funeral, she moved to Scottsdale, Arizona, and has never returned to Skagit County, Washington—not even for a visit.

———————

AT ABOUT THE same time that Arnold Ashley was decapitating ducks and Rubin Kosomovitch was gagging on golf balls, Noah Odell was sprawled on the living room sofa, looking up dirty words in a battered and dog-eared 1937 edition of *Webster's International Encyclopedic Dictionary*. Noah was bored literally to tears. Looking up words in this thick, heavy book of knowledge that his mother had purchased at a rummage sale was something he often did whether or not he was bored, but because it was Saturday afternoon and because it was bucketing rain outside, he had absolutely nothing to do *but* look up words. His ankles were stacked comfortably on the sofa's arm rest, and his muddy, high-topped tennis shoes were resting just the width of a frog's hair from an embroidered elbow doily. His mother was due back from her morning trek to the Gold Hill post office at any second, and Noah was torn between getting up, removing his shoes, and placing them outside on the front porch, or leaving his feet where they were and causing a boredom-breaking ruckus when his mother walked in. He knew what she would say— something like "Noah Odell, take your filthy shoes off that couch right now!"—and if his response wasn't immediate, she would more than likely send him to the lilac bush in the front yard to cut a switch that would be used on his backside.

Noah was fourteen, but he still got switched when he did things that he wasn't supposed to do. That didn't happen too often these days, luckily, but still occurred occasionally. He had, in fact, been sent to the lilac bush twice already that month: once for muttering "goddammit" when he stubbed his bare toe on a loose piece of kitchen-floor linoleum, and a second time for stupidly calling the unmarried and effeminate Reverend Balch, pastor of the Gold Hill Methodist Church, a "faggot," while in the presence of his mother. Noah had learned early that the size of the switch he cut would directly determine the magnitude of the switching he would receive.

The smaller the lilac branch, the more ferocious the switching, so he usually opted for larger ones. Moreover, he knew that protest only prolonged the agony. More often than not, he would go to the lilac bush without complaint when ordered, sever a limb with his Boy Scout knife, and making sure the smaller branches were whittled cleanly away, return to take his medicine like a man. His mother would then order him to lower his pants—including his underwear—and grab his knees. The pain was intense, but if he scrunched up and held his breath, it wasn't unbearable. Lowering his pants and scrunching up twice in one month was enough, Noah decided. He sat up, carefully removed the muddy tennis shoes and set them on the planking beneath their covered front porch just outside the door, then returned to the couch and his dictionary.

Outside, a steady, unfriendly drizzle was falling from a gray, unfriendly sky. It had been falling, day and night, for months. Noah could barely remember when it *hadn't* been drizzling. He walked to school in the rain. He walked home *from* school in the rain. He went to sleep and woke up with rain falling on the roof. Southern Oregon summers were wonderful—long, hot, sunny days, each one filled with the smell of grassy-banked rivers and madrone-covered hillsides and live oak trees baking in the heat. Southern Oregon summers were short, however. In October it usually started raining, and from then until May, and sometimes right on into June, it drizzled constantly. Unless southern Oregonians simply stayed inside for seven rainy months (and there were some who did), they were always wet and often muddy. KEEP OREGON GREEN, read a thousand southern Oregon highway signs. *Oregon doesn't need any goddammed help staying green*, Noah thought to himself, and as he had already done a dozen times that day, he wished that the drizzle would stop and the sun would come out. "And if I wish in one hand and crap in the other," he said out loud, "I know which one will fill up first." If his mother ever heard him say *that*, he might just as well go pitch a tent under the lilac bush and move in.

Noah heard the front door open and close softly, and a few seconds later his mother entered the living room. At thirty-nine, Ethel Odell was a small, busty, dark-haired woman, who resembled her son—from the neck up at least—so closely that no one could possibly doubt the consanguinity of the relationship. They both had the same raspberry-tinted cheeks; wide-set, greenish-brown eyes with long lashes; slender, large-lobed, almost elfin ears; and a long, strong, straight nose that divided their respective faces into two separate entities. A smattering of freckles marched randomly across their rosy cheeks, and they both sported a shock of dark brown hair that curled and cowlicked up from their scalps in every direction. Had not Ethel Odell insisted on monthly haircuts for both herself and Noah, in fact, their brunette canopies would have surged toward the heavens in tangled emancipation, a barrier no mere plastic comb could ever dominate. Noah knew that his mother said a small prayer during church service every Sunday morning, thanking the Lord that neither she nor her son had ever contracted head lice. In rural Oregon, the tiny insects were an irritating pestilence from which many children suffered. Searching for lice in Odell hair would be like searching for the proverbial rat in the woodpile. Usually accompanying the prayer was a quiet shudder as she visualized the prospect of lice. Bugs of any sort or size were one of the few things she could not deal with logically.

Smiling, Mrs. Odell removed a damp scarf from her hair and took off her old gray cotton coat, soggy from the drizzle. She hung both on a nail behind the door to dry.

"Is my little man finding something to do?" she asked. "Why don't you go see what your friends are up to today?"

"Not finding much, Mom," Noah answered, snapping the dictionary closed on the word "bollocks" and placing it on the floor beside the couch. "And I don't want go out in the rain. And stop calling me little. I'm bigger than you are!"

She sat next to Noah on the couch and tried unsuccessfully to brush a few feral strands of hair back from his forehead. He certainly was bigger than she. Last year, Noah had undergone a major growth spurt, shooting up five inches and gaining twenty pounds between February and the last of November. Norman Bell, the husky math teacher and football coach at Gold Hill High, had taken notice. He had knocked on the Odells' front door uninvited one Saturday morning and asked Mrs. Odell if Noah could try out for the next year's team.

"That boy is a natural fullback," he said. "He's gonna bust a few heads next year, I know it for a fact."

Ethel Odell listened politely.

"Coach Bell," she said quietly when he was finished, "please listen carefully. I will not allow my son to take part in violent activity of any sort. If you ever come near Noah again talking about football, or anything else that means busting someone's head, it will be *your* head that gets busted. Do I make myself clear?"

Having been in the business of training young men to bust heads for nearly fifteen years, the coach recognized a precarious situation when he saw one and took heed. The subject of Noah playing football never came up again. He hadn't much wanted to play anyway because running around in the rain and mud clad in uncomfortable shoes, heavy padding, and an ill-fitting helmet while a group of boys twice his size tried to smash him into mush was basically a pretty stupid way to spend time. He had been secretly pleased nonetheless, when someone other than his mother had noticed his extra height and weight.

Mrs. Odell removed a crumpled envelope from the front pocket of her blouse and handed it to Noah. "It's a letter from your Uncle Bud," she said with a resigned tone. "He's bought a ranch of some sort and wants us to come live with him."

Wham—just like that! If there was one thing Noah could say about his mother, it was that she didn't beat around the bush when she had something to say. He opened the envelope with anticipation. A letter from his cheery and affable uncle was always something to look forward to. Bud was not the cleanest of men or the most picturesque, but he was nonetheless Noah's favorite person in the world next to his mother. Habitually dressed in grubby bib overalls, a sleeveless undershirt, and scuffed leather boots, he usually concealed the smell of sweaty and infrequently washed armpits with a strong dose of bay rum and shaved only enough to keep from being arrested for vagrancy. A large nose and fanlike ears decorated three sides of his leathery face, and a thin, white knife scar—the result of a barroom brawl over a pretty señorita, or so Bud claimed—ran a crooked path southward from the top of his forehead to the bottom of his cheek. He also had a notable beer belly, one that usually strained his overall straps to the breaking point and reminded Noah of a large, ripe watermelon.

Bud was on Noah's "favorite person" list for two main reasons. First, he was a mellow, good-natured sort of man who incessantly seemed to look at the bright side of life and usually offered a grin to everyone he met. Second, and just as important, he always included a five dollar bill in each of his letters for what he called "Bub's gettin' around money." Noah saw that this letter contained no cash, however. It was just a single sheet of unlined tablet paper with his uncle's unmistakable and almost unreadable scrawl meandering like the tracks of a besotted chicken from edge to edge. As with all of Bud's correspondence, it was short and to the point:

> *deer sis an bub. how are you both. i am fine. im riteing to tell you this. i now own a ranch in tularosa new mexico. a nice plase but not to many tree but no dang rain and lots of chikens an some cows to. now that I have a good big hom and land I wood like you and bub to come liv heer. bub can be a cowboy and I shur can use sum help. if so ill send bus fair. sel that old dang car. sinserly Clarence w. Boggs (your brother)*

Noah read the letter slowly, and then read it again. He glanced up at his mother, who hadn't said a word since handing it to him. That was always a bad sign. She wasn't smiling either, and that was even worse. He didn't really know what to say, so he said nothing, but the word "cowboy" kept charging across the back of his eyeballs at full gallop with "ranch" not far behind. Noah had no trouble in reaching two quick conclusions: first, that Bud's letter was a divine gift sent especially to him by an angel in heaven, if such existed, and second, that if he played his cards right and didn't totally screw up, he might, within a very short time, see the last of the stinking, perpetual Oregon rain.

NOAH DIDN'T EXPECT his mother to make up her mind right away—one way or the other—about her older brother's invitation and she didn't disappoint him. Always a logical, pragmatic woman, she had steadfastly refused to be impulsive where the welfare of her son was concerned. Noah knew in his heart that if things stayed the same, the odds of leaving Oregon were not in his favor. Since his father's passing ten years earlier, he had been raised without the benefit of permanent male companionship or assistance and had survived quite nicely. Toward the end of each month when the last of their Social Security income had been spent on some unexpected levy, things sometimes got a bit iffy, but his mother earned a few extra dollars each month by hemming and patching other women's dresses or working as a part-time checker at Cogswell's Grocery. Their small, shingled, two-bedroom frame house with a cedar-shake roof and indoor plumbing on a corner lot just across from the high school hadn't cost much when they bought it and was now completely paid for. And even though Mrs. Odell hated to accept outright donations, Bud sent money every month. Noah knew his mother worried, but they had managed to get by for a long time without borrowing or stealing. Not once in fourteen years had either of them ever gone without a meal, so why should things change now?

When Noah thought about it, he realized that what he knew about his uncle was pretty limited. Bud and Noah's mother had grown up on a red dirt Oklahoma farm that produced barely enough food to support the family. He had quit school at the end of the sixth grade to work in the cotton fields (the consequence of this early departure was a corruption of the spoken language that would give an English teacher a bad case of the shudders), and when he left home at seventeen, he had moved west to New Mexico and had been there ever since. Noah had no idea what Bud's hobbies or interests were, and neither he nor his mother had ever been to New Mexico, let alone to his uncle's house. He had once asked his mother what Bud did for a living and had gotten a brusque reply that bordered on rudeness.

"It isn't really any of our business, is it," she had snapped. Noah had wisely decided to let the matter drop.

Nonetheless, Bud had helped Noah and his mother considerably since 1947. In addition to the cash he sent, he dropped in at least twice a year, just to make sure his sister and nephew were OK. He and his old Studebaker pickup would appear in the Odell's driveway unannounced, usually during late spring and then once again in the autumn. They never knew he was coming until he drove up and often didn't know he was leaving until an hour before he left. He generally stayed at least two weeks, but because he was a competent carpenter and passable appliance repairman, he spent most of the two weeks working. There was always plenty to build or repair at the Odell household.

At some point during his visits Bud always offered his sister a sizable wad of cash, which she would always refuse until he said something like, "It ain't fer you, Ek, it's fer Bub, yonder," or, "Dang, Sis, his shoes is got holes in 'em an' thet shirt he's wearin' is gettin' downright raggedy." Because Ethel Odell could not abide the thought of her son going around in rags or worn-out shoes, she normally accepted the donation reluctantly but without further complaint or mention.

On the other hand, Bud had two major blemishes that Noah's mother didn't appreciate. First was his passionate affection for beer. His favorite brand was Lucky Lager, and he consumed several bottles every day whenever possible. He was also a true "connoisseur of the blaspheme," or so Reverend Balch had once said, and when he was angry—which happily wasn't really that often—Bud could curse so formidably that he would literally blister paint. His sister tolerated the beer, but she was adept at shaming her brother for his swearing. Noah had seen Bud hang his chin sheepishly on his chest while Mrs. Odell's tongue lashed him like a cat-o'-nine-tails. She was not essentially a religious woman, and she attended the Gold Hill Methodist Church more for Noah's sake than hers. She just detested cursing—like some people detest liver and onions. Noah's mother also assumed quite rightly that Bud's bad habits would eventually rub off on her son if the two spent much time together.

If Mrs. Odell's opinion of her brother was sometimes miscible, Noah's was just the opposite, and the more he thought about the matter, the more he relished the idea of living with his tarnished but benevolent uncle. His grandparents on his mother's side were long since dead, and so they had no living relatives from the Boggs family left to consider except for Bud. There were a few Odells still around over in the center of the state near Bend, but Noah and his mother steered clear of their clannish relations, and that included Grandpa Ira and Grandma Mabel. Not a single one of them, his mother had once informed him, had attended his father's funeral, and not a single one had ever come to Gold Hill for a visit or even sent them a letter.

A week had passed since Bud's invitation had arrived, however, and Noah's mother had said little about moving except for one short conversation that took place after supper three days earlier. He had been reading his math workbook and listening half-heartedly to a Floyd Patterson–Archie Moore heavyweight title match from Chicago on the radio when Mrs. Odell came into the living room from the kitchen. She sat down on the sofa next to him.

"When your father died in 1947," she said, clasping her hands in her lap and getting right to the point, "I promised myself that I wouldn't ever do anything foolish that might cause us trouble, or worse, leave us out in the cold without so much as a pot to pee in."

Noah closed his math book and stared at his mother, a bit startled. He hadn't ever heard her use the word "pee" before. Occasionally she might say "drat," but that was about as raunchy as Ethel Odell ever got.

"I've kept that promise as best I could," she continued. "We may not have much, but we're both healthy and we have a roof over our heads and there's food on the table every day. It might be only beans and fried potatoes, but we aren't starving."

Noah started to say something, but Mrs. Odell held up her hand and went on.

"Let me finish. I know that you want to go live with your Uncle Bud, and in a way I suppose I do, too, but moving to a place we've never heard of, or never been to, or never even seen pictures of would be doing something foolish. We don't know anything at all about New Mexico!"

Out of one ear, Noah could hear the crowd on the radio roaring and the announcer shouting something about Patterson knocking out Moore in two minutes and twenty-seven seconds of the fifth round. He forced himself to block out the radio noise and concentrate on looking directly into his mother's eyes. He honestly didn't know if she was trying to convince him or herself that they shouldn't move, but it sounded like the latter.

"New Mexico is the forty-seventh state in the Union," he said confidently. "It's between Arizona and Colorado and Texas, and a small part of it sits along the border with Mexico. The capital is Santa Fe and the biggest city is Albuquerque, and it has deserts and mountains and lots of Indians, and it doesn't rain much." Goddam, dictionaries were wonderful!

It was Mrs. Odell's turn to look startled. "Well, you've certainly done your homework." She stood up and switched off the lamp at the end of the sofa. "And now, little smarty pants, turn off the radio and brush your teeth and then go to bed! You've got school tomorrow."

THAT HAD BEEN on Tuesday. Now it was Friday evening, and things hadn't progressed any further. Noah stood bare chested with his hands above his head in front of the large bathroom mirror, carefully searching the soft, pale skin of his armpits for even the slightest evidence of underarm hair while thinking about New Mexico and considering what to do next. Most of his friends—at least those he had seen naked or in swimsuits—had tufts of dark, wiry hair sprouting from beneath their arms, but Noah's pits were still totally hairless. A month earlier, as an experiment, he had coaxed a neighbor's mangy, long-haired black dog to within petting distance with a cracker, and while scratching the animal's head with one hand, he clipped a large hunk of fur from its back with the other using a pair of his mother's sewing scissors. Later that afternoon—with the bathroom door locked and a homemade wooden wedge jammed between door sill and the door itself for good measure—he stripped to his underwear and gingerly pasted a thick clump of black dog hair into each of his armpits with a glob of quick-drying model airplane glue. He stood sideways in front of the mirror, raising and lowering each of his arms over and over, admiring the manly flash of black against white, until after several minutes his armpits started to prickle with pain as the hardened glue began to pull and pinch and gouge the tender skin to which it was now firmly adhered. It took twenty agonizing minutes of rubbing and peeling to finally remove the glue and fur mixture from underneath his arms, but Noah was nonetheless impressed with his own cleverness. He had seen the future and the future was him . . . with hairy, smelly, masculine armpits.

Noah put on his shirt and left the bathroom—disappointed that he had not found even the slightest hint of fuzz growing under his arms—and flopped down on the living room sofa while he waited for supper. He realized that he needed to do something—though he didn't know what—to prod his mother into reaching a positive decision about New Mexico. He imagined himself as a cowboy, sitting around a campfire, roping cows, riding the range, doing whatever it was cowboys did all day. Never mind that he had never seen a range, let alone a real cowboy, and what he knew about cowboys was about the same as what he knew about football, which probably wasn't enough to fill the bunghole of a flea. He got up and walked to the small bookshelf where they kept a King James Version of the Holy Bible and their beat-up copy of *Webster's International*. Noah opened the latter to the *C* section and flipped through it until he located the word "cowboy" on page 223.

> **cowboy:** A hired hand who tends cattle and performs other duties on horseback; a performer who gives exhibitions of riding and roping and bulldogging; someone who is reckless or irresponsible (especially in driving vehicles); a cattle herder; a drover; specifically, one of an adventurous class of herders and drovers on the plains of the western and southwestern United States.

Noah understood most of the definitions quite clearly, although he had no idea what "bulldogging" meant, and the bit about "reckless or irresponsible" was a little mystifying. He was too young to drive a vehicle, but he had certainly been called reckless and irresponsible by his mother on a number of occasions. Did that make him a cowboy? He thought not, and read on:

A cowboy is an animal herder who tends cattle on ranches in North America, traditionally on horseback, and often performs a multitude of other ranch-related tasks.

There was a lot more about historical cowboys and cowboy traditions, but Noah figured that once he got to New Mexico, the easiest way to find out what cowboys did was to ask his uncle. Getting to New Mexico, of course, was the hurdle. He thumbed through the pages of the dictionary until he came to the *N*'s and then turned the pages slowly until he found New Mexico. He had already read through the information a number of times over the past week, but once more wouldn't hurt.

New Mexico (Spanish: Nuevo Mexico): The 47th state of the Union (1912), New Mexico is located in the southwestern region of the United States. It is bordered on the west by Arizona, on the north by Colorado, and on the east by Texas. Inhabited by American Indian populations for many centuries, it has also been part of the Imperial Spanish viceroyalty of New Spain, part of Mexico, and a U.S. territory. Among U.S. states, New Mexico has the highest percentage of Hispanics, comprising both recent immigrants and descendants of Spanish colonists. It also has the fifth-highest total number of American Indians after California, Oklahoma, Arizona, and Texas. The tribes represented in the state consist of mostly Navajo and Pueblo peoples. The climate of the state is highly arid, and its territory is mostly covered by mountains and desert. At a population density of 15 per square mile, New Mexico is the fifth most sparsely inhabited U.S. state. The first known inhabitants of New Mexico were members of the Clovis culture of Paleo-Indians. Later inhabitants include the Anasazi and the Mogollon cultures.

Out of curiosity, Noah flipped backward to the *A* section and looked up "Anasazi." There wasn't a lot to read.

Anasazi: A group of early American Indians who inhabited Colorado, Utah, Arizona, and New Mexico. They often lived in caves and in underground shelters known as pit houses but sometimes constructed large, above ground towns which Spanish settlers called "*pueblos*"—such as Chaco Canyon in New Mexico—and cliff cities such as Mesa Verde in Colorado.

The dictionary would have probably offered more information on the Anasazi and New Mexico if Noah had bothered to search further, but what he had already read provided him with two important facts: the state was arid, which meant that it didn't rain very much, and it had lots of Indians, which probably meant—at least according to the western movies he'd seen—that there were lots of cowboys around.

With all this in mind, Noah began to carefully formulate a plan of action. Over the years he had charted his mother's strengths and weaknesses like a sea captain might chart a newly discovered island. He also knew how to avoid the former and aggravate the latter to his best advantage. Ethel Odell was a strong woman and a tough mother, but there were chinks in her armor through which she could be manipulated. Noah had discovered three, in fact. He could play upon her sympathy, irritate her discomfort, or flagellate her disgust. Knowing full well that moving to New Mexico was not a forgone conclusion and that he would get only one chance, he decided—just to make sure—to do all three.

3

Dead Soldiers, Sow Bugs, and Garter Snakes

Bottled beer—beer that has been provided by breweries for human consumption in glass bottles, or beer that is sold commercially or traded or bartered in glass bottles—has soothed man's palate and eased his mind since the sixteenth century. Naturally, anything that has been around that long doesn't remain unchanged. In the sixteenth century, for instance, wayfaring strangers, wandering minstrels, itinerant monks, poverty-stricken serfs, commoners, knights so bold, and all the king's horses and men could drink from only one type of bottle—a heavy, black glass receptacle stoppered with a cork or wooden plug. In Middle English it was known as a *botel*; in Middle French, *boteille*; and in Medieval Latin, *butticula*, and it was often used, when empty, to bludgeon unruly wives or mouthy older children who had not yet learned that it wasn't wise to sass Pa when he was half in the bag.

Modern beer drinkers have a much wider choice from which to choose. "Stubbies," for instance, are short, fat bottles that can be packed into small spaces for transporting. Beer isn't usually transported very far before being drunk, however, so "stubbies" aren't any more popular than any other bottle. Standard beer bottles, or "longnecks," provide a long cushion of air that absorbs the pressure of carbonation and eventually reduces the risk of explosions. Most beers, of course, don't have time to explode before they are consumed, so nobody really cares. "Growlers" are one-half-gallon glass jugs of beer. Growlers hold way more beer than longnecks or stubbies, so naturally, real men who sweat, spit, fart, have hair in their armpits, and work for a living prefer "growlers."

When empty beer bottles—whether they are stubbies, long-necks, or growlers—are thrown out of a car window and alight without shattering on the weedy, gravel shoulders of a city street, county road, or state highway, they automatically become "dead soldiers." Nobody seems to know exactly why discarded bottles are called dead soldiers because they aren't really dead, just empty, and not a single one of them was ever in the army. Nonetheless, every Saturday morning during southern Oregon's rainy months, if Noah Odell wasn't doing something else, which he usually wasn't, and so that he might have a little extra spending money to squander on Big Hunks or Baby Ruths, he collected dead soldiers from the muddy shoulders of half a dozen county roads and state highways around Gold Hill. He carried them in an old gunnysack, and when the sack was full, he would haul them down to Cogswell's Grocery, where he received two cents each for the stubbies, three cents each for the longnecks, and a nickel each for growlers. It was hard work, and he often came home smelling like a brewery and covered from head to foot with mud, but he didn't really mind. It got him out of the house and put spending money in his pocket.

His mother minded plenty, of course, and if there had been a better way for Noah to make a few bucks during the rainy season, she wouldn't have let him anywhere near the highway, let alone allowed him to handle dozens of filthy beer bottles, most of which were half-filled with dead bugs pickled in smelly, anonymous liquids.

"Young man," Mrs. Odell had objected when he had first broached the idea of collecting dead soldiers, "you don't need money that badly. We are not in the poor house and you aren't wearing rags, and I won't have you picking up other people's garbage!"

"They're just old bottles, Mom, not garbage. And I *do* need money for things. I can't even buy you a nice birthday present and I need to start saving for Christmas and my fishing reel is busted and besides that, all my friends have money for candy bars and I don't."

Mrs. Odell had finally given in and allowed Noah to collect bottles, mainly because there simply *wasn't* a better way for her son to make spending money during the winter. The reason, of course, was the uninterrupted, imperishable drizzle that fell continually from the gray Pacific Northwest sky from October until the first of June and sometimes later. During the summer, Noah could mow lawns or pull weeds or move piles of junk for the neighbors, but for the rest of the year, like most of the other boys he knew, he suffered from the rainy day, southern Oregon blues. Consequently, Mrs. Odell swallowed her pride on Saturday mornings and let her son paw through the weeds along the roadsides for several hours, carrying his heavy, stinking gunnysack. She always made him bathe when he came home, but the odor of stale beer and rotting insects in his hair and on his clothes often lasted for days.

Noah knew that the uninterrupted, imperishable drizzle, at least in his mother's case, led to discomfort, both physical and monetary. If the rain wasn't dribbling through their worn-out cedar-shake roof and warping the linoleum floor in the living room, it was causing mildew to form on the kitchen baseboards. Both situations meant a handyman's visit and another bill Mrs. Odell had to pay if Bud wasn't around to repair the damage. Worse, when the rains began in late October, in came the critters, thousands of them—earwigs, sow bugs, daddy longlegs, tree frogs, and garter snakes—through the rotting holes in the baseboard caused by the previous year's rain that Bud had missed on his *last* visit. If there was anything Mrs. Odell disliked worse than drinking and cursing, it was crawling, slithering, slimy, germ-covered vermin.

Noah's plan went into effect on Saturday morning. He pulled on his tattered old raincoat, picked up his gunnysack from the porch, and told his mother he was off to collect dead soldiers. He had discovered long ago that the most productive area around Gold Hill for discarded bottles was the wide shoulder of Route 99, a paved, two-lane highway that connected the town of Rogue River in the north to the sprawling lumber mills in Central Point. Loggers and sawmill workers vastly preferred growlers over stubbies or longnecks. After twelve hours of cutting, hauling, or sawing up giant ponderosa and sugar pine logs, a regular bottle of beer wouldn't even wash away the sawdust in a lumberman's mouth, let alone quench his thirst.

At least that's what Noah had always imagined, although he couldn't remember exactly why. He had met only one real lumberman in his life and that was Buford Betts, the father of his best friend, Ricky Betts. Mr. Betts was a lumberjack, but he didn't really look much like what Noah thought a lumberjack should look like. Instead of a towering, dark-eyed, black-bearded pillar of a man, with broad shoulders and bulging muscles gleaned from long hours of swinging a double-bitted ax in the dense pine and fir forests of southern Oregon, Mr. Betts was skinny and extremely short, even when wearing his caulked leather logging boots, which laced up almost to his knees. His head was entirely bald and he had no facial hair to speak of except for the two giant, bushy black caterpillars that doubled as eyebrows and danced up and down above his eyes when he talked. He was also slightly crooked, mainly from the waist down, as the result of having been struck by the front fender of a logging truck. Mr. Betts drank growlers, of course, because all lumbermen preferred growlers, and he swore a lot because all lumbermen swore, but somehow he hadn't ever given Noah the impression of being a man who each day lived on the cutting edge of danger.

Three hours after leaving the house, Noah returned home covered with mud and soaking wet but richer by two dollars and twenty cents. He left his gunnysack on the porch, took a hot bath in the old claw-foot tub in the bathroom, and then helped his mother pin the hem on a taffeta dress she was mending for a neighbor. Hemming wasn't a task he ever relished. Stripping to his underwear, he had to pull the dress over his head, then turn very slowly with his arms out while his mother knelt at his feet and pinned the hem evenly with a hemming guide. If one of his friends ever saw him so attired, he would be the laughing stock of Gold Hill High.

As he stood in the living room, arms parallel to the floor and his mother at his feet, humming to herself as she worked, Noah felt like Jesus Christ being crucified on the cross, wearing a pink taffeta dress with a light blue flower design. He was careful not to say much about his bottle-hunting excursion that morning. He said even less at supper, toying with his food and staring off into space every few minutes.

"I know you like black-eyed peas," Mrs. Odell said from across the table. Noah hardly ever toyed with his food. "Are you getting sick?"

"I feel fine, Mom," he answered gloomily. "I was just thinking about that big snake I saw today. Maybe a rattlesnake, but I couldn't really tell. He was coiled up in an old tire that was full of bugs and spiders." Noah had never even seen a picture of a rattlesnake, but he squirmed perceptibly anyway and then added casually, "I just wondered if he was poisonous, that's all."

Ethel Odell froze with a spoonful of black-eyed peas halfway to her mouth. Her typically raspberry-colored cheeks were as pale as a freezing nun's buttocks.

"Where on earth . . . !" she stammered.

"Out on the highway," Noah said, suppressing an urge to giggle. This was too easy. "He was a big one. Probably five feet long." Noah spread his arms wide. "Don't worry—I didn't touch him or anything."

He scratched the spot on the back of his neck that just before dinner he had pricked with a pin in the bathroom until it bled.

"And I got a tick today, Mom. He bit me on the neck and swelled up with blood before I picked him off." He turned and showed the spot to his mother. "I put some iodine on it so it doesn't hurt anymore."

For a moment Noah though he'd gone too far, but his mother just sighed and they finished dinner in silence. Before bed, he got a stern lecture about getting too close to snakes and was ordered henceforth to carry a large stick with him on bottle-hunting forays. The next morning at breakfast, however, he knew he'd made some progress because his mother brought up the subject of Bud's letter herself.

"Do you really want to go live with your uncle, Noah?" she asked. "You'll have to change schools and leave all your friends behind. Dickens and your parakeets can't come either, so they'll all have to stay here."

"We couldn't take Dickens?" Noah was a bit startled at the thought of leaving his big yellow tomcat behind. Dickens had been around since kittenhood, when they had found him mewing pitifully on their back porch one summer evening. Bud had been visiting at the time and had muttered, "What the dickens is makin' all thet racket?" before scooting his chair back from the supper table and opening the screen door. There was the kitten, probably no more than three weeks old. They never found out where he came from, but the name Dickens stuck. "I could make him a basket and. . . ."

"We can't take him," his mother said sternly. "They wouldn't allow him on the bus, so you would just have to find him a good home here. And what about Ricky? He's your best friend, isn't he?"

Noah looked up and met his mother's stare. For a second, he wavered. Ricky Betts *was* his best friend, or had been before he moved a few weeks earlier to the town of Prospect, more than thirty miles away. He and Ricky had certainly enjoyed some high times and exciting adventures together, though most people who knew them would probably agree that "gotten into a lot of mischief together" was a more accurate description.

When Noah was ten, for instance, Bud had given him a Red Ryder BB gun for Christmas. Ricky had also gotten a BB gun, and when summer arrived, they had spent many hours wandering the oak- and madrone-covered hillsides around Gold Hill, hunting whatever savage beasts they could find. Mostly it was dairy cows, though they were careful to shoot them in their rear half only—which really caused them to jump but didn't actually hurt anything—and only when no one was looking. Occasionally they bagged a street light or a window in an abandoned building, but one July afternoon, when Ricky tried to add a large, striped skunk to his list of trophies, their hunting adventures came to an abrupt end. Ten seconds after the first BB hit the skunk, both boys were in full and chaotic flight toward home, screaming their heads off as the powerful thiol compounds from the animal's anal glands turned their eyes and nasal passages into pockets of pain. Scrubbed raw in cold tomato juice baths once a day for a week, both boys permanently lost their taste for big game hunting. The BB guns went to Red Ryder heaven and were never seen again.

Another escapade gone wrong had been an evening excursion to a gloomy, three-story Victorian mansion situated on an overgrown lot at the north end of Gold Hill. The house had been built in the 1870s and certainly looked its age. Dozens of giant live oak trees dotted the property, and in places the undergrowth was so thick that it almost blocked the view of the rambling old house from the street. On more than one occasion, a pale white face had been seen peering from one of the upstairs windows, but the lights never seemed to be on, even at night. Everyone said the place was haunted, and there wasn't a kid in town who would even walk by the house alone if he or she could help it.

Except for Noah and Ricky, who on a warm autumn evening after supper climbed through the saggy barbed-wire fence that ran along one side of the property and crept quietly toward the dilapidated old structure. Using the huge oak trees as cover, they were careful to dodge the thick patches of poison oak that grew under the trees. Their BB guns had been confiscated, but both boys were armed with slingshots made from Y-shaped Pacific madrone branches and strips of old bicycle tires.

Ten feet from the Victorian's lopsided back porch, Ricky stopped and took a marble-sized pebble from his pocket. He placed it in the leather pouch of his slingshot, pulled back the rubbers, and let the stone fly toward the back door. When nothing happened, he reached for another pebble. Then he stopped, sniffing the air like a dog.

"Somethin's burning," he whispered. "Stinks really bad."

"I smell it," Noah whispered back. "Do ghosts stink?"

"Don't know," Ricky said. "I ain't never seen no ghost."

The creaky voice that came floating out from the gloomy darkness of the overhanging porch was high-pitched and laced with irony and spite.

"I'm cooking up two nosey boys just like you," it said, "and you're gonna be next."

Ricky shouted "ugghhh!" at the top of his voice. He jumped a foot straight into the air and promptly peed his pants. Noah gave a little screech and headed for the fence at a dead run with Ricky stepping on his heels. They plowed straight through the flotillas of poison oak that covered the lot and slowed down only when the old Victorian was a block away and out of sight. They were both shaking so badly that their teeth rattled when they talked.

"Let's go tell the constable!" Noah rattled, trying to catch his breath.

"But we wasn't supposed to be there," Ricky countered. "We'll get in big trouble. Besides, I cain't let nobody see I got wet britches."

"But they're cooking people!" Noah almost shouted. "We've gotta tell *somebody*! Nobody's gonna look at your darn pants."

They found Constable McCoy in his small office next to Morrow's Hardware and spluttered out their tale, leaving out the part about the slingshot and about Ricky peeing his pants. When they finished, the constable just grinned.

"That old lady sure has got a sense of humor," he said, shaking his head and trying not to laugh. "Listen boys, what you smelled was old Granny Pillows burning her garbage. She puts it in a barrel out back and burns it once a week. And I'll be straight with you. She's an eighty-one-year-old woman who pays her taxes and likes her privacy, and neither one of you should have been on her property." Constable McCoy walked them to the door. "Granny Pillows is a nice old lady that never hurt a flea, and she just wants to be left alone," he said. "I'm not gonna tell your parents, but you boys need to mind your own business."

Noah and Ricky kept their noses clean after that little exploit, at least for a while. It took them three weeks just to get rid of the worst case of poison oak either of them had ever had. A year later, however, Ricky did precisely what he had been told not to do a thousand times by his parents; he played with matches. He played with them on the tinder-dry hillside just north of Gold Hill on a scorching August day during one the hottest, driest summers in southern Oregon's recent history. Native grasses that covered the hillsides around town had turned a dark, parched brown from drought, and the live oaks and madrones were desperate and despairing for a drink. A dozen fire trucks and fifty volunteer firemen from Central Point and Medford fought the blaze for eighteen hours as it crept ever nearer to the houses on Gold Hill's northern outskirts. When it was finally put out, Constable McCoy interviewed Ricky's parents and then interviewed the parents of all the children who lived near the spot where the fire had started, but learned nothing. Noah was the only one besides Ricky who knew the real story, and he kept his mouth shut. Luckily, the blaze was extinguished before it could destroy anyone's home, and though Gold Hill reeked of smoke and charred wood for months afterward, no real harm had been done. When Ricky's dad got a better job offer from the logging company that ran the big sawmill in Prospect, the family moved. Noah knew he would miss his best friend, but he was secretly relieved.

Noah thought about Ricky Betts and Dickens and of his uncle's wide grin and large ears and his swearing and of a ranch and cowboys and campfires and horses. Carefully, he put his right hand under the table and removed the straight pin he had swiped from the sewing session the previous afternoon and had threaded into his jeans just below the knee where it wouldn't do any damage. Holding the pin between his thumb and first finger about half an inch from the point, he jabbed it into his leg as hard as he could. Two giant tears, real huckleberry-sized tears of pain, slithered down his cheek and onto his shirt. God dang, that hurt!

"I want to be a cowboy, Mom!" said Noah, feeling slightly sick to his stomach. "I want to be a cowboy, and I can't do it in the rain!"

4

A Journey of a Thousand Miles
Always Begins with Some Kid Throwing Up

In the year of our Lord 1626, Dutchman Peter Minuit pur-chased the island of Manhattan from the Lenape Indians for sixty guilders and some junky beads and trinkets that he picked up for a song at a yard sale in Amsterdam. By today's standards, sixty guilders would have been equal to about a thousand dollars, and de heer Minuit got a darn good deal anyway you look at it, unless you happened to be an Indian.

The Odells' two-bedroom frame house on the corner of Jacoby Street and Sixth Avenue, with its worn-out cedar-shake roof and oversized front lawn, sold within a week of being put on the market. The buyer was a sweaty, overweight retiree from Los Angeles named Benjamin Bakker, whose shiny, bald head reminded Noah of a giant onion. De heer Bakker, too, got a pretty good deal, and he had the $2,500 in cash that Mrs. Odell was asking for the house right there in his wallet. He made it clear that he wanted to move in immediately. Ethel Odell made it clear that she wasn't about to move until the first week of June so that Noah could finish the school year. Benjamin Bakker acquiesced, knowing a losing battle when he saw one.

Mrs. Odell wrote lots of letters and made a flurry of telephone calls from Gold Hill's only public telephone booth, which was attached to the outside wall of Cogswell's Grocery. She sold their old, green Nash Ambassador, with the rusty fenders and broken door handles, to a used car dealer in Central Point. They rarely used the vehicle anyway, mainly because it was always breaking down or wouldn't start when it was needed, and Gold Hill was so small they could walk everywhere they wanted to go. The greasy salesman at the dealership gave Mrs. Odell just thirty dollars for the Nash, but it was a relief to be rid of the thing.

A pair of parcels wrapped in brown paper arrived from Bud a few days later. The smaller of the packages contained two Greyhound bus tickets and three crisp, one-hundred-dollar bills. The larger package held a pair of hand-tooled leather cowboy boots with cream colored tops and pointed toes. HECHO EN MEXICO was stamped on the soles, and they were exactly Noah's size.

Noah finished his freshman year at Gold Hill High without any problems. He didn't tell many people he was leaving, mainly because he didn't think anyone would care. In the meantime, he took care of several exigent tasks that had to be completed before they left. First on the list was to find a new home for Dickens, long and trusted friend, who, if nothing else, kept the house and yard free of rodents. He wasn't very handy at dispatching bugs, frogs, or snakes, but the Odells hadn't seen a mouse in years. The tom's relocation turned out to be easier than Noah had expected. On the day before their departure, he was to deliver Dickens to the Gold Hill Grange, in whose spacious halls the overweight old cat had been promised a cozy future terrorizing a rampant population of mice and rats.

Finding a new domicile for a matched pair of light green parakeets named Lopsy and Dopsy, presented as a birthday gift to Noah by an acquaintance of his mother, proved to be more difficult. Twice he canvassed the neighborhood but was unable to find anyone willing to adopt the birds, neither of which could talk nor even sing. Both of them, in fact, would much rather bite the finger that fed them than perch on it. They were disliked even by Noah's mother, who had been victimized more than once by the "proffered finger syndrome" from which the pair suffered.

His last hope was loony old Mr. McKnight, a sort of hermit who lived just up Jacoby Street from the Odells in a ramshackle, two-room cabin made from scrap lumber and tar paper. The cabin sat on a small, untidy lot blanketed with blackberry bushes, poison oak, madrone trees, and junk. Mr. McKnight was an ancient, withered fellow, perhaps seventy-five, whose only clothing seemed to be filthy bib overalls and leather boots with flapping soles and whose long white hair and full white beard were always dirty and wildly unkempt. No one seemed to know much about the old man, but Noah had learned from Mrs. Malloy—the librarian at the Gold Hill Community Library—that Mr. McKnight had once been a gold miner. Now, however, he seldom left the confines of his cabin, at least in daylight. People around the neighborhood all agreed that Mr. McKnight was loony because on the rare occasions that he was seen in public, he was always talking to himself. Muttering to himself would be a more apt description. The last time Noah had seen the old man, in fact, was just before dark on a late autumn day when they had passed each other near the driveway leading to Noah's house. Mr. McKnight was having an animated conversation with some invisible entity, muttering things like, "Whar in hell d'you leave the mule?" and, "We surely hit the mother lode this time!" Noah politely smiled and said hello as the old man passed, but Mr. McKnight just kept walking and muttering, gesturing delicately in the air with gnarled hands as though he were explaining a complicated math problem to a group of students.

Noah dreaded going anywhere near Mr. McKnight's cabin, but a week before they were to leave for New Mexico and having had absolutely no success finding the parakeets a new home elsewhere, he cranked up his courage, walked up the street to the old man's dilapidated house, and knocked loudly on the door.

"Who that be?" The gruff, muffled reply scratched its way with great difficulty through the old boards and ripped tar paper that covered the cabin walls.

"It's Noah Odell, Mr. McKnight," Noah answered loudly. "I'm your neighbor. My mom and I live down the street."

For almost a minute there was no further sound or movement from inside the cabin. Then suddenly the door swung open and Mr. McKnight stood there scowling. He wore nothing but dirty socks and a decrepit undershirt that barely covered his private parts, and Noah caught a strong whiff of body odor and musty clothing mixed with the aroma of rotting garbage and freshly brewed coffee. The old man's long white hair flew out from his head in every direction, and his beard was filled with what looked like small pieces of oatmeal. Noah had never seen anything quite like the half-naked apparition standing in front of him.

"Whatever yer sellin' boy, I ain't wantin' none," Mr. McKnight said. "Ain't got no money anyways."

"I just wanted to talk to you for a minute," Noah said, getting right to the point. "My mom and I are moving to New Mexico, and I'm trying to find someone who'll take my parakeets. They're nice and they love people and they aren't any trouble at all to take care of." Noah had long since given up being truthful about Lopsy and Dopsy.

"What'n hell's a parakeet?" the old man asked. He scratched his crotch with an arthritic, claw-like finger.

"A bird," Noah said. "Parakeets are colored birds that come from the jungle. I have two of them."

"They good to eat?" Mr. McKnight asked, breaking into a grin. His broken, yellow teeth gleamed with saliva. "Like chickens? Ain't had no chicken since I cain't remember when. Ate a goddam dog once, though, guts and all. Damn tasty, too, when yer hungry."

"Parakeets are kind of small," Noah said, robustly wishing he was someplace else. "Way too small to eat."

Mr. McKnight stared vacantly into Noah's face. "Cain't eat 'em, then I don't want 'em," he said, and slammed the cabin door.

Noah did not look back as he hurriedly walked down the hill to his own house, but he half expected Mr. McKnight to come storming out of the cabin at any second, swinging an ax or brandishing a butcher knife and muttering about dinner. Safely home, he sat down on the steps of their small front porch and tried to think of a solution. Earlier, he had seriously considered just releasing the parakeets into the bushes, but his mother had said no.

"Those two poor little creatures would most certainly die a slow, cruel death from starvation if you just let them go," she said. "They don't know how to find food and probably don't even know what water looks like if it's not in a bowl."

Noah closed his eyes and concentrated. In his mind he formed a picture of a skinny old man with a long white beard dressed only in dirty underwear. He was sitting at a dinner table in front of a greasy plate, clutching a knife and fork in his twisted hands. A pile of small bones lay to one side of the plate next to a dog's head, and the old man's beard was dotted with small blue and green feathers. Mr. McKnight was grinning and licking his lips. Noah's eyes popped open. He knew what he had to do.

An hour later, while Mrs. Odell visited a friend down the street, he carried the cage containing the malicious birds outside and set it on the lawn. He made sure no one was nearby, and then, wearing a pair of old garden gloves, he carefully removed Lopsy and Dopsy one at a time from their cage and stuffed them beneath an over-turned galvanized washtub on the grass.

Dickens had been watching curiously from the porch. "I need some help saving these birds from a slow death by starvation," Noah told the big tom. "You interested?" He lifted one edge of the washtub and shoved Dickens underneath with the two birds. Five minutes later, he got rid of the cage by flinging it into a thick patch of poison oak and blackberry vines in the shallow canyon behind the house. He gave Dickens a scratch behind the ears and told him to keep his mouth shut.

When Mrs. Odell returned from her visit, she noticed the missing cage immediately. "Oh good," she said, with a noticeable tone of relief in her voice. "You found a home for the parakeets. Who took them, honey?"

"Some guy with whiskers, Mom," Noah answered. "He said he liked birds a lot." The subject was dropped. Well, it wasn't *exactly* a lie. If Mrs. Odell happened to notice the tiny blue and green feathers clinging to one corner of Dickens's mouth, she didn't mention it.

Noah's final task—other than packing his toothbrush—was to say farewell to a rock-throwing, cat-kicking, snotty-nosed, seventeen-year-old bully named Skeeter Johnson. Skeeter lived with his mother, three sisters, and an older brother named Jimmy in an old, gray house six blocks away from the Odells on the same street. Skeeter was not very smart. He had been held back in the fourth and fifth grades and was the oldest kid in his class by far. Worse, he was just plain mean. On numerous occasions, and for no apparent reason other than having a contemptible nature, the six-foot-tall Skeeter had pounded Noah's nose to a bloody pulp after school. The worst of the bullying had taken place on a day two years earlier during summer vacation. Noah had been practicing basketball by himself on the paved court at the high school a block away. He was concentrating on his shooting so much that he hadn't seen Skeeter and Jimmy enter the court and come up behind him. Noah had been holding the ball over his head in preparation for a long shot, when Skeeter simply grabbed it out of his hands.

"Git outta here, you little bastard," Skeeter said, bouncing the ball. "We're gonna play and we don't need no little crap-head watching." He tossed the ball to his brother, took a step forward, and with absolutely no warning, slapped Noah in the face.

Noah was just twelve and half Skeeter's size. Nonetheless, he foolishly took a feeble swing at the larger boy. Skeeter just grinned and then proceeded to beat Noah's face and head so badly that at the end of thirty seconds his eyes were almost closed and his shirt was covered with blood. Crying and in pain, Noah stumbled out of the basketball court and ran home, where his very angry mother cleaned him up, put him to bed, and then went directly to Constable McCoy's office to file charges.

And that was as far as it went. Two days later, the constable came by the house and notified Ethel Odell that Skeeter's mother and sisters were prepared to swear in court that Skeeter and Jimmy hadn't left the house on the morning Noah had been beaten. There was nothing more he could do.

"And don't try to do anything about this yourself, Ethel," Constable McCoy warned. "Just leave it alone and try to keep Noah as far away from Skeeter as possible. That's a real mean family down there, and there's no telling what they might do."

Skeeter hadn't bothered him much during the past year because of his sudden growth spurt, but after years of hateful abuse, Noah had cultivated a smoldering hatred for the older boy. He now planned to bestow a crumb of long-awaited justice where it was sorely needed.

Noah waited until the morning before their departure for New Mexico. Most of their belongings had already been packed into half a dozen sturdy cardboard lettuce boxes, wrapped with heavy twine, and shipped via Greyhound bus to C.W. Boggs, Tularosa, New Mexico. Dickens had been tearfully delivered to old Mrs. Bell at the Grange, the yard had been cleaned up, and the grass had been mowed for the last time. Noah told his mother he had to say good-bye to someone, then walked to a preselected spot behind a madrone tree along the street halfway between his house and the Johnsons'. He didn't have long to wait. Within half an hour, he spotted Skeeter heading toward him with a basketball—Noah's ball no doubt—underneath his arm, headed for the concrete basketball court at school.

Noah waited out of sight behind the madrone tree until Skeeter was ten feet beyond him. Then, with a goose egg–sized boulder launched from an oversized slingshot especially manufactured for the occasion, he got in his parting shot, so to speak. The rock hit Skeeter right between the shoulder blades with a satisfying *thunk!* The bully screeched and fell flat on his face. Noah stuck the slingshot in his back pocket, ran to where Skeeter lay moaning on the street, and kicked him as hard as he could in the ribs.

"Bye-bye, scrotum face!" Noah said loudly, so that Skeeter would know it was him. "I hope you hurt for a year!"

He had found the word "scrotum" in the dictionary quite by accident when he was ten and thought it a grand word, although he hadn't been able to figure out exactly when or where to use it until now. On the same day—again by accident—he had found the word "penis," which was much more descriptive than "wee-wee," which is what his mother called it, or "whizzer" or "pecker" or "yer tool," which is what Uncle Bud liked to say. He had never seen a penis that whizzed or pecked or could pound a nail, and he had seen quite a number of them during the last several years because beginning in junior-high, all boys had to shower after P.E. every day, and all the showerheads were in one icy-cold, concrete-floored room in the gym.

He gave Skeeter another vicious kick in the ribs. "Don't steal anyone else's basketball, penis nose!" he said even louder than before, and then he turned and ran for his house.

An hour later, Constable McCoy knocked loudly on the Odells' front door. Surprised to see officialdom on the porch, Mrs. Odell politely invited him into the living room. Trying to look as innocent as possible, Noah joined them.

"I won't be but a minute or two, Ethel," the constable said. "Sorry to hear that you and Noah are leaving Gold Hill. The town's gonna miss you'all." He looked at Noah and grinned. "With you and Ricky Betts both gone, I guess I can board up the jail and retire."

Constable McCoy took off his hat and looked at Noah. "Skeeter Johnson told his mom that Noah tried to brain him with a rock down the road a piece this morning. Skeeter's mom says she's gonna press charges. I just wondered if you'all knew anything about the incident."

Mrs. Odell turned and gave Noah a stern look. "Noah, did you hit Skeeter Johnson?"

"Nope," Noah lied. His face was as much a model of innocence as he could make it. He had practiced his speech and his innocent look at least a dozen times in the past hour, knowing that the constable would arrive sooner or later. "Why would I hit Skeeter? We're almost best friends."

"Noah hasn't left the house this morning," Mrs. Odell said, with a knowing smile breaking across her face. "He's been with me every second. I'll swear to that in court."

Noah paused for a count of five. "I bet he got hit by a meteor!" he said, trying to sound excited. "The radio said Oregon was getting a meteor shower this month. I'll bet anything that's what happened."

Skeeter Johnson had picked on many children over the years besides Noah, most of them too small, or too afraid, or too well brought up to fight back and Constable McCoy knew it. Not once, however, had he been able to prove that Skeeter had done anything wrong. According to his mother, brother, and sisters, Skeeter was always at home when the few offenses that were reported took place.

"Know what, I'll bet you're right, Noah," the constable said kindly. "I heard that story on the radio, too. I'll bet Skeeter was just in the wrong place at the wrong time. Probably a miracle that he didn't get hit in the head and killed, though he's gonna be real sore for a few weeks. I'll have a talk with his mother."

The constable left, wishing them both a good trip to New Mexico. Mrs. Odell looked Noah in the eye and then poked him on the chest with her finger.

"Young man," she said sternly, "if you ever do something like that again, I will snatch you bald. You could have killed that boy." Noah made one last glorious trip to the lilac bush, and it was worth every step.

At four o'clock the following morning, Ethel Odell roused her son from bed and made sure he washed his face and cleaned his ears. She stripped the bed linen and stuffed it into the emptier of the two additional lettuce boxes that would go with them on the bus. They ate the fried egg sandwiches that Mrs. Odell had made the night before, had a last look around, switched off the lights, locked the back door, and left the key under the welcome mat for the new owner. An hour later, after a short walk to the bus station half-dragging, half-carrying the lettuce boxes and making a tremendous racket in the process, Ethel and Noah Odell were seated on a smoke-belching, forty-one-passenger Greyhound "Highway Traveler" bus headed south toward cowboy land.

———————

ANYONE WHO ACTUALLY believed the famous Greyhound radio commercial, "It's such a comfort to take the bus and leave the driving to us," and out of naïveté or desperation found himself or herself or themselves aboard one of the airless, antiquated, diesel-belching, slightly post–World War II buses on a cross-country trip during the summer will assure you it isn't something they wished to do more than once. Seat-wise, the vehicles weren't particularly uncomfortable, but they were noisy and had neither air-conditioning nor toilets. Passengers who suffered from claustrophobia, asthma, hay fever, high blood pressure, bladder infections, or incontinence were just out of luck. So were fourteen-year-old boys who had earlier washed down a cold-fried-egg-sandwich breakfast with a very large glass of water. Noah managed to control his urges until the bus stopped in

Ashland, where he made a beeline for the station's lavatory, scattering like bowling pins the elderly passengers waiting in line to board.

That was just the beginning. On the twisty, two-lane highway through the Siskiyou Mountains south of Ashland, the combined stench of diesel fumes, cheap perfume, and stale fried chicken and boloney sandwiches in brown paper bags was lethal. Noah's normally placid tummy began to whirl and churn ten miles from the Ashland station, and by the time the Greyhound crossed the California state line near Hornbrook, it had progressed to the destruct stage. Scrunched down in a window seat and unable to get a proper breath of fresh air, Noah had no choice but to throw up, first down the collar of a crotchety senior citizen in the seat in front of him, then into, or at least toward, a sickness bag thoughtfully provided by the Greyhound company for just such emergencies. Ethel Odell apologized to the gentleman who had been the target of her son's liquid loquacity. She then had Noah lie on the seat with his head in her lap, vomit-spotted cowboy boots pointed toward the ceiling. She bathed his face with a wet handkerchief and placed a cool palm on his forehead.

Noah slept for an hour or so, but the worst was yet to come. Like chicken pox, spewing one's breakfast into one's lap in the crowded confines of a circa-1950s "Highway Traveler" was contagious. Just north of Eureka, the morning's events repeated themselves (the old man in front had by this time changed seats), and within thirty seconds a bus filled with queasy passengers had joined together in disgorging a malodorous chorus of "When the Guts Begin to Groan" across the foggy, northern California landscape. The smell inside the nearly airless Greyhound would have floored a pig, had one been present. In Eureka, Shively, Willits, and even as far south as Geyserville, the Nauseating Tabernacle Choir, under the direction of Noah Odell, tossed their cookies in the greatest upchuck festival ever to play the Golden State. By the time the Greyhound arrived around midnight at San Francisco's gloomy terminal, unused sickness bags were as rare as teeth on a chicken.

The remainder of the trip was pretty hazy. Thirty-six hours of noodle soup, mushy crackers, and filthy bus station bathrooms later,

Noah's nausea finally abated. Somewhere around Bowlin's Wild Indian Trading Post and the large, white sign that said LAST GAS FOR 100 MILES in eastern Arizona, he fell asleep and slept the rest of the way to Albuquerque. During a three-hour layover in the hot, stuffy downtown Albuquerque bus station, he conked out on a wooden bench and only vaguely protested when his mother pushed him aboard another bus for the final two-hundred-mile-long leg south to Tularosa. The next thing Noah remembered was a gentle shake on the shoulder and his mother telling him to look out the bus window. Uncle Bud, badly needing a shave as usual, was slouched against the rear fender of his old pickup, a battered fedora hat pushed to the back of his head. He held a bulging brown paper bag in his arms. As they stepped off the bus into the hot sun, Bud greeted them with an ear-to-ear grin.

"Well, yer finally here," he said, setting the bag in the truck's bed before slapping Noah on the back and giving his sister a bear hug. "Dang bus is two hours late." He took a good look at his nephew and shook his head. "Yer lookin' a little peeked, Bub. You comin' down with somethin'?"

"I threw up in four states and I haven't had much to eat," Noah said truthfully. "And I stink. And my clothes are dirty and I feel like I got run over by a bus instead of riding in one."

"We're sorry about being so late Clarence," Mrs. Odell said, giving her brother a peck on his cheek and then putting her arm around Noah, "but you know buses are never on time. We're here now, though, and glad to have our feet back on solid ground."

Bud retrieved the paper bag from the pickup's bed and reached inside, pulling out a brightly colored Mexican shawl and an elegant, hand-carved leather handbag that he presented to Mrs. Odell. He then reached in once more and pulled out a brand-new ten-gallon straw cowboy hat.

"Gotta wear this when yer cowboy'n," he said, handing it to Noah. "Sun'll boil yer brains in a minute if you don't."

Noah put the hat on. Just like the pair of boots, it fit him perfectly. It was also about the best thing that could have happened to a sleepy, half-sick, very smelly wannabe cowboy who had just barely survived the absolute worst journey of his life.

———————————

WHILE BUD HELPED the bus driver remove the badly squashed lettuce boxes from the belly of the Greyhound, Noah took his first look at downtown Tularosa. There were perhaps a dozen businesses of one kind or another situated on the two-block-long section of the main drag that he could see. On one side of the street Noah spotted a Tastee-Freez, a Texaco gas station, and a feed store, and on the other, a Woolworth's Five-and-Dime, a small grocery store, and a run-down movie theater called "The Ranger." The few side streets he could see from the bus station were unpaved, dusty lanes lined with squat, flat-roofed houses that seemed to bake in the sun like loaves of brown bread. Half-naked children played and squealed in dirt yards while scrawny dogs yapped out their encouragement at full volume. Some of the houses were shaded by towering green trees, but try as he might, Noah could not spot a lawn or a hedge.

The only people Noah could see besides the screaming children were those waiting at the bus station. Most of them were dark-eyed, brown-faced men dressed similarly in long-sleeved shirts, faded or dirty jeans, and cowboy hats. Near the station doors, Noah saw several men he assumed were Indians. They, too, were wearing blue jeans and boots but had brightly colored blankets draped across their shoulders, and instead of hats, they wore red or blue scarves wrapped round their foreheads just above the ears. As the bus passengers milled about, waiting for their luggage, wooden tomahawks and small drums and beaded moccasins appeared from beneath the blankets and were offered up for sale with lethargic disinterest.

Noah spotted a group of dark-haired boys a little older than he was leaning against a mud-colored wall across the street and watching a young blonde girl riding past on a bicycle. The tallest of the boys shouted something indecipherable as she passed. Undaunted, the girl flipped the speaker an extended middle finger as she turned the corner out of sight.

"You stay away from thet bunch, Bub." Bud had come up quietly behind him, carrying a lettuce box on his shoulder. "Them fellers ain't anyone you need to know." He dropped the box into the truck bed with a *thunk*. "Ain't keerful, they'll hand you yer butt on a tortilla."

"What's a tortilla?" Noah asked.

"Never mind," Bud answered. "Jest you keep as far away from them boys as possible. They ain't too warmhearted toward gringos."

"What's a gringo?" Noah asked, but his uncle ignored him.

"Climb on up in there," he ordered, gesturing toward the back of the pickup. Noah saw that his mother was already seated in the cab. "Put on yer hat an' let's head fer the wrench."

Bud jockeyed the pickup out of the bus station's parking lot and onto the unshaded main street. Noah could feel little rivers of moisture start to dribble down his chest and armpits, and by the time they reached the edge of town, the skin on his face stung from the terrific heat even though he wore his new hat pulled low over his forehead. Looking back, he spotted a welcome sign that said TULAROSA, NEW MEXICO, POPULATION 934. He could also see a translucent curtain of heat waves rising up from the flat, hot land on either side of the highway. Here and there a bright green field of corn or hay interrupted the otherwise sparsely vegetated landscape, but they were few and far between and disappeared altogether within a mile of the city limit sign. The last vestige of civilization was the Cactus Drive-In, a decrepit outdoor movie theater occupying a large dirt lot overrun with garbage and knee-high weeds on the left side of the highway. The dirty, forty-foot-high movie screen was marred near the bottom by several large holes, and at least half of the speaker poles in the parking area had been nudged over into forty-five-degree angles, probably by automobile bumpers. Tularosa, New Mexico, Noah decided, was a very small, very hot town in the middle of a very large, very hot desert.

Fifteen minutes later, Bud braked heavily and yelled out his window for Noah to hang on. As the vehicle swerved left off the pavement onto a rutty dirt road, Noah grabbed hold of Bud's heavy toolbox, propped his feet against a lettuce box, and braced himself.

Dust billowed up in great brown clouds as the pickup's wheels hit the dirt, and Noah heard his mother shouting at Bud to slow down. When the pickup's left front tire hit a giant pothole almost deep enough to bathe in, Noah's tailbone bounced against the metal pickup bed hard enough to make him yelp.

They passed a row of old, battered trailer houses. Across the road from the trailers sat a cluster of ramshackle but occupied shacks, many with rusting automobiles crouched indolently in their front yards. Laundry drooped from clotheslines, and piles of weathered lumber, empty cans and bottles, rags, and other human debris lay everywhere. A mile from the highway, they drove by a small, neat dairy farm with a herd of thirty or forty black-and-white spotted cows standing in the shade of an old barn. Noah tried to concentrate on what he was seeing, but his teeth were rattling like seeds in a gourd and his eyes were filled with dirt.

Another mile passed. The only other car they saw was a dusty, olive-green sedan, its motor running and windows closed, parked in one of the road's few wide spots. As Bud slowed down and edged by the sedan with only a few inches to spare between fenders, Noah saw a large white star on the driver's door with the words "U.S. ARMY" printed underneath. The words were barely readable because of the cloud of dust that the Studebaker was churning up. Noah tried to see inside as they went by, but the only thing he could make out were two shadowy shapes sitting in the front seat.

Finally Bud turned off onto an even narrower, dustier road. Two hundred feet along, he navigated the truck through a pair of tilted gateposts made of old railroad ties half-buried in the ground. A rickety barbed-wire fence ran in both directions, and a hand-printed sign nailed to one of the posts stated: BOGGS RANCH, NO SAILS MEN. On top of a steep rise a hundred feet past the sign, Bud came to a stop. Road dust churned up by the tires settled back onto the breezeless earth like a dingy blanket. Noah's hair was gritty and at least two shades lighter from its coating of dirt.

"Well, there's the kettle wrench," he said proudly. Then, not forgetting his nephew was in the back, he stuck his head out the window and shouted, "There's the wrench! Somethin', ain't it?"

Noah stood up and looked over the pickup cab. Nestled below in a shallow depression and surrounded by hard-packed, weed-covered earth was a rambling, one-story, mud-colored house. Brown mud plaster had peeled off the walls like sunburned skin in some places, and Noah saw that several of the dozen or so blue-framed windows were cracked. Adjacent to the house were several small wooden sheds and a large, newly-constructed pole barn built of raw lumber. Inside the open doors of the barn, Noah could see a stack of hay bales. Fifty feet behind the house was a wooden privy with a crescent moon cut in the door. To the rear of the outhouse, perched crookedly on the side of the depression, was a wooden corral containing a dozen or so skinny, humpbacked cattle. Beyond that, the land leveled away into the flat, cactus- and greasewood-blanketed Chihuahuan Desert of southern New Mexico. Through the heat waves Noah could just barely make out a low range of purplish-blue mountains in the far distance.

"Well, Bub, Sis, whaddya think?" So that he wouldn't have to keep sticking his head out the window, Bud opened the driver's door. "See them kettle yonder? Them's Brahmas. Meanest sons a bit . . . meanest dang critters in the world, but they're worth a hunnerd bucks apiece on the hoof. We got us six hunnerd acres here, an' if it ain't the sweetest six hunnerd acres I ever seen, then I'm a monkey's bee-hind."

Bud got out so he wouldn't have to keep swiveling his head back and forth when he talked. "Course most of it ain't got much growin' on it, an' it ain't got many trees, but it's still dang purty."

The fact was, Noah noticed, there were no trees at all. He could see all the way to the horizon, and there was nothing growing that was taller than his knees. His mother started to say something, then changed her mind and clasped her hands in her lap.

"Fine house, too," Bud went on. "Little run-down mebbe, but them walls is two feet thick. Thet ain't no problem anyways . . . hey you!" Bud waved his left arm back and forth to get Noah's attention. "Two strong fellers like us oughta be able to fix it up good, huh?"

He climbed back in, slammed the door, and ground the starter, and the pickup lurched down the hill, throwing up another boiling cloud of dust. Noah was flung backward onto a lettuce box. A small flock of chickens that had been loitering unseen in the shade of the driveway weeds scattered wildly. Noah noticed that a big, mean-looking speckled rooster with half its feathers missing didn't bother to move, even though the Studebaker passed within a couple of inches of its tail.

Bud parked in front of the house and helped his sister climb down into the yard. He hurried to the front door and swung it open. At the precise instant that Mrs. Odell's attention swiveled toward the house, the rooster charged across the yard, gave a great, flapping leap, and pounced triumphantly and squarely upon her shoulders. Mrs. Odell shrieked and ran for the house, flinging the rooster away with a backhand swipe. As she reached the door and pushed it open, a two-inch-long desert cockroach with its antennae waving frantically scurried across the knotty pine floor inside. She stopped and clasped her hands together across her bosom. She closed her eyes and exhaled a little gasp.

"Don't worry about them bugs, Ek," said Bud. He stomped the roach into brown mush, winked at Noah, and patted his sister on the shoulder. "I got me some mousetraps in town today. An' I'm sure sorry about ol' Ee-ho. He's muh watch-chicken. Get used to you and Bub in a day or two."

"Ee-ho's kind of a strange name for a chicken," Noah said. "It sounds sort of Indian?"

Bud glanced at his sister, who was several feet ahead of them, examining the living room furniture. "Tain't Indian," he answered, his voice so low that Noah could barely hear him. "Real name's Ee-ho-day-puda—least thet's what the man sold 'em to me said. Call 'em Ee-ho fer short 'cause his whole name's kinda hard to spit out lest ya talk some Mexican." Again he glanced at Ethel Odell's back, then winked at Noah. "Means somethin' purty bad anyways, which I ain't gonna tell ya what, an' you ain't gotta say nothin' to yer ma neither."

The exterior of the old adobe ranch house left a bit to be desired, but the inside was neat, cozy, clean, and pleasant. The huge, low-ceilinged living room was at least thirty degrees cooler than the outside air. It contained an old but comfortable sofa, an easy chair, various lamps, and a long, heavy wooden table with six sturdy wooden chairs around it. The walls had been freshly painted white, and even the old potbellied stove in one corner had received a new coat of blacking.

The kitchen was equally large and well-tended. A battered electric range with an oversized oven slouched against one wall, its top covered with cooking pots and pans. Next to the stove was an ancient refrigerator, also battered but humming with life. Next to that was a deep, metal double sink with a faucet on either end. The waist-high counter and oversized cupboards were made of rough-cut lumber and obviously hand built, but they were sturdy and also freshly painted.

"Hired me an ol' Mexican woman to come clean up the house last week," Bud said proudly. "Did a damn fine job, 'cept fer missin' a few bugs. Got her husband an' son to paint all the walls in ever' room so things'd be good as new fer you an' Bub."

Bud continued with the tour, pointing out the freshly coated walls and the recently scrubbed floors in each section of the house as though they were fine pieces of art. To one side of a long, cool hallway were two spacious bedrooms, each containing a metal bed frame and a mattress and box springs covered with a heavy, faded quilt. Another quilt was folded neatly at the foot of each bed. There was also a handmade chest of drawers in each room, with a small, windup alarm clock on top. An enameled chamber pot sat on the floor next to each of the beds. The smaller of the two bedrooms had a window that looked out on the weedy backyard.

"You'll git this'un here, Bub," said Bud, pointing to the bedroom with the window. "And, Sis, you git this'un right here, next to the boy's. Mine's on tuther side of the house so's I don't keep nobody up snorin'."

On the opposite side of the hallway was a single door leading to a partly finished bathroom that contained a deep metal tub, a metal sink with hot and cold faucets, and an enamel toilet. There were wooden pegs in the walls for hanging towels and a small, square mirror hung from the wall above the sink.

"This here's the throne room," said Bud, gesturing at the space. "Fer a day er two we gotta use the privy out behind the shed, but it won't be long till you kin sh . . . till you kin do yer business in style."

Ethel Odell looked at her brother without smiling but still made no comment as she turned and walked back toward the living room. Before Noah could follow, Bud grabbed his arm. "An' watch it when ya sit down in the outhouse, Bub," he whispered. "They's a whole nest a black widders livin' down the hole."

5

Life on a Kettle Wrench

Food writer Lucius Beebe once mentioned to some friends that "a gourmet can tell from the flavor whether a woodcock's leg is the one on which the bird is accustomed to roost."

Alimentary physicist Albert Einstein wrote, "An empty stomach is not a good political advisor."

Master chef and cookbook author James Beard stated, "A gourmet who thinks of calories is like a tart that looks at her watch."

Jack-of-all-trades cum kettle wrencher Clarence William Boggs once told a sixty-year-old, overweight taco temptress who waited tables in a mediocre Mexican restaurant near Silver City, New Mexico, that "food jest ain't food lest it's got some jalapeños er red chile er green chile in it, neither."

Noah's mother, who was none of those things and had never been quoted by anyone in her life, wiped the corner of her eye with the corner of her delicate white handkerchief.

"That stew is just too spicy to eat, Clarence," she said. "What on earth did you put in it?"

They were seated at the long wooden table in the living room. It was nearing seven o'clock, and the desert outside was finally beginning to cool off. Through the open front door, Noah could hear the loud *bup-wee-bop* call of what his uncle had told him were cotton-top quail.

Noah had to agree with his mother about the stew. The first bite he took had caused his tongue to tingle; a second bite caused it to crawl down his throat. Unable to proceed past his tonsils, it had curled up in a ball and was now throbbing with pain and hoping for last rites. Noah took a large gulp of water and filled his mouth with cornbread.

Bud looked innocently down at his bowl and then at the spoonful of stew he held suspended halfway to his mouth.

"Spicy? Don't taste spicy to me. Mebbe you jest got a hot bite." He returned to his meal, mindless of his sister and nephew who sat filling up on cornbread and water.

After supper, Bud left to feed the cattle and the flock of chickens. Noah wanted to go along but was ordered to stay and help his mom with the dishes.

"Feedin' the livestock'll be yer job all the time in a couple a days," he said, patting Noah on the shoulder. "It's part of yer learnin' if you wanna be a cowboy. But yer ma's tired and needs some help, so git busy with thet dish towel."

Once Bud disappeared into the semidarkness of the evening outside, Mrs. Odell placed one arm affectionately around Noah's shoulders and gave him a healthy squeeze.

"From now on, I'll do the cooking," she promised with a smile on her face. "I know everything is so . . ." she searched for the word, ". . . strange, but we can get used to it if we try."

"I like it here, Mom," Noah answered honestly. "It's gonna be fine. We'll fix the place up real good. And it won't be any problem at all to get rid of those spiders."

Mrs. Odell's arm dropped. Her smile galloped off. Automatically she looked up, searching the ceiling for webs.

"What spiders?" she asked in a deadly low voice.

Noah knew he had already put his foot in it, so he answered truthfully.

"Black widows, Mom. There's some in the privy. You've just got to give the door a good kick before you go in . . . to let 'em know you're coming."

Mrs. Odell walked into the living room and sat on the sofa, eyeing the cushions meticulously for intruders before she did so. She pulled her already moist hanky from a sleeve and spread it neatly on her lap. Then she began to cry. Just a few tiny little tears—tears about the size of spiders' eggs but tears nonetheless—rolled down her cheeks.

One of these stupid days, Noah thought to himself, *I'll learn to keep my stupid mouth shut.* He sat down next to his mother and put an arm around her shoulders. "Uncle Bud and I will get rid of the spiders, Mom," he said. "And the real bathroom will be done in a couple of days. We'll be OK till then."

AT BREAKFAST THE following morning, Mrs. Odell served up a large platter of scrambled eggs, buttered oven toast, and fried bacon. Noah ate like a starved lion, asked for seconds and then thirds, and then washed everything down with a large glass of water. When he finished, Mrs. Odell cleared his dishes and then sat down next to her brother, a determined look on her face.

"D'you see them army people yesterday when we was comin' home, Bub?" Bud asked Noah before his sister could speak. Bud's fork was piled high with scrambled eggs and pieces of some unidentified, bright green vegetable and was poised above his plate, ready to be delivered into his mouth at the first opportunity.

Noah nodded. "They looked like they were lost," he added. "I couldn't see who was inside the car."

"Weren't lost," Bud said. "I seen 'em a couple a times in the last week er so in 'bout the same spot. Army's all over the place round Alamogordo 'cause there's a big base a couple a miles west, but they don't come up here much." He motioned in the general direction of the desert to the west with his forkful of eggs, careful not to shake any off. "They's been some talk 'bout the army kickin' people off their wrenches way out yonder, but I cain't see what thet has to do with—"

"Clarence!"

Bud stopped talking and looked at his sister.

"Clarence, we need to have a talk."

Bud set his egg-laden fork down carefully onto his plate and leaned back in his chair, a puzzled look on his face. Mrs. Odell got right to the point.

"If you will faithfully promise to finish the bathroom as soon as possible and . . ." she searched the ceiling again, ". . . get rid of those bugs *and* that evil-hearted rooster, Noah and I will stay. Otherwise, we'll pack our clothes and go back to Gold Hill tomorrow. I will not have my son eaten alive or bitten by spiders or ravaged by a chicken."

Noah knew his mother was probably bluffing, but his stomach gave a little doodah at the reference to another possible bus ride across half the country. He looked at his uncle. Bud was studying his plate. Even the chickens that had been scratching just outside the living room window next to the table had stopped crooning and gurgling to each other.

"Now don't go gittin' yerself in a tizzy, Sis," he said. "Me an' Noah'll get busy on them things this mornin', won't we, Bub?" He looked at Noah and winked. Bud always winked with the eye that had supposedly been cut in a barroom brawl, giving him a slightly lopsided look. "We'll finish the plumbin' ourselves," he continued, "an' we'll pick up some bug stuff thet'll send them critters straight up to bug heaven real quick. As fer thet rooster, he's the best dang watchdog in Tularosa an' won't nobody never steal nothin' while ol' Ee-ho's on the job. Give 'em a few days an' he'll quiet down, hokeydokey?"

It was one of the longest speeches Noah had heard his uncle make in years. Mrs. Odell looked apprehensive but nodded her head. Careful not to rattle the silverware or scrape his chair or make the least noise that would disturb the delicate armistice, Noah left the table and quietly began to wash the dishes. Bud grabbed his hat and headed for the door.

"Gotta go check the lower forty," he said as he left. "You help yer ma."

Noah wanted to ask forty what, but he didn't have a chance. Outside the window, the hens once again began their melodic gurgling as they lacerated grasshoppers and red ants.

An hour later, when the dishes had been done, the kitchen had been cleaned, the beds had been made, and the newly painted furniture had been given a swipe with a damp dust rag, Bud magically reappeared at the front door.

"All done, Bub? Where's yer ma? Whaddya say we git on to town and look at thet car?"

Noah gave the last chair a final wipe. "What car?" he asked. "You're getting a new car?"

"Yer ma's gonna git one, if the price's right, so's you an' her can git to town when I ain't around. Where's she at? Time's a wastin'."

Mrs. Odell appeared from the back of the house carrying her new leather purse over her shoulder. A scarf was tied down over her hair. "I'm right here, Clarence. Where's that nasty rooster?"

Bud glanced over his shoulder at the yard and shrugged. "Ain't here," he said. "Probably seein' to them hens of his. You all go hop in the truck an' we'll git. Gonna be hot today, Bub, so wear yer hat."

Cautiously, Mrs. Odell stuck her head out the door, looked both ways, and then quickly strode to the pickup and opened the door. Noah climbed into the back and sat on Bud's toolbox, his new cowboy hat shading his face. He was not looking forward to another trip over the rough, dusty, two-mile-long road that connected the ranch to the main highway. Things hadn't changed overnight, though, and by the time they reached the pavement twenty minutes later, he was once again covered hat to boots with dust. He also felt like his eyeballs had been jarred loose from their sockets by the constant jouncing.

Ortega's Used Cars occupied a weed-filled lot at the south end of Tularosa. An unpainted, one-room frame building with a dirty window in front and OFFICE painted over the door was the only structure on the lot. Fifteen or twenty automobiles in various states of repair sat neglected among the weeds and broken beer bottles, tin cans, and old newspapers. Some of the cars had flat tires, and all of them were covered with half an inch of dust. If there was a single vehicle on the lot that didn't have a dent, cracked windshield, or smashed taillight, Noah couldn't spot it.

Bud parked halfway down the front row of automobiles and got out. He opened his sister's door and helped her step down, then motioned to Noah to climb down out of the back. The door marked OFFICE opened. Through it, like a giant bag of Jell-O hanging from the chest of a triple-chinned fellow half its size, squeezed the largest belly Noah had ever seen. It quivered and jiggled when it left the confines of the office doorway and seemed to roll forward, dragging the triple-chinned fellow along behind.

"How joo bean, Señor Bod?" Pedro shouted the greeting from thirty feet away. His baggy pants were held up by bright red suspenders, and his once-white shirt looked as though it had been washed in a mud puddle.

"Dis joo eseester?" Pedro shook hands with Bud, smiled at Mrs. Odell, and patted the top of Noah's head with a huge, sweaty hand.

"This is her, Pedro. We come down to have a look at thet Ford."

Pedro's smile now went from ear to ear and made his head look like it came apart on hinges in the middle. He turned and waddled toward the far end of the lot, motioning everyone to follow. With each step he took, the earth shook dramatically and a little cloud of dust swirled up around his ankles.

Pedro halted in front of a light blue Ford sedan with big chrome bumpers. The tires were bald and one taillight was smashed, but the windshield was unbroken and had at least been cleaned of dust sometime in the past six months. With a grunt, Pedro opened the driver's door and motioned for Mrs. Odell to slide in. Looking a bit uncertain, she did as he asked. She honked the horn, turned the steering wheel back and forth, and then climbed out and brushed the dust off her dress. Shaking his head, Pedro squeezed and grunted himself into the driver's seat. He pumped the accelerator a couple of times, turned the key in the ignition, and pushed the starter button. The engine caught with a healthy roar. The fat man folded his hands across his massive middle and a satisfied look settled on his face. He goosed the gas pedal once or twice, closed his eyes, and smiled contentedly.

After a few moments, Bud thumped the salesman on his shoulder. Pedro shut off the Ford's engine and retracted himself from the front seat with difficulty. The sedan gave an audible sigh of relief.

"How much you askin', Pedro?" said Bud. "Car's kinda beat up."

The fat man spoke to a point somewhere on the distant horizon. "Tell joo whot," he said, "because joo Bod's eseester, I'm gonna let joo have dis Fart for tree hunnerd dollars." He clasped his hands behind his back and cracked his fingers, a pleased look on his face.

Mrs. Odell looked at her brother. Bud scratched his four-day-old beard, kicked a tire, walked around the Ford once, and then propped one foot on the front bumper.

"Amigo, thet ain't no deal," he said. "Thet's jest plain robbery."

The pleased look on Pedro's face turned to one of astonishment, then sadness. He hooked his thumbs underneath his suspenders and closed his eyes.

"Hokay," he said. "Two hunnerd feefty. *Mi esposa*, she gonna keel me."

Bud took his sister's arm and motioned Noah to head for the pickup. "They's a good lookin' Chevy fer sale down in Alamogordo," he said. "Leastwise they won't try an' rob us blind."

"Hokay, hokay," Pedro said hurriedly. In the end, even as he whined about his angry wife and starving children, he took a hundred dollars cash for the Ford and threw in the hubcaps for good measure.

While Noah and his mother drove back to the ranch in their new car, Bud made a trip to the hardware store in Alamogordo for plumbing supplies. He was back at the ranch in an hour, the bed of the Studebaker bristling with different lengths of pipe and copper tubing. Obviously trying to fulfill his promise to finish the new bathroom as quickly as possible, he carried his toolbox inside and went directly to work.

Bud was an adequate, if not admirable, carpenter, but the fact that he had very little expertise in the plumbing business became quickly apparent. Noah had been delegated to chopping weeds in the front yard until he was needed in the bathroom, but when his uncle dropped a three-foot-long steel pipe wrench on his foot, he heard the loud *clunk* even through the wall. Mrs. Odell was just around the corner at that particular moment, so Bud said nothing anyone could hear. Instead, he hopped around on one foot, gritting his teeth and cursing under his breath. As he gimped back and forth, trying gamely not to swear out loud, he kicked over a freshly opened Lucky Lager longneck that he had placed on the floor next to his tools. The bottle went spinning away on its side, spewing its foamy, amber contents everywhere.

"Well, goddam!" Bud shouted, unable to help himself. Five seconds later, Mrs. Odell appeared in the doorway.

"Clarence!" Her voice was stern. "Stop that cursing!"

"Don't git yer dander up," Bud spluttered. "Dang thing bit me!" He motioned at the wrench, then at his foot, then at the mess on the floor. "Dern near busted muh foot."

Noah could hear the exchange between his mother and uncle and thought it prudent to keep his head down and his mouth shut. Ten minutes later, Bud came out of the house carrying a flashlight in one hand and the wrench and several short pieces of pipe in the other. He had opened another beer, which he had stuffed into the top of his overalls for safe keeping. He dropped the wrench and pipes in the dirt, set the beer bottle on a windowsill, squatted down, and shined the flashlight into a narrow opening in the concrete foundation. It wasn't a door exactly, but more like a small, square hole, two feet wide on each side. Satisfied there were no rattlesnakes or scorpions lurking in the darkness, Bud lay down in the dirt, and with the wrench in one hand, turned over on his back and scooted himself under the house. All Noah could see protruding from the hole were his uncle's boots, toes pointing at the sky.

Several minutes later, Bud's disembodied voice floated out of the hole like smoke. "Gimme a hand here, Bub," it said. "Han' me them pieces a pipe an' thet beer and don't drink none neither."

Happy to abandon the weeds, Noah dropped the hoe and hurried over. He picked up the pipe sections from the dirt, knelt down, and placed them one by one into Bud's outstretched hand. He did the same with the cold beer. He heard a *glug, glug, glug*, then a few *clank*s and *clonk*s. The toes of Bud's boots waved back and forth as he struggled to put pressure on the wrench handle.

"See thet yeller handle out yonder?" Bud's voice floated out of the hole again. "When I holler, give 'er a twist."

Noah spotted the yellow handle a few feet away and nearly hidden by weeds. It was attached to a rusty pipe, one end of which protruded from the wall of the house, while the other went directly into the ground. The handle had no hose attachment and was obviously a shut-off valve.

A moment later, his uncle shouted "Let 'er rip!" Noah twisted the handle counterclockwise as far as it would go and heard the sound of water rushing through the pipe. Suddenly, a fountain of dark brown, nasty-looking liquid spurted from the hole as something burst under the house. It soaked Bud's upper half completely. Crab-like, he scuttled out from beneath the house, banging his head brutally on the concrete foundation as he emerged.

"Dirty, rotten, cow-humpin' sonofa . . . !" Bud started to spout, then with a massive effort suppressed the rest of the phrase. "Turn thet dang thing off!" he ordered Noah. He was sopping wet from the waist up and a trickle of blood dribbled onto his overalls from the head wound. Noah hurriedly twisted the faucet handle in the opposite direction and the spurting ceased.

Bud rubbed his forehead with a grubby hand, smearing blood and dirt over his entire face. He dropped his chin to his chest, and Noah knew he wasn't praying.

Just then, Ethel Odell stuck her head out of the window.

"Good heavens, Clarence!" she said, staring at her bruised and bleeding brother. "What on earth have you done to yourself?"

"Ain't nothin' that a good cussin' won't fix," Bud muttered. "Jest leave me be fer a minute or two, Sis, an' I'll be hokay."

"You come in here right this minute and let's get you cleaned up," Mrs. Odell ordered. She looked at her son. "Noah, go mind your p's and q's somewhere else for a while. You can help your uncle later."

Noah snuck a glance at Bud. He saw his uncle wink, even under all the blood and dirt.

"You go on an' do yer rat killin' somewheres else, Bub," he said softly. "An' keep one eye peeled fer rattlesnakes 'cause they's a whole bunch of 'em around."

Noah turned and trotted toward the driveway, grateful to be released from the drudgery of chopping weeds. He heard his mother say, "Rattlesnakes?" in the form of a question, followed closely by a muttered, "Oh, good Lord!"

It was the closest he'd ever heard her come to swearing.

6

Starvin' Marvin, Crazy Deeter, and the Meanest Dang Cheekn in the World

The vast Chihuahuan Desert of southern New Mexico, named the Jornada del Muerto or "Journey of the Dead" by early Spanish conquistadors, is a barren landscape of cactus, yucca, and sand in which few humans ever tread voluntarily. Most of the animals that live in this arid region are nocturnal out of necessity, staying in their burrows or dens during the daytime and venturing out for food and water only after the sun has gone down. Surprisingly, however, once darkness has set in and the earth has cooled to a habitable temperature, the desert floor becomes an interstate highway of critterdom, all of them searching for the rodent version of a brew pub or *ristorante*.

It is accepted fact that the deadliest of all these nocturnal creatures is the sleek and silent *Crotalus atrox*, the western diamondback rattlesnake. Often reaching lengths of six or more feet, it is sometimes called a "coon-tail" because of the black bands of pigmented scales circumnavigating its tail just above the rattles. Venomous hunters, diamondbacks move almost unseen through the desert night, gliding from one rocky outcrop or grassy hummock to the next. Their flickering tongues constantly "sniff" the evening air for the telltale odor of prey.

A principal entrée on a diamondback's dinner menu is the wide-footed pocket mouse, *Peromyscus klodhopparii*, a dull-witted desert rodent so lacking in natural instincts that it doesn't have the sense to scurry away when a coon-tail slithers by. It prefers instead to investigate the curious movement yonder. Once the mouse makes eye contact with the rattlesnake, it is quickly hypnotized and bitten, and because diamondback venom is the most toxic of all the rattlesnakes' venom, the pocket mouse, of course, doesn't stand a chance. Once deceased, it is swallowed whole and slowly digested for up to a week in the snake's elongated stomach.

Coon-tails are voracious eaters and will not only dine on wide-footed pocket mice but all other suitably sized desert creatures as well, of course. There are literally hundreds of different kinds of rodents residing in the Chihuahuan Desert, most of them various species of mice and rats. One example is the woodpecker mouse, *Perognathus gnokgnokensis*, so named because of an unusual protuberance on the back of its skull that closely approximates, when seen from a distance at least, the crown or "topknot" of a ladder-backed woodpecker.

The woodpecker mouse is far more intelligent than its wide-footed cousins and tends to stay well away from predators, but occasionally it will still find itself caught in the hypnotic stare of a coon-tail. Nature has provided this feisty little desert dweller with some unusual natural protection, however. Its pelt, for example, consists of an extremely dense inner layer of fur overlaid by layer after layer of tough and almost impenetrable outer guard hairs that make "Woody" (as it's sometimes called by biologists) a tough-skinned little fellow, indeed. More importantly, and for reasons as yet undiscovered by scientists, the woodpecker mouse seems to be totally immune to rattlesnake venom.

When a diamondback rattlesnake strikes, its lower jaw unhinges and two needle-sharp folding fangs snap forward and lock into a vertical position. As the fangs pierce the skin, a deadly stream of venom is automatically injected into the hapless victim through tiny openings in the tip of each fang. Most small animals normally die within seconds after being bitten, but such is not the case with the woodpecker mouse. Because of its thick pelt, it is seldom actually punctured by a rattler's fangs, and since it is immune to the venom anyway, it won't die even if penetration does occur.

But a rattler's strike is hard and fast, and often the tiny wood-pecker mouse is knocked unconscious by the blow. Thinking its prey is dead, *C. atrox* then unhinges its jaws even further in order to swallow the mouse whole. But as the rodent slides into the heat of the snake's throat cavity, the initial shock of the strike wears off and the uninjured rodent wakes up scratching and biting. Its struggles are so violent that often it renders great tears in the anterior end of the rattler's esophageal canal. Instinctively realizing it has erred, the rattler then painfully stretches itself out on level ground and regur-gitates the mouse as quickly as possible. More often than not, the snake is successful and within a few seconds the mouse is able to scurry away, wet and bruised but still quite alive.

A similar example of natural defense occurs in the battle of wits between the tiny false-tailed whipper lizard, *Slenarius phakunitt*, and the much larger, night-prowling Gila monster, *Heloderma suspec-tum*. The latter—an ugly, sluggish reptile covered with rough, black-and-orange splotched skin—is the only known poisonous lizard in the United States. When hunting false-tailed whippers (or any of the other small lizards it preys upon), *H. suspectum* is deliberate and cautious. Utilizing a heat-sensing device in the middle of its fore-head to locate *S. phakunitt*, it moves oh-so-slowly toward the smaller lizard until it is within a few inches. Then, with a lightning-quick lunge, the Gila monster makes its move, hoping to catch the whip-per in its horrible, venom-dripping jaws.

That final lunge of *H. suspectum* is fast, but the almost alien reflexes of the whipper are faster. Even as the Gila monster's gap-ing jaws are closing, the smaller lizard, sensing imminent danger, is able to flip itself sideways and present its long blue tail as a tar-get. Usually, it is this thin denouement upon which *H. suspectum*'s jaws close, and at the first sign of pressure, the tail immediately self-amputates. The whipper then disappears into the darkness to begin growing a new tail (which only takes a few weeks), and the Gila monster is left without its dinner.

All of this illustrates quite clearly that the unattractive Gila mon-ster can always get a piece of tail, but the magnificent diamond-back rattlesnake can barely get its pecker up. Such is life in the wild.

Noah Odell was thinking of life in the wild and wild things as he walked up the driveway toward the main road. He was thinking specifically of wild rattlesnakes, *searching* for wild rattlesnakes to be exact, on the ground alongside the lengthy driveway to Boggs Ranch. He had never actually laid eyes on a rattlesnake and wasn't really sure that he wanted to lay his eyes on one. Nonetheless, Noah figured that he should at least know what a rattlesnake looked like, just in case. In case of what, he didn't have a clue.

He didn't have to search long. As Noah passed between the weathered railroad ties that marked the Boggs Ranch boundary, he heard a loud, raspy buzz coming from a cluster of bushes off to his left. Cautiously, he moved to the edge of the driveway, keeping well clear of anything that might offer a place to hide. The snake, however, was blatantly conspicuous. Six feet from the gatepost, the two-foot-long, greenish-brown reptile was coiled loosely atop a flat sandstone boulder. Its wicked-looking triangular head was raised slightly, and a slender, forked black tongue stabbed repeatedly in and out of its mouth, rummaging the air for Noah's scent. A row of diamond-shaped dark splotches embellished the snake's back, and its black striped tail ended in a chain of small, cream-colored rattles. Every time Noah moved, the rattles snapped into action.

Not quite sure what to do next, Noah debated between returning to the house and telling his uncle—and consequently his mother, who would probably throw a giant hissy fit and order him to stay inside the rest of the day—or fetching a large stick and committing great bodily harm to a dangerous animal. In the end, he did neither. Simply observing the creature's movements, Noah discovered, was fascinating. With its heavily scaled head and neck resting lightly on its coils and its beady black eyes never leaving Noah's face, the rattler seemed quite content to bask in the bright sunlight in full view. If Noah moved, the rattles vibrated; if he remained motionless, the raspy buzz stopped. After five minutes, the snake had had enough. As if to say, "OK, you've ogled me and I've ogled you and now I'm going home," it leisurely uncoiled itself and slithered off the sandstone boulder and across the hot sand into the shade of the bushes.

Grinning smugly because of his daring but also wondering if he had made a stupid mistake by not dispatching what he knew to be a deadly hazard to both humans and cattle, Noah returned to his walk. He had gone perhaps half a mile when he saw a horse and rider coming toward him. As they drew closer, Noah recognized the horse as a palomino; it was the same color as Trigger, the horse that Roy Rogers rode. Its mane and tail were well brushed, and the rider, who looked about Noah's age, was wearing jeans, a white shirt, and a cream-colored, ten-gallon cowboy hat with a very high crown. The skin on his face was almost white, with a pale smattering of freckles across his nose and under his eyes.

The palomino came to a halt a few feet away. "Howdy, kid," said the rider in a high, almost squeaky voice, looking down. "You thet new kid lives with Mr. Boggs? Where's yer horse?"

Noah mustered up his best Gabby Hayes drawl. "Howdy," he answered. "Don't have a horse. Wish I did, though."

The other boy took his feet out of the stirrups, slung one leg over the saddle horn, and slid from the palomino's back. He was several inches shorter than Noah and extremely skinny. His ten-gallon hat sat far down on his head, nearly touching the tops of his ears.

"Name's Marvin," he said, holding out his hand. "Marvin Couch. We own thet there dairy ranch yonder." Marvin gestured toward the highway with his thumb, then pushed back his huge hat and wiped his forehead with a sleeve. He dropped the palomino's reins to the ground. "Stay, boy," he said over his shoulder. "This here's Jake," he added. "He's muh horse."

Noah introduced himself. "How come Jake doesn't have a bridle?" he asked, pointing to the braided rope around the nose and ears of the palomino. The reins were attached to the rope directly beneath the horse's chin.

"You from the city, kid?" Marvin said. "Old Jake don't need no bridle. Thet there's an Injun hackymore."

"Are you an Indian?" Noah asked Marvin. He certainly didn't look like an Indian. Barely five feet tall including the big hat, he looked like a starving midget with a smart aleck mouth who was about to receive a busted lip if he called Noah "kid" once more.

"Course I ain't no Injun," Marvin said. "Where you from, anyway?"

"Oregon," Noah answered. "Where *you* from, Hicksville?"

Marvin thought for a moment. "Ain't never heard of Hicksville," he said. "We come up from Texas when I was jest a kid. Whaddya think of thet mean cheekn?"

Bud's maltreatment of the English language made him sometimes difficult to understand, and Marvin's nasal twanginess wasn't that far behind.

"What's a cheekn?" Noah asked, puzzled.

"What's a *cheekn*?" His voice had risen an octave. "Well, dang, yer sure from the city, ain't you? Cheekn! Cheekn!" Marvin flapped his arms and made clucking noises. "Cheekn! You got the meanest dang cheekn I ever seen! Like ta scairt old Jake till he puked!"

The sun rose in the east. Chicken! Rooster! "You mean Ee-ho!" Noah said, finally understanding what Marvin was asking. "My uncle's rooster. Yep, he's mean all right. Chased my mom into the house on the day we got here. Now she won't come out if he's anywhere around."

"Thet's what I jest said," Marvin grunted, rolling his eyes. "Thet's the meanest, dangest cheekn I ever seen!"

His point made, Marvin walked over to Jake and patted his neck. He took off his hat and scratched the back of his neck. His light blonde, almost white hair was thick and chopped short in a crew cut. Noah picked up a rock and flung it toward a dead soldier lying in the weeds. He missed on purpose because it was worth two cents if he ever needed it.

Marvin broke the silence. "It's too dang hot to jest stand here doin' nothin'. Was you headed somewhere important?"

"Nope," Noah answered truthfully. "I was looking for rattlesnakes."

"Lookin fer *rattle* . . ." Marvin rolled his eyes again. "Wanna go see my brother?"

"Where's your brother?" asked Noah.

"Don't nobody know," Marvin answered, shaking his head. "He's crazy. An' he pees his pants. You gotta promise not to laugh, though, 'cause Ma don't like it when people laugh at Deeter. She says he cain't help bein' crazy."

The offer was too tempting to pass up. Noah promised he wouldn't laugh. Satisfied, Marvin looped the reins over Jake's neck. He backed off a few feet and then took a running jump at the palomino's side. With a tremendous effort, he grabbed the saddle horn with his left hand, then grunted and crawled upward to where he could hook his left toe into the stirrup and swing his right leg up and over the saddle.

"You ever rid a horse before?" Marvin asked when he finally straddled Jake's back. He looked down at Noah. "Ol' Jake'll carry double if you ain't very heavy."

After the cheekn fiasco, Noah was not about to show any more signs of weakness. "Sure, lots of times," he said. "Nothing to it."

Marvin told Jake to stay and then motioned for Noah to hop on. Noah took a deep breath, stepped back a few feet as he had seen Marvin do, then charged toward Jake's back. Two seconds before collision, the palomino decided he didn't particularly want to be pounced on by a perfect stranger. He lunged backward, causing Noah to land squarely on his neck instead of his back. Jake jumped backward again at the impact. Noah grabbed the nearest thing handy, which happened to be Marvin, and both boys landed in a dusty heap next to Jake.

"Well, gol-danged horse!" Marvin spluttered, as they untangled themselves and stood up. He spit out a mouthful of dust, looked around, then picked up a three-foot length of discarded two-by-four lying next to the road. Board in hand, he approached Jake, shouted "Whoa!" and then fetched the horse a clout to the side of his neck that made his knees wobble and his golden tail stand out straight. Marvin tossed the board back to the roadside, and then once again he ran, crawled, grunted, hooked, and swung his way aboard Jake.

"Try 'er again," he ordered Noah. "Bet ol' Jake won't move now."

Old Jake was large, but he certainly wasn't stupid. This time, even when the perfect stranger unintentionally kicked him in the flank while crawling and grunting his way up behind Marvin, the palomino didn't move a muscle.

ACCORDING TO THE 1937 edition of *Webster's International Encyclopedic Dictionary*, some of the most fascinating people in mankind's long and intemperate history have been crazy.

For example, there was Gaius Julius Caesar Augustus Germanicus, shortened officially by decree to just Caligula. When he was a child, Caligula wore army boots and accompanied his father on military campaigns. As third emperor of Rome from AD 37 until AD 41, he made his horse a member of the Roman senate. Once during the Roman Games, Caligula ordered his guards to throw an entire section of the crowd into the arena so he could watch them being killed and eaten by lions and tigers and bears, oh my. As a sexual pervert, he ripped his own unborn child from his sister's womb in a temper tantrum—while she was still alive. He was finally assassinated by his own guards with help from a group of concerned Roman senators who concluded that their emperor was a walking loony toon if there ever was one, and utterly out of control.

Another historic lunatic was Francisco José de Goya y Lucientes, known to friends and family as just plain Frank because it was a bit inconvenient to go around saying things like "Francisco José de Goya y Lucientes, please pass the salt," or "Francisco José de Goya y Lucientes, get off your duff and take out the garbage!" A court painter for the Spanish Crown during the late eighteenth and early nineteenth century, Frank was considered to be the greatest artist of his time and was also known as the last of the "Old Masters." In later years—suffering from deafness, lead poisoning, boredom, warts, and a complete lack of sexual fulfillment—Frank went totally bonkers and retired to his house just outside Madrid. There, on the plaster walls of his cottage, he painted his fourteen famous *Black Paintings*, the most notable of which is *Saturn Devouring His Son.* Today this graphic depiction of the Roman god Saturn consuming the bloody, headless carcass of little Johnny (along with Frank's other gruesome paintings from the same period) is housed in the Museo del Prado in Madrid. Frank himself has been housed in a cold, stone box in the same city since his death 1828.

Then there was Grigori Yefimovich Rasputin, better known as the Mad Monk and sometimes as Tootin' Rasputin (though no one called him that to his face) because of his daily diet of beet gruel and three-week-old bread. A semiliterate peasant, debaucher, and off-his-rocker mystic who lived in Russia during the late 1800s, Rasputin practiced a doctrine of salvation and religious fervor combined with extreme sexual indulgence. Not so bad, really, except that as friend, advisor, and "holy man" to Tsar Nicholas II, Rasputin had a stranglehold on the Russian government. When he appointed a group of similarly inclined, off-their-rocker mystic debauchers to high political posts and eventually undermined the imperial government, the Mad Monk was deemed a stinky fish egg in the pot of political caviar. In 1916, after surviving a stabbing attack by a prostitute that left his entrails hanging from a gaping stomach wound, he was poisoned by an assassin. The poison didn't work, so a group of Russian nobles led by Prince Felix Yusupov shot him four times. Then they threw his body in the river and held it underwater for ten minutes. Then they crushed his head with a set of weight lifter's dumbbells. That killed him.

In Noah's opinion, Marvin's brother Deeter beat all of those other fellows hands down.

"Howdy, Pa." Marvin's father was in the front yard when the two boys rode up on Jake. Like his son, Mr. Couch was small, skinny, and wore a large, cream-colored hat with a skyscraper crown.

"This here's the kid what owns thet mean cheekn down the road. This here's my pa." Noah slid down off Jake's back and shook Mr. Couch's extended hand.

"Glad to meet you, son," Mr. Couch said. "Call me Heze if you want. Your uncle's told us all about you. Y'all go on inside. Lunch is fixed and on the table."

Marvin's mother was also short, but unlike her husband and son, she was chubby and rosy cheeked. She was wiping her tiny hands on a dish towel when the boys entered the house through the kitchen door.

"Ma, this here's Noah, the kid what owns thet nasty cheekn," Marvin again made an introduction. "This here's my ma." Mrs. Couch smiled and extended her damp hand, which Noah shook.

"We're glad to see you, Noah," she said. She pointed to a big kitchen table. "Lunch is ready. You boys wash your hands and sit."

They washed their hands in the kitchen sink and sat down at the table. Marvin's father came in, washed, and joined them. Mrs. Couch set a platter of cornbread and a huge pot of pinto beans on the table and then left the room.

"Where's your brother?" Noah whispered. "Doesn't he get to eat?" Marvin nodded and whispered back. "Jest hold yer horses and he'll be along."

At that moment, Mrs. Couch returned to the kitchen, gently pushing her other son in front of her.

"Told you so," Marvin muttered under his breath. "Ma had to get 'em out of his cage."

Deeter was certainly all Marvin had cracked him up to be. He was about sixteen, but a flattened nose and wide, horselike lips made his face seem much older. He was dressed in fuzzy pink bunny pajamas, complete with ears and a fluffy white tail. When Deeter was seated at the table directly across from Noah, his mother wrapped a short length of rope around his waist and tied him to the chair. He began to moan and wave his arms above his head, swaying back and forth to some unknown and esoteric melody that only he could hear. Noah had to admit that he was a wonderful specimen of a crazy person.

"Deeter, can you say hello?" Mrs. Couch asked softly. Deeter drooled and waved his arms. One pajama sleeve was already dripping bean juice from where it had been dipped in the bowl of pintos. "Ollalllallla," Deeter said pleasantly.

"You men go ahead and dig in," Mrs. Couch said. She placed a cereal bowl filled with scrambled eggs on the table in front of her son and began to feed him with a spoon. No one else seemed to notice the drooling, moaning spectacle across the table, so Noah tried not to notice either. He concentrated instead on spooning cornbread and pinto beans into his mouth and focused on Marvin's oversized hat, which Marvin hadn't bothered to remove when he sat down.

Noah's concentration was suddenly shattered by Deeter's loud sneeze. Mrs. Couch had just finished stuffing his mouth with scrambled eggs, and there they came, spewing across the table like a swarm of giant, yellow bees. A large piece of goo caught Marvin square in the forehead, and both Noah and Mr. Couch were hosed down with wet, yellow mush. Marvin wiped his face with his shirt sleeve and continued eating. So did his dad. Noah saw that a large piece of the scrambled egg was floating in his bowl of beans. He used a piece of cornbread to remove it. Deeter's mother proceeded to refill her son's mouth with another spoonful of food.

Five minutes later, Deeter sneezed again. This time, Noah saw it coming and had time to duck before the egg mush came whistling by. When he looked up, Marvin was wiping his hat off with a napkin.

"Hazel, whyn't you take the boy into the living room until we finish," Mr. Couch told his wife. "Looks like he's got a case of the sniffles."

Nodding, Mrs. Couch untied the rope around Deeter's waist and helped him to his feet. As he stood, a dark stain spread around the crotch of his bunny costume. The odor of warm urine filled the room.

"Oh, Deeter, now look what you've done," said his mother. "You know you're supposed to tell Mama when you have to go." Deeter flailed and moaned and drooled, having a wonderful time as his mother pushed him out of the living room.

With Marvin's crazy brother in another room, they were able to eat in peace. Noah learned that the Couch dairy had a herd of forty adult black-and-white Holstein cows and a dozen new nursing calves. The cows had to be milked twice a day, and the milk was then delivered in cans to Hawthorne's Dairy in Alamogordo, where it was pasteurized, bottled, and sold. Most of the milking was done by machines, but several of the older cows had to be hand-milked because of their easily irritated udders. Marvin was in charge of the nasty chore known as mucking—cleaning a hundred pounds or so of wet, smelly cow manure out the barn each morning and evening with an oversized metal squeegee known as a mucking rake.

"Git used to the smell after a while," Marvin told Noah. "Jest kinda hard to git off yer boots, is all."

When they finished their beans and cornbread, the boys excused themselves and meandered out to the front porch, where they collapsed onto an old wooden swing in the shade.

"What's the matter with Deeter?" Noah asked. "Is he sick?"

"He's jest crazy, thet's what," Marvin answered. "He was born thet way. Ma and Pa says sometimes God works in mysterious ways, an' thet everthin' happens fer a reason."

"Does he really live in a cage?" Noah asked.

"Kind of a cage," Marvin said. "Sort a like a big baby crib. Ma says it's so he don't hurt hisself."

"Does he always sneeze like that during meals?"

"Course not." Marvin brushed a final chunk of scrambled eggs from his hat with his sleeve. "Sometimes he pukes up his guts instead."

Noah didn't get home until almost dark. Marvin insisted that he stay to watch the milking, which was just fine with Noah since he had no overwhelming desire to return to weed chopping or plumbing a bathroom. Mr. Couch kindly drove his old pickup up the dusty road to Boggs Ranch, just to make sure it was OK with Mrs. Odell if Noah stayed. Deeter didn't make another appearance during the afternoon, but Noah could hear him moaning and gurgling away through the open windows of the house.

Late in the day, when the last cow teat had been squeezed dry by Mr. and Mrs. Couch working in tandem alongside the electric milking machines, the last smelly cow pie had been mucked from the barn, and the concrete floor had been washed down with a hose, Marvin retrieved Jake from a nearby corral. Using a metal milk carton to stand on while they mounted, the boys climbed onto the palomino's bare back and trotted through the dusk toward Boggs Ranch. As they passed through the gateposts, Noah searched the ground for the rattlesnake he had encountered earlier, but he saw nothing. At the top of the rise, Marvin pulled Jake to a halt and carefully scanned the yard below.

"Where's thet danged cheekn at?" he asked quietly. "We ain't goin' no closer till I find out where he's hidin'."

Noah searched the yard as well. Ee-ho and his flock of hens were nowhere to be seen.

"Roosted, probably," Noah whispered back. "Up on the roof or maybe in the barn."

Marvin took one more look, then kicked Jake in the side. Reluctantly, the horse trotted down off the hill.

"You ain't such a bad kid," Marvin said as Noah slid to the ground. "Didn't laugh at Deeter or nothin'. Most everbody laughs when—"

At that moment, from beneath a large weed where he had concealed himself to await such an opportune moment, Ee-ho launched his body at Jake's head, screeching like a demon. Jake nearly reared over backward before Marvin could regain control. Noah let go of Marvin's waist and allowed himself to quickly slide backward off Jake's back onto the driveway and jump out of the way of the frantic, prancing horse before it happened again.

"I knew thet dang cheekn was round here somewheres!" Marvin squealed, his voice again raising a full octave. Not waiting for another attack, he kicked Jake into motion and galloped off up the driveway. With the palomino gone, Ee-ho turned his aggression on Noah. Noah waited until the strutting, squawking fowl got within two feet, then drop-kicked the rooster back into the weeds fifteen feet away, violently removing another quarter of his remaining feathers in the process.

NOAH DIDN'T SEE much of his new friend for several weeks because he was occupied from dawn till dusk each day, helping his mom turn the old house into a comfortable home, chopping weeds, or assisting Bud with what seemed like an endless list of chores around the ranch. He *did*, however, find time to look up "crazy" in *Webster's International.*

crazy: Affected with madness or insanity; foolish; totally unsound; possessed by inordinate excitement; bizarre or fantastic; characterized by weakness or feebleness; broken, weakened, or disordered in intellect; shattered; demented; deranged.

Marvin had been right. Deeter was undoubtedly crazy, at least in Mr. Webster's opinion.

Among Noah's principal chores were the care and nourishment of the chickens. Once a day, usually in the morning, he fed the flock half a bucket of cracked corn and made sure they had plenty of water. In the afternoon, he collected eggs from the nesting boxes and loose piles of hay in the barn. Another of his jobs was to feed the herd of Brahmas a sixty-pound bale of alfalfa hay each day in the early morning, then once the cattle had eaten, he had to herd them out of the corral's back gate and into one of several large, fenced pastures for the rest of the day. There, they were allowed to graze on the wild grass and shrubs that somehow managed to survive in the sandy soil. The herd always wandered back by itself in the late afternoon, thirsty and irritable, and another of Noah's daily tasks was to make sure the galvanized metal water barrels in the corral were filled with fresh water from a faucet next to the house. He soon discovered that what he had called "cows" on several occasions were actually steers and weren't really as mean as his uncle had claimed on their first day at the ranch. The animals were nonetheless smelly and stupid and certainly not to be trusted. Bud warned Noah never to let himself get caught between the cattle and the corral rails if he didn't want to get squashed, and never to stand directly behind one of the animals if he didn't want to get pooped on or farted to death.

Noah's primary task, however, at least for the time being, was to assist Bud as he plumbed the bathroom. The ranch had its own deep well and water pump, so they only had to hook up the ingoing water lines to the stool, sink, and tub, and to connect the drains for all three to the pipes that carried waste to the cesspool out back. Bud had no further problems underneath the house, and the project was finally completed the following Saturday. Mrs. Odell showed her appreciation for the new bathroom by baking a three-layer chocolate cake topped with thick pecan icing.

"We'll knock down thet old privy jest as soon as the weather cools down some," Bud said. "We kin cut up most of them boards fer firewood so's we don't have to haul nothin' off, and we kin fill up thet crap hole with dirt." He wrinkled his nose and grinned. "Gonna be a stinky job, but nothin' you cain't handle, hey Bub."

While Bud and Noah took care of the outside tasks, Mrs. Odell focused her attention on the local battalions of insect and spider species that had probably resided in the old house for decades. With bug spray in hand, she went on the rampage each morning, filling every crack, hole, and fissure with Roach-B-Gone. By 10 a.m., the wooden floors were littered with dying vermin, feet up and antennae waving feebly. Bugs that somehow managed to escape the crack-by-crack slaughter and were foolhardy enough to make a break for freedom met a decisive and untimely finish at the bugger end of Mrs. Odell's fly swatter. Word got around quickly. A week after completion of the bathroom, the beetle body count had dropped to almost nothing.

Next, it was Ee-ho-day-puda's turn. The big, ugly rooster was truly an unusual fowl, guarding his front-yard domain with a determination no bulldog had ever developed. His only failing, really, was that often he unfortunately attacked first and asked questions later. Ee-ho never bothered Bud and, after getting slammed into the air a couple of times by Noah, decided a less tenacious victim was preferable. Which was, of course, the sturdy but petite Mrs. Odell. She could hardly set foot outside before Ee-ho arrived in full battle dress, eyes glittering, wattles puffed out like the fins of a blowfish. With his tail feathers spread wide apart and his head down, the rooster would attack from ambush whenever an opportunity presented itself. Knowing his mother as he did, Noah figured her patience would soon be at an end. When that happened, Ee-ho should take out an insurance policy and see to his personal affairs. The world's best guard chicken or not, he wouldn't be long for this world.

Early one morning in mid-June, before the desert heat became unbearable, Mrs. Odell was outside washing the new panes of glass that Bud and Noah had installed in the ranch house windows the previous afternoon. She seemed not to notice as Ee-ho silently strutted from weed patch to weed patch behind her, waiting for just the right moment to attack. After thirty seconds or so, and without so much as a by-your-leave, the rooster gave a loud screech and launched himself at the back of Mrs. Odell's head.

Noah had always said—and his uncle would certainly agree—that woe and despair would quickly and without mercy manifest itself upon the poor soul who pissed off Ethel Odell. Unbeknownst to anyone—least of all Ee-ho—she had been watching the rooster's reflection in the newly installed window glass. Just as the old bird launched himself from the weeds toward Mrs. Odell's head, she started to turn. Three feet into the flight, the rooster's feet and claws came out in front, and the big butcher knife Mrs. Odell had honed to razor sharpness snickered into sight from the pocket of her apron.

Ee-ho had been around long enough to know that attacking someone who was facing him—as Mrs. Odell was now—could produce dire consequences. At the last second, he tried hard to gain altitude and fly up over her head to the roof. Even with his wings pumping rapidly and his long, half-feathered neck extended for flight, however, he didn't have a chance. Rooster and butcher knife met formally and violently in midair. Ee-ho's head flew in a looping arc to land in the dust fifteen feet away, while his body, spurting blood from a cleanly severed neck, slammed into the house in a flurry of dust and feathers. It bounced, did three end-over-end backward somersaults, and lay still.

With the butcher knife held loosely at her side, Mrs. Odell stood quietly staring at the rooster's corpse. Then, with a tight-lipped smile on her face, she walked over and gingerly picked up a very deceased Ee-ho-day-puda by his rough, scaly rooster legs.

"You're as ugly as grandpa's toenails and probably as tough as an old boot," she said to the lifeless body she held out in front of her. "But I'm sure you'll make a wonderful stew."

7

Gold on Ladrón
and Brimstone in the Barn

It has always been a great mystery, in the typically non-mystifying world of Chihuahuan Desert wild-animal ecology, how the docile and timorous serpent-tailed kangaroo rat, *Dipodomys slitheropsii*, is able to stop a full-grown coyote in its tracks—even at the apex of the coyote's attack—with a simple movement of its tail and body. Researchers have observed the rat's peculiar predator-defying defensive actions on numerous occasions, and a film crew from the National Geographic Society was actually able to record it happening in 1953. In other words, scientists know how it happens but they don't know why it works. That, of course, is the mystery.

Serpent-tailed kangaroo rats are the largest of the twenty-three kangaroo rat species inhabiting North America. They are about fourteen inches in length (two thirds of which is tail), and like all kangaroo rats, they are surprisingly similar in appearance—except in size, of course—to Australian red kangaroos. Their powerful posterior limbs are almost twice the size and length of their front limbs, and their long tails—which are tipped with puffy white plumes—are used as stabilizers when hopping about the desert floor. Teddy-bear cuddly and exceedingly mild-mannered little creatures, even newly captured serpent-tails seldom try to nip researchers' fingers when they are handled.

How is it then that a six-ounce kangaroo rat can humble forty or fifty pounds of hungry coyote in the wink of an eye? It happens like this. By nature, serpent-tails are diurnal, preferring to scurry about the desert floor in search of seeds, small insects, and green shoots in the early evening while there is still enough light to see by. As they hop here and bound there looking for food, they are often spotted by coyotes, who also like to hunt in the coolness of evening. When a coyote sees a feeding kangaroo rat, it will instinctively utilize whatever cover is available to slowly and stealthily move inch by inch to within striking range. If the coyote can get within three or four feet of the rat without being spotted, it will make its final charge, actually pouncing on its prey like a cat pounces on a ball of catnip. Most other kinds of rodents do not stand a chance of escaping.

Serpent-tailed kangaroo rats are not other rodents when it comes to defense tactics, however. If the rat sees its attacker in time (and a kangaroo rat's vision is exceptional), it will, in the blink of an eye, actually flatten itself into the sand like a deflated balloon and snap its long, banner-tipped tail straight into the air. Amazingly, the instant the tail comes erect, the coyote stops dead in its tracks. Without hesitation, it will then slink away, tail between its legs, into the darkening evening, giving the flattened rat a wide berth and providing it the opportunity to scurry safely back to its hole.

Some vertebrate zoologists believe that coyotes that exhibit the SATBIL behavior (Slinking Away, Tail Between Its Legs) after encounters with serpent-tailed kangaroo rats are simply startled by the sudden appearance of the tail and the sudden disappearance of what they thought was about to be a tasty snack. Others think that the erect rat tail—which usually sways slightly from side to side— probably makes the coyote believe it has just blundered upon a deadly poisonous western diamondback rattlesnake (albeit a small one) that is about to strike. The problem is, of course, that because neither serpent-tailed kangaroo rats nor coyotes can talk, no one really knows why either animal does anything, and thus the actual reason for SATBIL remains a great mystery.

How it was that Clarence William Boggs, more or less unemployed handyman and jack-of-all-trades, owned a six-hundred-acre kettle wrench and was able to feed three people, a dozen kettle, and a flock of chickens (minus one rooster); keep his Studebaker and his sister's Ford in gasoline; and still have enough money to slip Noah a five-dollar bill every Friday afternoon with the warning, "Don't spend it all in one place, an' don't tell yer ma, neither," was also a great mystery. Noah hadn't ever actually *asked* his uncle about finances, mainly because he remembered his mother's curt warning about minding his own business. Nonetheless, he still wished he knew how Bud did it.

A week after Ee-ho's untimely death, Noah noticed that the flock of ranch chickens wasn't laying its usual compliment of eggs. Each day he had to search the barn longer and harder to locate even enough for breakfast. He mentioned the problem to his uncle one morning over his plate of pancakes and fried potatoes. Mrs. Odell was in the kitchen washing dishes. Surprisingly, Bud had been only mildly upset about the unfortunate demise of his guard chicken. He, too, knew Ethel Odell well enough to clearly see the writing on the wall if Ee-ho wasn't going to change his habits.

"I figgered thet was comin'," Bud said, scratching the stubble on his chin. "Them hens ain't got no rooster to keep 'em happy since yer ma got handy with thet dang butcher knife." He winked in Noah's direction. "They ain't gonna do no serious layin' till they git a boyfriend, so's we need to go find 'em one, pronto."

That was on Sunday. On Monday morning, Bud slapped his old fedora onto his head and told his sister that he and Noah were going shopping for a new rooster.

"This'un won't be so dang mean," he promised, "but them hens gotta have a sweetie or we won't be gittin' no chicken fruit, nohow."

Bud filled up the pickup at the gas station in Tularosa, and they drove south for ten miles to the much larger town of Alamogordo. Alamogordo looked nothing like Tularosa. For one thing, most of Tularosa's side streets were lined with tall cottonwoods, but Alamogordo had few trees of any kind. And where Alamogordo's streets were all paved, Tularosa's streets—except for the main drag—were dirt or gravel and usually blanketed with an inch of dust. The downtown business district in the larger city was at least a mile long and boasted everything from a giant Piggly Wiggly store to a sprawling, three-story brick courthouse and equally large city hall.

"This here's the county seat," Bud explained as they drove slowly through town. "Got lots a big stores so's if you ever need somethin' special, this here's the place to git it."

Bud pointed west, across the desert.

"Member we was talkin' 'bout a big army base? Well, it's over thet way. Them soldier boys got tanks an' jet airplanes an' rockets an' no tellin' what else. Always blowin' up somethin' 'cause you kin hear the booms from the wrench."

"I wonder if the soldiers are looking for space monsters and flying saucers," Noah commented. Bud glanced over to see if his nephew was joking, but Noah had a straight face and was obviously serious.

"Where'd you hear anythin' 'bout space monsters?" Bud asked with an "oh, poo" tone in his voice. "They ain't no sech thing."

"I heard it on the radio," Noah answered. "The radio said that a flying saucer had landed on the highway someplace down south of Alamogordo—somewhere called Oscuro—and that another one had been chased off by jet planes."

Noah hadn't heard any reports about actual space monsters, but stories about strange, plate-shaped flying objects being spotted in the area recently had been all over the radio newscasts during the past few days. His uncle wouldn't have heard them because he never listened to the radio. According to eyewitness accounts, one of the objects, shaped like an oversized gray dinner plate, had landed in the middle of the highway. When motorists tried to turn around and escape in the other direction, their car engines had mysteriously died. When the dinner plate took off again and flew away, the engines restarted by themselves, something Noah knew wasn't supposed to be possible. Another report said that a flying object shaped like a giant cigar had been chased by military fighter jets but had flown away at a speed no airplane could ever dream of reaching. And there had been dozens of sightings reported to the sheriff of bright green lights hovering over the desert at night. Noah figured if there were rocket ships flying around out there, then somebody, or some*thing*, had to be flying them. Only space monsters could travel in flying saucers from the stars.

"You jest don't believe none of thet stuff 'bout monsters," Bud said. "Only monsters we got round here is them dang cockroaches living at the wrench, an' I think yer ma got rid of 'em—leastwise, I hope she did."

At the south end of Alamogordo, they turned east on a narrow strip of pavement that ran toward a range of hazy, dark blue mountains in the distance. Twenty minutes later, Noah saw a sign that said CHICKENS FOR SALE tacked to a fence post on the main road. Bud turned onto the gravel driveway and parked in the front yard of a small farmhouse. An elderly man wearing faded overalls answered the door. When Bud told him what they needed, the old man led them to a sizable coop out back that was overflowing with chickens of every size and color.

"What kind of rooster was you lookin' for?" the old man asked Bud. "Whatever it is, I probably got it. If I ain't got it, I kin more'n likely steal it for you."

Bud grinned and looked over the flock in the coop. "Don't make much difference," he said. "We jest got us a bunch of lonesome hens thet need company bad." He looked at Noah. "You git to pick this'un, Bub, so's if yer ma don't like 'em, then you git the dang blame an' not me."

What Noah knew about roosters was about the same as he knew about football and rattlesnakes, but after staring at the flock of chickens milling about the pen for a minute or two, he chose a small, pure black rooster with a puffy topknot of feathers, haughty eyes, and glossy tail feathers that seemed to arch out of its stern like a feathery fountain of ink.

"That's a damn fine choice," the old farmer said, "and purty besides. That there's a silky, and he'll give your hens a good time, all right. If he don't perform, just bring 'em back." He accepted two dollars, cornered the rooster in the coop, and stuffed it gently into a gunnysack. Bud placed the sack and bird carefully in the back of the pickup and tied it down to the toolbox with a piece of string.

On the way home, Bud pulled off the highway into a wide spot and parked in the deep shade of a cottonwood tree. He felt around under the seat for his first-of-the-day longneck of Lucky Lager and popped the cap off with the opener he always carried in the pocket of his overalls. He took a long swig, then another, and then belched loudly and slumped back in his seat, eyes closed.

"Yer old enough to learn some things," he said finally, "and they's purty important, but you gotta promise thet you ain't never gonna tell a livin' soul 'bout what I'm gonna say."

Bud had the most serious look on his face that Noah had ever seen him wear.

"Thet means you cain't tell yer best friend and you cain't tell yer girlfriend and you cain't tell yer wife if you ever git one, least not fer a while. Yer ma already knows, but it's real important thet nobody else finds out."

"I won't ever tell anybody anything, I promise," Noah said. "But how come it's so important?"

"Kinda like this, Bub. They's a bunch of real bad cusses out there in the world, an' if one of 'em ever found out 'bout what I'm gonna say, we all might end up . . ." Bud let the sentence hang, but he ran his index finger across his throat and rolled his eyes back into his head. He looked totally silly, but Noah didn't laugh.

"Now, pay attention 'cause I ain't gonna tell you twice." Bud paused and cleared his throat. "'Bout ten years ago, right after yer pa died, I was deer huntin' in the middle a nowhere up by Belen. Local folks call the mountain I was on Ladrón Peak an' in Mexican thet means 'thief.' Ain't many people go up on ol' Ladrón 'cause the road's so bad it'll jangle yer brains, an' the rattlesnakes up there is thicker'n flies on a dead hog."

Bud stopped to let what he'd said so far sink in. He took a big swallow of beer and wiped the foam off his stubble of whiskers with the back of his hand.

"There's an' ol' story 'bout Ladrón," he continued. "Some people say a long time ago they was a gang of outlaws thet robbed a gold train and then hid the gold in a cave up on the mountain till they could come back fer it later when things'd cooled off. The story says thet they never made it back 'cause a couple a weeks later they robbed a bank in Los Lunas and all of 'em got caught by a sheriff's posse and got hung on the spot. Nobody ever found no gold, and nobody ever found no map. Probably wasn't nobody thet *really* thought they was any lost gold anyways. It was jest somethin' Pa and Ma told the kids to git 'em to sleep."

Noah was totally engrossed in his uncle's tale by this time. Bud downed the last swallow of beer, threw the empty beer bottle out the window, and reached under the seat for another.

"Anyways, I was out huntin' on the edge of one of them big, deep canyons up on Ladrón," Bud went on. "Thet country's jest plain mean. So dang steep, you kin skin your nose walkin' up a hill, an' they's canyons an' steep cliffs an' boulders everwhere. I was lookin' fer a big buck I'd shot at earlier thet mornin' an' I come across this cave. Couldn't see it from up above, but when I climbed down off the rimrock 'bout a hunnerd feet, there it was, big as life, hidden so's nobody could see it even from tuther side a the canyon. Started pokin' around inside, lookin' fer arrowheads, but they was so many rattlesnakes in it, I figured it must be a den. I was about to leave it be when I saw somethin' thet coulda been an old wooden box lyin' way back over to one side. Well, by now I'd got my curious bone tickled, so I got me a big club and crawled in real slow and started killin' rattlers. Killed thirteen of 'em and flipped 'em off to one side 'fore I got to where I could see . . ."

Here Bud paused. He sat his beer bottle on the pickup's dash, reached into the front pocket of his overalls, and pulled out a small cloth sack that had once held Bull Durham tobacco. He opened the sack's strings and dumped a shiny gold coin about the size of a fifty-cent piece into his hand.

"Fact is, Bub, it wasn't no kids' bedtime story about thet outlaw gold up on Ladrón Peak," Bud said, handing the heavy coin to Noah. "Sittin' way in the back they was an ol' wooden box fulla gold coins jest like this one, 'bout a hunnerd in all. This here's a twenty-dollar Liberty gold piece. Dang box wasn't heavy, but it didn't have no handles neither. Took me an hour jest to git the thing up the cliff to muh truck without droppin' it 'cause I was hangin' on to the box with one hand and climbin' up with the other'un. One slip an' I'd a been . . ."

Bud ran his index finger across his throat and rolled his eyes again.

Noah looked at the coin closely. On one side was a woman's head surrounded by stars and the date 1865, and on the other was what looked like an eagle holding a shield and the words "UNITED STATES OF AMERICA TWENTY DOLLARS" around the edge. For its size, it was extremely heavy. He could picture his beer-bellied, overall-clad uncle—rifle slung over his shoulder—trying desperately to cling to a steep canyon cliff with his fingertips while holding a large, unwieldy box of gold under his other arm. Noah wanted to laugh, but didn't.

"Thet's muh good-luck charm," Bud said. "Ever' one a them shiny little ladies is worth thirty-five American dollars if they was jest normal coins an' you could sell 'em somewheres, which you cain't do 'cause the government says a man ain't supposed to have no gold lest it's in his pocket watch."

Bud took the coin back from Noah. He dropped it back into the Bull Durham sack and put the sack back in his pocket. He looked a bit guilty as he related the next part of the story.

"Thet sorta brung up a problem, so's I knew I had to be kinda keerful 'bout what I did with what I'd found. Couldn't jest take all them coins down to the bank an' tell 'em 'here's a buncha gold thet I ain't supposed to have anyways, so don't tell the po-leece.'"

Bud took another big swallow of beer.

"I know this feller runs a pawn shop in Las Cruces, so I took one a them coins down an' showed it to 'em. He dang near blew a gasket when he saw it. Eyes lit up like a couple a kerosene lamps. He looked it up in a book an' it turns out thet coin wasn't jest any ol' gold coin, an' it was worth a whole bunch more cash money than thirty-five dollars 'cause they wasn't many of 'em ever made."

"Did you tell him where you'd found them?" Noah asked.

"Didn't tell 'em nothin' at first, 'cept thet it might be fer sale. Asked me how many I had, and I told 'em jest a couple. Later on, he liked to filled his britches when he found out I had a hunnerd of 'em."

"How come people can't have gold coins?" Noah asked. "What happens if you find some like you did and the sheriff hears about it?"

"Don't know why," Bud said, "but if the law finds out you got gold, they'll take it an' hand it over to the government an' probably throw you in the hoosegow. I didn't want thet to happen, so this

feller in Las Cruces an' me worked things out. Took some time, but
he sold all of them coins to some rich folks in Texas fer a whole lotta
money. He got some an' I got the rest, an' my share's all hid away in
my hidey-hole."

Bud paused and grinned at Noah.

"Anybody ever wants to know what I do fer a livin', jest tell 'em
some a this an' some a that, an' don't mention to yer ma I told you
'bout the gold. She's a stubborn woman an' won't take no money, an'
I promised her I wouldn't say nothin' till you was eighteen. It'll all
be yers anyway when I kick the bucket, leastwise what's left of it."
He grinned and added, "An' when you git it, don't spend it on bad
women er good liquor 'cause both of 'em's overpriced."

On the ride home, Noah thought long and hard about what Bud
had told him, trying to decide whether it was true or just another of
his stories. Bud *was* a good storyteller, or at least he had been when
Noah was still young enough to enjoy sitting on the couch next to him,
listening to the Clarence Boggs version of classic fairy tales like "Little
Red Riding Hood." He remembered that one in particular because his
uncle's version was so silly that even his mother had laughed.

LITTLE RED RIDING HOOD BY CLARENCE BOGGS

Once upon a time ago a buncha years back, they was this kid
with lots a red hair thet wanted to go see her granny, but her
ma wouldn't have none of it 'cause the kid didn't have no car,
an' granny's house was a long ways away over in thc woods.
So this kid got her dander up, an' told her ma she was in the
doghouse in her book, an' later on, she snuck outta the house
anyway an' took off fer granny's house 'cause she was a little
brat. She didn't pack no lunch er nothin'.

So there she went, walkin' down the highway, big as you
please, headed fer granny's, an' out jumped a big, mean wolf
wearin' sheep's clothin'. Well, this kid wasn't no dummy. Red
pulled out 'er gun and blew thet dang wolf to Kingdom Come.
Then she started off fer granny's again, but a witch flew outta
the trees on a broomstick an' tried to git 'er, but the kid was
a real sharpshooter an' shot 'er down like a dog. When she

got to granny's house, they made a buncha tacos an' had supper, an' then they visited quite a spell, an' then granny bought 'er a bus ticket so's Red could git home without no trouble. Only thing was, 'fore she got there, she ran into three pigs all livin' in the same house, an' they thought *she* was a witch an' begged 'er not to kill 'em. So she made 'em fork over ten bucks each an' then let 'em off with a warnin'.

In the end, Noah decided that his uncle was probably telling the truth about the gold, but maybe Bud wasn't and the coin he had was a fake. Either way, Noah decided that he couldn't ever tell anyone about Bud's secret, if there really was a secret not to tell about, because he'd promised he wouldn't.

———

WHEN NOAH CAME out to breakfast a few days later, his mother and uncle were already seated at the table. Both of them were beaming broadly as he sat down. All through the scrambled eggs and biscuits, Bud kept grinning and winking like he had something in his eye and was trying to coax it out with a smile. Noah glanced down at his fly to make sure it was closed.

"What's wrong with everybody?" he asked. He didn't really think that his arrival at breakfast could make everyone this giddy. His mother giggled and poured Bud another cup of coffee.

"Ain't nothin' wrong." Bud's eye fluttered like a butterfly as he winked at his sister. Grin. Wink. "We jest got us a new addition round here, thet's all."

Probably another cow, Noah thought to himself as he stuffed the last of his biscuit into his mouth. *Steer*, he corrected himself, *or some more chickens.* Despite the new rooster—who certainly was no Ee-ho-day-puda where guarding his ladies was concerned—coyotes had taken at least three laying hens over the past couple of days. He hadn't counted the flock yet this morning, so he didn't know what, if anything, had happened overnight.

"What kind of a new addition?" Noah asked politely. "Did you get another Brahma?"

"Nope," Bud said. "We got enough kettle fer now. I jest figured you oughta have some transport fer the summer, so I brung you a present an' . . ." He rose abruptly from the table and pointed to the front door. ". . . An' it's outside waitin'."

Noah made a dash for the door with Bud and Mrs. Odell hot on his heels like bloodhounds on a scent. Sure enough, the first thing he saw as he stepped into the bright sunlight was a small flock of three or four new white hens scratching in the dust near the black rooster.

"Ah, chickens!" Noah managed to say as cheerfully as possible.

"Thet ain't yer present, dumbo," Bud said, sounding slightly offended. "Think I'd bring you a dang chicken? *There's* yer present, yonder in the barn."

Noah looked to where Bud was pointing. Tethered by a rope around its neck to a hook in the barn door, ears flapping back and forth, and tail swishing this way and that way to ward off the flies, was . . .

"A horse!" Noah shouted. "My own horse!"

"Well, tain't quite a horse," Bud said. "Half-horse, maybe. Tuther half's a donkey. Thet there's a mule. Name's Brimstone. Figgered you oughta start learnin' how to be a cowboy."

Noah ran to where Brimstone was tied to the barn door. About three-fourths the size of Jake, he was dark brown and sleek, with white socks on three legs and a whitish blaze down his forehead. Obviously, he had been well taken care of because his hide was smooth and almost shiny. Noah scratched his floppy ears and patted his neck. The mule stood patiently, acknowledging only the presence of flies with an occasional swish of his tail or shake of his head.

"He ain't no spring chicken," Bud said, "mebbe fifteen, mebbe twenty years old, but mules is tough critters. This here feller'll carry you anywhere you want to go."

"How'd he get here?" Noah asked as he patted and scratched.

"Brought 'em home last night in the truck after you was in bed," Bud said, glancing over toward his pickup. A new galvanized metal cattle rack enclosed the back, and there was a gunnysack of fresh corn leaning against a rear fender. "They's jest one trouble. Man thet sold 'em to me don't know if he's broke to ride or not 'cause he jest used 'em for packin' supplies up to his huntin' camp. Best lemme try 'em out first to make sure."

Bud walked to the Studebaker and picked up a bridle from the floorboards in the cab. He hid it behind his back as he approached Brimstone and didn't let the mule see it until he was standing by his head. As gently as possible, Bud slipped the bit between Brimstone's teeth, looped the leather headband up and over his ears, and fastened the neck strap. The mule didn't seem to mind the bridle on his head and the metal bit in his mouth at all.

"Good ol' feller," Bud said quietly. He removed the rope around the mule's neck and led him away from the barn. "You jest keep on bein' quiet, and don' try no funny stuff." He handed Noah the bridle reins, moved around to Brimstone's left side, grabbed hold of his mane, and cautiously began to pull himself onto the mule's back.

Brimstone's ears suddenly flopped forward and then back flat against his head in that universal equestrian signal of displeasure, which in the body language of a horse means something like "Stop what you're doing, or I'll stomp your head into mush." Bud was half on, half off, trying to get a leg over Brimstone's back, when the mule jerked the reins from Noah's hand and swung his head around. For just a second, he eyeballed the foregathered meat and cloth that was trying to straddle him, then calmly buried his yellow teeth in Bud's left thigh.

Bud let out a yelp and whacked Brimstone hard on his nose with a fist. The mule let go, and Bud quickly dropped to the ground. Then, with a grunt and a mighty kick, he planted his boot in Brimstone's flank. The animal gave an explosive *whuhhh!* as Bud's foot landed, and then his ears went even flatter against his head. Before Bud could move, the mule's hindquarters swiveled to the left, and his left hind leg blurred into motion, popping Bud in the chest so fast that he never saw it coming. Clarence William Boggs, mule skinner, sat down hard, did a complete roll backward, and came to rest flat on his back fifteen feet away. Brimstone's ears went forward, and he stood there quietly, swatting flies to death with his tail.

Bud was on his feet and rubbing his chest by the time Mrs. Odell reached him. His face was beet red with a combination of pain and laughter.

"Don't never let nobody tell you a mule cain't kick without usin' both feet, Bub," he wheezed. "Looks like thet jackass don't wanna be rid, but leastwise I got his attention." He found his hat and brushed off the dust. "Well, Bub, you got yer work cut out fer sure."

Mrs. Odell had other ideas.

"Young man," she said, turning to her wide-eyed son, "you are not to go near that animal!" She turned to her brother. "Clarence, you'll have to get rid of him! Today!" She gave Brimstone a look that would have made a three-day-old corpse stand at attention and whistle "Dixie."

Bud wasn't having any. "Now hold yer dang bananas, fer Pete's sake! All mules kick an' this'un ain't no different, so let's jest give 'em a chance 'fore we jump off the cliff holdin' hands!"

Mouth open, Mrs. Odell stood speechless as her brother continued to rant.

"I give forty dollars cash money fer thet critter"—he reached into the pocket of his dusty overalls and waved a crumpled sheet of paper toward his sister—"an' I ain't gonna git rid of 'em without no fight. 'Sides thet, mules is always good critters to have round a kettle wrench like this'un. Me an' Bub'll break 'em, an' thet's final!"

The siblings stared hard at each other for a moment, both with their hands on their hips in defiance. Then Mrs. Odell set her lips and stomped into the house. Bud gave Noah a big wink.

"Gotta be strong with them dang women, Bub. Give 'em a chance, an' they'll run ya down like a kettle truck."

ONE OF THE two large stalls in the barn became Brimstone's new home. And breaking the mule to ride actually turned out to be a simple chore because, as Bud and Noah discovered the next day, he was already perfectly broke. Maybe Brimstone didn't like Bud's particular odor or the smell of adults in general, but every time he got close, the mule's ears would flatten and his stomach muscles would ripple in preparation for a kick. Bud's eyesight was as well-developed as his ability to cuss, and he stayed well clear of the animal's rear end.

Noah tried leading Brimstone near the corral fence so that his uncle could sit on the top rail and leap onto the mule's back, thereby staying out of range of that vicious left hook. Brimstone was far too smart for such nonsense. He waited until the precise moment that Bud made his move and then stepped away so suddenly that Noah simply could not hold him. Bud missed his target completely and landed on his knees. Just in time, he scuttled away through the dust as Brimstone aimed a kick at his head.

"Well, butter my butt and call me a biscuit!" Bud spouted after half an hour of useless maneuvering. He took off his hat and scratched his head. "You got any good ideas, Bub?"

What Noah knew about mules was the same as what he knew about roosters and rattlesnakes. It *was* his mule, however. Swallowing a big wad of anxiety stuck behind his tonsils, he said, "Maybe Brimstone thinks you're too heavy or something. Why don't I try to ride him?"

Bud glanced at the house. Mrs. Odell was nowhere in sight. He took the mule's reins and led him to the other side of the barn. "Hokay," he said. "Let 'er rip, but be real keerful an' don't git close to them hind feet." He rubbed his still-bruised chest.

While his uncle held the bridle reins, Noah eased along Brimstone's left side to a point just behind his left foreleg. Keeping one eye on the mule's ears and the other eye on his stomach muscles, Noah crouched down then took a big hop and clawed his way onto Brimstone's back. Brimstone just stood there peaceably, tail swishing.

"Well, if I ain't a baboon's bee-hind," Bud sputtered. The mule rolled his eyes into the back of his head, flopped his big ears this way and that, and smiled. Actually smiled. His lips retracted and his yellow teeth clacked together a few times. "Well, if I ain't a baboon's bee-hind," Bud repeated.

Noah took the reins and very cautiously kicked Brimstone in the sides and said, "Giddyap!" The mule promptly moved forward at a walk around the yard. "Whoa!" Noah ordered, and Brimstone politely stopped.

"Hey, Sis!" Bud shouted. "Git out here an' lookit yer son! Boy's one helluva cowboy, danged if he ain't!"

Mrs. Odell opened the front door and stepped into the yard. When she saw Noah hadn't been decapitated, a look of relief crossed her face. She didn't even bother to chastise her brother for his cussing.

8

The World
According to Marvin

Anyone who has driven U.S. Route 380 through the vast and desolate reaches of southern New Mexico's Chihuahuan Desert undoubtedly noticed that many of the cactus- and mesquite-covered hillsides to the right and left of the highway are lined with an unusual display of animal trails. The trails don't go up or down or diagonally, but instead, they run only horizontally across the slopes. This phenomenon, known as RPPF, or "repetitive parallel pathway formation," reminds many people of those beautifully terraced Indonesian mountainsides—built in the dawn of time by a race of tiny Balinese rice farmers known as Phorenshirs—that we've all seen in the pages of *National Geographic Magazine*.

Phorenshirs disappeared from Bali thousands of years ago, of course, but the retiring, deer-like mammals that create the unusual hillside trails in southern New Mexico are hopefully a long way from extinction. Scientifically termed *Odocoileus lopsideii*, but known to most people simply as "stubblybuks," their populations are sustaining, if not growing, and their range is extensive. Research done at New Mexico State University in 1949 concluded that viable stubblybuk habitat in New Mexico encompassed more than two hundred thousand square miles of Chihuahuan Desert and that the population in Otero County, New Mexico, alone numbered in the hundreds.

It's difficult at first glance for laymen to distinguish stubblybuks from common, floppy-eared mule deer—especially when they're standing on the side of a hill—but closer examination will quickly reveal the disparity between these two analogous species. Whereas mule deer are able to move laterally, vertically, horizontally, or diagonally across a hillside, stubblybuks can only go *around* a hill. The reason for this seemingly limiting motivation is that a stubblybuk's front and rear legs on one side of its body are nearly a foot shorter than its legs on the other side. The legs on a male stubblybuk's right side, for example, are shorter than the ones on its left side. Females are just the opposite, with shorter legs on the left side and longer ones on the right. Scientists believe that this evolutionary gender dissimilarity enables males and females to travel in different directions and consequently to make eye-to-eye contact when they pass instead of eye-to-anus contact, which would be the case if the legs on both sexes were identical.

The best time to observe and photograph these unusual, side-of-the-hill animals is in early July when they migrate to their breeding grounds in a rugged segment of southern New Mexico terrain known as Tierra de Luna. Less than ten square miles in size and located at the extreme northern end of the San Andres Mountains, Tierra de Luna is ideally suited for breeding. Perfectly sloped hills (important for stubblybuk ambulation), unusually plentiful browse, and clean, fresh water from several year-round seeps and springs all help create an atmosphere conducive to procreation. In addition, Tierra de Luna also provides an ample growth of tiny fairynipple orchids, *Cephalanthera areolas tinkerbellius*, arguably a stubblybuk's favorite type of browse. Fairynipples, of course, contain large amounts of intercorsium, a rare mineral known to stimulate sexual activity in browse-consuming mammals.

The breeding season lasts only about two weeks, but this fortnight of bizarre and often gravity-defying sexual hullabaloo is truly worth observing. Stubblybuk fornication scientists, animal copulation experts, and a host of wildlife whoopee voyeurs from all over the world come to scrutinize, monitor, and record. It is a celebrated and anticipated event, despite the terrific early July heat that has been known to boil chicken eggs in their shells and send *Crotalus atrox* slithering into the nearest deep hole in fear for its life.

Just as mating pairs of intercorsium-stimulated stubblybuks pay scant attention to the egg-boiling, snake-killing early July heat, neither did Noah and his new mule. Bud purchased an old and creaky but usable Mexican saddle for Brimstone from a rancher he knew, and made Noah saddle and unsaddle the animal until he could do it in his sleep. After a couple of mornings of practice riding around the ranch pastures and up and down the driveway, Noah was finally allowed to leave the nest. His first trip was to the Couch dairy, where he found Marvin mucking out the barn.

"Well, it ain't really no horse," Marvin said. He cautiously patted Brimstone's nose and scratched his neck. "Kinda purty, though, an' at least ol' Jake don't have to carry us both no more."

"He's half horse," Noah said, "and half donkey. Bud says he can't make babies because he's sterile."

"Jake cain't make no babies neither," Marvin said. "He got hisself castoorated so's he wouldn't git no mean streak."

"What's castoorated?" Noah asked.

"Thet's when somebody cuts off yer ... you know ..." Marvin pointed between his legs. "Thet way you ain't got nothin' to make babies with, so you cain't make none an' you don't git mean neither."

"Wouldn't that really hurt?" Noah asked, cringing at the thought of having his "you know" cut off.

"S'pose so," Marvin said, "but I ain't never been castoorated, an' I ain't plannin' on it, so's I cain't really say."

The rest of that day and all day, every day during the following two weeks, whenever Noah could get away from weed pulling and Marvin had finished with his barn mucking, they explored the surrounding desert landscape. Any place within five miles of Boggs Ranch or the Couch dairy that wasn't on private property was fair game. Usually they would leave early, just after morning chores, and return by one or two in the afternoon, before it got really scorching outside. Noah's mother often fixed them a large lunch, which they carried in cloth bags slung over their saddle horns, and Marvin's father insisted that both of them carry half-gallon canteens of water. They were ordered by Mr. Couch *and* Bud to always wear their hats and to stay off the main roads.

Noah learned a lot about the complex social apparatus of Tularosa during these long rides—at least as it was analyzed and defined by Marvin Couch. According to Marvin, there were three groups of people into which all of Tularosa's residents fell.

"First, there's the whites," Marvin told him one day as they plodded along side-by-side on their way home from a three-hour ride. "That's us." He gestured at Noah and then himself. "Some people say 'white men' stead a 'whites,'" he added, "but if 'whites' is good enough fer my pa, it's good enough fer me. The whites is up on top, an' they run things an' kin tell everbody else what to do if they want to."

Next on Marvin's totem pole of genetic preponderance came the Hispanos, known as "Hispanos" when they weren't present and as "Spanish people" when they were. "Them Hispanos call us whites 'gringos' when they're bein' nasty, or sometimes 'Anglos' when they want somethin'," he said, "but don't let 'em fool you 'cause Hispanos don't much like whites, and whites don't much like Hispanos."

Last and lowest according to Marvin were the Injuns, mostly 'Pache, who lived in small, filthy shacks on the 'Pache reservation and had hordes of starving children and an unquenchable thirst for cheap wine. An Injun's intelligence, claimed Marvin, was questionable, if not downright nonexistent. For the most part, whites and Hispanos did not get along and hardly spoke to each other unless they wanted to fight. The Injuns were excluded from this esoteric social anatomy altogether because neither whites *nor* Hispanos considered Injuns worth talking to or about.

"You ain't supposed to talk to no Injuns," Marvin told Noah, "'less you see one beatin' up on his wife er kids down in Tularosa, an' then you gotta tell 'em to stop 'cause us whites is supposed to protect women and children no matter who they is."

Most of the time, Noah didn't really understand what Marvin was talking about, but it was pleasant nonetheless just to ride along side-by-side, making conversation. In addition to their excursions around the nearby countryside, they were also allowed to ride into Tularosa if they stayed on the highway's shoulders, well away from traffic, and on Tularosa's dusty back streets. Mostly they made these trips on hot afternoons so they could visit the Tastee-Freez for a cherry Coke or soft ice cream cone.

On their first trip into town, Marvin stopped in front of the feed store and introduced Noah to three of his friends who were leaning against the front wall of the store in the shade. To Noah, they all looked alike—three tall, skinny, sixteen-year-olds wearing jeans, battered cowboy hats, and stovepipe cowboy boots. They were all chewing tobacco and paying little attention to where they spat the juice.

"Frank, Bob, Billy, say howdy to muh potner," Marvin said in his best Texas twang as they approached the three look-alikes. "Potner, shake hands with muh friends."

Obediently, Noah shook hands with the three and said howdy. He tried to be inconspicuous as he wiped the tobacco juice from his hand onto his pants. Later at the Tastee-Freez, seated on a bench in the shade, Noah asked Marvin why he hung around with boys who were older then he was. Marvin slurped the last of his cherry Coke up through the straw before he answered.

"Them ol' boys is pretty tough," he said, lowering his voice. "An' I wouldn't wanna tangle with 'em. They'd help us out if some a them Hispanos ever give us any trouble."

A week later, Noah found out exactly what Marvin meant by "trouble." They had ridden into Tularosa on a baking afternoon and, as usual, tethered Jake and Brimstone to a wooden loading dock on the feed store's shady side. They had ordered and eaten sugar cones of soft ice cream at the Tastee-Freez and were returning to their mounts. When they rounded the corner, Noah saw five boys standing in a semicircle around Jake and Brimstone, tossing small stones at their flanks. The boys all laughed when a sizable pebble connected and made Brimstone jump in pain and surprise. It was the same bunch, Noah remembered, that his uncle had warned him about at the bus station on the day of his arrival in Tularosa.

"Don't start nothin'," Marvin whispered. "Thet big guy's name is Zefo Montoya. Them Spanish kids is a mean bunch."

The boys around Jake and Brimstone were all smaller than Noah, with one notable exception. Zefo Montoya weighed at least thirty pounds more than any of his companions and stood a foot taller. He was dressed in tight, pegged jeans and a dirty white T-shirt. A pack of cigarettes was rolled in one sleeve of his shirt, and his long, black, greasy-looking hair was slicked back into a ducktail.

Trying to ignore the rock throwers, Noah and Marvin walked around the group of boys to where the animals were tethered. Marvin untied Jake first, but as Noah reached for Brimstone's reins, a pebble glanced off the back of his head. Laughter erupted behind him.

"¡Mira! Hey, bastardo!" one of boys shouted. "Zatchoo daddy?"

Noah didn't say anything, but the knot of fear in his stomach was big enough to flatten downtown Tularosa had it been inclined to roll that way. Once again, he reached for Brimstone's reins, and once again, a rock bounced off the back of his head.

"Hey man!" It was Zefo talking. "Hey, pendejo! Look at me when I talk to you!" Zefo moved to within a few feet of Noah. He stood perilously close Brimstone's rear end.

In the next few seconds, several things happened all at once. Doing his best to ignore Zefo, Noah fumbled with Brimstone's reins, trying to get them untied. Marvin heaved and grunted himself onto Jake's back. Frank, Bob, and Billy suddenly appeared around the corner of the feed store and stood quietly, watching the show. Noah glanced over, wondering when help was coming, and as he did, Zefo's right fist slammed into his nose. His hat went flying, and the next second he was lying on his back in the dirt, trying to focus his eyes. The blurs of Frank, Bob, and Billy just stood there, big wads of tobacco pooching out their cheeks.

If there was one thing Noah had learned from numerous encounters with Skeeter Johnson, it was never, ever to stay down where he could be kicked. He stood up quickly, fists clenched, nose bleeding a river onto his shirt. Obviously, Zefo was not expecting opposition or resistance because he looked truly surprised when Noah's hard, accurate haymaker caught him directly in his left eye. He grunted and took a step backward, no doubt preparing to tear Noah into small, edible pieces.

Unfortunately for Zefo, he stepped back right into Brimstone's hindquarters, and for the second time that summer, Noah saw the mule's ears go back and his hindquarters swivel and his left hind foot blur into action. There came a solid *whump!* and Zefo flew into the street like a sack of potatoes, a look of sheer disbelief spreading across his face. He landed ten feet away, face down in the dirt. The T-shirt he had been wearing was bunched up into his armpits, and crumpled cigarettes were strewn everywhere in the dust, like pieces of broken chalk. Zefo lay without moving, but Noah could hear his mournful moans.

Ethel Odell hadn't raised a fool, and Noah wasn't about to hang around to receive the plentitude of punches that would shortly have been dispersed about his head and body by Zefo's friends. He grabbed his hat from where it lay in the dirt, threw Brimstone's reins over his neck, and clawed his way aboard quickly. One of the other boys, braver than the rest, tried to grab the mule's bridle, but he was bowled into the side of the feed store like a football by Jake's massive shoulder as Marvin kicked him into motion.

Five minutes later, on the edge of town, they slowed from a gallop to a walk and assessed the damage. Marvin and Jake were unhurt, but Noah's nose was swollen to the size of an apricot and was still bleeding. His upper lip was cut and dripping blood as well. Brimstone hadn't been injured by the pebbles Zefo's gang had thrown at him, but he was winded and breathing hard from the long, hot gallop out of town.

"Dang, you got a mean punch, potner!" Marvin said. Obviously he hadn't seen Brimstone put Zefo on the ground and thought it had been Noah. Noah didn't tell him any different.

"How come those friends of yours didn't help out?" he asked, spewtering blood from his cut lip as he talked. "Looks to me like they were just plain chickens."

"Cheekns!" Marvin shot back. "Them boys? They wasn't cheekns. They jest wasn't enough of 'em."

"Not enough of them!" Noah shouted. "There were three of them! How many does it take to help out their friends?"

Marvin reined Jake to the right, trying to stay clear of Noah's bloody spittle. He pushed his way-too-big hat onto the back of his head and hooked a thumb in his belt.

"Didn't mean they wasn't enough a *them*," he clarified. "They wasn't enough a them Hispanos. Them ol' boys jest didn't wanna spoil all our fun."

9

Little Green Men
in the Malpais

O f all God's marvelous creatures roaming the sandy wilderness of the Chihuahuan Desert in southern New Mexico, *Lethopterus leapii horniculus*, the common jackalope, is without a doubt the most maligned and misunderstood. The species was initially discovered in 1603 by Spanish conquistadors from Mexico City, who were exploring present-day New Mexico around White Sands, and ever since, these oversized jackrabbit cousins with sharp, ten-inch-long bony knobs protruding from their heads have been victimized by fables and falsehoods. Some parables declare, for instance, that jackalopes have razor-sharp claws and three-inch-long fangs and, when cornered, will rip their unsuspecting attackers into tiny pieces. Others allege that they have the strength of animals ten times their size and can travel on flat ground at speeds reaching ninety miles per hour. Finally, there is an old wives' tale asserting that a jackalope's milk has miraculous healing powers, and that it's toenails, if ground to a powdery consistency and mixed with prune juice, offer astonishing sexual prowess to those who drink it.

The truth, of course, is that jackalopes are none of these things. They are most certainly shy, secretive, and cagey, but what creature wouldn't be retiring if it had once been hunted and trapped, almost to the point of extinction, by postcard photographers during the early twentieth century. Supernatural creatures, however, with extraordinary fighting powers and the ability to transform wimps into studs through the oral consummation of powdered podiatric proteinaceous keratin, they are not.

Until just a few years ago, an annual jackalope roundup, head-quartered in the small town of Corona, New Mexico, was aimed at acquainting people with the habits and habitats of these creatures in an effort to save them from total extinction. Environmentally minded people from all walks of life attended the three-day roundup by the hundreds, putting Corona on the map as the jackalope capital of the world. Unfortunately, not a single jackalope was ever actually *seen* during one of these events, let alone rounded up, and it was cancelled because of the lack of attendance in 1955.

The almost daily riding trips made by Noah and Marvin into Tularosa for cherry Cokes at the Tastee-Freez were cancelled, too, at least for the foreseeable future. The boys knew that Zefo and his friends would likely rip off their arms if they showed their faces in town, so they gave the place a wide berth. Noah had told his mother and uncle what had happened as soon as he got home, mainly because it was difficult to lie about getting in a fight when your schnozzle was spurting enough blood to provide Sunday dinner to a castle full of vampires. Mrs. Odell wanted to visit the sheriff and have Zefo arrested, but Bud's cooler head prevailed.

"Sheriff wouldn't do nothin'," he said, "'cause thet ain't the way things work hereabouts. Zefo'd jest say he wasn't nowhere around, anyway. Spanish kids an' Anglo kids jest gotta settle their own problems. Things'll work out, jest wait an' see. Ol' Zefo'll git his due one a these days."

With access to the Tastee-Freez interrupted at least until things settled down, the boys began roaming farther and farther into the desert west of the ranch. There was little chance they could get lost because the Sacramento Mountains looming in the east would always let them know which way they should go. Bud told them about a place he'd once found while hunting antelope called Aguilar Spring that lay ten miles straight west from the ranch.

"They's arrowheads an' broke Indian pots all over the place out there," he said. "Indians hunted in these parts 'fore Tularosa was ever heard of." To get there and back, Bud told them, they would have to ride a total of twenty miles across country without any roads to follow, twice the distance Noah had ever ridden in one day before.

Aguilar Spring was a challenge neither Noah nor Marvin wanted to pass up. They planned the trip for a Saturday morning, and on the day of departure, with full canteens and sacks of peanut butter and jelly sandwiches slung over their saddles, they set out right after chores were done. Bud loaned them a small compass and a box of wooden matches for emergencies and told them to follow the fence to the gate at the end of the Boggs property then ride straight west for two hours. When they reached a lava flow, or malpais, they should turn left and follow the edge of the flow south until they came to a stand of large cottonwood trees. Aguilar Spring flowed out of the desert sand beneath the trees. On the ride back, they could simply reverse their course and follow their own tracks home, or they could follow the compass needle straight east toward the mountains until they intersected the highway or spotted the tall cottonwoods of Tularosa.

With Noah and Brimstone leading the way, the boys did as they had been told. They went through the Boggs's gate and headed west, checking the compass every ten minutes or so to make sure they were on the right heading. As they plodded along through the rapidly increasing heat, Noah thought about Zefo Montoya. He wondered if Zefo and Skeeter Johnson could somehow be related, since they were both the biggest bollocks on earth. He was so pleased with himself for finally discovering a use for the word "bollocks"—which was even better than "penis face" for describing people like Zefo and Skeeter—that he barely noticed Marvin come up alongside him.

"You figger there's really a God somewheres," Marvin asked, "or Jesus? Somebody thet looks after you an' makes sure you don't git in no trouble if yer good, an' can make mountains an' lakes an' stuff like that, an' boss angels around, an' take you up to heaven when you die?" Long horseback rides seemed to transform him into an unlikely philosopher.

"Guess so," Noah answered. "My mom says there is anyway. I don't know what Uncle Bud thinks. He never says anything about God except when he's swearing. When he swears a lot, Mom calls him a heathen. I don't think heathens are supposed to believe in God."

"Well, if there *is* a God or a Jesus somewheres," Marvin said, "how come He made Deeter crazy? Whyn't He make 'em walk normal and talk normal like me. Then I'd have a regular brother thet didn't pee his pants and puke up his guts."

"Didn't your mom say that God works in mysterious ways?" reminded Noah.

Marvin thought a moment. "He sure as heck made Deeter mysterious, all right. Started rollin' around on the floor of his cage this mornin', screechin' like he was bein' skint alive. Wouldn't quit neither till Ma threw a bucket of cold water on 'em."

Marvin made Jake walk a little slower so he wouldn't get ahead of Brimstone.

"What if there ain't no God or no Jesus though?" he asked. "*Then* who made Deeter crazy?"

Noah had no answer to that one, so he said nothing. It didn't stop Marvin from prattling on.

"Coulda been the Devil, I guess, but I cain't figger out why the Devil'd bother messin' with somebody like Deeter." Marvin removed his hat and scratched the top of his head. "'Sides thet, if there ain't no God or no Jesus then there probly ain't no Devil neither." Once again, he slowed Jake down so they could ride side-by-side.

"You think there's a heaven?" he asked. "Where you think it's at?"

"Well, if there's a God, then there's probably a heaven, I guess," Noah said. "Everybody says it's up in the sky somewhere. The minister at our church in Gold Hill said that heaven isn't a place that living people can go. He said that only dead people can go to heaven, and if you weren't a good person when you were alive, you wouldn't be a good dead person when you died and wouldn't go to heaven anyway unless you were a movie star or somebody important."

"Trouble with that is ain't nobody got no proof there's a heaven. I bet yer minister ain't never been to heaven, so how's he know if you gotta be good to git in. I ain't never heard a nobody thet went to heaven and come back to tell about it, thet's for sure," Marvin said.

Noah couldn't think of anyone offhand either.

"Think there's a bad place, too? You think hell's a place thet bad people go to when they die so's the Devil kin rip off their arms and legs and maybe castoorate 'em, too?"

Noah didn't know anyone who had gone to hell and returned either, but several times during the past week he had wished Zefo Montoya would take a quick, one-way excursion to that fabled underworld location.

"What if you believed in heaven an' hell all yer life an' went to church ever' Sunday an' put money in the church bowl ever' time you went so's you wouldn't go to hell when you died, an' then when you died, you found out there ain't no heaven, an' there ain't no hell, an' there ain't no God an' no Jesus? Whaddya do then?"

Noah had to think about that one. "Well," he finally said, "if you die and go to heaven but there isn't one, then you wouldn't know there wasn't one anyway because you'd be dead. Same goes with hell and God and Jesus, I guess."

Marvin seemed to find solace in Noah's answer, and he reined Jake once again into single file. He was back alongside Noah in a few minutes.

"My pa says there's a whole buncha people in the world thet don't believe in God or Jesus or heaven or nothin' else," Marvin said. "Pa says all them people don't never go to church and don't sing hymns and don't have no Christmas, and they don't git no presents neither."

Noah looked skeptical. "How many is a whole bunch?" he asked. "I guess there are some people that probably don't believe in God or Jesus, but I don't think there's a whole bunch of them. At least I've never heard about it if there are."

"My pa says there's jillions of 'em. You ever heard of the Hay-rabs, or the Bood . . . somethings, or the Chinamen, or the Japs? None a *them* believe in God or Jesus or heaven, an' there's at least a jillion of 'em."

Noah had heard of Chinamen and Japs, but he had no idea what a Hay-rab or a Bood . . . something was. Before he could comment, however, Marvin changed the subject.

"How come yer uncle ain't got no wife?" he asked. "She die or somethin'?"

"Nope," Noah said. "He just never got married; at least he hasn't ever said anything about it if he did."

How and why it was that Clarence Boggs, at forty-one years of age, had never experienced the joys of matrimony, in fact, had been a topic of conversation in the Odell household since Noah was about ten. When they lived in Gold Hill, the subject of marriage would be broached by Bud's sister at least once during each of his visits.

"Clarence," she would ask, "when are you going to find some nice girl and settle down?" Or, "Clarence, why don't you ask that nice widow woman Mrs. Harris down the street if she wants to come to dinner tomorrow?" Or, "Clarence, I'm sure if you gave up drinking and cursing, you would probably blah, blah, blah."

Things had gotten so bad, Noah remembered, that Bud had finally brought a "nice girl" with him on one of his visits. Precisely where he found Minnie (they never learned her last name), Noah never found out. Somewhere on the dark side of forty, she was short and stout, with a pasty smile and thin, stringy, bleached-blonde hair. Her fingernails had been chewed into the quick and a hickey the size of a quarter embellished the side of her neck. Throughout the afternoon, Bud smiled flaccidly as Minnie's overworked mouth chatted mindlessly on about how when Honey Pot and her got married, they were gonna have a buncha kids, and boy, did she wish she had a bottle of beer, but Honey Pot wouldn't let her bring none, and how cute Ethel's house was, but she'd change this and she'd change that if it was hers. While Minnie talked, she squeezed Bud's arm like a monkey squeezes a banana, and tooted a series of quiet but smelly feminine flatulence into the hand-embroidered pillows adorning the sofa seat. The couple stayed just one afternoon, and both Noah and his mother were quietly thankful when they left before dinner. Once Bud's truck was out of sight, the pillows were quickly hung on the clothesline to air, and Noah's mother opened all the doors and windows in the house. A week later they received a letter from Bud postmarked San Francisco announcing Minnie's return to Oklahoma. Noah could imagine his uncle grinning widely while he wrote it. The subject of marriage had not been brought up since.

"He ain't one of them faggots, is he?" Marvin asked.

"Of course he's not a faggot," answered Noah, slightly incensed at the question. "He just doesn't want a wife, that's all. Bud says most women are more trouble than they're worth." Marvin seemed satisfied and once again dropped back into single file.

Two hours after leaving the ranch, the boys reached the malpais, just as Bud had said they would. Probably half a mile across, it was a wide, black, fifteen-foot-high tumbled river of hardened lava running north and south as far as they could see. There was no volcano or cinder cone to be seen, so the lava had obviously just flowed from a hole in the earth somewhere to the north. It looked impossible to cross on horse- or muleback, and even people on foot would have had difficulty finding a way to the other side. Not one plant grew on the flow, not even a cactus. Noah had never seen anything like it.

Following instructions, the boys turned left and followed the jagged, meandering edge of the malpais toward the south. Twenty minutes later, they spotted the grove of cottonwood trees they'd been told to look for. In the deep shade beneath the trees, a small seep of water formed a shallow pool in the bottom of a sandy gully. The pool was filled with back swimmers and other water bugs, but it was clear and cold. They let Jake and Brimstone drink their fill, bugs and all.

When they had eaten their sandwiches, they left the animals tied in the shade and began a search of the desert around the spring for Indian artifacts, keeping their eyes peeled for rattlers. The sand within a hundred yards of the water had been picked clean, but farther out they found several small but skillfully chipped obsidian arrowheads half-buried in the sand. They also found pottery shards, most of them a rusty color and without markings, but a few decorated with brightly colored zigzag lines or pictures of animals. Some of the shards were the size of their hands. They put the obsidian points and larger pieces of pottery in one of the lunch sacks for safekeeping.

In a shallow depression beneath a giant mesquite bush, Marvin stopped and motioned for Noah to come closer. "Bet those is jackalope tracks," he whispered, pointing to a set of smudged impressions in the sand at his feet.

"What's a jackalope?" Noah asked, also whispering.

"Cross between an antelope an' a jackrabbit," Marvin said. "They got horns an' big sharp teeth an' claws an' kin run faster'n a horse."

Noah was skeptical. "Have you ever actually *seen* a jackalope?"

"Nope," Marvin answered truthfully, "but thet don't mean nothin'. I ain't never seen no Chinamen neither, but my pa says they all make dang good food. Only trouble is none of 'em believe in God er Jesus."

Noah studied the tracks. He couldn't tell from looking at them whether the animal that made them was big or small. "Why do you think those are jackalope tracks?" he asked. "They look too messed up to tell *what* they are. And why are we whispering?"

"Thet's what them jackalopes do," Marvin whispered. "Mess up their tracks so's nobody knows they're around. An' we're whisperin' 'cause if one of 'em *is* around, we don't wanna git 'em mad at us."

―――――――

THE BOYS STARTED toward home about midafternoon without seeing a jackalope. It was baking hot, but Jake and Brimstone were full of water, and the boys had their wide-brimmed hats to keep the sun off their faces. Marvin led as they headed east, following the compass toward the hazy mountains in the distance. They'd ridden no more than a mile when Marvin pulled Jake to a halt and pointed to something in front of them. Noah followed his finger. He could see flashes of bright green that seemed to be moving back and forth across the sand.

"Ain't supposed to be nobody out here," Marvin said quietly. "Pa said they ain't no roads at all, and if we got stuck, they'd have to come git us with a horse."

"Maybe they're soldiers," Noah said. "My uncle said there was an army base out here somewhere."

"Soldiers ain't got no clothes thet color," Marvin said. "Bet they ain't soldiers."

Curious but not necessarily afraid, the boys dismounted and tied Jake and Brimstone to a large bush. They crept slowly and quietly toward the movement ahead, keeping low and staying behind the mesquite and cactus when they could. A hundred yards away, they dropped into a shallow gully and were able to walk stooped over to a point perhaps fifty yards from where they thought they had seen the green flashes. Marvin took off his hat and motioned Noah to keep low. He peeped carefully over the top of the gully's rim, a reconnaissance that lasted less than five seconds before he dropped back down beside Noah with a startled look on his face.

"You ain't gonna believe what I jest seen!" Marvin's voice was high-pitched and shaky. He stood up again for another quick peep, and then, wearing a look of total disbelief, collapsed on the sand next to where Noah squatted.

"They's a spaceship an' a bunch of green space monsters walkin' around out there!"

Noah removed his hat and carefully peeked over the gully's edge. Marvin hadn't exaggerated. The five bright-green, two-legged beings he saw had massive round heads and were gathered around what looked like a rocket ship lying on its side. Three of the creatures carried small gadgets that looked like ray guns. Noah had read enough Flash Gordon comic books to know what space monsters and ray guns looked like. These were them, no doubt about it.

Marvin grabbed hold of Noah's pants and pulled him down. "We gotta go tell somebody!" he squeaked. "Bet they're invaders from outer space an' they're gonna blast people into bits!" Marvin, too, read Flash Gordon comic books.

Noah suddenly remembered the stories he'd heard on the radio about strange flying objects spotted around Alamogordo that summer. "They look like space monsters all right," Noah whispered, "but maybe they're just lost or hurt. Let's get closer so we can see what they're doing."

"I ain't goin' no closer," Marvin whispered back, shaking his head violently. "They see us, they'll blast us with them ray guns!" Jamming his hat down as far as it would go, Marvin started crawling back the way they had come.

Noah didn't follow immediately, torn between his curiosity about the green beings and his fear of getting caught and zapped into pink goo. He finally decided that Marvin was probably right. Maybe it was time to leave and go tell somebody before they were spotted. Noah, too, jammed his hat down low and started back on all fours toward the spot where Jake and Brimstone were tied. He had gone no more than a few yards, though, when he caught a glimpse of bright green movement to his right. He glanced up and saw another of the green beings, this one with both arms raised in surprise, standing not twenty feet away. It was watching him crawl up the gully.

Noah stood up. He knew it was time to fly. "Run or they're gonna get us!" he shouted to Marvin, and he charged out of the gully away from the creature, his legs churning like a windmill. Marvin didn't need a second invitation. He bolted up and out of the gully as well, half a second behind Noah. Noah chanced one glimpse back over his shoulder and saw the bright green creature point the small gadget it carried in its hand in his direction. He dodged around a large bush and made a beeline for his mule, expecting to be fried into toast at any second.

———————————

WHEN THE TWO exhausted and excited boys finally reached Boggs Ranch later that afternoon on two thirsty and winded equines, they poured out their story to the first person they saw, who happened to be Noah's uncle. Mrs. Odell was shopping for groceries in Alamogordo. Bud was skeptical. Nonetheless, he agreed that the authorities should be notified.

"Ain't got no idea what you boys saw out there, but they's no sech thing as space monsters," he said. "Don't sound normal, though, so's let's head into town and you kin tell the sheriff what you told me, jest in case."

They stopped at the Couch dairy and found Marvin's dad forking hay into feed bins in the barn. Once again, the boys told their story about little green men carrying ray guns to a skeptical ear.

"Coulda been a plane crash," Mr. Couch said, "but I think you two got too much sun and saw a mirage. I'll get my hat and go with you anyway, though."

Twenty minutes later, Bud parked the pickup in front of the small sheriff station on the east side of Tularosa. As they walked toward the door, he gave Noah and Marvin a quick lecture about telling the truth.

"Screw on yer ears an' pay attention," he said. "When you talk to the law, you got to tell 'em what you know, not what you think. Don't say no space monsters tried to eat you, 'cause that ain't what happened. Jest tell 'em the truth an' don't say nothin' else less yer asked."

Inside the station, a dark-skinned, mustachioed sheriff's deputy wearing a khaki uniform sat at a small desk on one side of the room. His short hair was prematurely gray, as was his waxed and manicured handlebar mustache. Two jail cells with floor-to-ceiling bars occupied the other side of the office. Both cells were empty.

The deputy looked up without a smile when they came in. "Howdy, Clarence. Howdy, Heze," he said. He looked at Noah and Marvin.

"Deputy, this here's muh nephew, Noah Odell." It was the first time Noah had ever heard his uncle use his entire name. "He's muh sister's boy. You know Marvin. Bub, Marvin, say howdy to Deputy Mendoza."

Noah and Marvin did as they were told. They got a long, hard stare in return.

"Heard you two got into some kinda scuffle with Zefo Montoya and his bunch last week," Deputy Mendoza said. "Nobody's sayin' much, but Zefo's got three busted ribs, and he's hobbling around on a crutch."

Noah's spirit did a feisty little tap dance of happiness around the room, bouncing off the walls as it went, though his body didn't move a muscle.

"Don't know what you hit him with, but the word's out he'll be looking for you as soon as he can walk properly. I'd stay as far away from those boys as I could get if I was you."

The deputy looked at Bud and Mr. Couch. "That what this is all about?"

Bud shook his head. "This ain't got nothin' to do with thet," he said. "Thet little pachuco got what he had comin'." He nodded to Noah. "Tell 'em what you boys saw, and 'member what I said 'bout monsters."

Between them, Noah and Marvin got the story out in less than five minutes. Deputy Mendoza listened intently until they were finished.

"I wouldn't doubt it a bit if you'd seen a bunch of little green men and a spaceship," he said, spinning the ends of his mustache between his fingers. "That's a real weird place out there on those lava beds, and we've been getting all kinds of reports of colored lights and strange-looking objects flying around." He got up and walked across the room to a bulletin board. He removed a piece of yellow paper tacked to the board and brought it back to the desk.

"But I happen to know what you saw didn't come from outer space," the deputy continued. "We got this on the teletype yesterday morning. Which one of you two can read?"

He handed the paper to Noah. "Out loud," he ordered. Noah did as he was told, and read:

> July 10, 1957. The Office of Public Safety at White Sands Proving Ground is hereby notifying all law enforcement agencies in Otero County that a short-range ballistic rocket being tested at White Sands Proving Ground went off course yesterday morning and crash landed ten to fifteen miles west of Tularosa near the geologic basalt formation known as the malpais. OPSWS has not yet located the exact site. Law enforcement agencies in the area are requested to contact this office if any sightings are reported. The rocket is not explosive but should not be approached by civilians because of toxic gasses.

"What you boys saw was a bunch of army scientists trying to figure out what went wrong with their rocket," the deputy said. "I know for a fact that they wear bright green suits with oversized helmets so they won't get gassed. What they had in their hands was probably some kind of gas-measuring device."

"How'd they git way out there?" Bud asked. "Aguilar Spring ain't right next to the highway."

"Army probably flew them in by helicopter from White Sands. They're a pretty secretive bunch out there, and they don't tell us donkey spit if they don't have to. They sure as heck won't advertise in the newspaper if one of their rockets goes off course and lands on public land."

Bud and Mr. Couch thanked the deputy for his time, shook hands, and shooed Noah and Marvin out the door and back to the pickup. The mystery seemed to be solved, at least to Deputy Mendoza's satisfaction. On the ride home, it was Noah and Marvin's turn to be skeptical, however.

"You think he was right?" Noah asked as he and Marvin sat on the rusty toolbox in the bed of the Studebaker. "About that thing being an army rocket?"

"Dunno," Marvin answered. "Mebbe. Mebbe not. Dang scary lookin', whatever it was."

"What are we going to do about Zefo and his gang?"

"Dunno 'bout thet, neither. Keep outta town, I guess. Mebbe he'll get ran over by a truck."

"Maybe he'll get blasted by monsters," Noah said.

"Mebbe he'll git blasted *an'* ran over by a truck," Marvin added. They both started laughing.

"I think they *were* space monsters," Noah said. "And I think that *was* a spaceship."

"Me too," Marvin said. "But don' tell yer uncle or my pa. They ain't gonna believe nothin' we got to say till them things start blastin' people to bits by the hunnerds."

10

The Meeting of the Moos

W hat happens when, in the middle of the southern New Mexico desert, God in all of his wisdom creates 275 square miles of absolutely useless, granulated, cosmically vetted white stuff that looks like sand and feels like sand and stings the hell out of your eyes when it gets in them like sand but really isn't sand? It's not snow either because the temperature outside is 110 degrees Fahrenheit in the shade, and snow would last about as long as a snowball in hell would last, which is about 0.12 seconds on the Richter scale.

Here's what happens. The white stuff, whose scientific designation is $CaSO_4 \cdot 2H_2O$, or crystallized gypsum dust, sits there for about twenty million years not bothering anyone until humans invent the automobile. Pretty soon after that, somebody out looking for Indian arrowheads or photographing jackalopes or something similar tries to drive his car out into the middle of the stuff that looks and feels like sand, and he bogs down to his axles and gets hopelessly stuck and then looks around and shouts, "Eureka! After someone saves *us* by towing us back to the highway with a mule, we must save this white wilderness of $CaSO_4 \cdot 2H_2O$ for future generations!"

The next thing you know, along comes the U.S. National Park Service. They build some shelters and a couple of fire pits, and they pave the entrance road and parking lot, and they haul in a couple of portable plastic bathrooms and put up a couple of signs saying PORTABLE PLASTIC BATHROOMS, THIS WAY, and voila! Before you know it, a national monument that attracts six hundred thousand or so tourists a year is born.

Among those tourists on a hot afternoon in mid-July 1957 were Noah Odell and Marvin Couch, both of whom were totally overwhelmed by their first sight of the great white wilderness known as White Sands National Monument. The malpais had been mind-blowing, especially with the addition of green space monsters with ray guns and rocket ships, but the towering white dunes of pure white gypsum stretching as far as the eye could see and dotted only here and there with an occasional yucca plant was about the strangest thing either of them had ever seen.

"Dang, I ain't never seen nothin' like this!" Marvin said as they drove past the monument headquarters and into the first of the dunes. "My pa ain't never brung me out here!" The two boys were riding in the back of the Studebaker. Bud was driving, and Mrs. Odell, looking a bit awed by the remarkable scenery, was on the passenger side of the bench seat. Marvin's mouth was agape. "Like it snowed ever'where," he managed. "I ain't never seen no snow up close neither, but I bet this is what it looks like if I *had* seen some up close, which I ain't."

Bud parked the truck near a picnic shelter in the heart of the monument two or three miles from the main highway. There were half a dozen other shelters scattered about the day use area, all of them occupied by picnicking families with children. Surrounding them in all directions were hundreds of steep-sided, sugar-white dunes, some of them several hundred feet high.

Bud helped his sister out of the cab and told Noah and Marvin they could climb down from the back. "Git out yer ear trumpets an' listen up," he said before letting them go exploring. "When yer ma's got dinner ready, she'll holler. Meantime, don't go nowhere you cain't see the truck. You kin git lost out here real quick, and the buzzards'd be pickin' their teeth on yer bones 'fore we ever found ya."

"Buzzards ain't got no teeth," Marvin said.

"Don't be no damn smart aleck," Bud said. "Jest don't git lost er we'll have to cart yer dried-out carcasses home in a gunnysack."

With that cheery thought in mind, the boys hastily removed their boots and rolled up their pant legs and set out to scale the largest dune in the neighborhood, a towering pile of sculpted, crystallized dust perhaps three hundred feet high. Climbing up the steep slope was difficult because for every five feet they gained in elevation, they slid back three in the quicksand-like gypsum. When they finally reached the top, they collapsed on their faces, thoroughly exhausted.

Noah heard a giggle and looked up. A slender, very pretty girl wearing light blue shorts and a blue sweatshirt was watching them with a smile on her face. Her dark brown hair was cut so short that it was almost boyish, and a spattering of tiny freckles trotted across her nose and cheeks from one ear to the other.

"Hi," Noah said. "What's so funny?"

"You boys are funny, that's what," she said. Her voice was soft and low pitched. "You looked like two monkeys trying to shinny up a giant banana."

"Howdy, LaDonna," Marvin said.

"Hi, Marvin," she said cheerily. "Ready for school to start? Who's your friend?"

"Ain't never ready fer school to start," Marvin said. "Don't know when it starts and don't care much neither. This here's Noah. He lives out by me. This here's LaDonna. Her dad owns Hawthorne's Dairy in Alamogordo."

"Ernest Renan said, 'The simplest schoolboy is now familiar with truths for which Archimedes would have given his life,'" LaDonna said, smiling at Marvin. "Be happy. School starts on September 15, so you have two months of freedom left. Hi, Noah. Do your parents own a dairy, too?"

"Nope," Noah answered. "We have a bunch of cows, though. Brahmas mostly, but I don't think I'd want to milk one."

LaDonna giggled again. "They're really called Brahman," she said, "and they came from India a long time ago. Cowboys just call them Brahmas, though." Noah noticed that when LaDonna spoke, the freckles on her cheeks seemed to dance a little jig. It was fascinating to watch. "Since we're all sort of cow people," she continued,

"I guess we could call this a meeting of the moos. Moo I have a moo-ment of your time?"

"Sure you moo," Noah said, "as long as it's in July and not in Moo." Both he and LaDonna started laughing. Marvin didn't get it, and Noah didn't feel like explaining.

"I saw you in Tularosa once," LaDonna told Noah. "You were in front of the feed store riding a mule. My dad won't let me ride into town. He says I wouldn't be safe if I was alone."

"I'm with your dad," Noah said. "We got jumped by Zefo Montoya and his gang a few days back."

"Zefo Montoya isn't a nice person," LaDonna said. "He likes to beat up people who are smaller than he is. Is that what happened to your nose? It looks kind of lumpy."

Noah started to answer, but Marvin butted in.

"You think *he* looks bad, you shoulda seen Zefo," he said. "He ain't gonna be walkin' right fer a while."

"Somebody told my mom he was on crutches. Did you do that?" LaDonna sounded skeptical.

"Dang right, he did it!" Marvin interrupted again. "Ol' Zefo never saw it comin' neither. One second he was standin' there bein' a cow's hiney, an' the next second he was eatin' dirt an' cryin' fer his ma."

Noah just shrugged and didn't correct Marvin's version of the story. It was way too late for the truth. "The only trouble is Zefo probably wants to rip our hearts out and feed them to the coyotes."

"Wow!" LaDonna said. "Remind me never to get into a fistfight with you." She giggled. "Let's forget about Zefo. Want to go explor-ing? There's lots of things to do at White Sands." She motioned at the surrounding sea of white dunes. "Some of the animals here are pretty strange."

"Sure," said Noah, "but we have to stay where we can see my uncle's pickup. If we get lost, the buzzards will pick their teeth with our bones."

"I don't think buzzards have teeth," LaDonna said, "but we can do that easy. We'll just stay on top of the dunes and make a big cir-cle around the picnic area. Did you know the kangaroo rats here are white?"

Noah's knowledge of the kangaroo rats at White Sands was about the same as his knowledge of roosters and rattlesnakes and mules, though he'd learned a lot about Brimstone over the past several weeks. He hadn't even known White Sands existed until the previous afternoon when his uncle had told him they were going there for a picnic. LaDonna walked a few feet along the crest of the dune, examining the sand at her feet, then suddenly flopped down on her stomach. She motioned for Noah and Marvin to come over. When they were similarly situated on their stomachs next to her, she pointed at a tiny line of tracks in the gypsum.

"To catch a kangaroo rat," she said, lowering her voice, "we have to follow its tracks across the sand until we find out where it's hiding." LaDonna put her nose only a few inches from the sand. "I think this is the track of a serpent-tailed kangaroo rat. It's sort of common around here. Now we just have to make sure which way it's going."

"How kin you tell which way a rat's goin'?" Marvin asked.

"You have to look for the signs," LaDonna whispered, putting her finger to her lips.

"What kinda signs?" Marvin asked, whispering as well.

"Little bitty signs," she said and once again put her nose close to the gypsum. "They're kind of hard to read, but they say 'Kangaroo Rat Went This Way.' There's one right there!"

Marvin put his nose close to the sand and looked hard. So did Noah. LaDonna started giggling. Too late, the boys realized they'd just been had.

"When you two geniuses figure out that rats can't write," she said, rolling on her back in the gypsum and laughing hysterically, "we'll go try and catch one."

———

LATE IN THE afternoon, with the sun sinking quickly toward the hazy, purple western horizon, the three of them were once again atop the large dune upon which they had met earlier in the day. They had completed an entire circuit of the picnic basin, keeping to the tops of the highest dunes and always staying within sight of the cars below. LaDonna hadn't been joking about the kangaroo rats. Most of them *were* white, or nearly so, and therefore difficult to see against the white gypsum unless they were moving. They had caught several by following their tracks, locating the holes they were hiding in, and then digging them out of the sand with their hands. Noah was amazed at how they could flatten themselves into the sand and erect their white-plumed tails so quickly.

An hour before dark and with her parents' permission, LaDonna had joined them for a tasty picnic dinner of fried chicken, coleslaw, and fresh homemade bread at the picnic table beneath the shelter. After supper, they had helped Mrs. Odell clean up the mess and then once again clambered up the dune to watch the sunset. The late afternoon sky was a deep turquoise blue, and there wasn't a breath of a breeze. Looking out across the sea of dunes, Noah thought about the beautiful Oregon beaches, half a day's drive from Gold Hill, but eighteen hundred miles away from White Sands.

"It reminds me of the ocean," he said. "My mom and I used to go to the ocean once a year, at least when our car would run and we had any extra money. We would stay in an auto court and collect seashells and walk along the beach for hours."

"I ain't never seen no ocean," Marvin said. "Closest thing we got to any oceans is Elephant Butte Lake over by Truth'n Consequences. Pa took me over once to go fishin', an' I sat down on some dang cactus an' thought I was gonna croak it hurt so bad."

"I haven't seen one either," LaDonna said, "but I will someday. I want to live by an ocean, someplace where it rains every day and where I never have to milk another cow."

"You'd like Oregon then," Noah said. "One thing it's got lots of is rain. It used to have cows too, but they all got drowned because it rained so much."

"It sounds like my kind of place," LaDonna giggled. "Want to hear a poem I wrote? It's about rattlesnakes."

"Plenty a rattlers round here, thet's fer sure," Marvin said. "Cain't go nowhere without seeing a dang snake."

"Sure," said Noah. "Poetry is nice. I had to read 'The Raven' by Edgar Allan Poe in eighth grade English class. It wasn't about snakes, but it was pretty good."

LaDonna clasped her hands in front of her, closed her eyes, and recited:

Behold, the kingdom of the snake,
where sun flays skin and bleaches bone.
Of misty dew one shan't partake,
and glacial morn is seldom known.
Beware the fool that walks unbid,
for death lies waiting on the dune.
The final dark can't be undid,
Step lightly, neath the cold, pale moon.

Noah felt a cold shiver tickle his spine. Marvin was carefully examining the sand around him. "Wow," Noah said appreciatively. "Pretty spooky, but pretty good. Do you like snakes?"

"I can't stand snakes," La Donna answered, making a face. "Especially rattlesnakes. They bite our cows on their ankles all the time and cause them to swell up. Then Dad has to call the veterinarian and the cow stops giving milk for a few weeks. Sometimes they even die." LaDonna shuddered. "The poem just sort of popped into my head. My mom says I must have a tiny little demon that lives in my brain and tells me when things need to be written down. I think he's probably green with a long, gray beard and horns and hair growing on his toes. I've got a whole drawer full of poems and stories at home that just came out of nowhere." Her voice dropped to a low murmur. "Want to hear a ghost story? I know a good one about Pavla Blanca, the White Lady of the Dunes."

"If it ain't too scary," said Marvin. "We gotta ride home in the back a Mr. Boggs's truck in the dark."

"It's not real scary," LaDonna said, "especially since it isn't even dark yet. Anyway, I'd rather meet a ghost than a rattlesnake, or worse, a space monster. Some people say that space monsters have been landing out in the desert."

Noah and Marvin glanced at each other but didn't say anything. They had already met the space monsters. LaDonna was right. They weren't much fun.

"OK, here we go then," LaDonna said, pulling up her knees and wrapping her arms around them and clasping her hands in front. "A long time ago, there were some Spanish conquistadors that came to White Sands from Mexico City looking for treasure. They weren't looking for treasure in White Sands exactly, but this was one of the places they discovered while they were searching. The conquistadors were trying to find a place called the Seven Cities of Cibola, where all the houses were supposed to be made of gold and the window frames were lined with jewels."

"What's a conquistador?" Marvin interrupted.

"A Spanish soldier who lived a long time ago," LaDonna said. "They rode horses and wore heavy armor and had funny looking helmets. They actually brought the first horses to America. Some of the ones they were riding got away and had babies and that's where all our horses came from."

Marvin looked a bit skeptical but let her continue.

"The conquistadors reached the edge of White Sands in the year 1540, probably right around here someplace," LaDonna said, "but then they were attacked by a band of Apaches. One of the conquistadors was killed. His name was Hernando, and he had gotten married just before he left Mexico City. His friends all escaped the Indians, but they had to leave Hernando's body out there in the sand." LaDonna pointed dramatically to the west. Her voice softened as she told the next part of the story.

"Hernando's new wife was a beautiful young woman named Mañuela. She was the daughter of a Spanish prince, so she was also a princess. When the conquistadors returned to Mexico City and told her that Hernando had been killed, she could only think of one thing. She had to ride north and try and find his body and then give it a proper burial."

Listening to LaDonna quietly relate the tale of Mañuela, Noah suddenly realized that her soft, low-pitched voice was almost hypnotizing. He glanced over at Marvin. Marvin's mouth was open and his eyes and attention were focused like a beam of light on LaDonna's face.

"Poor Mañuela," she continued. Her mesmerizing voice was now barely a whisper. "No one would go with her—not her father, not the conquistadors, not even her best friends. She begged them desperately, but no one wanted to leave the safety of Mexico City." LaDonna dramatically placed her hand over her heart. "So on a dark night while everyone in the hacienda slept, Mañuela saddled her best horse and rode north like the wind. Day and night, she galloped until she finally reached El Paso."

Here LaDonna paused. As the sun crept toward the edge of the horizon, the surrounding white desert began to take on a surreal golden glow. Noah and Marvin sat spellbound, waiting for her to continue.

"That was the last time anyone saw her," she whispered. "Indian legends say that Mañuela reached the great white wilderness but couldn't find her husband's bones because the coyotes had carried them away. Supposedly she died out there, all alone and grieving for her lost Hernando, and now every night, her beautiful ghost haunts White Sands. She wears a long, white wedding dress and cries out the name of her lost husband as she wanders across the dunes. Apaches call her Pavla Blanca, the White Lady."

Noah shuddered as a cool breath of wind blew across the top of the dune. LaDonna was staring into the west, shading her eyes with her hand.

"Look," she whispered. "She's here."

Noah and Marvin looked. They saw nothing at first, but then, at the crest of another tall dune two hundred feet away, a misty white shape seemed to form and reform itself as it moved slowly across the backlit horizon. Noah felt the hairs on the back of his neck stand straight out.

LaDonna suddenly screamed and toppled over backward, causing Noah and Marvin to jump six inches straight up into the air. She threw herself off the crest of the dune and rolled down the steep slope, arms and legs flailing. Noah and Marvin followed, trying unsuccessfully to stay upright in the deep gypsum. At the bottom, they all lay breathless and panting. LaDonna was curled up like a ball, her shoulders shaking hard as though she were sobbing. Noah put his hand on her shoulder.

"Are you hurt?" he asked. "Do I need to get your dad?"

LaDonna uncurled herself and sat up. She was covered from head to foot, including her short hair, with white gypsum dust, and if she hadn't been shaking so hard with laughter, she would have looked like a ghost herself.

"I told you it was a good ghost story," she said, trying to catch her breath, "but I lied about it not being scary."

═══════════

"Dang, thet was skeery," Marvin said. He was seated on a blanket next to Noah in the back of the Studebaker, and he had to talk loudly to be heard above the noise created by the engine and the hot night wind rushing by. "Thet thing sure didn't look like no dust devil I ever seen."

"I don't want to go back and find out," shouted Noah. "I'll trust what LaDonna said about it being a dust devil. She's been there lots of times before."

"LaDonna's OK for a girl," Marvin said. "She knows about Deeter and don't laugh. Her ma and pa's nice, too. They buy all our milk ever' day."

"Does she live in Alamogordo?"

"Nope. Lives 'bout halfway between Tularosa an' Alamogordo. Place where they put the milk in bottles is in Alamogordo, though. We could ride down to the Hawthorne's fer a visit if you want. Ain't thet far."

"That would be fun," Noah said. "I like her, and besides, I don't know anyone else in Tularosa. What do *you* think that thing was at White Sands if it wasn't a dust devil?"

Marvin thought a minute before answering. "Mebbe it really *was* the ghost of thet White Lady," he said, "but it coulda been one of them space monsters like we seen out by Aguilar Spring."

"Yeah, but this one wasn't green," Noah said. "And I didn't see any ray gun."

"Mebbe he took off his green skin so's he could sneak up on us. Thet's probably what they look like when they're nekkid. Mebbe he was gonna git close an' blast us into goo. When you wanna ride down to LaDonna's place?"

"I can't go tomorrow because Bud's giving me a driving lesson," Noah said.

"Yer gonna learn to drive?" Marvin said. "You ain't got no license an' you ain't old enough to git one neither."

"I know, but he wants me to know how to drive anyway. He says it's part of learning to be a cowboy."

"Only thing a cowboy drives is a horse," Marvin said. "Mebbe a tractor when he's balin' hay."

"Well, a cowboy has to know how to drive a pickup so he can haul his horse to where the cows are."

"Not when he's jest fourteen," Marvin said. "Sheriff sees what yer doin' an' he'll haul you off to jail."

"I'm almost fifteen," Noah said. "I'll be fifteen on September 11. I can get a permit to drive when I'm fifteen, at least that's what Bud says. First, I have to learn *how* to drive so I can pass the test."

"Dang, thet's jest two months away," Marvin said. "Whaddya want fer a present?"

Noah thought for a second. "It sounds dumb, but what I really want is to not see any more ghosts or space men or Zefos or mean roosters," he said.

"Thet ain't no real present," Marvin said, "but if you find it somewheres, git me one, too."

NOAH'S MIDMORNING DRIVING lesson the next day took place on a lonely, deeply rutted gravel road inappropriately named Tule Road that turned off the main highway just north of the Tularosa town limits and ran west into the Chihuahuan Desert. It didn't really go anywhere, and no one knew why it had been constructed in the first place, but Tule Road had very little traffic, so it was a perfect place to train a new driver.

Bud parked the pickup in a wide dirt pullout alongside the road and killed the engine. He climbed out and ordered Noah to slide over behind the wheel, and then he climbed into the passenger's side.

"They ain't nothin' to drivin'," he said. "You jest gotta know how to work the gears and the clutch at the same time. An' the brakes a course. An' you gotta make sure yer mirrors is in the right place so's you kin see what's comin' in ever' direction."

Before Bud let Noah start the engine, he had him push in the clutch with his left foot and go through the gears, including reverse, half a dozen times. He showed him where the headlight switch was and the dimmer button on the floorboards, and he taught him how to use the emergency hand brake. Finally satisfied, he pulled a cold beer from beneath the seat, popped the cap, and took a long swig.

"OK, Bub, it's all yers," he said. "Git us from here to over yonder an' don't run over no dogs er old ladies in the meanwhile."

Noah drove west ten miles into the Chihuahuan Desert on Tule Road with no problems before Bud told him to stop and turn around. His uncle made him stop every half mile, turn off the engine, and then start and go again using the gears. Near the Tularosa town limits, Noah swerved to avoid a large rattlesnake—probably five feet in length—crawling slowly across the road. Bud didn't notice, and Noah didn't think it was worth the effort to point the snake out. Rattlers were a dime a dozen in this part of the world.

"Hokay, yer ready fer some town drivin'," Bud said when they reached the intersection with the main highway. "Turn right, an' if you see the sheriff, make like you ain't nobody 'cause you ain't got no permit yet."

Noah turned right onto the highway and drove at the speed limit into Tularosa, keeping one eye peeled for Deputy Mendoza's cruiser. Bud had him park parallel along the curb in front of the feed store, then park again in the parking lots at Woolworth's and the Tastee-Freez. When he had driven up and down every back street in town several times, Bud finally told him to pull over and they changed places.

"You got this drivin' stuff down purty good, Bub. Let's go git some vittles."

When they reached the ranch, Noah saw an official-looking, olive-green sedan with a large white star on the door parked next to his mother's Ford in the yard. It looked much like the same sedan he had seen parked along the road near the ranch on the day of his arrival from Oregon.

"Guess we got us some company, Bub," Bud parked the pickup next to the sedan. "You know anybody in the army?"

Noah said he didn't. "Maybe they're here because of those space monsters we saw out in the desert."

"You didn't see no dang space monsters," Bud said. "What you seen was jest what the deputy said you saw, which was some army people lookin' at a rocket."

In the living room, Mrs. Odell was serving coffee to two uniformed military officers who were seated at the big wooden table. One of them was a woman. They had both removed their hats and placed them on a chair. A long roll of paper was lying on the table. Both officers stood when Bud and Noah entered the room.

"Clarence, these nice folks are from the army," said Mrs. Odell. "They've been waiting to talk to you."

"Good morning, Mr. Boggs," the woman said, sticking out her hand. "I'm Major Paenin-Diaz, and this is Lieutenant Apodoca from the Judge Advocate General's Office at White Sands Proving Ground. We're lawyers."

Bud took the offered hand. "Howdy, Major. Howdy, Lieutenant," he said. "This here's my nephew, Noah, and you done met my sister. I got me a funny feelin' you two ain't here 'bout thet rocket these boys saw out by Aguilar Spring," Bud added.

The two officers gave each other a blank look. "No, sir," Major Paenin-Diaz said. "We haven't heard anything about anyone finding a rocket. We're here on another matter." She gestured to Lieutenant Apodoca, who removed a rubber band from the long roll of paper and flattened what seemed to be a large black-and-white photograph out on the table. He placed a salt shaker on one corner and a pepper shaker on another.

"Mr. Boggs," Major Paenin-Diaz continued, "you might have heard about the rockets that are being tested at White Sands. Most of them land exactly where they're supposed to, but occasionally one goes off course and lands outside of the Proving Ground." She glanced at Noah. "From what you just said, I can assume your nephew must have found one."

Major Paenin-Diaz walked to the table and studied the spread-out photo for a moment. "This is an enlarged high-altitude photographic map of the area around Tularosa, and this is your ranch, right here," she said, thumping a spot on the map with her index finger. "As you can see, it's several miles farther west than any of the other farm or ranch properties in this particular area."

Bud, Noah, and Mrs. Odell walked to the table and gathered round where they could see. "Didn't know thet," Bud said, "but then I ain't got no map like this'un to look at neither. What's yer point?"

"The point is this, Mr. Boggs. Because of the rocket testing, and because the army doesn't want anyone to get hurt, White Sands Proving Ground is expanding its present range. The army now owns or leases all of the public and private land due west of the western boundary of your ranch, clear to the San Andres Mountains, here." She pointed to another spot on the map.

Bud pointed to the wide, black shape on the map that was obviously the malpais. "You mean you own all thet land out by the lava beds and Aguilar Spring?"

"All of it except for your six hundred acres," the major said. "By executive proclamation signed by the president of the United States, we leased that entire section of land from the Bureau of Land Management last week."

"We was jest drivin' on Tule Road this mornin'," Bud said. "Army own thet too?"

"Tule Road," said the major, "will be gated and closed to all traffic within the month."

"You sayin' what I think yer sayin'?" Bud asked.

"I'm saying that the army would like to buy your cattle ranch, Mr. Boggs. They are prepared to offer you a generous sum and will move your household items and livestock to the location of your choice at their expense."

Noah looked at his uncle. Bud's face was expressionless as he removed his old fedora and scratched the back of his head. "Thet's mighty kind of 'em," he said. "But there's jest one problem. I ain't plannin' on sellin' the wrench." He gestured at Noah and Mrs. Odell. "We all kinda like it out here."

Major Paenin-Diaz was quiet for a few moments. "I'm sorry to hear that, Mr. Boggs," she finally said. "Is there anything I can do to persuade you to change your mind? The price the army is offering is ten thousand dollars. Could I at least ask you to think about it a few days?"

"Ten thousand's a load a money fer an old place like this," Bud said, "but right now I jest don't have no use fer more money than I already got. Don't need no time to think about things neither. Tell them folks who's doin' the offerin' 'thanks but no thanks.'"

"Mr. Boggs, do you know what the process of eminent domain is?" When Bud said nothing, Major Paenin-Diaz continued. "Eminent domain means that the state of New Mexico, if it has a good reason, can take a person's land without that person's consent. They still have to pay for it, of course, but in matters of national interest, the rules we all try to live by sometimes go out the window. White Sands Proving Ground is state land leased by the U.S. Army. The army has deemed your ranch necessary for the good of America's security. If you refuse to sell it, they will simply ask the state to condemn the property. If a state judge signs the condemnation request—and I promise you he will—you and your family will be evicted, plain and simple."

"Thet sure wouldn't be very neighborly, Major," Bud said calmly. "What's so dang important thet the army wants a little wrench like this'un? Ain't nothin' here but some kettle an' chickens an' a mule. An' us, a course."

"To be honest with you, Mr. Boggs, White Sands does not really want your ranch," Lieutenant Apodoca said. It was the first time he had spoken. "But it doesn't want one of its rockets falling on a citizen's house and killing somebody either. If there is no one living in the houses out here, then there is little chance of that happening."

Bud looked at the officers, shook his head, and then pointed at the door. "I know this ain't yer doin' but I'd jest as soon you all'd git 'cause right now yer 'bout as welcome as two whores at a church picnic. An' tell whichever donkey's dingdong decided this here kettle wrench was good fer anythin' but raisin' kettle thet he's dumber'n a stack a toes."

Without another word, the two army officers put on their hats and rolled up their map and left. When Bud heard their car start, he sat down at the table and stared out the window at the dust cloud caused by the retreating army sedan. Neither Noah nor his mother knew what to say, so they said nothing. Mrs. Odell went into the kitchen and returned with a frosty bottle of Lucky Lager. Noah blinked his eyes hard a couple of times. He couldn't believe that his mother had just brought Bud a beer.

"Now ain't thet jest the monkey's whiskers," Bud finally said. "I heard somethin' 'bout the army kickin' folks off their wrenches, but thet was way up north." He shook his head, took a swig of the Lucky Lager, and wiped his mouth with the back of his hand. If he noticed that his teetotalist sister had just served him a beer for the first time in recorded history, he didn't mention it. "Well, they sure as hell ain't gonna git this here kettle wrench, least not while I kin still holler fer Hannah."

"Who's Hannah?" Noah asked.

"Ain't got no idea," Bud said, giving Noah a wink. "Jest somethin' people say when they cain't think a nothin' else to say."

"Maybe they won't come back," Mrs. Odell said. "The major didn't really seem like a bad person. Maybe she'll just tell the army that you don't want to sell the ranch and that will be the end of it."

"Neither of 'em is bad people, probably," Bud said, "but it ain't them two I'm worried about, anyways." Bud tipped the Lucky Lager bottle up and took another long, deep swig. "Here's what we're gonna do," he said. There was a long pause as Bud collected his thoughts. "We ain't gonna do nothin' 'cause there ain't nothin' we *can* do 'cept worry ourselves down a hole, an' we ain't gonna do thet, neither." He looked at Noah. "Mebbe yer ma's right, Bub. Mebbe the dang army'll jest leave us be an' go bother some other poor fools."

"I don't think they're going to go away," Noah said. "Everything sounded too . . . official."

"I don't neither," said Bud, "but we'll skin thet cat when it comes meowin' round the back door."

11

The Miracle at the Ranger

Anna Sazi was in her kitchen. Anna's kitchen consisted principally of a fire pit surrounded by rocks in the mud floor of a shallow cave on the side of a low, rocky, cactus-covered hill in the middle of the Chihuahuan Desert. It was slightly more than one moon past the solstice in the year AD 1000, and it was goddammed hot outside, but Anna had a fire going in the fire pit anyway. With any luck, dinner would be arriving soon, and she wanted to be prepared. She stirred the coals with an old stubblybuk leg bone and threw on a few more twigs, all the while listening to the grunting of little Suzi Sazi and her older brother, Tommy Sazi, who were playing in the shade just outside the entrance to the cave.

Anna saw a dark shadow cross the cavern's mouth, and a few seconds later her mate, Sammy Sazi, came in. His hair was white with grime, and there were dozens of cactus spines sticking out of the thick calluses on his feet. He threw several serpent-tailed kangaroo rats and a couple of false-tailed whippers onto the mud floor in disgust, along with his stone hatchet, obsidian knife, atlatl, and several short spears tipped with flint points. "Don't even start," he grunted. "I've had a rough day."

"I hope you brought us something more nutritious than a few rats and lizards for dinner," Anna said caustically, with a look of scorn marring her dirty, smoke-blackened face.

"What you see is what you get," Sammy said sharply. "I did the best I could. This damn hot weather makes everything stick pretty close to their dens."

"What kind of a jerk hunter-gatherer are you, anyway? You have a mate and two hungry offspring to feed, and all you ever bring home are rats and lizards and maybe a stupid jackalope once in a while. Why don't you catch a stubblybuk or a grizzly bear or a giant sloth—something with a little meat on it? What do you do all day, sleep under a mesquite tree?"

Sammy Sazi grunted again and gave his mate an equally nasty look. "Giant sloths died out five thousand years ago, and I'm a little tired of listening to you complain all the time," he said. Sammy limped to the cave entrance, wincing as the cactus spines in his feet were pushed through his callouses and into the meat, and gestured at the barren landscape outside. "Take a look out there! We don't exactly live in the Garden of Eden. What do you want, for crying out loud—apple trees? Wine from water? Loaves and fishes?" He scratched a flea bite under the thick black mat of hair in one armpit. "You have a roof over your head and rabbit skins to wear and lizard soup in your belly, and you even had a bath three, no four, years ago. There are lots of Sazis out there in a helluva lot worse shape than we are."

Anna Sazi wasn't intimidated by her mate's bluster. "What do I want, you ask?" She was almost shouting. "I'll tell you what I want! I want you to get out of this idiotic hunter-gatherer business and become a farmer! Farming is all the rage up at Chaco Canyon, at least that's what everybody says, and if it's good enough for them, it should be good enough for us!" Two big tears—tears about the size of a dung beetle's ball of manure—rolled down her smoke-blackened cheeks, leaving squiggly pink trails all the way to her chin. "You could grow corn and beans and squash, and I could make beautiful pottery, and we could build our own kiva together and—"

"You can't go into a kiva," Sammy Sazi interrupted. "You can't get anywhere near a kiva. Women aren't allowed in ceremonial structures, and you know it."

"You're missing the point, you . . . you Neanderthal!" Anna Sazi shouted, growing angrier by the minute. "I just want to get out of this cave and live in one of those swanky one-room apartments in a three-story pueblo where we can have lots of friends and where our kids can learn some communication skills instead of just grunting when they want something!"

"Yeah, and what about the pollution problems those Pueblo people have to put up with?" Sammy Sazi demanded. "I've been told you can cut the wood smoke in one of those apartments with a flint knife. And how about the sanitary conditions? When they have to go to the bathroom, they don't even have bushes they can get behind for privacy because they've all been cut down for firewood. From what I hear, the people in Chaco Canyon don't bother to go potty outside, anyway. They just use the hallway or the living room floor whenever the urge takes them. Can't you just imagine the smell?"

The lobby of the Ranger theater on the main street in downtown Tularosa, New Mexico, had a smell that was hard to imagine, too. It was the stench of rancid popcorn and stale cooking grease and the stink of unwashed bodies and moldy walls and the reek of old vomit and dribbled urine, all united in a permanent odiferous aura that no amount of painting the walls or scrubbing the floors could ever remove.

No one really cared what the Ranger smelled like, though. Local residents went to the old theater to see movies, and after ten years of being shown in every indoor theater and outdoor drive-in in America, *Miracle on 34th Street*, starring Maureen O'Hara and John Payne, had finally arrived in Tularosa. It hadn't gotten lost in the mail or anything like that. The Ranger simply wasn't known for its first-run movies. The Ranger had never *shown* a first-run movie, in fact, or a second-run movie either, for that matter. The Ranger often didn't have movies at all. When the old Dodge flatbed that picked up the oversized film cans at the train station in El Paso and hauled them to the theater was not in working condition or had a flat tire, or the driver was too drunk or too sick or too pissed off to make the weekly run, the Ranger was out of luck. It had been out of luck this time for three long weeks because of a broken axle on the delivery truck. Management had posted a SORRY, NO MOVIES sign in the ticket booth window and padlocked the building's doors.

It was late July in Tularosa, not Christmastime. It was sizzling hot even in the shade of the towering cottonwood trees, not snowy and cold. Nonetheless, *Miracle on 34th Street*'s imminent showing on Saturday night and then every night of the week for two weeks after that was the talk of the town. To be honest, its popularity wasn't entirely because everyone had an overwhelming desire to watch a ten-year-old film about Christmas or Santa Claus or snow in New York City. Some Tularosa residents were waiting for Saturday night and the following thirteen nights with anticipation because, for the first time in three weeks, they could escape the heat of the street outside and spend ninety-six chilly minutes, plus previews of coming attractions and a brace of Daffy Duck cartoons, relaxing in air-conditioned comfort. The Ranger was the only air-conditioned public building in town. It was the place many Tularosa residents, especially those without their own air-conditioning, wanted to be on a hot night in late July. And when there was a movie showing that was less than twenty years old and hadn't been shown half a dozen times already, it was only icing on the cake.

Late July in southern New Mexico, of course, is actually much cooler than late June. July is when the massive cumulonimbus rain clouds, known more commonly as thunderheads, begin to gather in the afternoon skies over the Chihuahuan Desert. Bellies distended with millions of gallons of water from the Pacific Ocean, they mass together in flotilla form like square-rigged ships on a stormy sea, white sails billowing in the wind. As afternoon glides toward evening and turbulence in the upper atmosphere increases, the thunderheads begin to collide. Golden slivers of lightning flash toward the earth in response, and then, finally, it rains. This particular rain is not a drizzle, nor a downpour. It is a malicious, threatening black curtain of vertical force that may deposit a million gallons of moisture in five minutes on a single square mile of land.

Except that if you happen to live in the arid microclimate around Tularosa, New Mexico, you'll find it almost never rains, not even in late July. The curtain usually falls elsewhere. The vertical force lands on something else. The million gallons of moisture end up watering flowers in Socorro or filling up the Ruidoso River or turning the streets in Las Cruces into muddy canals. If Tularosa gets any rain at all, it can be measured in drops. A drop here and a drop there. Still, the weather gets cooler, at least by a few degrees, because of all the rain that has fallen elsewhere.

Noah didn't give a rat's bandana if he never saw another rain drop in his entire life, but when he and Marvin heard about the movie on Saturday, they knew they had to go see it. Air-conditioning was air-conditioning and a thing to be relished since neither of their houses had it. It was likely that Zefo and his gang would be at the Ranger as well, and that presented a problem, of course. They needed a plan that would allow them to enter and leave the theater without being spotted and subsequently ripped apart. Noah supposed a good place to start would be by asking his uncle if he had any ideas. He got his chance right after breakfast one morning when Bud said he had something to show him outside.

"You ever seen an Okie hep-yerself, Bub?" They were standing next to the Studebaker, and Bud had a length of old rubber garden hose in one hand and a galvanized metal bucket in the other. He kept looking over his shoulder at the house where Mrs. Odell was washing the breakfast dishes.

"Didn't think so," he said when Noah shook his head. "Yer ma ain't gonna tell ya 'bout things like thet."

Bud took a large jackknife out of the pocket of his overalls and opened the longest blade. "Okie hep-yerself's jest fer emergencies," he said, "when you ain't got no money an' yer outta gas. Jest don't let nobody see you usin' one, an' don't tell yer ma thet I told ya 'bout one neither."

He cut a five-foot-long section off the main piece of hose with his knife, took one last look over his shoulder, and then undid the gas cap on the Studebaker. "This here's how it works," he said. "Poke one end a the hose down the gas hole till it's in the tank. Then git yer bucket handy an' suck on the other end till the gas starts flowin'. Thet's all there is to it. When ya got a bucket full, pour it in yer car an' git gone."

Bud put the hose into the gasoline pipe of the truck, placed the bucket at his feet, and got down on his knees. He put the other end of the hose in his mouth and sucked as hard as he could. Seconds later, a spurt of gasoline filled the hose and his mouth at the same time.

Spitting and spluttering, he wiped his mouth on his shirt-sleeve then pulled the hose out of the gas pipe and handed it to Noah.

"Be keerful when gas comes outta the tank er you'll git a mouthful, an' the dang stuff don't taste like biscuits 'n' gravy. Give 'er a shot, an' don't smoke no cigarettes while yer doin' this neither 'cause you'll blow yerself to Kingdom Come."

Noah placed the bucket at his feet and then pushed one end of the hose down the gas pipe until he thought it was in the tank. Following his uncle's example, he kneeled in the dirt as low as he could get and took a deep pull on the end. Sure enough, a few seconds later he heard gasoline gurgling up the hose, and he quickly removed it from his mouth. Gas flowed freely into the bucket like it was coming out of a faucet.

"Yer purty dang handy with thet hose," Bud said with a grin. "You sure you ain't done this somewheres before?"

As they walked back to the house, Noah wondered where and when he would ever have need of an Okie hep-yerself. His uncle hadn't said it in so many words, but stealing gasoline from someone's car was obviously illegal and probably worth a month or two in jail. However, his mind really wasn't on gasoline theft. Noah explained the problem about Saturday night to his uncle. He already knew that neither Bud nor his mother wanted to see *Miracle on 34th Street*, and Mr. and Mrs. Couch didn't go to the movies because they couldn't leave Deeter by himself. Bud had volunteered to drive the boys to the theater and fetch them after the movie was over, but getting there and getting home was not really the dilemma.

His uncle scratched his chin. As usual, he was three or four days behind on shaving. "Way I see it there's jest *one* thing you boys kin do, Bub," he said. "Borrow some of yer ma's clothes an' fix yerselves up so's nobody knows it's you. Simple as thet." He thumped Noah's forehead with a finger. "Gotta use them brains, Bub. Nobody'd ever believe thet two big, strong boys like you two'd ever stoop to wearin' girl's clothes."

Marvin didn't like Bud's idea at all. To say he was adamantly opposed to dressing like a girl and going out in public, in fact, would be a grossly understated understatement.

"I ain't goin' nowheres dressed like no girl!" he spluttered when

Noah told him what his uncle had suggested. "No cowboy'd ever dress up like no girl an' I ain't gonna do it neither!"

"You got any better ideas?" Noah asked when Marvin finally stopped spouting about how he'd have to be dead and rotting before he would ever consider wearing a dress.

"How 'bout we jest wait till the movie gits goin', an' *then* go buy a ticket," Marvin said. "If it's dark when we go in, nobody kin see us."

"Yeah, but what if Zefo has somebody standing guard at the door?" Noah asked. "And we'd probably miss the cartoons and maybe not even get a seat at all."

In the end, Marvin caved because neither of them could come up with a better solution. Mrs. Odell had not been overjoyed with the whole idea either, but when Noah promised they would leave immediately if they saw Zefo in the theater, she reluctantly gave him permission to go. The following day, while delivering the morning's milk collection to Hawthorne's Dairy, Heze Couch told Mr. Hawthorne what the boys were planning, and Mr. Hawthorne passed the gossip on to his wife and daughter that evening at supper.

"For God's sake, give me the young man who has brains enough to make a fool of himself," LaDonna said dramatically, placing the back of her hand on her forehead as she quoted Robert Louis Stevenson. "Those two dressed up as girls is something I have to see, and I'm sure they won't invite me along so I'll have to invite myself."

She announced the news that she planned to accompany Noah and Marvin to the movies to Marvin's father the next morning when he delivered the milk, and asked if he would advise the boys.

"They aren't gonna like it," Mr. Couch said, but he grinned and said he would ask Noah's uncle to pick her up when Bud took the boys to the movie.

On Saturday evening at twenty minutes before seven o'clock, Bud turned his Studebaker into the Hawthornes' driveway and stopped in front of the house. LaDonna was waiting on the porch dressed neatly in jeans, T-shirt, and penny loafers. She tried to keep a straight face as she climbed into the back with Noah and Marvin. Noah had borrowed one of his mother's old paisley dresses and wore it with a lightweight cotton sweater and tennis shoes. A large green scarf tied beneath his chin covered his shock of brown hair. Marvin was wearing yellow pedal pushers and a pink satin blouse also borrowed from Mrs. Odell. He, too, covered his hair with a scarf and wore tennis shoes. Noah's mother had applied just enough bright red lipstick to the lips of both boys to make them look feminine.

LaDonna stared at the two for a long moment, doing her best to stifle an overwhelming desire to scream with laughter. "You both look absolutely marvelous," she finally said, able to suppress the scream and condense it into a giggle, only with the greatest of efforts. "I just adore that shade of lipstick, and I do hope I can have the name of your hairdresser."

"Don't rub it in," Noah said. "We just couldn't think of anything else."

"Yeah, an' if you ain't got nothin' nice to say, jest don't say nothin' at all," Marvin added. "Least we ain't gonna git ourselves kilt."

Ten minutes later, Bud dropped the three of them off a block from the Ranger. "You two're cuter'n a couple a hens wearin' curlers," he said to Noah and Marvin, grinning widely and winking with his knife-scarred eye. He told the trio that he would pick them up at nine o'clock sharp.

The inside of the Ranger was a palace of entertainment, where shoes stuck like glue to a floor tacky with a thousand spilled cherry Cokes. Unfortunate patrons who arrived late and had to sit in the ground floor orchestra section were often besprinkled with everything from stale popcorn to water balloons by those who sat in the balcony fifteen feet above. Nonetheless, it was cool inside the old theater, and the place was packed. Noah and Marvin received a few odd looks in the lobby, but they kept their heads down and, with LaDonna leading the way, found three seats together in the front row on the left. There was no sign of Zefo. When the lights finally went down and the Movietone News started, they knew they had it made.

The particular copy of *Miracle on 34th Street* shipped to the Ranger had been shown perhaps five hundred times in its ten-year life span. It was old and battered and brittle, and just as Fred Gailey was about to prove that Santa Claus did indeed exist and that he was actually in that very courtroom, the cellulose acetate filmstrip broke without warning. The lights came up, and the booing and catcalling started. When a minute went by and still no movie, the crescendo inside the theater reached epic proportions. Coke cups and empty popcorn boxes flew off the balcony into the crowd below, and people in the orchestra shouted insults and curses at those above. It was just then that a tall, dark shape wearing tight pegged jeans, clambered onto the ten-inch-wide balcony rail, unzipped his fly, and in a random but all-encompassing pattern, showered the crowd below with recycled Budweiser beer. It ran down the neck of a Presbyterian minister and stained the shirt of the high school principal. It prostrated a dozen boxes of popcorn, conquered a clutch of Cokes, and saturated a hundred square feet of teased, sculpted, and sprayed-on hairdos. Panic ensued below, and when the forty-second cloudburst finally ceased and anyone dared look up, there was Zefo Montoya, grinning from ear to ear.

"I showed you a miracle, *pendejos!*" he shouted, shaking the last few drops of spring-water wisdom into the catastrophe below. "I made it rain!"

Then Zefo created his second miracle of the evening by simply vanishing. One second he was there, and the next second—presto!— he was gone. Unfortunately, while he'd been hosing down the crowd below, he had also hosed down the rail upon which he was balanced precariously. As he started to turn around and climb down, his leather-soled loafer hit the slick spot on the rail and over he went, backward, into the semidarkness below.

By the time someone in authority got there, Zefo was not a happy camper. His twenty-foot fall had been partially broken by the four people he slammed into at the bottom, but he was still in bad shape. Doctors at Gerald Champion Memorial Hospital in Alamogordo later described his injuries as "severe." In addition to the three broken ribs he already had, he was diagnosed with having a broken collar bone, two broken arms, a compound fracture of the left tibia, a serious concussion, and various bumps, bruises, and contusions. Evidence gathered at the scene by Deputy Mendoza indicated that Zefo had drunk at least two growlers of beer by himself in the alley adjacent to the theater immediately before show time. Where he got the alcohol—since he was only sixteen and couldn't buy it himself—was anybody's guess. Further evidence gathered at the hospital in the form of smashed fingertips and size twelve boot prints on his face, indicated that probably not all of his injuries were caused by the fall.

A WEEK LATER, Noah came out of the barn after finishing his morning chores just in time to see a black-and-white Otero County sheriff's car come slowly down their dusty driveway and stop in the yard. Deputy Mendoza got out and waved Noah over.

"Your uncle around?" he asked. "I need to talk to him, and you, too."

They found Bud in the kitchen drinking coffee. Bud shook hands and introduced the deputy to Mrs. Odell, who asked him to sit. She poured another cup of hot coffee and set a platter of fresh, hot biscuits on the table.

"This is about Zefo Montoya," Deputy Mendoza said, munching a biscuit and sipping coffee. "I thought you might like to know that he won't be around for a while." He tried to suppress a smile. "When Zefo gets out of the hospital, which'll be three, four weeks at a minimum, he'll spend the next two years in the New Mexico Boys' School up in Springer. He was already on parole from the Boys' School on a charge of beating up a teacher, so now he'll stay there until he turns eighteen."

Noah had been right after all. Somewhere out there, floating around in the clouds, keeping His eye on things was an honest-to-goodness God.

"So no more Zefo Montoya?" Mrs. Odell asked.

"No more Zefo," the deputy said.

"What about those other boys?" Mrs. Odell said. "The hoodlums that hung out with Zefo. Are they still here?"

"They're still here," the deputy said. "But they don't have the courage to bother anybody without Zefo egging them on. He was the *jefe* who kept them from messing their diapers. Anybody looks at them crooked now that Zefo's gone, the whole bunch'll probably turn tail and run."

Deputy Mendoza took another swig of his coffee and looked at Noah.

"You're a lucky kid," he said. "You and the Couch boy, both. You're lucky that Zefo and his crowd didn't do more damage than they did."

He stopped and looked at his empty coffee cup. Mrs. Odell fetched the pot from the stove and poured another round.

"It's a fact that Spanish boys and Anglo boys in Tularosa don't always get along that well," the deputy continued. "There's always been a lot of fistfights and bloody noses and name-calling, and nobody really knows why but it probably has something to do with the color of your skin and what language you speak and how you dress and who can guess what else. Spanish kids call Anglo kids 'gringos' or '*chorras*'—not very nice terms—and Anglo kids call Spanish kids 'spicks' and 'greasers,' and those aren't very nice either."

"We certainly don't call other people bad names in this house," Mrs. Odell interjected. "At least not if I have anything to say about it." She gave Noah a hard glance. "Young man, have you called anyone . . . what Deputy Mendoza said?"

"No ma'am," Noah answered truthfully. "Neither has Marvin. I've never even heard those words before, at least not that I can remember. Besides, I don't even want to *think* about Zefo, let alone call him something bad."

"I'm sure you haven't called anyone anything," the deputy said, "and it's too bad things have to be that way, but that's the way they are and have been for longer than any of us has been around. There's one thing you should understand, though. Not all Spanish boys are like Zefo. Most Spanish boys are just like most Anglo boys—good, decent kids who do their best to get along with everybody. But there's always a rotten chile pepper in every sack, and that's exactly what Zefo was . . . rotten clean through and stinking to high heaven. Now he's gone and won't be back, and I think even his mother's glad he's not around anymore. She didn't say that in so many words, but I can tell she's relieved."

"I knew someone in Oregon like him," Noah said. "His name was Skeeter. He was a bully like Zefo."

"Sooner or later, all bullies take a big fall," Deputy Mendoza said. "In Zefo's case, it really was a fall. This Skeeter probably will too sometime."

Noah didn't mention that Skeeter had already fallen. He remembered the satisfying *thunk* of the river boulder connecting solidly with Skeeter's backbone, and the sweet ecstasy as he listened to the bully's moans as he lay writhing in the dirt.

"So now you've got to tell me something," the deputy said. "What was it you hit Zefo with that broke three ribs and put him in crutches?"

Noah was silent for a moment while he weighed his options. Should he stick with Marvin's version of the story—in which his right fist was chaos come a calling—or should he come clean and tell the truth? If he chose the former, would Bud and his mother keep quiet, or would they spill the beans making Noah out to be a liar? He decided it was probably safest to be truthful, and as briefly as possible without being rude, Noah related how Zefo had gotten his clock cleaned by Brimstone. When he was finished, Deputy Mendoza broke out in guffaws.

"Well, that sure tells me why Zefo wouldn't talk about what hit him," he said. "Admitting you got whipped by a jackass would be pretty embarrassing. Remind me never to get near that mule's rear end."

"Don't tell Marvin Couch," Noah said. "He thinks I'm the one that clobbered Zefo, and I don't want to disappoint him."

WHEN DEPUTY MENDOZA finished his coffee and left, Bud informed Noah that they had one more chore to take care of that morning.

"Gonna have a kettle drive," he said. "We gotta move them kettle over to another pasture, so's they kin git fattened up 'fore we sell 'em. High time you earned yer keep as a cowboy."

"Why are we selling them?" Noah asked. "Are they sick?"

"Course they ain't sick," Bud said. "Thet's what you do with kettle. You buy 'em young an' skinny, fatten 'em up, then sell 'em fer a profit. Then you buy some more an' do the same thing all over again."

"How far of a cattle drive?" Noah asked.

"Ain't far, 'bout three miles er so," Bud answered. "They's a farmer fella I know got a hay field over toward town thet's jest been cut. Still lots a hay in it, though, an' they's a water tank in it too. We gotta git 'em there, is all."

Bud told Noah to go fetch Marvin who had been volunteered by his father to help. Noah quickly saddled Brimstone and made the short ride to the Couch dairy. When he returned with Marvin and Jake in tow, Bud led both boys to the corral in which the small herd of Brahmas was milling about.

"This is the way cowboys done it in the olden days," Bud told them, "so clean the wax outta yer ear holes and listen. On a kettle drive, the fella thet leads the kettle to wherever they're goin' is the point rider. Thet's me." He patted his chest and pointed to the Studebaker. "Gonna put a little hay in the back, an' they'll follow me clean to the Devil's den."

Bud walked to the barn with the boys following, picked up a bale of hay, and carried it to the pickup. Noah opened the tailgate and Bud dropped the bale into the bed with a grunt.

"The fellas thet make the kettle move along is called drag riders, an' thet's you two," he continued. "Kinda dirty but nothin' you two cain't handle. The fellas thet ride alongside an' keep 'em from strayin' is called flankers. Thet's you boys, too, 'cause we ain't got nobody else."

He handed Noah and Marvin each a short piece of stiff rope with a knot tied in each end. "This here's yer kettle whip; if they git stubborn, whack 'em on the rear end. An' don't be afraid to yell at 'em neither. Kettle is jest plain stupid and yellin' don't hurt 'em one little bit."

"How come you know so much 'bout cowboy'n?" Marvin asked Bud. "You ever been one?"

"Dern tootin', I was," Bud said. "Ever hear a the Bell Wrench? Biggest kettle wrench in the state. Worked there fer three years when I was younger, an' it was dang hard work, too. Ain't somethin' I wanna do twice."

"Why was it hard?" Noah asked. He hadn't known Bud had worked on a ranch. He hadn't known Bud had ever worked *anywhere*.

"'Cause you rode yer horse all day fixin' fence posts, then you come home an' chopped wood an' branded cows an' shoveled horse apples, an' then ate beans fer supper, an' they didn't have no chile neither. Thet was all on Monday. On Tuesday, you did the same dang thing all over again. Got one day off a month. Jest ain't somethin' I wanna do twice," he repeated.

When Bud was satisfied that the two boys could handle their jobs, he backed the truck up until it was a few feet from the corral gate and told Noah and Marvin to mount up. He opened the gate, ran back to the truck, and started slowly toward the driveway. The steers just stood there, looking confused. Bud stopped the truck and motioned Marvin and Noah to come over.

"Looks like yer gonna have to give 'em a jump start," he said. "Ride in there behind 'em and push 'em outta the dang corral."

They did as they were told. At first, the steers just went round and round the corral with the two boys chasing behind them shouting as loud as they could. Finally, one of the bolder Brahmas discovered the yawning gate and out they went in a contagious mini-stampede, pushing, bawling, and climbing over each other as they all tried to get through the opening at once. They didn't follow the pickup as it drove slowly up the driveway, bed full of hay or not. Instead, twelve young Brahma steers went in twelve different directions at a dead run as if they were being chased by banshees. One charged into the backyard and right through a low-slung clothesline heavy with freshly laundered sheets and towels. Another plowed through the open barn doors, and Noah could hear it bouncing off walls and hay bales as it tried to find its way out. Bud saw what was happening and stopped the pickup again, only to have two steers almost run him down as they dashed up the driveway. Kettle chaos reigned, and only when Bud broke open the hay bale and threw several flakes onto the ground did they stop trying to escape from whatever invisible entity—probably a rattlesnake, since those creatures seemed to compete for crawling space in southern New Mexico—had set them off. Within a few minutes, all of the steers—including the two escapees that had run up the driveway—had recovered from their impulsive folly and were calmly munching away as if nothing had happened.

Noah's mother was not happy. The cotton clothesline had snapped without pulling out the posts, but her freshly washed towels and sheets were covered with dirt and scattered around the yard like so many old, brown rags. Noah and Bud helped her collect the filthy linens and pile them in a basket while Marvin kept an eye on the herd.

"Clarence, if you can't control those cows, they shouldn't be out of their pen," she scolded when they finished. "They might trample somebody!"

"Sorry 'bout that, Sis," Bud said. "Cain't figger out what made 'em git crazy like thet all of a sudden." He winked at Noah. "They ain't cows, anyways. Cows is the ones with ti . . . thet give milk. Bub'll be glad to help wash them clothes again after we git where were goin', wontcha, Bub?"

When the hay on the ground had been eaten, the boys remounted, and Bud once again started slowly up the driveway in the Studebaker. This time, the herd followed along without complaint. Serenaded by a chorus of whistles and yelps from Noah and Marvin, and an occasional whap on the butt with a knotted whip, the smelly herd of bawling Brahmas moved down the road toward their new home.

The three-mile trip took just under two hours. It was accomplished without further incident, even though the steers had to cross the paved highway that ran north out of Tularosa. When they reached the highway junction, Bud slowed until he was sure that no cars were coming from either direction and then yelled out the window for the boys to hurry the herd up. Once across the pavement, the dirt road down which they were traveling was fenced on both sides, making Noah and Marvin's job much easier.

A mile from the highway, the farmer who owned the hay pasture was sitting on an old John Deere tractor in the shade of his ten-gallon hat, waiting patiently for the herd to arrive. The barbed-wire gate to a large field of freshly cut alfalfa stubble was already open on the left side of the road, and as the pickup drew abreast of the tractor, the farmer motioned for Bud to block the road just past the opening. Bud stopped thirty feet past the gate and parked the Studebaker crossways. Once the steers had passed, the farmer started the tractor up and also parked it crossways, blocking the ranch road behind it. The Brahmas had stopped when the pickup stopped and now stood bawling and swatting flies with their tails. They were ten feet from the open gate, but even with Noah and Marvin yipping and yelping at the top of their voices, they refused to go through it and into the field beyond.

The farmer held up his hand for quiet. "Don't spook 'em boys," he yelled at Noah and Marvin. "Let's just all haze 'em toward the gate real slow, and they'll get the idea sooner or later."

On the farmer's signal, they began to close the circle. They waved their arms up and down but didn't shout, trying to coax the herd into the pasture without making them bolt again. The steers bolted anyway, suddenly, and for no apparent reason. One moment they were standing still, eyeballing the four people slowly moving toward them, and the next moment they were charging outward in all directions, exactly as they had done earlier at Boggs Ranch. The farmer was knocked to the ground, but he got up quickly before he could be trampled, and ran for the safety of the pickup. Bud also escaped the crush by jumping into the Studebaker, but Noah and Marvin were still mounted and had no place to go. They hung on for dear life as the Brahmas dashed back and forth between the tractor and pickup in mindless pandemonium, slamming into each other and Jake and Brimstone as well. Finally, one of the steers charged through the open gate and into the field, and like migrating gnus, the others followed closely in a rush. Even before the dust clouds caused by the commotion had settled back to earth, the herd was happily munching away in the alfalfa stubble, heads down and tails swatting flies.

Shaking his head in disgust, the farmer jumped down out of the pickup and quickly closed the gate to the pasture. He collected his trampled hat from the dirt and punched it back into shape.

"Cows are the dumbest dang animals that ever walked on this earth," he said, using his hat to slap some of the dust from his jeans. "Whatever you think a cow knows, he don't. Whatever you think a cow oughta do, he ain't gonna do it." He looked at Noah and Marvin. "You boys ever get a hankering to be full-time cowboys, you come see me first, and I'll do my level best to talk some sense into you."

12

Two Wraps and a Hooey

If there was one event during the summer that both young people and adults from every farm and ranch family in Otero County looked forward to more than any other, it was the annual Three Rivers Junior Championship Rodeo, held on the first Saturday in August. Sponsored by the Otero County Sheriff's Posse, free for everyone, and usually attended by several thousand contestants and onlookers, it took place in the dusty Three Rivers rodeo arena, ten miles north of Tularosa.

No one knew exactly why the tiny village of Three Rivers was called "Three Rivers." The place couldn't claim a dry creek bed, let alone a trio of waterways sizable enough to justify the designation "river." The entire population of the town numbered only seventeen on a busy day, so motels and restaurants were nonexistent. Contestants and their families who wished to spend Friday night at the rodeo grounds brought tents, bedrolls, and camp stoves, and slept out under the stars. There were no bathing facilities and only half a dozen smelly, fly-filled public privies were available at the arena, but no one ever complained. The event was one of just four annual junior rodeos held in the entire state of New Mexico, and it was the highlight of the year for local cowboys and cowgirls who wanted to dress up, show off, and strut their stuff.

Unusual in that it didn't discriminate because of age, race, gender, or experience, the rodeo was open to anyone eighteen years old or younger—male or female, Anglo or Hispano, high level of cowboy competency or none at all. Children of either sex, aged five and younger, for example, were grouped into the "Buckaroo" category. Assuming they were old enough to stand up without falling down, Buckaroos could enter the sheep-riding competition or the fence post–roping contest. "Peewees," boys and girls between the ages of six and eight, rode small calves and roped goats. Girls of any age who owned a horse, or could borrow one, ran the barrels or roped ribbon-bedecked calves, or both. Girls who didn't have access to a horse could lasso and hog-tie sheep or ride very small yearling steers, and boys in the eight to fifteen age group could enter the calf-roping, steer-riding, and wild cow–milking contests. Older boys, ages sixteen to eighteen, were allowed to ride bareback broncs and real bulls—albeit small ones—and with an accompanying adult hazer, they could also bulldog full-grown steers.

Marvin waited until the rodeo was slightly more than two weeks away before he wondered out loud one morning if Noah might want to enter some of the events. He didn't wait that long out of selfishness or meanness or even because he forgot. The thought simply didn't occur to Marvin that his friend might like to take part in Otero County's most popular annual get-together. Rodeo was in your blood, or it wasn't. Noah had never once even mentioned rodeo. City kids didn't know about rodeo, not even capable city kids like Noah.

"What do you do at a rodeo?" Noah asked, a bit puzzled. He had never even been to a rodeo, let alone taken part in one.

"Rodeos is what cowboys do fer fun," Marvin said. "An' if you ain't never rid no steer or roped no calf, then you ain't no cowboy, an' thet's fer sure."

Noah had never rid no steer or roped no calf, that much was certain.

"What do I have to do?"

"You gotta learn how ta ride hard an' rope fast, an' we kin practice everthin' right here."

Noah said he would ask his mother and let Marvin know later. He brought the subject up during supper that evening.

"I won't have you doing anything dangerous," Mrs. Odell said. She had never been to a rodeo either. She looked at her brother. "Clarence, can you get hurt riding in a rodeo?"

Bud used two fingers to scratch an itch in his three-day-old stubble. "You kin git hurt walkin' to the barn if you step on a rattler er fall in the cesspool an' git drownded," he answered. "Ain't many people git hurt at rodeos, though, lest yer ridin' bulls." He looked at Noah. "You plannin' on ridin' any bulls, Bub?"

Noah was not planning on riding bulls and said so. Mrs. Odell made him promise that he wouldn't do anything dangerous and said he could go if he was careful. Before he went to bed, just to make sure he knew what he was getting into, he looked up "rodeo" in *Webster's International*.

> **rodeo:** Rodeo is a sport that arose out of the working practices of cattle herding in Spain, Mexico, and later the United States, Canada, South America, and Australia. It was based on the skills required of the working vaqueros, and later, cowboys of what today is the western United States, western Canada, and northern Mexico. Today it is a sporting category that consists of several different timed and judged events that involve cattle and horses, designed to test the skill and speed of the human cowboy and cowgirl athletes who participate.

While he was at it, Noah also looked up "castoorated" and "Hayrab" but couldn't find a listing for either. Next, he flipped to the *J*'s and looked up "jackalope."

> **jackalope:** Also called "antelabbit," "aunt benny," and "Wyoming thistled hare," jackalopes, *Lethopterus leapii horniculus*, are hares with horns. Shy and retiring mammals, which are found mainly in the deserts of the American West, they may resemble a miniature version of a jackrabbit–American

pronghorn antelope hybrid but are actually their own species. Contrary to folklore, jackalopes possess neither unusual strength or speed, and their milk and toenails do not contain magical medical remedies.

Well, Marvin had been partially right at least, Noah thought to himself, although the whole jackalope thing sounded pretty darn fishy. He flipped to the *H*'s and looked up "heaven."

heaven: The expanse of space that seems to be over the earth like a dome; firmament—usually used in plural; the dwelling place of the Deity and the blessed dead; a spiritual state of eternal communion with God; a place or condition of utmost happiness.

Nothing new there, although Sunday communion—the act of drinking warm, sour grape juice and eating a stale saltine cracker that had been stuffed into his mouth by the minister while everyone in the church looked on—was perhaps the most boring ritual of many boring rituals in the Methodist Church, and Noah simply could not imagine taking communion forever, with or without God being present. Lastly, he looked up the word "hell."

hell: A nether world in which the dead continue to exist; the nether realm of the Devil and the demons in which the damned suffer everlasting punishment; a word often used in curses or as a generalized term of abuse.

Noah didn't know what "nether" meant and was yawning too hard and often to look it up. He brushed his teeth, said good night to his mother and uncle, and went to bed. As he waited for sleep, he hoped that when he finally died he would be provided with a third choice, one that would allow him to bypass both heaven with its blessed dead and eternal communion, and the everlasting pain and punishment in the nether world of hell. Both of them sounded like truly awful places.

The next morning, Noah told his friend that he had been given permission to enter the rodeo.

"Good deal," Marvin said. "We gotta git started."

Noah's first task was to learn how to rope. Marvin went into the barn and returned with two coiled hemp lariats.

"This here's a cowboy lasso," he said. "Twenty-eight feet long an' stiff as a cow's tail." He handed Noah one of the ropes. "Ain't easy to use, but you'll git the hang of it."

Marvin showed Noah how to make a three-foot-wide loop and swing it over his head with a rolling motion of his wrist. He illustrated how to hold the coils in his left hand and let them go as the loop snaked toward its target.

"Now you try," he said, pointing to a fence post ten feet away. "Rope thet pole yonder and then jerk it tight when you got it caught."

Noah formed the loop carefully in his right hand and coiled the excess rope in his left. He swung the loop over his head like Marvin had shown him and immediately knocked off his hat. He tried it without the hat and whacked the back of his head with the inflexible hemp so hard that he saw stars.

"You'll git it," Marvin said encouragingly. "Jest keep practicin'."

While Marvin offered advice, Noah kept trying. At the end of an hour, he could drop the rope over the fence post and jerk it taut nine times out of ten.

"Thet ain't bad fer a city kid," Marvin admitted. "Let's go try somethin' harder."

They walked to the corral where Mr. Couch kept the nursing Holstein calves isolated so they couldn't drink all of momma's milk, and climbed over the wooden rail fence. The dozen or so skittish calves inside the corral scattered in every direction.

"When you rope 'em, don't choke 'em er nothin'," Marvin instructed. "An' don't let go of yer lasso, neither, 'cause it'll git covered in cow flop."

Noah set out in pursuit of the calves, swinging his rope over his head while he tried to get close enough to throw it. The calves had other ideas. The corral was large enough that each time Noah came within twenty feet, they would simply trot out of lariat range. Finally,

Marvin joined in and shooed them back in Noah's direction. After fifteen or twenty tries, he finally dropped the loop over a calf's head and jerked it tight. When the noose tightened, the healthy, hundred-pound Holstein bull calf bolted, giving Noah a nasty rope burn on the palm of his hand. Remembering what Marvin had said, he tightened his grip and dug in his boot heels. The calf stood straddle-legged and quivering at one the end of the rope while Noah stood straddle-legged and quivering at the other end, unsure what to do next.

Marvin pulled a short piece of slender rope out of his pocket. It had a small, permanent loop woven into one end.

"This here's a piggin' string," he said. "It's what you hog-tie 'em with once you git 'em flanked."

"How do you get one flanked?" Noah asked.

"Show ya," Marvin said. "Jest watch."

Marvin threaded one end of the rope through the loop to make a larger loop about six inches across. He put the loop between his teeth and stuffed the other end of the piggin' string under his belt. He grabbed hold of Noah's rope and pulled the protesting calf toward him, caught it by the left and right leg where they attached to the body, and in one smooth motion flopped the protesting little bull onto its side. Marvin quickly planted his knee in the calf's flank, placed the loop of the piggin' string over one foreleg, pulled the two hind legs together and wrapped the piggin' string around all three— once, twice, three times. He finished the wrap with a half hitch knot, threw his hands into the air, and shouted, "Time!"

"Thet's called 'two wraps an' a hooey,'" he said, standing up and looking pleased with himself. "Calf's gotta stay tied fer at least six seconds."

"Wow!" said Noah, impressed by Marvin's skill. "Where'd you learn to do that?"

"Pa taught me," he said. "Pa used ta rodeo when he was a kid. I took second in calf roping last year. This year, I'm shootin' fer first."

Noah's numerous attempts at roping, flanking, and the "two wraps and a hooey" technique during another hour of practice could barely be called adequate, but considering it was his first day, he hadn't done too badly. When he went home for lunch, tired, dusty, and sore from slapping himself in the back of the head with the lariat so many times, he told his uncle about the calf-roping lessons.

"Jest don't let one a them kettle put a dent in yer noggin," was Bud's only comment. "Yer ma'd never let me forget it if you got kilt."

The next morning, after breakfast and after his chores were completed, Noah rode Brimstone to Marvin's instead of walking as he had the previous day. Jake was already saddled when he arrived, and they led their mounts into the corral that held the nursing calves. Still skittish from the previous day's practice, the young Holsteins kept as much space as possible between themselves and the boys.

For the next hour, they practiced hard, and Noah soon discovered that roping calves from the back of a moving animal was a lot more difficult than roping them from the ground. If he wasn't whapping Brimstone's ears or neck or hindquarters as he swung the loop over his head, he was thumping himself in the ear or across his back. And because he had to hold both Brimstone's reins *and* the coiled rope in his left hand, he was continually dropping one or the other or both. Marvin showed him how to knot the reins so they dropped only as far as Brimstone's neck and how to dally the end of the lasso around the saddle horn so it wouldn't be flung away when he threw the loop at a calf. Both tips helped some, but it was not an easy technique to learn.

The next part was even harder. Marvin explained that once Noah caught his calf, he had to quickly dismount, grab the rope, run to the animal, flank it, and then tie three legs together with the piggin' string. It was important that Brimstone moved steadily backward once the calf was roped, so that the lariat was kept taut around the calf's neck. If it loosened, the loop would open and the calf would escape. To illustrate, Marvin chased down and roped one of the smaller calves. As the rope tightened around the calf's throat, Jake slammed to a halt and began to back up, keeping the lasso tight. Marvin jumped down and grabbed the rope with one hand, ran to the calf and flanked it, then popped the loop of the piggin' string over the calf's foreleg, made his wraps, and threw his hands into the air.

"Wow!" Noah said for the second time.

SINCE HIS ARRIVAL at Boggs Ranch in early June, Noah's physical appearance had changed considerably. He had grown another inch in height and had gained at least five pounds in weight. His arms and legs were rippling with stringy muscles from lifting hay bales and sacks of chicken feed, and he had exchanged his pale Oregon skin color for a deep, nut-brown New Mexico tan. Lo and behold, there was even a smudge of black hair—if you had a magnifying glass handy and looked closely—sprouting from each of his armpits.

But as the rodeo got closer, Noah began to have second thoughts about taking an active part in the event. Maybe his height, weight, and skin color had changed, but he still knew his limitations. He realized, for instance, that no matter how much he practiced between now and the first Saturday in August, he would have almost no chance at all of catching his calf in the calf-roping event. Brimstone didn't have a clue about what he was doing and neither did Noah. That really made little difference, but he didn't want to make a total fool of himself in the process of not having a clue about what he was doing. Roping a fence post or a stationary calf on the ground was one thing; roping a running calf from the back of a mule in front of a critical crowd was quite another.

And then there was steer riding, the second event that Marvin wanted him to enter. Noah had never ridden a steer. He had never even thought about riding a steer. He had never even thought about thinking about riding a steer.

"Thet don't matter none," Marvin told him. "All you gotta do is hang on, an' if you git throwed off, try not to git yer brains stomped on an' spattered all over the dirt."

"Do we get to practice?" Noah asked.

"Cain't practice fer real," Marvin answered, "'cause we ain't got no yearlin' steers. Don't know nobody with none neither." He pointed at the barn. "What we got is Hump."

Noah followed Marvin into the milking barn. In a far corner away from the milking machines, suspended on four ropes from the rafters, was a fifty-gallon steel oil drum. The bottom of each rope was connected to the barrel with a five-foot-long, four-inch-wide strip of inner tube. A tattered horse blanket was strapped to the top of the barrel with two pieces of rope. One of the ropes had a small loop at the top. A thick pile of hay had been spread on the concrete slab beneath the barrel.

"This here's Hump," Marvin said proudly, pointing at the contraption dangling from the rafters. "He's a buckin' barrel. Pa made 'em so's I could practice ridin' steers without gettin' stomped." He picked up a steel milk crate and placed it to one side of the barrel as a step. "Climb on, an' I'll show ya how it works."

Noah stepped up on the milk crate and then clumsily straddled the tipsy, bouncy steel drum, trying his best not to fall off.

"You kin only use one hand to hang on with," Marvin said, removing the milk crate. "Grab hold of thet loop. Cain't touch the steer with yer other hand neither, an' you cain't touch yerself, so make like yer wavin' at yer ma."

Noah grasped the rope loop tightly with his right hand and held his left hand above his head. Marvin tied one end of a lasso to the nearest piece of inner tube and stepped back fifteen feet or so, playing out the lariat as he went.

"You ready?" he said.

"Ready for what?" Noah asked.

"Fer steer ridin' practice," Marvin said, and with that, he gave the lasso in his hands a terrific tug. The barrel jumped sideways, and Noah promptly tumbled off into the pile of hay.

When Marvin finally stopped laughing, he replaced the milk crate next to Hump. "Gotta hang on better'n thet," he said, shaking his head, "'cause you gotta ride for eight seconds. Try 'er again, an' this time hold on with yer knees, too."

Noah tried to rub the pain out of an elbow that had collided with the concrete floor when he landed. Once again, he stepped onto the crate and climbed aboard the barrel. This time he squeezed the metal hard with his knees, just like he was riding a galloping horse. Marvin moved the crate out of the way, returned to his lasso, and gave it another hard pull. The barrel jumped sideways, but Noah was ready and stayed aboard.

"Now yer learnin'!" Marvin shouted. He gave the rope another hard tug, and another, until the barrel was bouncing up and down and from side to side on its inner tube springs like a drunk pig on a pogo stick. Noah squeezed knees, groped rope, and waved as hard as he could, but five or six seconds later, he landed hard on the concrete again. He sat up and spit out a mouthful of hay.

"Why does anyone want to ride a stupid steer in the first place?" he asked.

"'Cause it gits you in practice fer when you turn sixteen and kin ride bulls," Marvin said.

The boys took turns trying to throw each other off the bucking barrel for an hour and then went back to roping calves in the corral. Marvin used a stick to draw a large square in the dirt at one end of the enclosure. He told Noah that in a real rodeo arena it was called a roper's box, and it was where a cowboy and his horse waited behind a string barrier for a calf to be released. The calf itself was held in a wooden chute with spring-loaded doors and was given a twenty-foot head start before the cowboy could leave the roper's box. If horse and rider jumped the gun and broke the string barrier, they would get a ten-second penalty. In calf roping, receiving a ten-second penalty was like being given a death sentence.

"Yer time depends on yer timin'," Marvin said philosophically, although he hadn't meant to be philosophical and wouldn't have known what the word meant. "Cain't go too soon 'cause you'll break the barrier, an' you cain't go too late 'cause yer calf'll git away. Fer sure you won't hafta go first," he added, "'cause first-time ropers don't never hafta go first. You kin watch what the other fellas is doin' an' then you kin do the same thing, if they're doin' anything right."

―――――――――――

NOAH AND MARVIN practiced long and hard for the next two weeks, roping calves and riding Hump every day for at least three hours. They were covered with bruises from being thrown off the bucking barrel, but both of them had gotten considerably better at staying aboard for the required eight seconds. Noah tried without much success to teach Brimstone to back up when a calf was on the other end of the rope. The mule was not a roping horse and never would be. The best Noah could hope for, if he did get lucky and catch his calf, was that Brimstone would at least stand still and not try to follow him as he ran to make the tie-down.

LaDonna came to watch Noah and Marvin practice on the Thursday before the rodeo started. They hadn't gotten together since the movie, mainly because of rodeo practice. LaDonna, too, would be at Three Rivers—running the barrels on her horse Measles in the girl's barrel-racing event—but she practiced at home in a small arena near one of the milking barns. The large sack of freshly-baked chocolate chip cookies and gallon jug of sweetened lemonade LaDonna brought with her was a welcome break from their usual mid-morning snack of Mrs. Couch's cold cornbread and ice water, and was gone within minutes.

Sitting on a pile of clean straw in the milking barn, LaDonna watched while Marvin and Noah practiced their steer-riding skills on the inner tube–powered bull Hump, booing loudly when one of them fell off, applauding when they stayed on. After an hour of being bruised, battered, and dirtied from slamming into the concrete floor beneath the bull, the boys called it quits and collapsed next to LaDonna on the straw.

"I want to try," she said when they had time to catch their breath.

"Try what?" Marvin asked.

"I want to ride Hump," she said. "It looks like fun."

"Ain't no fun at all," Marvin said. "'Sides thet, girls cain't ride no steers. Ain't allowed."

"Who won't allow it?" LaDonna demanded. "Anything you can do, I can do and probably better."

"Don't know," Marvin admitted. "Girls jest ain't s'posed to ride steers."

"Ah ha!" she said with a disgusted look on her face. "'The most mediocre of males feels himself a demigod as compared with women.' Is that what you think? Simone de Beauvoir would spin in her grave if she was dead, which she isn't."

Marvin looked baffled. He looked at Noah for help but Noah was staring at a point in the distance trying hard to keep from laughing.

Prudently Marvin decided to give up the argument and let LaDonna have her way.

"OK, OK, you kin ride Hump," he said, holding up his hands in surrender, "but don't git mad when you git bucked off and bust yer head. An' don' say we didn't tell ya 'cause we did."

Marvin motioned for LaDonna to follow him to the metal bull. He placed the milk carton underneath one side and pointed. "To git on 'em, ya gotta step on thet an' hold on here an' . . ."

Before he could finish the sentence, LaDonna was already aboard, swinging on so easily that the barrel hardly moved with her effort. She grasped the rope loop in her right hand tightly and locked her knees around the barrel's metal sides.

"Don't hold back just because I'm a girl," she said, grinning. "Maybe you and Noah both should pull on the rope."

Marvin stepped back, playing out the pull rope as he went. When he was fifteen feet away, he gave the lariat a mighty tug, fully expecting to see LaDonna go tumbling off head first onto the concrete.

She didn't. Instead, she let go of the handle loop with her right hand and held both arms over her head.

"You can do better than that!" she shouted. "Show me your muscles!"

For the next two or three minutes, Marvin did everything he could to dislodge LaDonna from Hump's back, all to no avail. Finally, totally winded and panting hard from the effort, he dropped the pull rope, walked to the pile of straw where Noah was still staring at a point in the distance, and collapsed. LaDonna hopped off the barrel as easily as she had hopped aboard, and joined them.

"That was fun," she said calmly, not even breathing hard. "Let's do it again when you've rested."

―――――――――

ON FRIDAY AFTERNOON, the day before the rodeo started, Bud and Noah lifted the galvanized cattle rack onto the pickup bed and secured it with bolts. They removed Bud's toolbox and replaced it with half a bale of hay. Noah covered the hay with a tarp so that Brimstone wouldn't eat it all on the trip to Three Rivers. The mule's bridle and saddle were piled on top of the hay along with the bedroll Mrs. Odell had made Noah using two old wool blankets and a pillow. A supper box of fried chicken, pinto beans, and corn on the cob went into the pickup cab. When they were ready to go, Bud backed the Studebaker up to the barn and, with four two-by-six wooden planks, made a narrow bridge up to the pickup's bed. With hardly any coaxing from Noah, Brimstone calmly walked up the planks and into the truck as though he had done it a thousand times. The boards went into the pickup bed alongside the bale of hay.

Mrs. Odell came outside to say good-bye. She gave Noah a hug and kissed him on his forehead. "Clarence will stay with you boys until bedtime," she said, "and we'll be there early tomorrow morning and bring breakfast."

"Marvin don't like scrambled eggs, Mom," Noah said, remembering the phalanx of yellow mush that Deeter had sneezed across the table. "Maybe we could have biscuits and bacon instead?"

"Biscuits and bacon, it will be," she said, giving him another healthy squeeze. "Promise me you'll behave yourself tonight and brush your teeth before bed."

"I'll see to thet, Sis," Bud chimed in, giving Noah a wink. "Won't let 'em chase no women er drink no liquor neither, lest I git to come along." He escaped to the pickup before Mrs. Odell could make a comment.

The rodeo arena was bustling when they arrived at about four o'clock. Noah had never seen so many horses all together in one spot. There were Appaloosas and palominos and buckskins and bays and roans and chestnuts, all being led, fed, watered, or ridden by young cowboys and cowgirls dressed in their best cowboy or cowgirl clothes. Horse trailers and pickups with cattle racks were parked everywhere. The dust cloud from the foot and car traffic blanketed the rodeo grounds like a brown fog, and temporary holding pens filled with bawling calves and bleating goats added a near deafening barnyard hullabaloo to the scene.

Noah spotted Marvin and his father parked beneath a colossal and ancient gray-barked cottonwood tree near the arena. Jake had ridden to the rodeo grounds in style in Mr. Couch's one-horse trailer, which was now detached and parked next to his pickup. The palomino was tethered a dozen yards away and was munching on a flake of hay. His saddle and hackamore and several coiled lariats lay on the ground beneath the tree. Marvin had set up a small pup tent and was gathering dead and broken cottonwood limbs for an evening campfire. Bud parked the Studebaker next to Mr. Couch's truck and helped Noah lead Brimstone down the plank bridge from the pickup bed to the ground. They put the mule's saddle and bridle next to Jake's gear under the tree, and Noah staked Brimstone out a few yards from the palomino.

"They ain't got no waterin' tanks on this side of the arena," Marvin informed Noah, "so's we gotta walk 'em over yonder when they need a drink. Figgered we could take 'em after supper."

Noah gave Brimstone a flake of hay and removed his bedroll and canteen from the pickup, then helped Marvin gather more firewood. Bud took two cold beers from a small ice chest and handed one to Mr. Couch. Chatting about cows, the two men wandered away toward the arena to register Noah and Marvin in their individual rodeo events and to examine the stock. The boys squatted down in the shade of the cottonwood tree.

"You scairt?" Marvin asked. "I was so scairt my first year rodeo'n I thought I was gonna puke."

"A little bit," Noah admitted. "I just don't want to mess up, and I probably will. I really don't know what I'm doing, and I haven't had enough practice."

"You kin stay on Hump longer than I kin," Marvin said encouragingly. "You'll probably win the dang steer ridin'. Anyways, we jest gotta compete against kids our own age 'cause them older boys got their own category. An' don't never tell LaDonna I said so, but she's better'n both of us. Probably win hands down if they'd let 'er ride."

"How many boys do you think there will be?" Noah asked.

"Last year they was thirty kids thet was ropin' calves, mebbe, an' twenty ridin' steers. 'Bout ten was purty good, an' ever'body else got throwed off quick or missed their calf."

That didn't make Noah feel much better, but it was nice to know that the competition didn't number in the hundreds. They left the shade of the cottonwood and walked through the dust to the arena, where Marvin showed Noah the roping box and calf chute. He also pointed to the individual wooden-gated bucking chutes at the opposite end of the arena, behind which the steer- and bull-riders would mount their animals.

"You gotta ride 'em for eight seconds," Marvin reminded him again. "You ain't got no spurs, but I brung an extra pair thet you can use so's you can make yer steer buck better. The harder you gouge 'em with yer spurs, the better he bucks."

Noah thought about that one for a minute. "You mean you spur him because you want him to buck harder so he has a better chance of bucking you off?" he asked. "That's pretty dumb."

Marvin pointed to a large wooden box on stilts above the arena. "Up there's where the judges sit at," he said. "You kin git twenty-five points if yer ride's perfect, an' it ain't never gonna be perfect. Judges'll give you more points if yer steer really bucks hard. If he don't buck at all, you don't git nothin'."

"How do you get off if you stay on for all eight seconds?" Noah asked. He was afraid he already knew the answer.

"Well, if you ain't got no ladder handy," Marvin said with a grin, "you got two ways of gettin' off. You kin fall off an' land on yer head, or you kin jump off and land on yer feet."

They returned to camp and found Bud and Mr. Couch waiting for them. The fried chicken, beans, and corn on the cob were spread out on the tailgate of the Studebaker along with paper plates and a platter of cornbread, courtesy of Mrs. Couch. Bud found two more Lucky Lagers in the cooler and two ice-cold Cokes. He handed each of the boys a soda and uncapped the beers.

"You boys dig in," Bud said. "Gonna be a long time till breakfast."

They dug in. When they finished twenty minutes later, not a crumb or a drip of anything remained. Bud and Marvin's father loaded everything back into the pickups. Mr. Couch stacked cottonwood branches in a shallow hole surrounded by stones near Marvin's tent.

"We're gonna head on home," he said. "Its gettin' late, and I'll bet those animals are thirsty, so you boys best get 'em watered." He gave

Marvin a small box of wooden matches. "Wait'll you get back to light that fire, and don't go anywhere once it's lit."

Bud handed each boy his competitor's identification: a large square of white cloth with a black number printed on it, and two safety pins stuck in one corner.

"Pin these on come mornin'," he said. "An' keep away from them cowgirls 'cause they ain't nothin' but trouble."

Marvin and Noah said good-bye and watched until Bud and Mr. Couch had driven off. They untied Brimstone and Jake and led them toward the large, metal watering troughs on the other side of the arena. It was nearly dark, and the dust cloud that had filled the air all afternoon was finally beginning to settle. Several other people were already watering their horses at the large metal trough, so they waited a few feet away until they were finished. Three older boys leading their horses lined up behind them.

"You gonna rope goats with the girls, buddy?" one of the boys asked loudly. Noah looked around. All three were laughing. "Marvin, how come you're hangin' round with somebody that rides a jackass?" More laughter.

"Howdy, Gary," Marvin said. "This here's muh friend, an' the only jackasses round here is the ones we're talkin' to."

"That ain't very friendly," Gary said, grinning. "You looking to get thumped?"

Marvin thought for a moment. "You heard what happened to Zefo Montoya?" he asked.

"Yeah, I heard he fell off the balcony at the movie theater. What about it?"

"Before thet," Marvin said.

"Sure, somebody hit him so hard they busted three of his ribs," Gary said. "Probably some trucker got tired of his lip. So what?"

"Wasn't no trucker," Marvin said, poking his thumb at Noah. "This here's the kid thet done it."

Gary glanced down at Noah's boots, then up at his hat, and then at Brimstone. "You put Zefo Montoya in the hospital?" he asked. "You don't look tough enough."

Noah said nothing, but he tried to look tough. Gary and his

friends stared quietly for a few more moments then turned and led their horses into the semidarkness toward another trough. They weren't laughing anymore.

"Are you trying to get me killed?" Noah asked Marvin when the older boys were out of earshot.

"Cain't let nobody make fun of yer hor . . . yer mule," Marvin said, "an' Brimstone's a whole bunch smarter than he is, anyways. Thet there's Gary Bishop, the one beat me in calf ropin' last year. He's fifteen an' his pa's rich, an' sometimes he's kinda snotty."

The horses in front of them finished watering and were led away by their young owners. Noah and Marvin led Jake and Brimstone to the trough and let them drink. When the animals had drunk their fill, the boys led them back to camp and fed them both another flake of alfalfa. Marvin lit their campfire, and they sat on the ground next to it, talking about the morning and listening to the quiet murmur from the other camps around them. By nine o'clock, the only noise was an occasional low-pitched grunt from one of the Brahma bulls or a muffled whinny from someone's horse. Jake and Brimstone had settled down nicely at the end of their long tethers and were quietly munching the few whisps of hay left over from their evening feed. Tired but not sleepy, Noah said good night and laid out his bedroll a few feet from the dying campfire, removed his boots, shirts, and jeans, and crawled in. He could hear Marvin in his pup tent trying to get comfortable on the hard ground.

"Don't forget to drape yer rope round yer bedroll," Marvin said from inside the tent. His voice was muffled and sleepy.

"Why would I want to put a rope around my bed?" Noah asked, a bit baffled.

"Ever' cowboy on earth knows you gotta put a rope round yer bed in case a rattlesnake comes crawlin' by, lookin fer a warm spot," Marvin answered. "Ain't no rattler nowhere gonna crawl over a rope 'cause it tickles his belly and rattlers don't like to have their bellies tickled."

Noah was dubious, but he wasn't willing to take the chance that Marvin might be misinformed. Rattlesnakes were fascinating but deadly, and they weren't something to be trifled with. Wearing only his underwear, he clambered out of his blanket, fetched his lariat from where it was hanging on the horn of his saddle, and draped a ten-foot loop around his bedroll. Feeling a bit silly but also slightly safer, he went back to bed. Two minutes later, he rolled onto his back and groaned.

"I didn't brush my teeth," he said, more to himself than to Marvin, trying to decide whether he should get up again and do it or stay in his blankets. "I promised my mother I would."

"Jest one day won't make no difference," Marvin muttered from inside his tent. "'Sides thet, if you git bucked off and git yer head stomped on by one of them steers, you ain't gonna have no teeth to brush anyways."

13

Even Cowboys Get the Scairts

Saturday morning dawned bright, clear, and with every indication of being another blistering day. There was not a cloud in the sky nor the slightest indication of a breeze when Noah and Marvin climbed out of their bedrolls just after daylight. Noah had gotten very little sleep. He had lain wide-eyed and fully awake until midnight, thinking about the next day's events, and just when he started to get drowsy, a family of night-crawling ants discovered the mountain of flesh in their midst and decided it would be great fun to play hide-and-seek in his hair. At first, Noah just brushed them away, but friends and relatives soon began to show up, all anxious to join the festivities. When one ant bolder than the rest crawled into his underwear, he jumped up, brushed himself off as best he could, shook out his blankets, and joined a protesting Marvin in the cramped confines of the pup tent.

Marvin's dad arrived around seven o'clock with a freshly baked coffee cake, a thermos of hot chocolate, and a jug of cold milk, all courtesy of Mrs. Couch. He was followed a few minutes later by Bud and Mrs. Odell. Bud hopped out and quickly opened the Studebaker's tailgate so that Mrs. Odell could lay out a pan of fresh-made biscuits and another of fried, crispy bacon.

"Yer ma outdid herself this mornin'," Bud said. "Them biscuits'd make a dead hog git up an' dance a jig."

At that moment, LaDonna arrived with her parents in a new Chevy pickup truck pulling a shiny, two-horse trailer with HAW-THORNE'S DAIRY painted on the side in large, red letters. LaDonna was dressed in black jeans, a light green shirt, and boots. Her Stetson was the same color as the shirt. Noah and Marvin helped her unload Measles—a perky, brown-and-white Appaloosa mare with a very short mane and a white, lightning-shaped blaze down the middle of her face—from the trailer.

"You two are crazy," LaDonna said when they had backed the Appaloosa—already saddled and bridled—carefully down the ramp and tied her snugly to the pickup. "Why would anyone want to sleep on the ground in the dirt and the bugs and the snakes when they could sleep in a comfortable bed at home?"

"Wasn't no snakes," Marvin said, "'cause we was roped in. Wasn't no bugs neither 'cept fer the cockroach thet kept me awake all night with his snorin'."

"Why were you roped in?" LaDonna asked. "Roped into what?"

Again Marvin patiently explained about how no rattlesnake in his right mind would crawl over a rope because it tickled his belly. LaDonna started to say something, then thought better of it and simply rolled her eyes instead.

"It wasn't all that bad," Noah said. "It was kind of nice to sleep out and look at the stars."

LaDonna gave a great sigh, closed her eyes theatrically, and recited: "Art is everywhere you look for it, hail the twinkling stars for they are God's careless splatters."

"Did you just make that up?" Noah asked, impressed.

"I got it second hand," LaDonna said. "Domenikos Theotoko-poulos made it up in the sixteenth century. He was a famous Greek painter who lived mostly in Spain. People called him 'El Greco.'"

"How come you know stuff like thet?" Marvin asked. He hadn't understood a word of the famous quote, but he, too, was impressed, at least with LaDonna's almost magical use of words.

"I read a lot," she answered, smiling. "Everybody should read a lot. Books are food for your brain and nectar for your soul."

When the last of the biscuits and bacon were gone, and the dishes and camp gear had been stored in the trucks, LaDonna left with her mother to enter herself in the barrel-racing event while Noah and Marvin led their mounts to the watering trough for their morning drink. They saddled and bridled the animals when they returned, but left them tethered in the shade of the cottonwood. Mrs. Odell pinned Noah's contestant number to the back of his shirt, then helped Marvin with his. Marvin's dad handed Noah a set of old, well-used spurs with stubby, silver rowels for the steer-riding competition. He showed him how to attach them to the heels of his boots.

"Wouldn't wear 'em when yer ridin' yer mule," Bud warned. "Ol' Brimstone wouldn't much care to git skewered with them things."

Just before nine o'clock, they all walked to the rodeo arena to find seats for the Grand Entry, traditionally the first event in all rodeos. The stands filled quickly with spectators, and by the time Miss Three Rivers Rodeo and her four attendants entered the arena on their prancing, farting, lathered horses, there was standing room only and very little of that. Dressed in matching bright blue western costumes topped with cream-colored Stetsons, the queen and her court galloped around the stadium's inner perimeter, waving enthusiastically at the crowd and almost brushing the wooden rails with their boots. Behind them, thirty uniformed riders from the Otero County Sheriff's Posse joined the gallop, each of them streaming a colorful banner from a wooden lance. Next came a troupe of mounted rodeo clowns in garish costumes, followed by half a dozen rodeo officials and smiling local luminaries. After three full laps, all of the riders slowed to a walk and then lined up side-by-side in the center of the arena. A two-cowboy color guard carrying the American and New Mexico flags and mounted on perfectly matched, pure-white horses was the last to enter the enclosure. The crowd of fifteen hundred in the stands rose as one and placed their hands over their hearts as the colors were presented to the melody of "The Star-Spangled Banner" blaring out over the loudspeakers.

When the Grand Entry participants had exited the arena, the announcer called for the "Buckaroos"—boys and girls five and younger—to begin their events. The first was the sheep-riding contest. One at a time, each Buckaroo was lifted onto a wooly white sheep and held in place by rodeo clowns on either side. Bedecked with cowbell necklaces around their necks and bright ribbons twisted into their wool, the ewes were not particularly overjoyed to have thirty or forty pounds of giggling child suddenly straddling their backs. At a signal from an official, each sheep was released from its lead and given a mild jolt with an electric cattle prod. Bucking and bleating, it would charge down the arena at a gallop while clowns on each side tried to keep their young rider upright. It was hilarious to watch, and by the time every Buckaroo had gotten a ride, onlookers, clowns, and rodeo officials were holding their sides in laughter.

The second and last event for the Buckaroos was fence post–roping. Each child was given a shortened hemp lasso and then placed in a line in the middle of the arena seven or eight feet apart. In front of each roper was a two-foot-high, upright wooden post on a stand. At the sound of the buzzer, the Buckaroos could rope away, and the first one to rope his or her post three times in a row would be declared the winner. The signal was given. Lariats flew in every direction, and within seconds, there was a mob of crying, shouting, fighting children in the dusty arena trying to untangle themselves or their neighbors. The crowd in the stands was rolling in the aisles.

The Buckaroo events were followed by the "Peewee" events, which were followed in turn by half a dozen girls-only roping events. Halfway through the "goat grab," LaDonna poked Noah in the side and motioned for Marvin to come closer.

"We have to go," she said. "Barrel racing is up next, and steer riding is after that."

The moment Noah had been dreading was at hand. Bud shook his shoulder and whispered, "Give 'em hell, Bub" so that his sister couldn't hear. Mrs. Odell just smiled and mouthed "good luck." Marvin led the way out of the stands and back to camp to where Jake, Brimstone, and Measles were tethered. Leading their mounts, they returned to the arena and walked to the large, dusty holding area directly behind the bucking chutes. The two boys tied Jake and Brimstone to a corral post, but LaDonna looped the reins over Measles's head and checked the saddle cinch for tightness. As the rodeo announcer made the first call for the girl's barrel race, she swung aboard the Appaloosa in a single smooth motion without even using the stirrup.

"Good luck," Noah said. "I'm sure you'll take first place."

LaDonna smiled down at him and waved. "I always do," she said quietly, and touched Measles's sides with her boot heels. The horse shot forward like a jackrabbit toward the arena entrance gate.

"Does she really always win?" Noah asked, as Marvin led the way toward an unoccupied spot near the arena fence where they could watch the race.

"She ain't never been beat while I been rodeo'n," Marvin answered. "Thet dang horse of hers kin fly. Last year she woulda set a new state record 'cept she knocked over a barrel and got a five-second penalty. Still won the race, though. Nobody else even got close."

LaDonna was the tenth racer to run the triangle-shaped, three-barrel course. Noah had never watched a barrel race, but he could see clearly from the instant that she and Measles exploded from the starting gate that this year would be no different than past years. He had never seen anyone who could ride as well as LaDonna could—not even Marvin, who was a pretty good horseman him-self. Stretched low over Measles's neck, she seemed to be molded to the Appaloosa's back like an oblique extension of the animal's back-bone. She wore no spurs on her boots and unlike many of the other barrel racers, she didn't need to whip Measles on her hindquarters with a quirt or the ends of the reins in an attempt to obtain more speed. Neither did she grab the saddle horn for support on the turns like the other girls did. As a matter of fact, LaDonna did nothing at all except to lean forward over Measles's neck as though she were whispering endearments into the Appaloosa's close cropped mane. As horse and rider navigated the sharp turns around the three bar-rels at a full gallop, they seemed to be leaning at a forty-five-degree angle to the dusty arena floor. Marvin had certainly been right about Measles; the small brown-and-white mare with the white lightning blaze could definitely fly.

LaDonna's time was 18.76 seconds, a full six seconds faster than her nearest competitor and less than two seconds under the New Mexico state junior barrel racing record. When she left the arena, she came straight to where Noah and Marvin waited by the bucking chutes. Her freckled face was covered with dirt and her once light green shirt was now the color of light brown dust. She was grinning from ear to ear.

"That was really a great race, LaDonna," Noah said as she dismounted and tied Measles to a corral post. He gave her a quick hug, something he'd never done to a girl before. "I've never seen anyone who can ride like you can."

"Thanks, Noah. I won another belt buckle. I wish they would give saddles to the girls like they do to the boys. I have a whole drawer full of buckles."

At that moment, the loud speakers blared, calling the top three finishers back into the arena to receive their prizes. LaDonna left to collect her buckle, and following the lead of several other young cowboys, Marvin and Noah climbed to the top rail of the holding pen so they could see down into the chutes. Steer riding was next, and the name and number of each rider had been written in chalk on a large blackboard nailed to one leg of the announcer's booth. Marvin's name was in the seventh position on the board, which meant he would be number seven to ride. Noah's name was in the twentieth position. There were a total of twenty-three names on the board.

The first-, second-, and third-place winners of the barrel race were announced over the loudspeaker to thunderous applause from the stands. As the clapping and whistles died down and the girls left the arena, six half-wild yearling steers were driven from the holding pen behind the half-dozen bucking chutes into the chutes themselves. When each one had been secured behind its individual gate, two cowboys cautiously strapped a bull rope—a short length of line with a rawhide handle at the top—around its middle, just behind the shoulders.

As Noah sat on the top rail watching the steer-riding preliminaries being completed, he couldn't remember when he had felt so much gut-grabbing panic. If it had been possible to back out of the event without totally embarrassing himself, he would have done so without a second's hesitation. If a green space monster started blasting people into pink goo in the stands, he would have been pleased as punch. Noah wondered if he could somehow make himself throw up and thereby feign sickness.

"Now I'm scared," he whispered to Marvin. "I don't want to ride a steer."

"Ain't nothin' to be scairt about," Marvin said, unfazed by Noah's obvious anxiety. "Jest remember thet you gotta stay on fer eight seconds, and you cain't touch nothin' with yer free hand."

LaDonna joined them on their top-rail perch. The announcer called for the first steer rider—a boy about Noah's age who looked confident as he climbed to the top rail of the number one bucking chute and eased himself down onto the back of the steer—to mount up. Noah watched closely as he wrapped his right hand around the handle, took a deep breath, and nodded his head. The gate swung open and the steer shot out, dumping its rider head first into the dirt in less than five seconds. Immediately, a rodeo clown on foot and a rodeo official on horseback were there, shooing the steer away from the prostrate rider and out of the arena through the exit gate.

The second, third, and fourth riders met similar fates. The fifth rider out of the chute stayed aboard his steer for the full eight seconds but received only a disappointing sixteen points out of a possible twenty-five for a score.

"Steer jest didn't buck enough," Marvin said. "Them judges is gonna be real tough."

The final rider in the first group of six finished his ride on a very feisty steer but was disqualified for touching the animal with his free hand. Cowboys quickly drove another six steers out of the holding pen and into the bucking chutes. Marvin climbed down off the fence without a word and walked across the corral to the number one bucking chute. He climbed to the top and at a signal from the gate attendant, lowered himself carefully down onto the back of a large, tan steer. He wrapped his fist around the rawhide handle, pulled his hat way down over his ears with his free hand, and gave Noah a wave. Then he nodded his head, and the bucking chute gate swung open.

As the steer burst into the arena, Noah had to admit that Marvin really looked like he knew what he was doing. His left hand was high in the air, and he was raking the steer's side with his spurs even as the steer bounced and bucked and twisted down the arena. When the eight-second buzzer sounded, Marvin let go of the bull rope and bailed out gracefully, managing somehow to land on his feet and keep his hat on in the process. The crowd applauded loudly as his score of twenty-two out of twenty-five was announced over the loudspeakers.

When Marvin returned to the holding pen fence, LaDonna patted him on the back.

"That was great!" she said. "You're in first place. I bet your dad will be happy."

"Jest got lucky," Marvin said modestly. "Thet steer wanted to git me off his back real bad. Least I didn't git stomped on."

Even though several other riders stayed aboard their steers for a full eight-second ride, Marvin's high score kept him in first place. The nearest score belonged to Gary Bishop, who received an eighteen from the judges. With only one rider in front of him, Noah suddenly found himself no longer nervous but actually anxious to get the whole thing over with. When number nineteen took a nose dive into the dirt and cow manure two seconds into his ride, Noah climbed to the top rail of the number two bucking chute. He vaguely heard LaDonna shout, "Good luck!" and Marvin's "Ride 'em, potner!" but didn't look around. With help from the cowboy attendant, he eased himself down onto the back of a small, dark gray steer and grasped the rawhide handle of the bull rope as tightly as he could. As ready as he would ever be, he raised his left hand over his head and nodded.

For a fraction of a second after the gate swung open, the steer didn't move. Then Noah felt its muscles bunch between his legs, and the animal exploded into the dusty arena in a twisting, neck-snapping frenzy. Ten thousand rides on Hump could never have prepared him for the next few seconds. With his legs flopping back and forth like rubber flaps as the steer gyrated up and down and sideways, Noah didn't have to worry about spurring. He had no idea where his left hand was or his hat either for that matter. From the initial surge out of the chute until he felt himself slam into the ground flat on his back, in fact, everything was just a blur of motion and color, and then pain.

The next thing he saw was the garishly painted face of a rodeo clown looking down at him through the dust.

"You OK, cowboy?" said a kindly voice. "Can you stand up?"

"I'm OK, I think," Noah said. He took the offered hand and pulled himself to his feet. "Just kind of dirty." As Noah picked up his dust-covered and badly squashed hat, he could hear the audience in the stands shouting and applauding loudly. The rodeo clown helped him to the exit gate.

"Damn good ride, son," the clown told him quietly, "but you'll need to change your shirt 'cause you landed in cow flop."

Noah left the arena and limped back to the holding pen fence to where his friends were waiting. The crowd was still applauding.

"Told ya you'd probably beat me," Marvin said, a wide grin on his face.

"Beat you?" Noah said. "I got creamed. I couldn't have been on more than a couple of seconds."

LaDonna pointed at the board on which the names of the riders were written. Behind Noah's name and number was a twenty-three with a circle around it, one point higher than Marvin's twenty-two.

"You're in the lead, you fool!" she grinned. "You're probably going to win a saddle!"

"You went way past yer eight seconds," Marvin said. "Told you yesterday, you gotta git off yerself if you ain't been throwed off."

"I never even heard the buzzer," Noah said, astonished. "I don't remember anything except hitting the ground." He turned around so Marvin could see the drying cow manure on the back of his shirt. "I landed in a cow pie."

"You done drew a real feisty steer," Marvin said, ignoring the green stain. Cow manure on your clothing was nothing new to someone who worked in a dairy every day. "He was all over the arena, an' you kinda went with 'em like you were stuck to 'em er somethin'. Thet's the kinda ride them judges like."

The last two riders were both bucked off within seconds of leaving the chutes. When the last steer had been shooed out through the exit gate, the announcer asked that Noah, Marvin, and Gary Bishop step into the arena. They stood side-by-side as the officials organized their notes. Gary said nothing, so Noah ignored him.

"Ladies and gentlemen, cowboys and cowgirls," the announcer's voice finally said over the loudspeakers, "third place in the steer-riding competition, with a score of eighteen points, goes to Gary Bishop from Tularosa." The crowd applauded enthusiastically. Miss Three Rivers Rodeo entered the arena and presented Gary with a hand-carved leather belt and a small silver buckle. She gave him a big smile and a peck on his cheek.

"Second place," the announcer continued, "with a score of twenty-two points, goes to Marvin Couch, also from Tularosa." The crowd applauded again as Marvin accepted a large, oval-shaped, silver belt buckle from the rodeo queen. He, too, got a smile and a peck on the cheek.

"And first plaaaccce," said the announcer, drawing out the last three letters of the word for more effect, "for one of the better rides we've seen here in a couple of years, with a score of twenty-three points, goes to . . ." The announcer looked at his notes to make sure he had the right name. ". . . Noah Odell from Tularosa. This cowboy's a newcomer to rodeo *and* to New Mexico."

The crowd roared. A rodeo official appeared from behind the announcer's stand carrying a brand new, hand-tooled leather saddle with a silver concho on each fender and a silver-encased saddle horn. Noah couldn't believe his eyes. The queen took the heavy saddle from the official and presented it to Noah with a girlish grunt. She pecked his cheek and smiled, then wrinkled her nose.

"Don't get close to anyone until you take a bath, kid," she whispered in her sweet, high school voice. "You smell like a cow barn."

The announcer informed the crowd that the day's next event would be the junior boy's tie-down calf roping. He advised all entrants to get their horses and gather at the gate to the roper's box. A group of twenty or so young calves was herded into one of the holding pens and then loaded, one by one, into the long, narrow runway that led to the calf chute. LaDonna wished them both luck, swung up on Measles, and left to join her parents in the stands.

Noah and Marvin quickly walked to where they had tied Jake and Brimstone earlier that morning. Bud was there waiting on them. He gave Noah a bear hug and shook Marvin's hand.

"Well, Bub, you sure showed 'em what yer made of," he said. "Yer ma's proud as a peacock with a new hat." He patted Marvin on the shoulder. "Yer pa's proud too, son. You both done real good."

"What'd Mom say when I got bucked off?" Noah asked. "Was she scared?"

Bud grinned. "Nah, she weren't scared," he said. "Jest a little nervous mebbe, till she seen you git up with yer head still attached to yer neck bone."

Bud pointed at Noah's spurs and reminded him to take them off. Noah sat in the dirt and undid the straps, then handed the spurs to his uncle.

"Where's yer new saddle at?" Bud asked.

"The man said I could pick it up later," Noah said, "so I wouldn't have to carry it around. He's got Marvin's buckle, too."

Bud wished them good luck in the calf-roping event and returned to the stands to rejoin his sister and Marvin's dad. The boys untied Jake and Brimstone and joined the small crowd waiting at the gate next to the roper's box. Several of the boys stared hard at Brimstone and a few laughed, but Noah just ignored them. He saw that there were only sixteen names listed on the blackboard. Marvin's name was at the top of the list, and Noah's was second to last. The final roper was Gary Bishop.

"OK with me," Noah said, glad he was almost last. "Maybe it'll rain and I won't even have to rope."

"Don't never rain round here," Marvin said. "Jest watch what everbody's doin' an' do the same thing."

Noah couldn't watch anything at all from where he was standing, so he wished Marvin good luck and led Brimstone past the crowd to the heavy, wooden rail fence enclosing the arena. He squatted down and found that he could see clearly between the rails both into the roper's box and the arena. The announcer called for the first roper to enter the roper's box. Marvin and Jake walked slowly through the gate. His lasso loop was already formed in his right hand and the coils and reins were in his left. A piggin' string was clenched between his teeth with the end tucked into his belt. Marvin rode Jake to the middle of the box and made him back up until his hindquarters were touching the wooden rails. An official hooked a string barrier across the mouth of the box. Marvin took a deep breath and nodded his head.

Slam! The noise of the spring-loaded calf-chute gate opening made Noah jump. The calf came out at a run, a lightweight cord attached to his neck. When the animal hit the end of the cord, it popped loose and the string barrier across the roper's box dropped. A split second before the barrier dropped, Marvin kicked Jake into motion. The lasso was already swinging above his head as Jake hit full gallop.

The calf was fast, but the big palomino was faster. Forty feet away from the chute, Marvin's rope dropped over its neck, and even before Jake slammed to a halt, Marvin was already on the ground. He caught the rope in his right hand, ran to the calf, and flanked it. One, two, three wraps with the piggin' string, and Marvin threw up his hands.

Marvin stood up, turned his back on the calf, and walked away. Jake backed up slightly, keeping the lariat tight. Six seconds later, the timekeeper sounded the buzzer.

"A time of ten point seven seconds for our first roper," the announcer said. The crowd clapped and whistled. "Ladies and gentlemen, that's about as good as it gets."

Marvin walked back to the calf with a grin on his face. He removed his lasso from around the animal's neck and pulled the piggin' string loose. He didn't bother to remount but simply led Jake to the exit gate. As he came out, the second roper was called in. Marvin came directly to where Noah squatted by the fence. The smile on his face galloped from earlobe to earlobe.

"Kin you beat thet?" he said. "I ain't never roped no calf under fourteen seconds before. I musta been nice to some little old lady."

"What?" asked Noah. "What little old lady?"

"I cain't remember bein' nice to one lately, but my pa always says that if yer nice to little old ladies, good luck'll come yer way."

"Well, you're nice to my mother," Noah said. "Maybe that's who it was."

"Yer ma ain't no old lady," Marvin said. "Least not old enough to have any luck. Musta been somebody else."

Slam! The spring-loaded doors on the calf chute opened again, and the second roper left the roper's box at a gallop. Noah and Marvin squatted down so they could see. After a long chase down the arena, the cowboy and his horse finally got within range, but he threw his loop to the right just as the calf dodged to the left. The crowd sighed a collective "oooohhh" of commiseration as the lariat missed by a yard.

By the time it was Noah's turn, only eight riders had caught their calves, and none had achieved a time anywhere near Marvin's 10.7 seconds. Noah handed his hat to Marvin and placed his borrowed piggin' string between his teeth. He mounted Brimstone and formed the loop of the lasso in his right hand, and when the announcer called his number and the gate swung open, he rode slowly into the roper's box. He backed Brimstone against the rear rails of the box as he had seen the others do. "Ready as I'll ever be," he said to himself, and he nodded for the official releaser of calves to open the gate.

Slam! The doors to the calf chute opened with a *clang*, and the calf shot forward. Noah didn't try to prejudge the roping box barrier but simply waited until he saw the barrier string drop before he kicked Brimstone forward. The mule was forty feet out into the arena and not gaining much ground when something totally unexpected happened. For no apparent reason, the calf simply stopped dead in its tracks. Noah didn't hesitate. He pulled Brimstone to a halt ten feet away, threw his lasso, and when he saw it drop over the calf's neck, he quickly reined Brimstone back until the rope was taut. The calf just stood there, frozen. Noah hopped down, grabbed the rope in his right hand, and ran to the calf. He threw it onto its side, made a sloppy two wraps and a hooey around three legs, and threw up his hands. Brimstone stood still exactly where Noah had left him. His head was down and he was swishing flies with his tail, but the rope between him and the calf was tight.

Noah stood up. The calf wiggled but wasn't able to shake the piggin' string loose, and when the six-second buzzer sounded, the crowd applauded but with lots of laughter mixed in. Noah couldn't have cared less.

"Seventeen seconds flat," the announcer said with a smile in his voice, "which puts this cowboy and his ropin' mule into ninth place."

Noah left the arena and joined Marvin at the fence.

"What'd you do to thet calf?" Marvin asked. The last roper, Gary Bishop, was preparing to enter the roper's box. "Ain't never seen nothing like thet before."

"I knew he was getting too far ahead," Noah said, "so I just whistled at him and he stopped. I think he liked me."

Marvin gave Noah a questioning look, but at that moment the calf chute slammed opened, and Gary Bishop rocketed out of the roper's box on a beautiful buckskin gelding with a black mane and tail. He reached the string barrier a split second after it dropped and was on top of his calf almost instantly. Noah saw his lariat fly over the calf's neck, and as it did so, the obviously well-trained buckskin slammed on the brakes. Gary hit the ground at a run, caught and flanked the calf, and tied it in one smooth motion. When he threw up his hands and stood up, the crowd roared in approval.

"Uh oh," Noah heard Marvin say. "Danged if ol' Gary ain't got me beat again!"

Just at that moment, Gary's calf gave a little jerk, and almost in slow motion, the piggin' string wrapped around its legs flopped loose. A millisecond before the six-second buzzer sounded, the calf stood up and bawled for its mother. A great howl of sympathy arose from the stands.

"Roper number sixteen has been automatically disqualified because of a mis-tied calf," said the announcer. "His tie-down time of nine point four seconds would have been a new state junior rodeo record." Another howl of disappointment came from the crowd.

Noah looked over at Marvin. He was sitting in the dust with his back against the rails. His hat was in his lap and a massive look of relief decorated his face.

"I ain't gonna do this anymore," Marvin said. "Jest too dang much . . . too dang much bother."

"But you won," Noah said, not feeling sorry for him a bit. "And you beat Gary Bishop! You probably won a new saddle."

"Probably," Marvin said. "Only trouble is, Jake don't need no new saddle, an' I don't need no more bother." He stood up and slapped the dust off his jeans with his hat. "My rodeo'n days is over, fer sure."

Gary Bishop walked up leading his gorgeous buckskin. Noah noticed that the horse's saddle was adorned with silver conchos and that Gary's name was carved into the leather fender above the stirrups.

"Nice job of roping, Marvin," Gary said. He glanced at Noah. "You too, buddy," he added, almost as an afterthought.

"Thanks a lot," Noah answered. "I'll sure remember this afternoon every time I climb up on my brand new saddle." He was hot and dirty and smelled like cow manure, and it was late on a Saturday afternoon, so why not rub it in a little.

Gary was too busy making excuses to notice.

"My damn horse didn't keep that rope tight enough," he said, switching his attention back to Marvin. "He hasn't ever been much good anyway. My dad says he'll buy me a new one for next year's rodeo."

"If yer horse ain't no good, you sure ain't never gonna win nothin'," Marvin said.

At that moment, the announcer requested that Marvin and the second and third place ropers enter the arena to collect their prizes. He stood up and put on his hat.

"Mebbe you oughta ask yer pa fer a jackass," he said. "Ol' Brimstone here's probably got some relatives thet might be right up yer alley."

14

Two Knives Anna Fork

If there were any such thing as a pocket of soup instead of a bowl of soup or a cup of soup, and if you could pour it in your pants pocket or vest or jacket pocket and carry it with you and take a sip or a slurp while you played tennis or test drove a new Ferrari or went to the movies or worked in your office each day, what kind of soup would you carry?

"I'd carry some tomato soup," said the first fool, "because my doctor says tomatoes are diuretics that will keep your bowels spotlessly clean. My doctor also says that tomato soup contains lycopene, which is healthy and good for me and may keep me from getting pregnant or catching cancer or having shingles."

"I'd carry some chicken noodle," said the second fool, "because chicken noodle soup has been proven to contain some as-yet unidentified component that actually keeps you from getting colds and sinus congestion. Have you ever seen a chicken with the sniffles or a noodle with a bad cough? I haven't."

"First thing right off," Clarence W. Boggs might say, "I'd put in some chile. Soup jest ain't soup, lest it's got some chile in it."

Red or green, Azteca or Hatch Valley, Anaheim or poblano, fresh, canned, dried, fossilized, petrified, putrefied, or preserved in salt and buffalo lard, chile peppers were Clarence Boggs's second most pronounced and unbridled addiction after beer. We're not talking about chili with an *i*, as in chili con carne, which is a prepared dish made mostly of hamburger meat, kidney beans, and tomatoes. Bud's addiction was chile with an *e*, as in chile pepper or chile pod, the spicy fruit of a plant domesticated in what is now Ecuador more than eight thousand years ago. He could eat chile anytime, anywhere, and with anything. Peanut butter, jelly, and green chile salsa spread on a corn tortilla ("pub-a-jilly," he called it) was his favorite lunch, especially if it was accompanied by a bowl of pinto beans laced with red chile powder. He seemed to be totally immune to capsaicin, the main ingredient in 8-methyl-*N*-vanillyl-6-nonenamide compounds—collectively called "capsaicinoids"—which give some varieties of chile peppers a heat index that would burn the face off of Satan. Bud could drink Tabasco sauce straight from the bottle and never bat an eye, and he could—and often did—devour pickled jalapeños by the dozen.

Noah's uncle no longer asked his sister to prepare or handle chile at mealtimes, nor did he ask her or Noah to share his passion. Still, there was always chile of some kind on the table at every meal, and Noah had to admit that Bud's version of red enchiladas— made especially for Noah and his mother with a mild homemade red chile sauce—were delicious. First, his uncle would deep-fry a dozen blue corn tortillas in a large skillet filled with sizzling lard, wrapping them in dish towels when they were crisp so as to soak up the grease and keep them warm. When all the tortillas had been fried, he would stack four of them on each plate and place a fistful of shredded cheese, chopped lettuce and tomatoes, and several spoonfuls of red chile sauce between each tortilla. On top, Bud would spread a final handful of cheese, lettuce, and tomatoes, followed by two eggs fried sunny-side up in another skillet. The kitchen often reeked of stale grease for days afterward, but the wonderful taste of the enchiladas made it well worth the stink.

When fresh chile was available—which it was from March through November in southern New Mexico—Bud kept two or three gunnysacks of red and green pods hanging from nails in the barn. Every Sunday morning, he would build a wood fire in the bottom half of an old fifty-gallon steel drum someone had sawed in two, place a grill over the flames, and roast and peel enough pods for the coming week. "You gotta cook 'em till the skin's dang near black, so's you kin peel it off real easy," Bud told him. "Cain't eat the skin 'cause it'll give you a bad case a the farts, an' you cain't eat the seeds neither 'cause you'll get a chile plant growin' in yer belly." Bud showed him how to lay a grilled chile pod on a piece of plywood, slice it down one side, open it up, and sort of slide the seeds out with the back of a table knife. "Kinda like guttin' a fish," Bud grinned. Noah had tried helping him peel the chile once, but the pungent and overpowering smell of hot capsaicin set his eyes to watering almost instantly, and he had to stop.

On the Sunday following the Three Rivers rodeo, Noah was sitting comfortably on the couch in the living room with his dog-eared encyclopedic dictionary in his lap, trying to catch up on his definitions. He turned to the C section and flipped the pages until he found the words "chile pepper."

> **chile pepper:** A finely tapering pepper of various sizes and colors and special pungency, first domesticated in Ecuador about 6,000 BC. In addition to adding taste and spiciness to food, chile also acts as a digestive, especially in starch-heavy diets. They may also help in the management of arthritis pain, herpes zoster (shingles)–related pain, diabetic neuropathy, post-mastectomy pain, and headaches. Christopher Columbus was one of the first Europeans to encounter chile and is responsible for the vegetable's introduction into Europe and the rest of the world.

There was a lot more, but at that point Bud walked through the front door from outside, slapping dust off his overalls with his hat.

"Ain't got but jest a couple a chiles left in the sack," he said. "Not enough to bother roastin' fer sure. Let's you an' me sashay on up to Mescalero this mornin' an' restock the pantry while yer ma does some shoppin'."

"Where's Mescalero?" Noah asked.

"Tain't far," Bud said. "'Bout an hour's drive east, up in the mountains."

"Sure," Noah said. "If it's OK with Mom." An excursion with his uncle was always an adventure.

They left before it got too hot—Bud and Noah in the Studebaker, and Mrs. Odell in her Ford. While Noah's mother continued on straight south to the Piggly Wiggly store in Alamogordo, Bud turned east onto Highway 70—the highway to Mescalero—at the north end of Tularosa and headed straight toward the Sacramento Mountains. The road climbed steadily, and the more altitude they gained, the greener and lusher the land became. An hour later, they had left the Chihuahuan Desert far below and replaced it with fir-covered hillsides and tiny, meandering streams. It wasn't green by Oregon standards, Noah concluded, but it was a far cry from the parched landscape around Tularosa.

"This here's all Apache land," Bud said, gesturing with a half-empty beer bottle at the landscape rolling by outside. "You ever heard of Geronimo?"

Noah had read a little about Geronimo in school. He nodded his head and started to ask a question about the Indians he'd seen at the bus station on the day he arrived, but Bud didn't give him the chance.

"Well, Geronimo was a big Apache chief. Don't think he ever lived here but jest visited some." He took a swig of beer. "Cruel people, them Apaches. Used ta pick up little white babies by their feet an' slam their heads against a rock."

"Why'd they do that?" Noah asked, feeling a bit queasy at the thought.

"To kill 'em, a course," Bud said. "Why else'd somebody slam yer noggin against a dang rock fer?"

Before Noah could ask any more questions, Bud slowed down and turned onto a paved side road and then immediately turned again into a wide dirt driveway. A large sign printed all in capital letters read:

APACHE INDIAN CULTURAL TOURS
FRIDAY, SATURDAY, SUNDAY, JULY 1–AUGUST 24
RESERVATIONS AVAILABLE AT TRIBAL OFFICE
HORSEBACK RIDES, FRESH TOMATOES, AND GREEN CHILE FOR SALE

Bud parked in a dirt parking lot next to a dusty Dodge pickup. Past the lot, Noah could see an Indian teepee painted with colorful symbols and designs and a corral with fifteen or twenty well-fed horses milling around inside. The horses were already saddled and bridled, and their reins had been knotted over their necks so they didn't dangle. Beyond the corral, a small, neat adobe house sat beneath a grove of pine trees. Several barns, sheds, and other outbuildings were also scattered about the property.

A man came out of the teepee and walked toward them. Noah stared, though he knew it was impolite. Tall and very brown with shoulder-length gray hair, he looked to be about Bud's age. His dark chest and arms were painted with red and brown stripes, and his only clothing was a piece of buckskin that encircled his torso from waist to knees and a pair of leather moccasins that came up past his ankles. A colorful feather headdress rode the back of his head like a giant parrot on a perch. His face was fearsome, decorated with vivid red and black designs. He held a long, slender wooden lance in his left hand.

"Bub, this here's Two Knives Anna Fork," Bud said when the apparition was a few feet away. "Two Knives, this here's my nephew, Noah."

Two Knives Anna Fork held up his right hand, palm forward.

"How, paleface white boy," he said. "You bring'um wampum to chief?"

Noah glanced at Bud, but his uncle's face under a three-day stubble of whiskers gave no indication of what he was thinking. Noah did the first thing that came to mind. He held up his own right hand, palm forward.

"How," he said, trying to remember some of the cowboy and Indian movies he'd seen. "No got'um wampum." He shrugged and held out his empty hands.

"Well, that's not really important, young man," Two Knives Anna Fork said in a clear, deep voice, "although a century ago, you would have undoubtedly left my lodge without your scalp. I'm glad you've come to visit my humble home, with or without wampum."

He shook hands with Bud, and slapped him on the shoulder.

"And you as well, Clarence. I haven't seen you in at least three months."

"Jest been busy round the wrench," Bud said. "Things is goin' along purty good. Gonna need some more calves 'bout November, soon's this herd's sold off, but today I'm jest buyin' chile."

"Chile, I have lots of," said Two Knives Anna Fork. "And believe me if you dare, this year my chile is *hot*. Best crop I've had in years."

He looked at Noah. "Please pardon my flair for the theatrical," he said, "but I must have my little crumb of humor occasionally." He touched the paint on his face and chest. "This is for the tourists, a large group of which I am expecting in about an hour. An assemblage of German teachers has come to see the red Indians—as they call us in Europe—at play, no less. Who could have imagined?"

"Are you really an Indian?" Noah asked.

"I am indeed an Indian," he said, tugging at a strand of his long gray hair then slapping his bare painted chest with the flat of his hand. "A full-blood Mescalero Apache and a member in good standing of the Yogoyekayden clan."

"You don't really sound much like an Indian," Noah said. "At least you don't sound like the ones I've seen in the movies."

"I am what you might call an 'educated savage,'" Two Knives Anna Fork said. His face was bubbling with humor, his dark eyes hopping up and down and sideways as he tried not to laugh out loud. "I earned my bachelor's degree at Harvard, attended Oxford University in England on a Rhodes Scholarship, and presently have found employment as a tenured full professor of anthropology and cultural history at New Mexico State University." He gestured at the teepee and the corral. "This is what I, and a couple of other educated savages of my acquaintance, do for entertainment during the summer. We offer insights into Indian culture—principally Mescalero Apache culture—through lectures, food, horseback rides, and physical manifestation." He looked Noah up and down. "And what do you do, young white boy with a scalp that begs to be taken?"

Noah didn't really know how to answer that one. "Well," he said, thinking quickly, "I'm trying to be a cowboy, and I was the junior steer-riding champion at the Three Rivers rodeo yesterday."

"Commendable," said Two Knives Anna Fork, "truly commendable. I'm not so sure about being a cowboy because I understand cowboy wages are extremely low, but steer riding is a difficult and sometimes dangerous pastime. Do you rope calves and ride broncs as well?"

"My mom probably wouldn't let me ride a bronc," Noah said, "but I took ninth in the calf roping. And I really stank."

"Ninth isn't that bad at all," the Indian said. "You shouldn't depreciate yourself that way."

"No, I mean I really stank," Noah said. "When I got bucked off my steer, I landed in a big pile of cow manure. Nobody wanted me to get anywhere near them."

Two Knives Anna Fork laughed. "Obviously, you are well on your way to being a cowboy," he said. "You certainly have a cowboy's sense of humor." He gestured toward the teepee. "Now, why don't you two come into the lecture hall? I'm just about to enjoy a bowl of extremely good posole, and I hope you'll join me."

"Thet's sure obligin' of you," Bud said. He hadn't contributed a word during the long exchange between Noah and Two Knives Anna Fork, but his face too was energetic with potential laughter. "Yer posole's mighty tasty."

"What's posole?" Noah asked politely.

"It's a kind of soup," Two Knives Anna Fork said, "an Indian soup made with onions, dried corn, pieces of pork, and, of course, red chile. It won't stop you from catching a cold or developing cancer or shingles, and it won't keep your heart beating strongly, but it is surprisingly flavorsome, nonetheless."

Bud fetched two cold beers out of the truck, and the three of them walked to the teepee and went inside. A small wooden table stood against one wall, the top occupied by a covered, cauldron-sized cooking pot, a stack of pottery bowls, and a container of metal spoons. About a dozen or so folding chairs had been set up in a semicircle around a small dais. Two Knives Anna Fork motioned them to help themselves. When they had filled their bowls they all sat on folding chairs and ate. Noah thought the posole was probably the best soup he'd ever eaten and said so.

"I'm pleased you like it," Two Knives Anna Fork said. "Good posole is a joy to eat and a sorrow to create unless you know exactly what you're doing. The secret is in the chile and the herbs, of course. If the chile is too hot, your mouth will fall off. Too much oregano and it will taste like something a buzzard would eat. If the chile is too mild and there is too little oregano, it will taste like something a buzzard *wouldn't* eat."

The Indian stood up and walked to the table. He ladled more posole into his bowl and motioned Bud and Noah to do the same. "I'm sure you're curious about my name," he said when they were seated again, "although you are too polite to ask. Everyone is curious about names. Take yours, for instance. You are obviously from a family that reads the Bible and appreciates the legend of Noah and his ark."

Noah shook his head. "I don't think my family read the Bible much," he said. "We went to church on Sundays, but my mom said it was just so I wouldn't be a heathen when I grew up." Noah glanced over at Bud, but he was busy filling his mouth with posole. "She told me I was named for Noah Webster. He invented the first dictionary. I think my dad just wanted me to be smart."

"A splendid namesake," Two Knives Anna Fork said, "and a worthy aspiration on your father's part. I, on the other hand, was given my somewhat unusual appellation because my parents had an abstruse sense of humor. My father was a White Mountain Apache, and my mother was a Mescalero. Neither tribe can boast a reputation for being exceptionally witty or amusing. My parents, however, were different. They thought it terribly humorous that their only son would never have to suffer from lack of name recognition among his peers, no matter what his chosen profession might be. In other words, a name such as Two Knives Anna Fork is not forgotten easily."

He put a spoonful of posole into his mouth. "It isn't uncommon for the Navajo to give their male children female names because theirs is a matriarchal society. It is unusual, however, among the Apache. As I said, my parents were different. If it's more convenient, you can call me Two Knives. I don't use my Christian name, so don't ask me to tell you what it is."

"Do Apaches really live in teepees, Two Knives?" Noah asked.

Two Knives smiled. "The Jicarilla Apache and Kiowa Apache were buffalo hunters in the old days," he said, "and they lived in teepees made from buffalo skins. But most of the other Apache tribes lived in brush shelters called wickiups."

He stood up and walked to the dais, where he picked up a large photograph. He held it up so both Noah and Bud could see. It was a black-and-white picture of two Indian men standing next to a small, round hut covered with sticks and grass. "As you can see," he said, "a wickiup would simply be too small to hold fifteen or twenty tourists, so we use a teepee instead. It's just a small fib, really, and no one but you has ever asked."

Two Knives returned the photograph to the dais. "You would have no way of knowing this," he said, "but strangely enough, the word 'Apache' is not really an Apache word. It is a Pueblo Indian word, probably Zuni or perhaps Hopi, meaning 'enemy.' The Apache word for Apache is 'Inde' which simply means 'the people.'"

"Why did Pueblo Indians call the Apaches enemies?" Noah asked.

"Because we were," Two Knives said. "Apaches were hunters and warriors, not farmers. If a band of Inde needed corn to make tortillas, they took it from the Pueblo Indians. If they needed cattle or slaves, they stole the cows and kidnapped Pueblo people or even Spaniards, and then later, white settlers. It made little difference to the Inde if they killed the owners of the cattle or the families of the slaves in the process. Later, when they needed horses and rifles for war against the white people, they took them from the U.S. Army. Taking what they needed was much more efficient than trading, mainly because the Apache had nothing to trade with."

"Did the Apache like horses?" Noah asked. Horses were something he knew a little about.

"Indeed they did," Two Knives said. "Or at least they *needed* them. Apaches were ferocious and unforgiving combatants who could run fifty miles without stopping and without water. What they could not outrun, however, were the horses of the U.S. Army. They needed horses to compete equally in battle, so they stole them. Legend says they were excellent horsemen."

"Did the Apache really kill little children by slamming their heads against rocks?" Noah asked.

Two Knives threw back his head and laughed. "Ah, I see your uncle has been acquainting you with some of our charming Apache family customs," he said. "Unhappily, the Chiricahua Apache did occasionally bash captive white children's brains in by smashing their heads against hard surfaces, most commonly large sandstone boulders." He shrugged his shoulders and looked directly at Noah. "It was usually done to children who were being too noisy or asked too many foolish questions. They also stripped some of their captured enemies naked and then tied them spread-eagle over red ant hills and let the ants crawl into their bodily orifices and eat their fill, but as far as I know, neither custom has been practiced in the past several years."

When they finished eating and had placed their dirty bowls and spoons in a box underneath the table, Two Knives led the way outside to one of the larger sheds. When he opened the door, Noah could see row after row of bulging gunnysacks, each with a red, yellow, or green tag hanging from its mouth. The robust odor of the chile was almost overwhelming.

"Green is for mild," the Indian explained, "which means it won't burn your mouth at all. Yellow means medium, which for the weak at heart is still much too spicy. True chile aficionados such as your uncle demand only the bags with the red tags. Red-tag chile is fiery hot—not just the seeds, but the meat of the chile itself. If you or I ate a pod from one of those bags, we might possibly have to have our tongues amputated."

"An' thet's jest fine with me," Bud chimed in. "Thet means more fer yers truly." He stuck his head in the doorway of the chile shed and took a deep breath. "We'll take three sacks of them red tags."

Two Knives picked up a red-tagged bag and handed it to Noah. He handed another to Bud and then took one himself. By the time they had walked to the Studebaker and dumped the sacks into the back, Noah's eyes were burning from just the smell coming from the sack he was carrying. Bud took his wallet out of his front overall pocket, but Two Knives shook his head vehemently and told him to put it away.

"You know I will never accept your wampum, Clarence," he said, "and I would thoroughly appreciate the gesture if you would simply stop offering. Whatever I have is yours for the asking."

"A man oughta be able to pay fer his own dang chile," Bud said, but he put his wallet away and shook Two Knives's hand.

The Indian looked at Noah and smiled. "I owe your uncle a great debt," he said, "one that I can never repay. But I'll let him provide an explanation if he wishes. In the meantime, come back anytime. You'll always be welcome on the Apache reservation, even if you do ask a lot of questions."

————————

As they drove slowly down the mountain toward Tularosa, Noah thought about what he had learned from Two Knives and then about the Indians he had seen at the bus station the day he and his mother first arrived. He asked Bud if the bus station Indians had been Apaches.

"Naw, them fellas is kinda make-believe Indians from down in El Paso," Bud said. "They come up once a week er so an' sell cheap stuff to the tourists. Most a what they sell is jest plain junk."

Noah badly wanted to know what the "great debt" was owed to his uncle by Two Knives, but he wasn't sure Bud would tell him. Still, he had nothing to lose by asking. The worst that could happen was that his uncle would tell him to mind his own "beeswax."

"S'pose ya wanna know why Two Knives won't let me pay fer nothin'?" Bud asked before Noah could get the question out of his mouth. "Well, it weren't much an' I wish he'd stop claimin' it was." He paused for a moment as if trying to decide where to begin.

"This here's whatcha gotta remember, Bub, an' yer ma probably ain't never gonna tell you, so's I will. Ever' thing on this earth was put here to be ate by somethin' or to do the eatin'. If you got any say-so in the matter, you dang sure wanna be the one thet's doin' the eatin' an' not the one what's gettin' ate."

Bud reached down under the seat and got another beer. He told Noah to steer while he opened it with his pocket opener.

"Two Knives is a nice feller, but a couple a years back, he got hisself in the kinda fix where he was gonna git ate. Happened over by Hot Springs on a back road thet leads up into the mountains an' goes all the way across the Black Range to Silver City. I was out huntin' rabbits an' my shotgun was sittin' in the seat next to me, an' I come around a corner an' there was a couple a cars parked in a wide spot. First thing I saw was four fellas kickin' this other fella on the ground."

Bud took a swig of beer to keep his throat moist. "Sure didn't seem like much of a fair fight, so's I pulled up behind the cars an' grabbed my shotgun and got out. 'Bout that time, the four thet was doin' the kickin' started yellin' fer me to git. I told 'em I wasn't goin' nowhere and mebbe they oughta move on back a ways."

Bud shook his head. "Man's gotta be purty dang stupid to go after somebody holdin' a shotgun, an' if brains was dynamite, them fellas didn't have enough between 'em to blow their nose 'cause thet's jest what they did. Here they come, runnin' over toward the truck, yellin' and shakin' their fists like they was the biggest, meanest monkeys in the tree! Gun wasn't loaded with nothin' but bird pellets, so I shot two of 'em in the ankles an' was gonna shoot the other two, but they turned tail and skedaddled so fast they was blowin' smoke outta their bee-hinds."

Noah started laughing as he tried to form the picture in his mind. Bud took another swig of beer and continued.

"Well, the fella they was kickin' was Two Knives. He was bleedin' like a stuck pig, but he said he could drive if I could help 'em git in his car. Didn't bother to check on them two I shot 'cause they was moanin' so loud I knew they wasn't dead, but I blew out all four tires on their car, jest in case. Anyways, Two Knives drove hisself to the hospital in Hot Springs with me followin' along, and that's purty much the end of the story."

"Why were those men kicking him?" Noah asked.

Again Bud paused to consider his next statement. "Listen, Bub, 'member what I said about there bein' a buncha real bad cusses out there in the world? Well, these was some of 'em. Two Knives told me he'd been over to Silver City visitin' friends and figgered he'd take the long way home through the mountains. Said he'd stopped jest to look at some flowers an' these four pulled in an' started beatin' on 'em fer no reason. Mebbe they didn't like Indians or mebbe they jest wanted to beat somethin' up." Bud shrugged. "Neither one's much of a reason fer dang near killin' somebody."

"Did you tell the sheriff?" Noah asked.

"Nope, didn't tell nobody nothin' 'cause thet's the way Two Knives wanted it. He told the doctor he'd got throwed off his horse and hit a tree. When they patched 'em up, I drove 'em back to the reservation an' got one of his friends to keep an eye on 'em. Two other friends drove over an' got his car the next day. Ever since then, my money jest ain't no good when he's around."

"What happened to them?" Noah asked. "I mean the people who beat Two Knives up."

"Didn't much care what happened to 'em an' neither did Two Knives. Two of 'em probably had lots of trouble gittin' round fer a while, though. Mebbe next time they's out lookin' to beat somebody up, they'll 'member what happened to 'em last time."

"I like him," Noah said. "Two Knives, I mean. He talks a lot, but at least he has something to say."

"I like 'em, too," Bud said. He threw the empty beer bottle out of the Studebaker's window and reached under the seat for another. "Now let's you an' me git thet chile home an' roastin' 'fore I start havin' the 'I ain't had no chile this mornin'' heebie-jeebies."

15

When Army Lawyers Are Outlawed, Only Outlaws Will Need Army Lawyers

Theres an old Apache folktale about roadrunners that Inde mothers tell their papooses when they're trying to get them to take their naps. The story has different twists and turns in different Apache clans and families, but it generally goes like this:

One day, when everything was new, Roadrunner was sitting on a tree stump in the vast Chihuahuan Desert, watching the world go by. Every time an animal of any sort would pass his stump, Roadrunner would chatter out the animal's name and ask him what he was doing. He did this because he knew many, many things. He knew many, many things because roadrunners can run very fast, and very fast runners can be in ten places at once. If roadrunners can be in ten places at once, they see many things and can be very helpful to those who, by nature, are not so fast.

Roadrunner was watching the world from his stump when a stubblybuk passed by, tilted at a forty-five-degree angle on his oddly formed legs. Roadrunner chattered out, "Stubblybuk, I see you and I hear you. What are you doing?"

"I'm looking for food," the stubblybuk said, "but it has been a dry summer, and I can't find any. Can you help me?"

Roadrunner thought for a moment. "I saw a very generous patch of fairynipples this morning growing on the side of a hill down by the canyon," he said, and he gave the grateful creature directions to the patch of tasty delectables.

A raccoon soon passed by, and Roadrunner again chattered out, "Raccoon, I see you and I hear you. What are you doing?"

"I'm searching for my children," said Raccoon. "All four of them started chasing butterflies this morning, and they wandered away from our den and now they're lost. Can you help me?"

Roadrunner thought for a moment. "I saw your babies not twenty minutes ago by a large mesquite bush on the hill, gnawing on an old jackalope carcass," he said, and he told Raccoon how to find her children.

After a while, a grizzly bear passed by, and Roadrunner chattered out, "Grizzly Bear, I see you and I hear you. What are you doing?"

"I'm bored and I'm looking for ground squirrels to chase," Grizzly Bear said. "Can you help me?"

Roadrunner thought for a moment. "There were two ground squirrels playing tag near the cactus forest about an hour ago," he said. "They asked me if I had seen a bear they could hide from." He gave Grizzly Bear directions to the spot and wished him luck. He silently wished the ground squirrels luck as well because they would become a midmorning snack if the bear caught them.

Soon, a tall, ferocious-looking Apache hunter with a bow and a quiver of flint-tipped arrows passed by the roadrunner's stump. Roadrunner chattered out, "Inde Hunter, I see you and hear you. What are you doing?"

"I'm hunting roadrunners," the Apache said, "and I haven't seen any this morning. Can you help me?"

"Why are you hunting roadrunners?" Roadrunner asked, a bit taken aback.

"I want to eat one so that his spirit can join with my spirit, and then I, too, can run very fast and be in ten places at once. And then, when I can be in ten places at once, I'll know many, many things, and I can be helpful to everyone and probably become the chief of my tribe."

Roadrunner considered what the tall, ferocious-looking Apache had said. "Inde Hunter," he finally chattered, "I'm a roadrunner, and you can eat me if you can catch me." With that, Roadrunner put his long, slender legs into high gear and dashed away so fast that the hunter saw only a flash of rusty brown flying across the desert floor. Unfortunately, Roadrunner was watching the hunter over his shoulder as he ran and didn't see the large sandstone boulder in front of him. He struck the rock so hard that his head went flying one way and his body, the other.

"Stupid bird," the Apache said to himself, shaking his head and flicking bloody pieces of meat and brains off his leather jerkin with a forefinger. "Only a roadrunner is dumb enough to think that anyone might ever want to eat such a worthless creature. I'm sure he would taste like stale kangaroo rat droppings, and besides that, I'm allergic to feathers." Satisfied with his little joke and happy to be rid of the chatterbox roadrunner that continually frightened off all the game in the area, the Apache hunter went back to his search for a stubblybuk or bear or a raccoon to shoot with his bow so that his family could have supper that night. "Swift the roadrunner may be," he said to himself as he walked away into the desert, "but he can't outrun a sandstone boulder." The Apache took a last look at the cloud of feathers that was just then settling onto the desert dust and shook his head. "He sure as hell ain't the sharpest arrow in the quiver, either."

The law of eminent domain—known as "compulsory purchase" in Great Britain and New Zealand, "compulsory acquisition" in Australia, and "expropriation" in Canada and South Africa—is the inherent power of a state to seize private property from its residents with due monetary compensation but without the owners' consent. It is a law that has been invoked numerous times in numerous places and is despised by just about everyone except the party that did the invoking. The people who crafted the law were not the sharpest arrows in the quiver either, but once it was crafted and invoked, not even a roadrunner—swift as he is—could escape eminent domain's tentacles if he happened to be the invokee.

"Here's what I figger," Marvin said, kicking Jake up alongside Brimstone. "I figger thet if you an' yer ma an' yer uncle don't want to leave yer house, then the army cain't make you leave 'cause the only thing they could do if you didn't was to shoot you er haul you off to jail, and they cain't do thet 'cause they ain't got no jails an' it's against the law to shoot people thet ain't in the army."

Bud had said not to worry about the whole "eminent domain" thing, and Noah was trying his best—with a lot of help from Marvin—not to. Marvin was philosophizing again, and it was difficult to concentrate on worrying about anything while he was prattling on.

"How do you know the army doesn't have jails?" Noah said.

"Jest common sense," Marvin said. "Who'd they put in 'em if they had any? Army ain't s'posed to arrest nobody thet ain't in the army 'cause thet's against the law, too. Least thet's what Pa says. Pa tol' me thet if yer in the army an' you do somethin' bad enough to git arrested for, they'll jest line you up against a wall somewheres and—*pow!*—they shoot you! Thet way they don't have to worry 'bout you doin' nothin' bad more'n once."

It was the last of August—more than a month since the army lawyers had visited the ranch—and nothing more had been heard from them or anyone else. The previous day, Noah and Marvin had helped Bud drive the now fattened and lazy Brahma herd out of the hay pasture and into a large cattle truck that was waiting at the highway intersection. The steers had cooperated without complaint or incident and were presently awaiting their future as round steak and taco meat at a slaughter house near El Paso. The driver had handed Bud a check for twelve hundred dollars for the cattle, and Bud had given the boys twenty dollars each for their help. Marvin suggested they ride to Tularosa the next day, stop and celebrate at Tastee-Freez, and then visit LaDonna at her parent's dairy ranch on the south side of town.

"I don't think the army shoots people just because they did something to get arrested for," Noah said. He reined Brimstone way over to the right edge of the highway shoulder so that Marvin and Jake could ride alongside them without getting hit by a cotton truck. Noah was mounted on his beautiful new rodeo saddle, and the comfort difference between it and the old Mexican saddle he had been using since Brimstone's arrival was huge. "Have you ever heard of anyone getting shot by the army?"

"Hunnerds a times," Marvin said without hesitation. "'Member all them Krauts an' Japs they kilt? Army kin do anythin' they want 'cept to shoot people thet ain't in the army or ain't Krauts an' Japs. Cain't throw 'em in jail neither 'cause they ain't got none."

They had ridden about a mile along the highway south of Tularosa. The land here was less desert-like and more agricultural than it was to the north; much of it was blanketed with irrigated fields of mature cotton and ripe corn. They had seen two rattle-snakes on the trip so far, both of them squashed flat on the highway.

"Dang snakes is ever'where," Marvin had commented as they gave the reptiles a wide birth so that Jake and Brimstone wouldn't spook at the smell. "Pa says don't ever put yer boots on less you shake 'em first 'cause a rattler might of crawled in 'em lookin' fer a mouse to eat."

"How far to LaDonna's?" Noah asked.

"Right yonder," Marvin said. He pointed ahead and to the right to a large, white house surrounded by trees that sat back several hundred yards from the highway. A sizable white barn and two or three smaller ones stood behind the house. There were dozens of dairy cattle grazing in the adjacent pastures. "Dang nice place, too," Marvin added.

As they trotted down the long driveway, Noah could see that the Hawthornes' ranch was manicured and well kept. The lawn in the front yard had been newly mowed, and there were flowers growing in raised beds along the edges of both the yard and driveway. LaDonna was on the shaded front porch with a watering can in one hand.

"Hey, moos!" she shouted happily when they got close enough to hear. "I was really hoping someone would come and save me from slow death by boredom."

"Hey yourself!" Noah shouted back. "I bet you just mooed the lawn. It looks really nice."

LaDonna laughed and came down off the porch and into the driveway. She scratched Brimstone's muzzle with her fingernails, and the mule smiled and clacked his teeth like he had when Noah had first climbed on his back. "You're such a sweetheart," she said in her low, soft voice, switching her fingertip to the soft skin just above the mule's eye and rubbing the spot gently back and forth. Brimstone leaned sideways and gave a long sigh. Noah caught just the slightest hint of a fragrant perfume that reminded him strangely of an open meadow filled with wildflowers. His mother had told him once that perfumes weren't supposed to shout at you as you walked by; instead, they were supposed to whisper "come closer, come closer." LaDonna had certainly gotten it right.

"You can tie Jake and Brimstone in the shade," she said, pointing to a large Russian olive tree growing alongside the driveway. "My mom just made some really good lemonade, and I bet you two are thirsty."

Suddenly, LaDonna stopped talking. She turned and ran inside and returned a few moments later carrying a pad and pencil. She put her finger to her lips asking for silence, then sat down on the porch swing and began writing. Two or three minutes later, she looked up and grinned.

"I wrote another poem," she said, glancing first at Noah and then at Marvin. "Want me to read it?" Without waiting for an answer, LaDonna cleared her throat and began to read in her soft, melodic voice:

Along came a cowboy
on a horse made from dreams;
his eyes filled with stardust,
his head full of schemes.
His name, it was Childhood;
his journey, quite brief.
Ride along, little cowboy,
'cause time is a thief.

"Did that come from your little green demon?" Noah asked. "It's really good."

LaDonna nodded. "I told you, things just pop into my head from out of nowhere."

"Cowboys don't ride horses made of nothin' but meat, bones, an' hide," Marvin said, unimpressed. "An' there ain't nobody named 'childhood,' neither."

"It's not a poem about a real cowboy," LaDonna said patiently. "It's about how life changes every day even though it doesn't seem to change at all. Didn't you ever wonder why you can only be fourteen once instead of twice or three times? Or why tomorrow never comes because when it gets here, it's always today and tomorrow is still out there in front of you where it always was?" She patted Marvin's shoulder softly. "Sometimes you have to turn words into pictures in your mind and let them take you where they want to."

Marvin looked confused, and LaDonna changed the subject with no transition sentence whatsoever. Noah could almost hear the cogs in her head mesh smoothly together as she double-clutched the conversation in a different direction. "Who are your heroes?" she asked. "Who do you really admire?"

"Ain't got no heroes," Marvin said. "Least I cain't think a none."

"You must have heroes," LaDonna said. "Everybody has heroes. Don't you read comic books? Robin has Batman, Tess Trueheart has Dick Tracy, Jimmy Olsen has Superman. . . . I could name twenty more."

She folded her hands in her lap and closed her eyes like she was about to recite another poem.

"Ernest Hemingway said that it's harder to find heroes as you get older, but they're still necessary. Everyone should have heroes whether they're young or old or in the middle. All of us need someone to look up to and respect."

"Who's Ernest Hemingway?" asked Marvin. "An' what heroes does Batman and Dick Tracy and Superman look up to?"

LaDonna's eyes popped open, and she gave Marvin a tolerant smile.

"Ernest Hemingway is a famous author," she said. "He's written all kinds of wonderful books about heroes, so he should know what he's talking about. And Batman and Dick Tracy and Superman don't have heroes because there's nobody they *can* look up to, so they'll probably die mean, lonely old men with no friends at all to bury them or care that they're gone."

"Still cain't think of no heroes," Marvin said.

"How about your dad?" Noah chimed in. "You're always saying nice things about him. How he does this and how he says that and how he knows something else."

Marvin considered Noah's question. "Hadn't even thought of Pa," he said. "S'pose he's kinda my hero, least when he ain't yellin' at me to clean up my room or help Ma with the dishes."

"I knew it," LaDonna said smugly. She turned to Noah. "I bet I can guess who yours are."

"I've never thought much about it," Noah said. "My dad died ten years ago, so I can't use him, and Uncle Bud isn't exactly the hero type. My mom would probably say he's more heathen than hero."

"I'll bet you think the Lone Ranger and Marshal Matt Dillon are heroes," she said, "and probably Gene Autry and Red Ryder and Hopalong Cassidy and Lash LaRue and John Wayne." She ticked the names off her fingers like she was counting cows in a field.

Noah grinned, impressed with LaDonna's knowledge of Hollywood cowboys. "Well they all have pretty good comic books and make good western movies," he admitted. "Who are *your* heroes?"

LaDonna didn't hesitate. "Anyone with a brain and something interesting to say," she said. "Right now, I'm reading Ernest Hemingway. He's kind of old, but he's really talented. Have either of you read *The Old Man and the Sea*?"

Noah and Marvin shook their heads.

"You'll probably read it in school this year. I have three copies, so if you want to borrow one, you can."

The three of them spent the next two hours sitting on the porch swing, sipping ice-cold lemonade and talking about everything from the upcoming school year to Zefo and his fall into infamy at the Ranger. Noah told LaDonna about the visit a month earlier from the White Sands lawyers, the process of eminent domain, and the possibility that the army might try to take the ranch.

"What's your uncle going to do?" she asked. "He should buy a rifle and fight them off."

"He already has a rifle," Noah said. "But I don't think my mom would let him shoot anybody. Bud said we'll just wait and see what happens before we skin the cat."

"What cat?" LaDonna asked. "Why would your uncle want to skin a cat?" She didn't wait for an answer. "My Dad had a run-in with the army at White Sands once. They wouldn't let our milk trucks deliver on the base because we mostly used drivers from Mexico, and they didn't have security clearances. They couldn't get them either because they weren't Americans. Dad finally had to hire a white American man to deliver the milk on the base all the time." She set her glass on the floor of the porch. "And speaking of Mexico, let's go talk to my friend Manuelo. He's a bracero."

"What's a bracero?" Noah asked.

"Thet's one of them things my ma wears on her . . . thet's somethin' my ma wears," Marvin said. "Why'd we want to talk to one of them for?"

"That's a brassiere, silly," LaDonna said, giggling. "Braceros are farm workers from Mexico who work in America. They can only stay here for a little while, and they can't bring their families. Manuelo told me he makes lots more money here than he could ever make in Mexico, but he only gets to see his wife and children every six months. He said he gets really lonely sometimes."

LaDonna invited Noah and Marvin into the Hawthorne's large, cool house, and the boys said hello to her friendly and talkative parents, who were drinking coffee in the kitchen. They went straight out the back door and walked to the nearest of the smaller barns. Inside, Measles was in a stall by herself, as were several other riding horses. LaDonna opened the stall door of a small, liver-colored roan with four white socks and a large white patch on his rump.

"This is Goose," she said. "He's the one I ride when I don't want bugs on my teeth." She grinned and slipped a bridle over Goose's ears and fastened the neck and chin straps. She led him out of the barn and around the house and into the front yard where Jake and Brimstone were tied. Once in the driveway, she entwined her fingers in the horse's mane and with one smooth motion swung effortlessly onto his bare back.

"Wish I could do thet," Marvin said, as he clawed and grunted his way onto Jake's saddle.

"Your jeans are too tight," LaDonna said, "and you need a smaller horse."

The three of them rode back up the driveway to the highway then turned north toward Tularosa. Two hundred yards from the Hawthorne ranch, they turned left on a rutty farm road that led into a large field of ready-to-be-picked cotton. The view across the field was as if someone had sprinkled each tall, green plant with oversized white marshmallows. A small, dark-faced man wearing dirty white clothing and a frayed straw cowboy hat was stooped over between two rows of cotton plants, dragging a long canvas sack between his legs. As he moved forward, both hands were blurs as he plucked the cotton out of the bolls and dropped it into the mouth of the sack. When they reached the edge of the field where the man was working, they stopped and dismounted.

"¿Cómo estás, Manuelo?" LaDonna said to the man as he stood upright. "¿Hace mucho calor, sí?"

"Sí, señorita," the man said, smiling, "mucho calor." He removed his sweat-stained straw cowboy hat and wiped his brow on a dirty sleeve. Noah noticed that the backs of his hands were bloody. "Su español es muy bueno."

"Gracias, señor," La Donna said. "This is Manuelo from Hermosillo. It's a big city in Mexico." She gestured at Marvin and Noah. "Estos son mis amigos de la puebla."

Noah waved and said hi. Marvin nodded but looked at the Mexican with suspicion, trying to pigeonhole him in one of his people categories.

"He told me my Spanish is pretty good," La Donna said, "and I told him you were my friends from Tularosa."

"How much cotton does he pick in a day?" Noah asked. "It looks like really hard work."

"He once told me he picks four to five hundred pounds every day," LaDonna said. "Each sack holds about a hundred pounds if he packs it in. He gets paid three dollars for every sack he picks, and he works six days a week."

"Why are his hands bloody?"

"Cotton bolls are hard, and they have really sharp spikes," LaDonna answered. She carefully pulled one off a plant and handed it to Noah. The white cotton inside was soft and fluffy, but the spikes on the boll itself were sharp as cactus spines.

"¿Quieres probar la pizca del algodon?" Manuelo asked Noah. "Es mucho trabájo."

"Manuelo wants to know if you want to try picking," LaDonna translated. "He says it's a lot of work."

The Mexican untied the wide cotton-sack straps from around his waist and stepped over the bag into the next row. He motioned for Noah to straddle the sack, and then he tied the straps around Noah's hips with the sack's mouth gaping open between his legs. Manuelo showed him how to carefully pluck the white cotton fluff from the boll without getting plant leaves or snapping off the boll itself, then he stepped back and lit an evil-smelling cigarette he took from a crumpled pack in his shirt pocket.

"*Bueno*," he said. "*Comenzar*."

Noah stooped over and tried to pull a handful of cotton from the nearest boll. Immediately he felt a stab of pain as one of the spikes punctured his finger. He was more careful the second time and managed to pull the cotton out of several bolls without further injury, but when he attempted to step forward up the row to the next plant, he couldn't budge the nearly full cotton sack dragging between his legs.

Manuelo laughed and rattled off several rapid-fire sentences to LaDonna in Spanish.

"I think he said you should stick to being a boy and leave the real work to old men like him." She took a tissue out of the pocket of her jeans and dabbed Noah's bleeding finger. "You need to stop anyway if you don't want to bleed to death before you get home."

It was nearly noon when Marvin and Noah told LaDonna good-bye and started back toward town, and almost two o'clock when Noah rode Brimstone down off the rise above the ranch and into the yard. Deputy Mendoza's white patrol cruiser and a dark blue New Mexico State Police sedan were parked next to Bud's pickup. With a knot in his stomach, Noah dismounted and led the mule inside the barn in the shade and tied him to a post. He pulled off Brimstone's saddle and sweat pad and hung them over a rail on one of the stalls. At that moment, Deputy Mendoza and a tall state police officer dressed in a dark blue uniform came out of the house. When they spotted Noah, they walked across the yard to the barn. The state policeman kept glancing over his shoulder at the ranch house as though he feared being shot from ambush at any moment.

"Hi, Deputy Mendoza," Noah said. He looked at the other officer, but no introduction was forthcoming. "Why do I get the feeling you didn't come all the way out here to drink coffee?"

"I wish I had," the deputy said. "Noah, this is kind of important, so listen carefully. You and your mother need to talk some sense into your uncle before he does something stupid."

"Sense about what?" Noah asked. "Is this about the army wanting to take the ranch?"

"Unfortunately, it is," Deputy Mendoza said. "Your uncle told me you already know what's happening, so I won't explain, but here's the lowdown. The army made Clarence a fair offer for this place, and he turned them down. Yesterday, government lawyers filed a Declaration of Condemnation under the eminent domain law with the state of New Mexico. We delivered the notice to your uncle just now. There's a hearing in front of a judge tomorrow morning at nine o'clock. It's at the courthouse in Alamogordo, and your uncle needs to be there. He'll have a chance to speak on his own behalf and try to convince the judge to dismiss the case."

"What does 'condemnation' mean?" Noah asked, struggling with the word.

"It's complicated," the deputy said. "The land that White Sands Proving Ground sits on is leased from the state of New Mexico by the army. Because of all the rocket testing that's been going on, the army has asked the state to say that no one can live here because it's too dangerous. In other words, they want your uncle's ranch condemned. If a state judge signs the declaration, it means that you'll have to pack up your belongings and leave."

"What happens if we don't leave?" Noah asked. "Can the army just kick somebody out of their house for no reason?"

The state police officer finally spoke up. "No one wants to kick anybody anywhere, son, but the law says if you don't leave on your own, we have to make you leave. It's an unpopular law that nobody likes, but it's still the law, and if a judge tells us to evict you, then you'll get evicted."

"Your uncle says he won't move," Deputy Mendoza said, "and he says he won't go to the hearing tomorrow either. You're a smart kid. You need to convince him to at least go in front of the judge and say his piece." He glanced at the state police officer. "And if he loses, you need to convince him not to do anything dumb. Tell him to just buy another ranch somewhere else so that nobody gets hurt on this one."

"You don't know my uncle very well," Noah said. He walked past the two officers without speaking further and went into the house. Bud and Mrs. Odell were in the living room seated at the big table. A sheaf of official-looking papers was lying on the table between them. Noah pulled out a chair and sat down next to his uncle.

"You heard what them two had to say?" Bud asked, nodding toward the window. It was more of a statement than a question.

Noah could hear the two police cars leaving. "Deputy Mendoza told me he gave you the papers telling us we might have to leave."

Bud nodded again at the documents on the table. "Dang cat's meowin' at the back door," he said, scratching his unshaven face, "so's I guess it's gonna git skint."

Mrs. Odell put her hand on her brother's arm. "Clarence, I want you to go to that hearing tomorrow. Someone has to tell the army that this is our home and that they can't just take it away for no good reason."

"Mom's right," Noah said. "Deputy Mendoza says you have to go see the judge and fight."

"Deputy Mendoza's the one what jest give us the paper's tellin' us we gotta move," Bud said, pounding the stack of papers with his index finger. "What's he know 'bout this, anyways?" He got up and went into the kitchen. Noah heard the refrigerator open and close, and his uncle returned carrying an open bottle of beer.

"He's just doing his job," Noah said. "I think he's the one that has to make sure we leave—him and that state policeman."

"What about tomorrow, Clarence?" asked Mrs. Odell. "If you won't go to the hearing, I will. We have to stick up for ourselves at least."

"I'll go, too," Noah said. "It's better than just giving up."

Bud took a swig of beer and then wiped his mouth with his sleeve. "Yer both part a this wrench, an' you got a right to git in yer ten cents' worth," he said. "An' jest so's you know, I ain't gonna give up. Army wants this wrench, they'll git it when I'm deader'n a slow toad at a truck stop."

"Don't say silly things like that!" Mrs. Odell said. Her voice had a sharp edge to it that Noah had heard all too many times in the past. "Let's do things one at a time, and the first thing we have to do is to go to that hearing tomorrow."

Bud scratched an armpit and thought about it for a few moments. "Hokay," he said, "we'll go tell 'em our side." He chugalugged the rest of the beer in one long swallow. "Ain't gonna do no dang good though 'cause them army people done got their minds made up already."

BUD CAME OUT to breakfast the next morning looking almost presentable, considering the fact that he hadn't owned a suit or even a sports jacket since 1947 when he attended Carl Odell's funeral. He was dressed in clean bib overalls, a worn denim shirt with a frayed collar, and a wrinkled brown tie with pictures of apples and pears on it. He was clean shaven and had made a halfhearted attempt to shine his boots, albeit not very successfully. Mrs. Odell, dressed in a light green dress and a green hat, ordered him to remove the tie and brush the dust off his hat and not to even think about drinking a beer until after they returned from the courthouse. Noah wore his Sunday-best shirt and pants and his old school oxfords instead of boots. His mother had made him wash his haystack of hair the night before, and he had combed it down as best he could.

Before they left, Noah opened his battered copy of *Webster's International* and looked up "eminent domain." The definition was pretty much what the army lawyers had said it was, and Noah discovered that the United States wasn't the only country that had such a law. He flipped the pages to the *C* section and looked up "condemn." There were several definitions, but two caught Noah's eye. One was "To declare or judge unfit for use or habitation" and the other was "To appropriate (property) for public use." Noah read the definitions to Bud just to make sure his uncle knew what he was up against.

They took Mrs. Odell's Ford to Alamogordo instead of Bud's pickup so that Noah wouldn't be filthy and windblown from riding in the back. At the courthouse, an efficient-looking woman behind a desk pointed them toward the courtroom in which the hearing was to be held. The room was large and airy with a dozen rows of bench seats in the middle facing the judge's raised dais that sat against one wall. On one side of the dais was the New Mexico state flag with its big red sun and rays on a yellow background, and on the other, the American flag. When they entered, Noah was happily surprised to see not only Marvin and Mr. Couch standing inside the courtroom but LaDonna and both her parents as well.

While Bud and Mrs. Odell took seats in the front row of benches, Noah joined LaDonna and Marvin. "How did you know this was happening today?" he whispered. "I didn't have time to tell anyone."

"Deputy Mendoza told Marvin's dad after he left your house, and Mr. Couch told us about it when he delivered the milk last night," LaDonna whispered back. "My dad thought we should come and help out if we could."

"I'm really glad you're here," Noah said. "My uncle doesn't think anybody can help us, but I'm still glad you came."

At that moment, a sheriff's deputy entered the courtroom through a side door, and Noah made a dash for his seat between Bud and his mother. LaDonna and her family took seats in the back next to Marvin and his dad. Noah spotted the two lawyers from White Sands sitting behind a low table on the left side of the courtroom, and he saw Deputy Mendoza standing off to one side with his arms folded across his chest. There were a dozen other people seated in the courtroom, but Noah didn't know any of them.

The side door opened again, and a heavy-set man wearing a long, dark robe entered the room. "All rise," the deputy ordered. "The Twelfth Judicial District Court of Lincoln and Otero Counties is now in session, the Honorable Leon M. Capella presiding."

Judge Capella eased his considerable bulk into the chair behind the dais, lifting the hem of his robe up to his knees before sitting down. "Please be seated," he said. He picked up a sheaf of documents on the dais in front of him and studied them. After a few moments, he turned his attention back to the courtroom.

"I'll try to keep this as simple as possible," Judge Capella said. "A Declaration of Condemnation has been requested by the state of New Mexico for the ranch property of one Clarence William Boggs." The judge looked down at the papers in front of him. "Said property consists of a six-hundred-acre parcel of land, a six-room adobe house, a two-thousand-square-foot barn, and various outbuildings. It is located approximately five miles northwest of the Tularosa town limits. Mr. Boggs, are you now present?"

"I'm here, Yer Honor," Bud said, raising his hand. "This here's my sister and her boy."

The judge nodded soberly toward Noah and his mother, and then continued.

"This Declaration of Condemnation was requested from the state on behalf of the United States Army at White Sands Proving Ground. Spokesman and attorney for the army is Major Imah Paenin-Diaz. Major Paenin-Diaz, are you now present?"

The major stood up crisply. "It's pronounced *Ee-ma*, Your Honor, with a long *e*. And I'm present, Sir."

"Interesting name you got there, Major, but I'm sure you've heard that before. Please—"

"I'm a mixture of Swiss and Mexican," Major Paenin-Diaz interrupted, speaking more to the courtroom than to the judge. "My father is from Geneva, Switzerland, and my mother is from Juárez. I speak both Spanish and German fluently."

"Fine," Judge Capella said, giving the attorney a prickly look. "Glad you made all of us aware of your colorful family history. Now if it wouldn't be too much trouble, please give this court a brief summary of the army's position on this matter and the purpose for requesting a condemnation declaration." Judge Capella glanced at the thick stack of papers on the table in front of Major Paenin-Diaz. "And no lawyer gobbledygook. Keep it in layman's terms so we can all understand what you're talking about."

Major Paenin-Diaz nodded. "Your Honor, the Tularosa property in question owned by Mr. Boggs borders the present eastern boundary of White Sands Proving Ground. This land has just recently been leased from the Bureau of Land Management and, because of its proximity to residential areas, is not now and will not be used specifically for research or project testing. However, the army has determined that Mr. Boggs's ranch lies within the range of certain rocket-powered projectiles that are presently being tested in other areas of the Proving Ground. Some of these projectiles contain toxic gasses and therefore constitute a danger to human life."

Major Paenin-Diaz studied one of the documents in front of her. "The army has deemed that because Boggs Ranch lies within the range of these projectiles, anyone residing on Mr. Boggs's property could be in danger if an accidental impact occurred. To remedy this situation, the army proposed in good faith to buy the property in question. Mr. Boggs was offered fair and adequate compensation. He was also offered assistance moving household goods and livestock if he was willing to sell. Mr. Boggs declined both offers."

"Exactly what does 'accidental impact' mean, Major Paenin-Diaz?" Judge Capella interrupted.

"These are experimental rockets, Your Honor. Occasionally they go astray and land where they're not supposed to land."

"Do they blow up when they land?" the judge asked.

Major Paenin-Diaz bent down and conferred with Lieutenant Apodoca. "Your Honor," she said after a few moments, "I honestly don't know if they carry explosives, and I'm afraid I couldn't answer the question if I did know because of national security issues."

"How much was the 'fair and adequate compensation' that was offered to Mr. Boggs?" Judge Capella asked.

"Ten thousand dollars," the major said. "According to local real estate values, the amount is almost twice what the property is worth."

"And what further arrangements has the army made concerning this compensation?"

"A savings account has been opened at the First National Bank of Alamogordo in the name of Clarence William Boggs, Your Honor. The compensation has been deposited into that account. Mr. Boggs will be provided with immediate access to the funds upon legal transfer of the deed to the state of New Mexico for the property in question."

The judge had no further questions. He motioned for Major Paenin-Diaz to be seated and looked at Bud.

"Mr. Boggs, I want you to clearly understand the law in this case. The army claims that you and your family could be injured or killed by falling military rockets if you continue to live on your ranch. Consequently, the state of New Mexico has the right, under eminent domain, to condemn your ranch as unfit for human habitation if you refuse to sell voluntarily, and to evict you and your family. Can you show good cause why this court should not sign the declaration to condemn your ranch?"

Bud removed his hat and stood up. Noah could see the dribbles of sweat rolling down his uncle's forehead.

"Yer Honor, I ain't got much to say 'bout this 'cause there ain't much anybody *kin* say. Ever' person in this room knows thet it jest ain't right fer one fella to steal somethin' from another fella thet don't belong to 'em, rockets er no rockets. In the old days, people thet stole things from other people was called 'outlaws,' and most of 'em got hung a long time ago." Bud looked over at Major Paenin-Diaz. "An' if them dang rockets is so dang dangerous, the army ain't got no dang business shootin' 'em off where they're gonna land on people anyways."

"Here, here!" someone in the rear of the courtroom said loudly. Noah thought it sounded like Mr. Couch.

The judge picked up a wooden gavel and softly tapped the dais. "Please continue, Mr. Boggs," he said.

Bud thought for a long moment before he spoke. "I was brung up to think thet if you worked hard an' kept yer nose clean, an' didn't break no laws—er leastwise not many—then whatever you done in yer life wasn't nobody's business 'cept yer own. Ain't nobody s'posed ta come along an' jest take what's yers jest 'cause they're in the army. If I was to take one a them tanks they got out there, they'd throw me in the hoosegow faster'n spit kin roll down a straw."

"Here, here, here!" several people shouted in unison. "They'd shoot you, thet's what!" Noah heard Marvin yell. The courtroom crowd broke into laughter and then applause. Again, the judge tapped his gavel on the table.

"I'll ask that visitors in this courtroom please remain silent," he said, trying to hide a smile. "Go ahead, Mr. Boggs."

"Ain't got no more to say, Yer Honor, 'cept this. Tryin' to git me off muh wrench is gonna be 'bout as easy as squeezin' butter outta roadrunner turds, I kin promise you thet."

Laughter and applause again broke out in the back of the courtroom, and the judge pounded the dais hard with his gavel this time. "Are you saying that you will refuse to abide by the authority and decision of this court?"

Bud glanced over at Deputy Mendoza. "I ain't got nothin' else to say 'bout nothin', Yer Honor." He replaced his hat and sat down.

The judge shuffled through the papers in front of him. He stared at the two army officers and then looked back at Bud. "Frankly, Mr. Boggs," he said, "I think this whole thing stinks. You were absolutely right when you said the act of stealing someone else's property used to be a hanging offense." He gave Major Paenin-Diaz another prickly stare. "But this is not the Old West and the state of New Mexico, in all its wisdom, has given me no other choice but to sign this Declaration of Condemnation that lies here before me." Judge Capella picked up a pen lying on the dais and scribbled his name at the bottom of the document. "Mr. Boggs, you and your family have two weeks to vacate the property in question, or you will be physically evicted by law enforcement officers. Please believe me when I say that I desperately hope you choose to leave."

16

Who's the Damn Fool
in the Outhouse with a Shotgun?

Once upon a time, a coyote was trotting through the sandy wilderness of the Chihuahuan Desert, gingerly hopping this way and tip-toeing that way so it wouldn't get a cactus spine or a mesquite thorn stuck in its paw. If the coyote got a spine or thorn stuck in its paw and couldn't pull it out with its teeth, it wouldn't be able to run. If it couldn't run, it couldn't catch a jackrabbit or jackalope or even a wide-footed pocket mouse for supper and therefore would go hungry. If it went hungry for very long, it would starve to death. Life was not a pleasant prospect for a coyote in the Chihuahuan Desert with a cactus spine or mesquite thorn stuck in its paw.

The sun was shining down brightly and hotly on this particular day, and the coyote was feeling parched.

"It would really be pleasant if a cloud floated across the sun and offered me some shade," the coyote said out loud to no one in particular.

At that very moment, a small cloud squirted into the sky from out of nowhere and covered the sun so that the coyote was walking in the shade. Clouds seldom showed their fluffy faces in this part of the Chihuahuan Desert, and it was a wonderful feeling. Nonetheless, the coyote wasn't satisfied.

"It would be even *more* pleasant," it said, again to no one in particular, "if an entire *sky* full of clouds would come by for a visit and provide shade for every living thing in the desert." The coyote thought about what it had just said. "At least for an hour or so," it added, realizing that a permanent sky full of clouds might not be such a good idea.

A few seconds later, the coyote looked up and saw dozens and dozens of huge, dark clouds sailing toward him. Soon, the blue desert sky was covered from horizon to horizon with clouds, and the entire desert basked in shade. Still, the coyote wasn't satisfied.

"I'm still hot," it complained loudly. "I really would like some rain to cool the desert floor and make the jackrabbits and jackalopes and mice come out of their holes so that they're easier to catch. I know it never rains in this part of the Chihuahuan Desert, but still, some rain would be *muy buenisimo.*"

Within a minute, the first rain drops began to fall from the cloudy sky. They fell until the sand was damp and cool and dozens of jackrabbits and several jackalopes and hundreds of mice and even a few western diamondback rattlesnakes and at least one Gila monster had left their holes and were frolicking among the cactus and greasewood like children at a birthday party. It's a coyote's nature, however, never to be satisfied.

"I would like a river to wash my paws in before I eat," this coyote said, feeling empowered. "And make it a big one because I've never seen a river, and I think it's time I expanded my knowledge of the natural world."

Quickly it began to rain harder and harder and harder. Suddenly a huge wall of muddy water came thundering down the arroyo in which the coyote was standing. He was bowled over and slammed time and again into the sand as the torrent tumbled him head over paws down the gully. Within minutes, the coyote had drowned, and his limp, battered body had been flung up on a sandy hummock. The rain stopped and the clouds disappeared and the sun came out hotter than ever. A few hours later, the coyote's carcass had disappeared, and the local buzzards were picking their teeth with his bones.

"An' don't tell me buzzards ain't got no teeth neither," Bud grunted, "'cause you ain't never seen down the inside of a buzzard's food hole, so's you don't know snot from green peas."

He and Noah struggled to shoulder the heavy and very smelly outhouse a foot to the left so that it was in the exact middle of the driveway. They could move it just an inch at a time because of its weight, and then only with the greatest difficulty.

"Point a thet coyote story is this," Bud continued. "If you got enough a somethin' already, don't git greedy an' ask fer anymore. Army's got way more land than they'll ever use, an' they sure as hell ain't got no use fer ours, so somebody's gotta stand up an' bite 'em on the butt an' git their attention." He winked at Noah with his scarred eye. "Guess thet somebody's us."

The job of dragging the rickety outhouse from its original position behind the house to the top of the driveway had taken almost two hours. First, Bud had lifted each side with a heavy crowbar fulcrum while Noah placed a greased wooden fence post runner underneath. Next, they shackled a tow chain around the bottom, and then, using low gear on the pickup, Bud slowly and carefully pulled the structure forward. As one set of fence posts ended, Noah replaced it with another set, then hurriedly ran back to carry the first set forward. It was slow, repetitive work, but the privy moved along steadily without turning over. Now, it stood like a guard shack—one with a crescent moon cut in the doorway—in the middle of the driveway, just over the rise above the house. Bud's Studebaker and Mrs. Odell's Ford were parked in the dirt on either side of the structure, effectively blocking incoming or outgoing traffic. As Bud was positioning the Ford in the grass and bushes alongside the outhouse, Noah had first heard, and had then seen, a pair of small diamondback rattlers slithering rapidly out of the way.

Ten days had passed since Judge Capella's ruling declared Boggs Ranch to be officially condemned. The only representative of the court they had seen was an unhappy Deputy Mendoza. The day before, he had parked his cruiser at the railroad-tie gateposts and walked slowly to the house. Bud had met him in the yard, and the deputy had handed him a piece of paper.

"That's a copy of the judge's order of eviction," he said stiffly. "It'll happen on the morning of Thursday, September 11, at nine o'clock. That's four days from now. I hope you'll leave peaceably. If you don't, you'll be arrested and taken to jail and charged with obstruction." Without another word, the deputy turned around and walked back to his car.

At lunch, Bud had informed Mrs. Odell that she and Noah would need to leave the ranch on Wednesday afternoon at the latest. "You kin stay in one of them auto courts in Alamogordo till this thing gits fixed one way er tuther," he said.

His sister was having none of it. "Don't you be stupid, Clarence," she said. "We're not going anywhere. If you plan on staying, then we will, too."

"Cain't stay," Bud said. "You an' Bub gotta git somewheres safe, case there's any shootin'."

"Shooting!" she said sharply. "You aren't going to shoot anyone, and no one's going to shoot you. This ranch isn't worth anyone getting hurt, and you know it. So does the army. There are other ways of doing things that don't involve violence."

Bud scratched his stubble. "You got any good ideas, now's sure's hell the time to git 'em off yer chest," he said.

"I think we should tell Two Knives," Noah volunteered. "I'll bet he could help."

"I cain't leave ta tell 'em," Bud said. "I go sashayin' round out there, an' them police'll be here quicker'n a goose kin fart."

"I can go," Noah said. "I know how to drive."

"Forget it, Bub," his uncle said. "Probly ain't nothin' he could do anyways. An' I don't want him gettin' in no trouble 'cause of us."

"I have a couple of ideas," Mrs. Odell said. "They might not work, but at least they could slow things down a little." She explained to her brother what she wanted him to do. "And don't mention us leaving again," she said. "We'll all go or we'll all stay, but Noah and I won't leave you here alone."

Moving the outhouse and the cars to block the driveway had been Mrs. Odell's first idea. "Now the police won't be able to drive anywhere near the house," she told her brother when the job was finished. "And if they can't drive, that means they'll have to carry or drag us out of the house and up the hill if they want us out. We don't want to make it easy for them, do we?"

Her second idea involved sitting down at the living room table and writing two short notes on lined tablet paper. She placed each note into an envelope and then sealed them both closed. She wrote a name on each envelope and handed them to Noah.

"I want you and Brimstone to deliver these right now," she said, "and don't ask questions. I have to stay here with your uncle or I'd go myself. And if you see the sheriff, don't tell him what you're doing. Just say you're out looking for bottles or hunting for rattlesnakes or something silly like that."

Noah saddled his mule and did as he was told, though it took most of the afternoon. He didn't see anyone he knew except for the people whose names were on each envelope. There was no sign of Deputy Mendoza or the army, although Noah wasn't exactly sure what the army would be driving. If they arrived in tanks, the outhouse and the cars parked in the driveway certainly wouldn't be much of a barrier.

When he got back to the ranch, he found his uncle filling in the smelly pit over which the privy had sat with dirt from the hillside above the house. Using an old wheelbarrow, Bud was dumping each load of dirt as near to the hole as he could get it, and then shoveling it in with a mucking scoop. The odor coming from the four-foot-wide, ten-foot-deep pit was ferocious. It was so bad, in fact, that Bud had tied a red scarf over his nose and mouth just so he could get close enough to push the dirt in. Noah gave the hole a wide berth as he rode Brimstone toward the barn. He unsaddled the mule, put him in his stall, and then grabbed another shovel and went to help his uncle.

By the time they were finished, it was late afternoon, and Mrs. Odell had pot roast and boiled potatoes with butter waiting on the table. At supper, Bud didn't talk about what might happen in the next few days. All he seemed to have on his mind was cattle.

"What we gotta figger out is what kinda steers to git," Bud said. "Brahmas is good, but so's Herefords er Angus. We kin git Brahmas up on the reservation fer ten dollars a head an' Herefords fer fifteen. Ain't got no idea what them Angus'll cost. Probably more'n they're worth."

"How do we get them back to the ranch?" Noah asked. "Are we going to make another cattle drive?"

"Only if we ain't got nothin' better to do fer four days than starin' at cow bee-hinds," Bud said, "'cause we'd have to bring 'em down from Mescalero. Nope, we'll hire us a truck an' haul 'em down. Jest take an hour er two thet way."

Noah was frankly glad that the subject of eviction hadn't come up because he had other things to think about. He felt very strongly that Two Knives Anna Fork had to be told what was happening, and he knew he was the only one who was going to tell him. He had a plan, but whether or not he could pull it off remained to be seen. When supper was over, he helped with the dishes and then took a long, warm bath in the big metal tub in the bathroom. At nine o'clock, he faked a yawn, told his mother that he was tired and going to bed, and headed for his room. It was about to become a long night.

Noah waited until his alarm clock said midnight, then quietly climbed out of bed, closed his bedroom door, and got dressed in the dark. He was tired, and it hadn't been easy keeping his eyes open until he was sure everyone else was asleep. He had done so by jabbing his leg with a pair of dull scissors from his mother's sewing box every time he started to drop off.

Barefoot, but with a pair of high-tops tied around his neck, Noah crept to his window and pushed it open. He had made sure earlier that the runners were well oiled so they wouldn't squeak. Trying not to make even the tiniest noise, he carefully climbed through the window and eased himself to the ground, hoping he wouldn't land on a scorpion or a rattlesnake or any of a dozen other unpleasant critters that crawled or slithered across the Chihuahuan Desert floor at night. Thirty feet from the house, he stopped and put on his sneakers and tied the laces, and then, hunched over and being careful not to step on a patch of loose gravel, he crept up the driveway toward the outhouse and cars. Everything behind him seemed dark and peaceful, and the only sounds he could hear were the raspy chirping of desert crickets and the yipping and yelping of a pack of coyotes as they squabbled over a fresh kill off in the distance. When he reached the top of the driveway, Noah looked back once more, then took a deep breath, hitched up his pants, and set about what he knew he had to do.

———————

THE WEATHER AT 8:55 a.m. on the morning of Thursday, September 11, 1957, in the Chihuahuan Desert, near the town of Tularosa, New Mexico, was pretty much like the weather had been on a thousand other September 11 mornings at 8:55 a.m. The sky was cloudless and robin's egg blue, and the temperature was warm enough for a T-shirt. The high for the day probably wouldn't exceed ninety degrees, and that was certainly a blessing if you were picking cotton or searching for lost rockets out in the malpais or had to physically carry a bunch of people out of a house and throw them into a police car and haul them off to jail.

Deputy Mendoza wasn't paying much attention to the weather, and he couldn't have cared less if the sky was robin's egg blue or buzzard-butt black. He was in a cranky mood, in fact, wondering why he had ever become a deputy sheriff in the first place, especially one whose job it was to kick law-abiding citizens off their own property. The people who were following the deputy in the small convoy of vehicles that turned off the main highway onto the road that led to Boggs Ranch weren't paying much attention to the weather either. Two uniformed state policemen in the second car were wondering if anyone at Boggs Ranch was armed, and if so, would they surrender their weapons peacefully, or would they play it like Baby Face Nelson and go down in a hail of gunfire. In the military jeep behind the troopers, five army MPs were crudely discussing the rounded attributes of the brunette waitress who worked at the Little Green Men Bar & Grill in Alamogordo. Behind the jeep, an Army Corps of Engineers corporal driving a heavy, olive green flatbed truck with a forty-nine-ton Caterpillar D9 chained to its bed was wondering how long it would take him and his humongous yellow machine to turn a six-room, one-hundred-fifty-year-old adobe ranch house into a pile of dust once the furniture and personal belongings had been removed and piled in the yard by the MPs. The one-star general in charge of the eviction operation had insisted that no furniture and no personal belongings such as clothing, hats, shoes, books, or pictures were to be destroyed if it was possible to remove them. The corporal was guessing about an hour overall, twenty-five minutes for the obliteration of the house itself. And in an army sedan behind the bulldozer jockey, Major Paenin-Diaz and Lieutenant Apodoca were talking about the upcoming trial of an army master sergeant accused of beating up his aged mother because she wouldn't spit shine his shoes. The major allowed as how some elderly people were so cranky that they deserved a few whacks on occasion just to keep them in line, but in this case, because the woman was almost ninety, confined to a wheelchair, and probably didn't have any spit left to shine with, the master sergeant would more than likely spend a few months in the brig.

Deputy Mendoza was certainly not expecting to see what he saw as he drove through the railroad-tie gateposts below the crest of the hill that overlooked Boggs Ranch. Blocking the driveway fifty feet in front of his cruiser was a large wooden privy with a crescent moon carved in the door. A half-dozen automobiles, including Clarence Boggs's Studebaker and a small, yellow school bus, were parked on either side of the outhouse, effectively blocking passage to the ranch. Four teenagers—three of them dressed in jeans, boots, and T-shirts, and one wearing a set of pink bunny pajamas complete with ears and a fluffy white tail—were standing next to the privy, smiling and waving. Three of them, at least, were smiling and waving. The one in the bunny outfit was smiling and flailing, his arms windmilling around his head like helicopter blades. Tied to the outhouse door by a rope knotted around his waist, he would flail in one direction until he came to the end of his tether, then turn around and flail the other way until he was stopped again.

When Deputy Mendoza saw what he wasn't expecting to see, he stomped the brake pedal on his cruiser all the way to the floor, stopping so quickly that his head snapped forward and bounced off the steering wheel. The state police car and jeep behind him were able to stop in time, but the flatbed truck with the forty-nine-ton monkey on its back didn't have a prayer. With its brakes squealing, the truck slammed hard into the back of the jeep, causing it to jump forward six feet and crash into the back of the state police car, which in turn smashed into the back of Deputy Mendoza's cruiser. Lieutenant Apodoca barely avoided rear-ending the truck by frantically swerving off the driveway and into the deep desert sand. When the lieutenant put the car in reverse and tried to back out, the sedan immediately sunk to its axles.

"¿Dónde aprender a conducir?" Deputy Mendoza yelled loudly in Spanish at the state police car as he opened the driver's door of his cruiser and stumbled onto the driveway. "Don't they teach you *cabrones* how to stop in police school?"

The state policeman, at whom the deputy's ire was directed, was having trouble opening his door. "Jesus H. Christmastime!" he yelled, finally wrenching the door open by sheer will power. He pointed at the corporal who was behind the wheel of the jeep. "You learn to drive in a school for the blind, soldier?" The MP got out and pointed helplessly at the truck behind him. Then he pointed to the smashed-in backside on the jeep and looked like he wanted to cry. One rear tire was going flat, and the vehicle's rear bumper was shaped like a malformed pretzel.

The only person who wasn't yelling at something was the state policeman who had not been driving. One hand was on the handle of his holstered side arm and the other was on his hip, and he was staring hard at the wooden structure blocking the road.

"Who's the damn fool in the outhouse with a shotgun?" he asked.

At the word "shotgun," everyone suddenly stopped shouting. The other state policemen quickly crouched down behind the sheriff's car, and the MP corporal scuttled back into his jeep. Deputy Mendoza remained standing, starting at what looked like the barrel of a gun poking out of the crescent moon cut in the privy's door.

"Probably Mr. Boggs," Deputy Mendoza said. "I want everybody to just wait right here, and let me do the talking." Normally he couldn't order the state police or the army to do anything, but since the eviction fell under his jurisdiction, everyone else had been placed under his command.

The deputy walked forward until he was twenty feet away from the privy and the four teenagers.

"Hi, Deputy Mendoza," Noah said, trying hard to stifle a laugh. The routine he had just witnessed was one of the funniest things he had seen in a long time. "You know my friend Marvin." He pointed to the flailing bunny outfit. "That's his brother Deeter, and this is LaDonna Hawthorne. Deeter's crazy, and LaDonna's dad owns Hawthorne's Dairy. My mom says you're all invited down to breakfast."

"Who's inside?" the deputy said stiffly, gesturing at the privy. He raised his voice. "If that's you, Mr. Boggs, put the gun down, and come out where I can see you before anybody gets hurt."

"Ain't nobody in there," Marvin said. "Too many dang black widows. Open thet door, yer gonna git bit fer sure if you ain't keerful."

"I think you need glasses, Deputy," LaDonna said. "William Bates once said 'the ways in which people strain to see are infinite, and the methods used to relieve the strain must be almost equally varied.' I bet my dad knows a good eye doctor if you need one."

"Ollalllallla," moaned Deeter, obviously having a wonderful time.

"I can see the gun," Deputy Mendoza said. "Mr. Boggs, please come on out."

"Whoops!" Noah said, slapping his forehead. He quickly opened the outhouse door and removed the dirt-blackened broom handle that had been sticking through the moon hole. "That's what we used to use to smash the spiders with. It must have fallen over when we dragged it up here."

The two state policemen, followed by the MPs, followed by the bulldozer jockey, followed by two very flustered army officers—one of which had a bloody gash on her forehead—joined Deputy Mendoza. One of the troopers carried a short-barreled pump shotgun. The MPs all had nightsticks and military-issue .45-caliber pistols in leather holsters hung from their belts. The bulldozer jockey was weaponless, but he was popping his knuckles and grinning in anticipation of the wide-spread destruction he was about to bestow upon the landscape.

"Yer in the kingdom of rattlesnakes, so ya wanna watch out where yer steppin'!" Marvin shouted. "Dang things up here is thick!" Noah was supremely impressed that Marvin actually remembered—and quoted—LaDonna's poem about snakes.

"Dammit, I told you people to stay put!" Deputy Mendoza said, glaring at the state police troopers, who were now examining the bushes and sandy terrain around them with great care. He turned back toward the teenagers.

"Noah, awhile back I said you were a smart kid, but right now, you're not showing me much. Where's your uncle? You know you're going to be evicted, so you may as well get Mr. Boggs, and we'll get this over with."

"I'm afraid that isn't exactly what's going to happen today, my friends," a deep voice behind them said.

Like miniature dancers on a music box carousel, Deputy Mendoza and his entourage swiveled in unison toward the voice. If they hadn't been hardened law enforcement officers and military policemen, tough bulldozer drivers, and experienced army lawyers, what they saw would have scared the bejesus out of them. Backlit against the bright morning sun were a dozen or so extremely tall, exceedingly muscular, half-naked apparitions, each one carrying a lever-action hunting rifle propped against his upper hip so that it was silhouetted against the sky. Each had a bandolier of ammunition strapped across his chest and was wearing nothing but a short leather jerkin around his waist and knee-high leather moccasins. The face of the tallest one was painted jet black, and his long, gray hair was in braids. The arms and legs and torsos of all of them were encircled with bright red stripes.

"Holy crap!" said the trooper with the shotgun. "Where in hell'd you people come from?" His voice was shaky and two octaves higher than normal.

"We appeared out of nowhere, naturally," the tall apparition with the jet-black face and the deep voice said calmly. "That's what Inde warriors do, you know. It was, in fact, because of that very reason that Captain William Simmons of the Fourth U.S. Cavalry lost the Battle of Red Butte Creek. He simply did not realize that suitably prepared Apaches can disappear and reappear at will and . . . ah, but that's another story. Right now, we are still in the middle of this one."

"Who are you?" demanded Deputy Mendoza. "And what are you doing here? This is an official police matter, and I'd advise you and your friends"—he gestured at the other apparitions—"to leave while you can. And keep those damn rifles pointed at the sky."

"My name is Two Knives Anna Fork," Two Knives said. "I am a full-blood Mescalero Apache and a member in good standing of the Yogoyekayden clan. I was educated at Harvard and Oxford, and I am a tenured full professor of anthropology and cultural history at New Mexico State University." He made a slight hand motion toward Noah, LaDonna, Marvin, and Deeter. "And these are my friends who have invited you to breakfast with their families. It would only be hospitable if you accepted or declined, but please do so promptly and with a modicum of politeness."

Deputy Mendoza looked more befuddled than angry. "Whether we eat breakfast or not won't change anything," he finally said, giving Two Knives an uncompromising scowl. "We're here to evict Clarence Boggs and his family and to bulldoze the house and barn flat, and that's exactly what's going to happen."

"Ah," said Two Knives. "Now we come to it." He slung his Winchester over his shoulder on its leather strap and reached into the waistband of his leather jerkin to withdraw a folded piece of paper. He opened the document slowly, almost as though he were savoring the moment to come, like a coyote might savor the moment an instant before he sunk his fangs into the juicy neck of a jackalope.

"This, Deputy, is an official document from the New Mexico State Court of Appeals, dated September 10, 1957. That was yesterday. It was filed and submitted by Mr. Boggs's attorney yesterday morning in Albuquerque."

Deputy Mendoza reached for the paper, but Two Knives wasn't through. "I've been ordered to present this document to the police officer in charge of the eviction process with the military attorneys representing White Sands Proving Ground being present at the time. I presume these are the officers in question?" He gestured at Major Paenin-Diaz and Lieutenant Apodoca.

"I'm Major Paenin-Diaz," Major Paenin-Diaz said. "This is Lieutenant Apodoca. What the hell are you talking about?"

Two Knives smiled. "That's certainly quite some name you have, madam. I *do* appreciate unusual names. I don't suppose your given name happens to be Imah?"

"It's pronounced *Ee-ma!*" the major said sharply. "With a long *e!*"

"Your parents must have had a wonderful sense of humor," Two Knives said. "But to answer your question, I'm talking about this." He held up the document. "The decision by Judge Capella to grant the condemnation of Boggs Ranch under the eminent domain process has been overturned by the New Mexico State Court of Appeals. All activity toward eviction is to cease immediately." Two Knives handed the paper to Deputy Mendoza. The deputy read it and handed it to Major Paenin-Diaz.

"As you'll notice, it has been signed by seven of the ten appeals court justices," Two Knives said.

"This just isn't possible!" said Major Paenin-Diaz, shaking the paper in Two Knives's face as she spoke. "How could anyone ram something like this through the Court of Appeals so damn fast? Appeals usually take weeks, if not months."

"I'm sure that's what the army was counting on," Two Knives said calmly. "But appeals do not take weeks if your brother happens to be the chief justice." He gestured at one of the apparitions standing next to him. "May I present Mr. Charles Tsisnah, Mr. Boggs's attorney and chief attorney for the Mescalero Apache tribe. He, too, is a Harvard alumnus, though his dislike for that wonderful center of higher learning is not fully understood by most of his colleagues. Possibly, it had something to do with the nickname—Redskin, I think it was—bestowed upon him by some of his fellow students, but that is only conjecture on my part. I apologize, but Mr. Tsisnah does not allow his true Indian name to be spoken in the presence of white people. Mr. Tsisnah's brother is Robert B. Tsisnah, chief justice of the New Mexico State Court of Appeals. His Honor was quite eager to join us this morning, but unfortunately, he was indisposed with other matters."

"I don't believe a word of this crap!" Major Paenin-Diaz said. She was close to shouting. "Deputy, this so-called document is a forgery. Half-naked people carrying rifles don't just walk out of the desert with a signed legal decision from the Court of Appeals."

"Looks pretty damn convincing to me," the deputy said, taking the court document from Major Paenin-Diaz before it got any more crumpled. He read it through once more. "You just stop and think for a minute now, Major. If you evict Mr. Boggs and tear down his house, and this turns out to be authentic, you'd be digging latrines in Alaska Territory next week, and the lieutenant there'd be handing you the spoon."

"Then the army will appeal to the state supreme court!" Major Paenin-Diaz shouted. "We're not through here yet by any means!"

"Major Paenin-Diaz," said the apparition named Charles Tsisnah, who had also slung his Winchester over his shoulder on its strap. He stepped forward and stuck his overly large Apache nose in the middle of the major's face. "Let me make our position perfectly clear. If the army pursues this foolish quest to remove my client from his lawfully gained land, we will immediately file a civil lawsuit against you, personally, and the Judge Advocate General's Office at White Sands, in general, for unnecessary and malicious harassment." The Apache took a step forward to accent his remarks, forcing the major to back up. "It will be for a considerable sack of wampum, I can assure you," he added. "I'm thinking maybe ten million dollars."

"You can't sue the government!" Lieutenant Apodoca said. He, too, was almost shouting.

"Just watch us," said Charles Tsisnah. "As an ancestor of mine once said, 'Swift the roadrunner may be, but he can't outrun a sandstone boulder.'"

While everyone except the Apaches—who nodded knowingly to each other—waited for the punch line, Noah looked around and saw that his uncle, his mother, the Couches, and the Hawthornes had all quietly walked up from the ranch house and joined the crowd. There were now almost thirty people standing around a smelly, wooden privy with a crescent moon cut in the door in the hot morning sun on top of a hill on a six-hundred-acre parcel of Chihuahuan Desert smack in the middle of nowhere.

Deputy Mendoza took off his hat, wiped his forehead with his sleeve, and then replaced the hat and smoothed one side of his handlebar mustache with two fingers. "This whole thing is over," he said.

He pointed to the two state policemen. "You two can go back to patrol. Major, take your MPs and your D9 and go home. We won't be bothering Mr. Boggs and his family any more than we already have."

The major started to protest again, then thought better of it. She turned crisply and headed back down the hill toward her stranded car. Lieutenant Apodoca was in quick step behind her.

Deputy Mendoza turned to Two Knives. "Why didn't you just bring this by my office yesterday and save us all a lot of time and trouble?"

"Ah, that was indeed an intentional oversight on my part, Deputy. The army and the state of New Mexico have wasted a lot of Mr. Boggs's time in the past few weeks and put him and his family through an enormous amount of trouble. It seemed only fitting to provide a smidgen of the same trouble to the people who made some very bad decisions."

"It was a damn fool thing to do, showing up out here armed to the teeth," the deputy said. "You or any of your people could have been shot. Some of these state troopers are too damned trigger-happy for their own good."

Two Knives made a tiny downward motion with his left hand. It was so slight that Deputy Mendoza didn't see it. "I'm sure you can somehow forgive our dramatic little presentation," he said. "We bloodthirsty savages must have our bit of fun occasionally." He gestured at the landscape. "Besides, even hotheaded state policemen can't shoot what they can't see."

Deputy Mendoza looked around. With the exception of Two Knives, the Apaches had evaporated into the desert like smoke.

"How in hell do you people do that?" the deputy said. "That's damned spooky!"

Two Knives touched the jet-black paint on his face and leaned forward as though to whisper into the deputy's ear. "Trade secret," he said without a smile and in a very low voice. "Geronimo would leave the Happy Hunting Grounds and scalp us both in a heartbeat if I told you."

It took nearly twenty minutes and the entire detachment of sweating, swearing MPs to finally free the army sedan from its partial entombment in the deep sand and get it back onto the driveway. When a small rattlesnake that had been keeping cool in a shallow burrow beneath a nearby bush shook his tail at the noisemakers and attempted to slither away, pandemonium ensued. One of the soldiers wrenched his .45 from its holster and was half a second away from spraying the surrounding bushes with bullets when his corporal literally tackled him to the ground and relieved him of his weapon. Ten more minutes passed, however, before any of the MPs would venture back into the sand to free the sedan, orders or no orders.

Deputy Mendoza and the state policemen required another fifteen minutes to pry out the crumpled bumpers on their patrol cars with borrowed crowbars and shovel handles so that they could be driven back to Tularosa safely. The bulldozer jockey slowed things down even more because without a proper space in which to turn around, and because soft desert sand lined both sides of the narrow track, he had to back the flatbed trailer carrying the D9 all the way to the main road at two miles an hour. No one could go anywhere until the flatbed reached the highway anyway, so while two of the military policemen changed the flat tire on their jeep, Bud coerced the other three plus the two state policemen and Deputy Mendoza into helping manhandle the outhouse off the driveway and out of the way.

Once the dust from the last police car settled and those who had parked their vehicles on top of the rise drove them down to the ranch house, Noah's mother called everyone to breakfast. The large living room table had been carried outside and set in the shade of the house and was now covered with platters of pancakes, biscuits, crispy bacon, fried potatoes, and a large pot of hot coffee. The Apaches had revaporated and were at the head of the line, all of them keeping a wary but reverent eye on Deeter, who had been tethered to the clothesline with a length of rope so he could moan and flail to his heart's content without hurting himself.

Noah, Marvin, and LaDonna took their time returning to the house. There was a lot to talk about.

"I can't remember when I've seen anything so funny," LaDonna said, trying to suppress a giggle. "It was like going to the circus."

"Specially when thet deputy finally seen us standin' in the road," Marvin said, "an' stopped so fast ever'body else crashed into 'em, and ever'body was yellin' at ever'body else. An' then, when them Injun's snuck up an' sca—"

"How did they do that?" LaDonna interrupted. "One second they weren't there, and the next second they were. It was like we were watching a magic act and—*poof!*—the rabbit came out of the hat!"

"Injuns is sneaky like thet," Marvin said. "Them an' jackalopes both. Jackalopes an' Injuns don't wanna be seen, you jest ain't gonna see 'em."

"Jackalopes aren't real," LaDonna snapped. "What on earth are you talking about, Marvin?" She turned to Noah. "Did you really steal your uncle's truck? Why didn't you come by and get me when you went up to see Two Knives?"

"Jackalopes is as real as snot in a cow's nose," Marvin interjected, slightly incensed at LaDonna's tone. He, too, turned to Noah. "How come you didn't git both of us?"

"It was the middle of the night," Noah answered. "And when I delivered the breakfast invitations that my mom wrote to your parents, I didn't know I was even going. Besides, I didn't want to get anyone else in trouble in case I got caught."

"I'm glad your mom invited us all to breakfast," LaDonna said. "She told my parents that if the army had to carry all of us out of the house and up the hill, maybe they would change their mind about the whole thing."

"It was a good idea," Noah said. "When she wrote the invitations, she didn't know that Two Knives was going to get an appeal from a higher court. Nobody knew anything until he knocked on the front door at four o'clock this morning. You should have seen the look on my mom's face when she came out in her bathrobe and saw a band of giant Apaches in full war paint and carrying rifles standing in our living room. The closest she's ever been to an Indian was to watch one in the movies."

Noah was about to describe his middle of the night trip to Mescalero in a stolen truck when he noticed that his uncle, standing together in the shade of the school bus with Two Knives and Charles Tsisnah, was waving him over. He told LaDonna and Marvin he'd catch up and joined the three men.

"I was just telling your uncle that I don't think you'll have to worry about an appeal to the state supreme court," the Indian attorney said. "I have a feeling that the threat of a ten-million-dollar lawsuit will make the army think twice before taking any further action. I believe they'll realize that your ranch just isn't worth the trouble, not to mention the bad publicity they would get."

"I ain't got the words to say a proper thanks fer what you done, Mr. Tsisnah," Bud said. "Without you an' Two Knives here, we'd all be in the hoosegow 'bout now."

"The pleasure was all mine," Charles Tsisnah said, smiling. "And theirs." He gestured at the other Apaches, who were making short work of the platters of food on the table. "It isn't often that we have an opportunity to practice being real Indians anymore. In fact, I can't remember when I've had so much fun. I truly wish I had a photograph of that state policeman's face when he turned around and realized that he'd been surrounded. The experience will be impossible to describe properly to my grandchildren."

Bud turned to Two Knives. "You an' me are all square an' even," he said. "Bub an' me'll be up in a week er so fer some more calves an' chile, an' I won't hear nothin' 'bout my money not bein' no good." He patted the wallet in his front overall pocket for emphasis.

"We can discuss that later, Clarence," Two Knives said, "but I'll look forward to seeing you both." He put a hand on Noah's shoulder. "And if I may offer a suggestion, you should be thanking your nephew here, not us. It took a great deal of courage to appropriate your truck and drive all the way to Mescalero in the middle of the night by himself. However, if he hadn't informed us about the situation when he did, Charles wouldn't have had time to drive to Albuquerque and make the appeal to his brother."

"Didn't appropriate nothin'," Bud said, giving Noah a lopsided wink. "He jest downright stole it. Didn't have no gas in it neither."

"I had to use an Okie hep-yerself," Noah said, looking a little guilty. "From somebody's car in Tularosa. We should go by and pay them for the gas I took."

"And what is an Okie hep-yerself?" Two Knives asked. "It sounds like it might be a useful device in certain situations."

Bud ignored the question. "Don't tell yer ma 'bout no Okie hep-yerself," he said to Noah. "She's rarin' to skin you alive jest fer stealin' the truck. Ain't no need to aggervate things none. Leastwise you got back without crashin' into anythin', an' yer ma oughta be thankful fer thet."

LATER THAT AFTERNOON, long after the Apaches had returned to the reservation in their school bus and the Hawthornes and Couches had said good-bye and gone home to do the milking, and after the chores had been done and supper eaten, Noah was in the barn scratching Brimstone's nose and feeding him pieces of a carrot he'd swiped from the refrigerator. He didn't hear Bud come in until his uncle cleared his throat. He leaned against the stall's wooden rails and hooked his thumbs underneath his overall straps.

"If we ain't gotta do thet again fer a while, it'll be too dang soon fer me," he said. "You an' yer ma was a big help." He reached into the breast pocket of his overalls and took out the worn Bull Durham sack containing the twenty-dollar gold Liberty coin. He handed it to Noah. "Didn't think I'd forget yer birthday, did ya? Sorry it ain't wrapped, but I ain't had much time to do no wrapping."

Noah slid the twenty-dollar Liberty out of the sack and held it up to the light shining into the barn through the door. The little golden stars circling the woman's head seemed to gleam and sparkle in the late afternoon sun.

"I forgot it was my birthday," Noah said. "But you told me this is your good-luck charm. You can't just give it away."

"Done brought me lots of luck," Bud said. "Probably more'n I deserve. Anyhoo, yer gonna need all the luck you kin git when you head fer school next week. Jest don't let nobody see it, not fer a while anyways."

Noah slipped the coin back into its sack and put the sack in his pocket. "I won't let anyone see it." A large tear—much larger than a spider's egg—rolled down his right cheek. He didn't bother to wipe it away. "Thank you," he said. "I can't believe I'm fifteen."

"You ain't a kid no more," Bud said. "Ya ain't a man neither, but yer gettin' closer. Ain't really a man till you dip yer knife in the mustard, but that'll come in time."

"I don't much like mustard," Noah said, slightly confused. "What does mustard have to do with being a man?"

"Never mind," his uncle grinned. "Some things you ain't gotta know yet."

Noah sat down on a hay bale. "Things got pretty scary around here this morning," he said. "It was funny, but scary. People with guns are scary."

Bud reached over and gave Brimstone a pat on his neck, being careful to keep an eye on the mule's ears, and then sat down beside Noah. "None of them rifles the Apaches was carryin' had bullets in 'em," he said. "Yer right, though, people with guns is scary."

"It just doesn't seem worth it," Noah said. "All the trouble that everybody went through, and we all just end up where we were before the whole thing started. Somebody could have gotten shot, and it would have been for nothing. What a waste of everyone's time."

"What we done this mornin' was somethin' worth doin'," Bud said, "an' we ain't lost nothin' 'cept a little time. Army got its butt bit real good, an' mebbe next time they'll think twice 'bout kickin' somebody off their land." He placed one hand on Noah's shoulder. "If you kin do somethin' worth doin' ever' day, then thet's one day you ain't wasted. An' you ain't got thet many to waste, anyways."

Noah looked at his uncle. "I guess you're right," he said. "Maybe now other people won't have to go through the same thing we did."

"Dern tootin', I'm right," his uncle said. He stood up and slapped the hay off his overalls with his fedora. "Now go git yer ma, and let's head fer town. I got a powerful need fer chocolate ice cream, an' tell 'er not to forget thet jar a jalapeños, neither, 'cause they ain't got none at the Tastee-Freez."

Epilogue

Exactly one week after what LaDonna later called the "Showdown at Outhouse Overlook," my Uncle Bud received a short, typewritten letter from the Judge Advocate General's Office at White Sands Proving Ground, notifying him formally and officially that because of "certain unforeseen circumstances which could not, and should not, be discussed in public, the U.S. Army, with the full concord and union of the state of New Mexico," was suspending their application to the state of New Mexico and the courts for condemnation of Boggs Ranch, "without further inquiry or action." Basically, the army used a lot of fancy words to tell my uncle that they had been scared spitless by Mr. Charles Tsisnah's threat of a ten-million-dollar lawsuit, especially when the chief justice of the New Mexico State Court of Appeals happened to be the plaintiff's attorney's brother.

Bud and I were both wrong about the army thinking twice about trying to take someone else's land, however. During the late 1950s and early 1960s, both the army and the air force, using the same strong-arm techniques that they tried on my uncle, successfully condemned several large and productive ranches bordering White Sands Proving Ground. Their tenants, some whose families had occupied the properties for more than a hundred years, were evicted. Boggs Ranch, with lots of help, had been able to fend off the eminent domain process. Others weren't so lucky.

I began my sophomore year of high school at Tularosa High in mid-September. It wasn't much different than school would have been in Gold Hill, Oregon, probably, except for one thing. Chiefly due to Marvin Couch's big mouth, the story of Zefo's three broken ribs and how his aggravation and annoyance at me had driven him mad, causing him to spritz and spatter several of Tularosa's finest citizens with *parfum de l'urine de Zefo*—thereby guaranteeing a second trip to the hospital with bootprints on his face and later a sorrowful return to New Mexico Boys' School—had spread quickly, and within a week, I had become somewhat of a teenage celebrity. Strangely enough, Frank, Bob, and Billy, who sort of turned out to be good guys, after all—despite their tobacco-chewing habits—never spilled the beans about what *really* happened at the feed store (maybe that was their way of "helping out their friends"), and probably out of sheer embarrassment, neither did Zefo's gang. As a result, the local bullies—and there were many hardcase tormentors in Tularosa's school yards (though none quite as brutal as Zefo)—gave me and my friends an unusually wide berth. As you might imagine, I suddenly had a lot of new friends.

The "Three Moos"—as LaDonna liked to call us—rode the same bus to school and had many of the same classes, so it was only natural that we hung out together. Hardly a weekend passed that Marvin and I weren't following LaDonna around on some half-baked excursion, doing our best to stave off the small-town doldrums. When Marvin finally convinced LaDonna that jackalopes truly were authentic creatures of nature, for instance, we spent ten full hours on our hands and knees out in the desert near the malpais searching for jackalope trails, jackalope tracks, jackalope droppings, and/or jackalope dens, all the while keeping a sharp eye out for patrols of army MPs—which by then had begun to make daily sweeps of the area in jeeps—as well as rocket ships and green space monsters with ray guns and big heads. You'd be unpleasantly surprised at how many nasty, dangerous-looking species of creepy-crawlies reside in shallow burrows scratched into the sand under mesquite trees in the vast Chihuahuan Desert of southern New Mexico. At least I was.

On another occasion, LaDonna decided that her bracero friend Manuelo needed a bicycle to get around town during his free time. We exhausted an entire weekend washing cars for fifty cents each in the Tastee-Freez parking lot in pursuit of the funds needed to buy Manuelo a second-hand bike, and we raised a grand total of three dollars. Two dollars of that came from Bud, who probably felt sorry for us and consequently "tipped" us an extra dollar fifty. Saint LaDonna was so irked by the lack of community participation in her project that she made a large cardboard sign that read PEOPLE IN TULAROSA ARE STINGY TIGHTWADS, which she taped to the glass showcase windows in the front of the Ranger theater. Because the movie delivery truck had broken down again, the sign stayed up for two weeks before the owners finally noticed and took it down.

Two Knives Anna Fork invited us to spend Christmas Day 1957 at his tidy little adobe house in Mescalero. LaDonna and her family and Charles Tsisnah and his family were there, plus the Couches (including Deeter, who spent much of the day tied to a tree in the front yard) and Deputy Mendoza and his girlfriend. The menu included an enormous pot of posole, potatoes wrapped in yucca leaves and cooked over hot coals in a fire pit, and a barbecued wild turkey basted with marinade made from beer, crushed piñon nuts, and minced green chile. Two Knives called it simply "Apache gobbler." I have no doubt, however, that Julia Child herself—had she ever tasted it—would have gladly and without the slightest hesitation farted "The Stars and Stripes Forever" at a high-school assembly in Topeka, Kansas, in exchange for the recipe. I can still see the glorious light of heaven explode in Bud's eyes when he took his first bite, and to this day, I can't recall having eaten anything quite as delicious.

My days as a cowboy in southern New Mexico were numbered, however. On April 1, 1958, my mother floored everyone by announcing that on June 1—assuming God was willing and the creek didn't rise—she would become the blushing bride of Mr. Bebe Billington, an old friend of Bud's who had visited the ranch on a number of occasions, almost all of them while I was in school. I'd met Bebe a couple of times and actually liked him, but I'd always thought he was dropping by to see my uncle, not my mother. I was told that I could spend the summer on the ranch if I wished, but in late August I'd be expected to join my mother and my new stepfather in Santa Fe, where Bebe owned and operated a small but successful construction company.

The two lovebirds were married, as scheduled, the day after school ended for the summer, in Juárez, Mexico, by a justice of the peace who didn't speak English. Bud and I were the only ones in attendance except for a three-piece mariachi band that Bebe hired to provide the wedding music. The happy couple honeymooned in Juárez for three days, then drove directly back to Santa Fe to set up housekeeping. I stayed with Bud and Brimstone on the ranch until late August, when I joined Bebe and my mother in their large and comfortable adobe house a few blocks from Santa Fe's historic plaza. I was allowed to keep my own last name, and I was told I should call my new stepfather "Bebe," not "Dad." I started my junior year of high school at Santa Fe High School two weeks later.

I enjoyed living in Santa Fe. It was a beautiful, historic city, filled with writers, artists, musicians, beatniks, and all sorts of other bohemian types, every one of them colorful, interesting people. I grew to love the smell of roasting chile and piñon-burning fireplaces in the autumn; the crisp, clean, icy winter air; and the melodic whisper of the quaking aspen forests up in the Sangre de Cristo Mountains as the spring wind blew softly through their new leaves.

Bud, Brimstone, LaDonna, and Marvin, however, were all in Tularosa, and it was there that I spent school holidays and most summer vacations during my remaining high school and college years. Without my mother's loving touch, the old ranch house quickly became run-down and messy, but unmade beds, dirty floors, and two weeks' worth of crusty dishes in the sink had little effect on my uncle's happy-go-lucky attitude as long as there were a couple of cold beers in the refrigerator and a sack of fresh chile in the barn.

Brimstone died of natural causes in July 1965. We buried him at the west end of the property in a deep grave that Marvin, LaDonna, and I dug by hand. Brimstone's death was a turning point in Bud's life, although I was never sure why. Two months later, he sold the ranch—rattlesnakes and all—to a retired schoolteacher from Albuquerque for a hefty profit and moved to the town of Socorro, New Mexico, a small college town in the Rio Grande valley, northwest of Tularosa, across the Jornada del Muerto. He rented a small, two-bedroom house on a quiet back street, and then—for some totally inexplicable reason—took a job driving a heavy dump truck for a U.S. Army contract development firm. His job was to haul two loads of gravel a day to a remote military construction site known as Stallion Range, which was located at the extreme northern end of what by then had become White Sands Missile Range. The round trip from rock crusher to Stallion Range was 140 miles. Bud told me later that he took the job simply to keep himself occupied.

I once made the run to Stallion Range with him in the big, noisy Mack dump truck that he drove. I remember an arid, rugged, nearly treeless landscape with massive lava flows and deep, eroded canyons everywhere you looked. Low, gray-green cholla cactus grew not in bunches but in forests, and the nearest thing I saw to water was a mud puddle in the road left by a watering truck in front of us that was making the same run. I had no military clearance, so while Bud hauled the gravel to the actual building site, I waited at the U.S. Army gatehouse with two friendly, laid-back military policemen. We passed the time by playing gin and shooting jackrabbits from the door of the guard shack with nonregulation .22 pistols the MPs brought from home. Later I discovered that the research laboratory and testing facility that Bud helped build at Stallion played an important role in the development of modern nuclear weapons, including the H-bomb.

Marvin and I didn't physically cross paths again much after 1965, mainly because of distance. Once out of high school—from which he graduated just by the seat of his pants—Marvin chose to attend college at New Mexico State University, the state agricultural college in Las Cruces, west across the Jornada del Muerto from Tularosa. LaDonna and I opted for the University of New Mexico, 160 miles north in Albuquerque, instead because I didn't have much of an interest in farming or raising cattle, and LaDonna was thoroughly

turned off by anything bovine—even a glass of milk. It took barely a
month at school for LaDonna's professors to discover what Marvin
and I already knew—that her intelligence quotient lay somewhere
between "inconceivable" and "immeasurable," and that her appe-
tite for, and comprehension of, both general and specific knowledge
about almost everything was voracious. In our freshmen and sophomore years—while I blundered my way through the basic college
carte du jour—LaDonna blasted through postgraduate courses in
English, creative writing, vertebrate zoology, genetics, journalism,
and history, effortlessly maintaining a 4.0 average while she did so.
By the time graduation rolled around—my graduation, that is—
she had skipped the bachelor's program entirely, taken a scientiae
magister and an MA and was just half a thesis away from her PhD in
English literature. She was invited to join Mensa International but
never filled out the application form; she told me that the members
were probably far too full of themselves for her simple tastes.

Much to everyone's surprise, LaDonna turned out not to be the
only escaped inmate from Tularosa's brainiac barn. Marvin ren-
dered friends and family speechless by undergoing an extraordinary metamorphosis during his sophomore year in college from
a cow-herding, manure-mucking, rodeo-loving cowboy with dirt
on his jeans and crap on his boots to a slide rule–toting, problem-
solving geek who studied six to eight hours each day and received
straight As in everything but English. After graduating with hon-
ors from New Mexico State, Marvin transferred directly to MIT in
Cambridge, Massachusetts, on full scholarship, where he earned a
master's degree and then a PhD in applied nuclear physics. When
he returned to New Mexico, he landed a high-end job in one of the
Strategic Defense Initiative (Star Wars) testing facilities located at
White Sands. Less than a year later, on a cold January morning, he
was killed in a two vehicle accident while on his way to work. Police
estimated that the Porsche 911T Marvin had been driving when he
collided head-on with an out of control tractor trailer rig hauling
Hatch Valley chile to supermarkets in Alamogordo was airborne
for nearly 250 feet before it landed upside down in a cotton field
alongside the highway. From what Heze Couch told me, Marvin

must have ridden the tumbling sports car all the way up and all the way down, just as though he was riding a bucking steer in the Three Rivers rodeo. The first rescuers on the scene told police that Marvin was still wearing his hat when they reached him.

Both Heze and Hazel Couch died in the late 1980s, but Marvin's crazy brother Deeter, confined to an institution for the mentally disabled in Albuquerque for much of his later life, outlived his brother and parents by many years, finally passing away in 2008. Today all three are buried side-by-side, next to Marvin in the Tularosa Cemetery. I stop by whenever I'm in the neighborhood, just to pay my respects, and Mr. and Mrs. Hawthorne—both of whom are elderly but very much alive and still living on the ranch just south of Tularosa—put fresh flowers on the graves once a month.

Zefo Montoya was released from New Mexico Boys' School in November 1959 but never returned to Tularosa. He tried to rob a mom-and-pop grocery store in Albuquerque at knifepoint a week after release and was shot once in the face and once in the groin (the latter "just for good measure") by the owner. The .22 pistol the owner used—which he kept stashed in the lower drawer of the cash register for just such an emergency—was an illegal Saturday night special, but when police examined Zefo's prior record, they chose to overlook the fact that the snub-nosed .22 with the sawed-off grip and filed-off front sight and serial number could have gotten the owner two years in jail.

When Zefo recovered, he was tried and convicted of armed robbery and sentenced to eight years in the state penitentiary. Six months later, he was kicked to death by his larger, meaner cell mate, who accused him of stealing cigarettes. I was told all this by former deputy Mendoza, with whom I had coffee in an Albuquerque shopping mall a few years ago. He told me he'd retired in 1978 after twenty-five years with the Otero County Sheriff's Department and that he spent most of his time gardening and looking after his grandchildren. He also said that he never did figure out how eleven full-grown, fairly large, well-armed Apaches managed to vanish virtually right in front of his eyes and that he still dreamed of the disappearing Inde warriors. I told him to forget it because there are some things regular people aren't meant to know, and if he didn't believe me, he should try following LaDonna around for a couple of days.

Bud passed away in the spring of 1979 while consuming a bowl of fiery chile *del diablo* and drinking a bottle of Dos Equis beer at a roadside Mexican restaurant in Socorro. He was sixty-three. The coroner said it was a massive heart attack, but LaDonna told me she prefers to think he was spirited away for an eternal chat by Old Cap Sayuhson, who just wanted someone knowledgeable about chile to talk to. Bud's funeral was held in Tularosa a week after his death and was attended by a noisy menagerie of cowboys, Indians, alfalfa and cotton farmers, braceros, and even a couple of sweet-smelling hookers from Alamogordo who seemed to know my uncle quite well. Two Knives Anna Fork arrived dressed in war paint and warrior regalia and, at my request, provided the eulogy. When the proper words had been uttered both in English and Apache, Two Knives laid a red-tagged gunnysack of fresh green chile pods on Bud's coffin before it was covered with dirt. Later on that same evening, he and I got roaring drunk at a local beer joint and talked about rattlesnakes, roadrunners, coyotes, and Bud, of course, until three o'clock in the morning.

Bud didn't leave a will when he died, but it didn't really matter. My mother and I were his only living relatives, at least as far as we knew, and she left the dispersal and disposal of his estate to me. Except for his battered old Studebaker pickup, a shotgun, his deer rifle, and a tin box of flint arrowheads, he had few personal belongings that he cared anything about. I kept the guns and arrowheads; gave a few drawers of worn bib overalls, wool socks, and chile-stained T-shirts to Goodwill; and donated the pickup to Two Knives Anna Fork for his chile business.

None of Bud's assets were ever found, of course, although the IRS and investigators from the New Mexico tax office launched a serious search. He had never trusted a bank in his life, so he had no accounts the bureaucrats could plunder, and other than about three hundred dollars in cash and change he had in his wallet when he passed away, Clarence William Boggs seemingly died broke. I knew better, of course. Years before, on a hot summer evening in June, he had drawn a detailed map on a piece of tablet paper and made me study it until I could have found the X in my sleep. A week later, that's exactly what I had to do. Bud woke me at midnight, pushed me into the driver's seat of the pickup, and ordered me to drive to what he called his "hidey-hole." An hour later, and with only a couple of wrong turns, I got us there. We didn't go in. We just sat and looked and talked about lost gold and listened to the coyotes howling their glee at the prospect of a moonlit night and a healthy jackrabbit population.

I didn't visit the hidey-hole again until several months after Bud's death, when I was sure the tax people had stopped looking. As it turned out, my uncle hadn't told me the entire truth about the Ladrón gold. According to a sheaf of scribbled paperwork I found, he had received eight hundred dollars for each of the forty-nine Liberty gold pieces from Ladrón Peak he'd sold in 1951. The pawn broker in Las Cruces had taken a ten percent finder's fee, which left Bud with a tidy sum of slightly more than $35,000 (about $344,000 in 2012 dollars). There was still about $15,000 in crisp one-hundred-dollar bills from the coin sale left, plus another $25,000 in fifty-dollar bills that he'd gotten for the ranch in Tularosa. All of it had been wrapped in wax paper and stacked neatly inside an airtight metal box.

The real treasure, however, was not the cash. Out of sight, under an old piece of canvas, I discovered another fifty gold twenty-dollar Liberty coins still cozied up to each other in the worm-eaten wooden storage box they'd originally been stolen in. Later that year, and mainly because the coins were part of a very limited and exclusive edition (only 1,234 were minted), each of the forty I decided to sell—offered one at a time to carefully selected numismatists in the United States, Canada, and Saudi Arabia—fetched an average price of nine thousand dollars. The money was always paid in cash. Invested wisely, it was enough to allow me to do anything I pleased for the rest of my life. The eleven remaining coins (including the one I still keep in the old tobacco sack) are increasing in value every day and should fetch enough to give my four grandchildren a healthy jump start in life—if they ever need it.

My mother passed away in 1998, at the age of eighty. She was still living in Santa Fe with my stepfather (who passed in 2003) in their two-hundred-year-old downtown adobe home when she died, and she was still as feisty as ever, despite the fact that arthritis often limited her activities. Before he died, Bud had always been a welcome guest, but he didn't visit very often because my mother wouldn't allow alcohol in the house. Bud said that staying with his sister was too much like staying in a church, and he preferred the church when it came right down to it because at least he could drink a little communion wine on Sunday.

Two Knives Anna Fork and I still keep in close touch, and we get together at least twice a year for a meal, a chat, a drink, and sometimes a few tears. Old but still spry, Two Knives retired from New Mexico State University years ago and is now a full-time chile entrepreneur. His Mescalero farm produces a fiery brand of internationally acclaimed red chile powder known as "Geronimo's Revenge." Last year, the all-Apache corporation he owns grossed ten million dollars from chile powder sales in fifty states and nineteen foreign countries. Bud would have been proud.

As for me, I never did get to be a cowboy, not a real one at least. It turned out that Two Knives and that old Tularosa farmer had been right all along. Cattle really *are* the stupidest animals on earth, and cowboys get paid way too little to take care of them. I own a small herd of horses and mules and spend a lot of time on horseback, but I ride for the pleasure of riding and not because I have to nursemaid a bunch of smelly, dim-witted cows. I should say I own two small herds, really, since LaDonna and I divide our time between a small, tidy hacienda on Costa Rica's beautiful Playa de Oro, where we spend our winters, and a red cedar summer house on twenty acres overlooking the Pacific Ocean, near Gold Beach, Oregon. Our children and grandchildren all love to ride and spend most of their time on horseback when they come to visit.

The tiny little green demon with a long beard and horns, and hair sprouting from his toes that has lived inside LaDonna's head since she was a child has kept her extremely busy for the past four decades. She self-published her first book of poems a year out of college and has never been anything but a writer since. Her analytical essays and disquisitional narratives have appeared in every major scientific and literary publication in the western hemisphere, including the *Mensa Research Journal*. Her latest mystery novel, *Murder in Jackalope County* (yeah, *that* El D Odell), topped the *New York Times* best-seller list for twenty-one straight weeks, and her agent and publisher are begging—literally down-on-their-knees *begging*—for another. LaDonna chose the unusual nom de plume El D without any help from me. Basically a modified acronym for "*el diablito*" which is Spanish for "the little devil," she claims it makes her sound dashing, mysterious, and just a little a bit naughty.

She still writes poetry, of course, and on our thirtieth wedding anniversary, she presented me with her latest endeavor—a lyric poem from her impish symbiont that she claims just popped into her head one morning at breakfast. I really thought it was one of her better efforts and a week later had the words burned into a myrtlewood plaque that now hangs in my office.

The Nexus continues to defecate.
Stupidity continues to replicate.
That's just the way things are going.
Too bad, isn't it?

My wife has a way of getting right to the heart of the bother. And speaking of bother, El D hasn't bothered to milk a cow—or even to get near one, in fact—since we took our vows in 1980, a year after Bud died. And I've learned to live with the bother of rain showers that keep both northwestern Costa Rica and southwestern coastal Oregon green, but I still don't much like to get wet.

—Noah Odell
Hacienda Brimstone,
Nicoya Peninsula,
Costa Rica, 2012